# DIVISIBLE MAN™

by

## Howard Seaborne

*For Vera, Blue Skies!*

*[signature]*

TWD™

FOR VERA,
GENE SXIES!

*[signature]*

# ALSO BY HOWARD SEABORNE

DIVISIBLE MAN

*A Novel – September 2017*

DIVISIBLE MAN: THE SIXTH PAWN

*A Novel – June 2018*

DIVISIBLE MAN: THE SECOND GHOST

*A Novel – September 2018*

ANGEL FLIGHT

*A Story – September 2018*

DIVISIBLE MAN: THE SEVENTH STAR

*A Novel – June 2019*

ENGINE OUT

*A Story – September 2019*

WHEN IT MATTERS

*A Story – October 2019*

A SNOWBALL'S CHANCE

*A Story – November 2019*

DIVISIBLE MAN: TEN MAN CREW

*A Novel – November 2019*

DIVISIBLE MAN: THE THIRD LIE

*A Novel – May 2020*

DIVISIBLE MAN: THREE NINES FINE

*A Novel – November 2020*

DIVISIBLE MAN: EIGHT BALL

*A Novel – September 2021*

DIVISIBLE MAN: NINE LIVES LOST

*A Novel – June 2022*

DIVISIBLE MAN: ENGINE OUT
AND OTHER SHORT FLIGHTS

*A Story Collection – June 2022*

# PRAISE FOR HOWARD SEABORNE

"This book is a strong start to a series…Well-written and engaging, with memorable characters and an intriguing hero."
    *—Kirkus Reviews*
    *DIVISIBLE MAN* [DM1]

"Seaborne's crisp prose, playful dialogue, and mastery of technical details of flight distinguish the story…this is a striking and original start to a series, buoyed by fresh and vivid depictions of extra-human powers and a clutch of memorably drawn characters…"
    *—BookLife*
    *DIVISIBLE MAN* [DM1]

"Even more than flight, (Will's relationship with Andy)—and that crack prose—powers this thriller to a satisfying climax that sets up more to come."
    *—BookLife*
    *DIVISIBLE MAN* [DM1]

"Seaborne, a former flight instructor and charter pilot, once again gives readers a crisply written thriller. Self-powered flight is a potent fantasy, and Seaborne explores its joys and difficulties engagingly. Will's narrative voice is amusing, intelligent and humane; he draws readers in with his wit, appreciation for his wife, and his flight-drunk joy…Even more entertaining than its predecessor—a great read."
    *—Kirkus Reviews*
    *DIVISIBLE MAN: THE SIXTH PAWN* [DM2]

"Seaborne, a former flight instructor and pilot, delivers a solid, well-written tale that taps into the near-universal dream of personal flight. Will's narrative voice is engaging and crisp, clearly explaining technical matters while never losing sight of humane, emotional concerns. The environments he describes…feel absolutely real. Another intelligent and exciting superpowered thriller."
    *—Kirkus Reviews*
    *DIVISIBLE MAN: THE SECOND GHOST* [DM3]

"As in this series' three previous books, Seaborne...proves he's a natural born storyteller, serving up an exciting, well-written thriller. He makes even minor moments in the story memorable with his sharp, evocative prose... Will's smart, humane and humorous narrative voice is appealing, as is his sincere appreciation for Andy—not just for her considerable beauty, but also for her dedication and intelligence...Seaborne does a fine job making side characters and locales believable. It's deeply gratifying to see Will deliver righteous justice to some very bad people. An intensely satisfying thriller—another winner from Seaborne."

—*Kirkus Reviews*
*DIVISIBLE MAN: THE SECOND GHOST* [DM4]

"Seaborne...continues his winning streak in this series, offering another page-turner. By having Will's knowledge of and control over his powers continue to expand while the questions over how he should best deploy his abilities grow, Seaborne keeps the concept fresh and readers guessing... Will's enemies are becoming aware of him and perhaps developing techniques to detect him, which makes the question of how he can protect himself while doing the most good a thorny one. The conspiracy is highly dramatic yet not implausible given today's political events, and the action sequences are excitingly cinematic...Another compelling and hugely fun adventure that delivers a thrill ride."

—*Kirkus Reviews*
*DIVISIBLE MAN: TEN MAN CREW* [DM5]

"Seaborne shows himself to be a reliably splendid storyteller in this latest outing. The plot is intricate and could have been confusing in lesser hands, but the author manages it well, keeping readers oriented amid unexpected developments...His crisp writing about complex scenes and concepts is another strong suit...The fantasy of self-powered flight remains absolutely compelling...As a former charter pilot, Seaborne conveys Will's delight not only in 'the other thing,' but also in airplanes and the world of flight—an engaging subculture that he ably brings to life for the reader. Will is heroic and daring, as one would expect, but he's also funny, compassionate, and affectionate... A gripping, timely, and twisty thriller."

—*Kirkus Reviews*
*DIVISIBLE MAN: THE THIRD LIE* [DM6]

"Seaborne is never less than a spellbinding storyteller, keeping his complicated but clearly explicated plot moving smoothly from one nail-biting scenario to another. As the tale goes along, seemingly disparate plot lines begin to satisfyingly connect in ways that will keep readers guessing until the explosive (in more ways than one) action-movie denouement. The author's grasp of global politics gives depth to the book's thriller elements, which are nicely balanced by thoughtful characterizations. Even minor characters come across in three dimensions, and Will himself is an endearing narrator. He's lovestruck by his gorgeous, intelligent, and strong-willed wife; has his heart and social conscience in the right place; and is boyishly thrilled by the other thing. A solid series entry that is, as usual, exciting, intricately plotted, and thoroughly entertaining."

—*Kirkus Reviews*
*DIVISIBLE MAN: THREE NINES FINE* [DM7]

Any reader of this series knows that they're in good hands with Seaborne, who's a natural storyteller. His descriptions and dialogue are crisp, and his characters deftly sketched...The book keeps readers tied into its complex and exciting thriller plot with lucid and graceful exposition, laying out clues with cleverness and subtlety...Also, although Will's abilities are powerful, they have reasonable limitations, and the protagonist is always a relatable character with plenty of humanity and humor...Another riveting, taut, and timely adventure with engaging characters and a great premise."

— *Kirkus Reviews*
*DIVISIBLE MAN: EIGHT BALL [DM8]*

# THE SERIES

While each DIVISIBLE MAN <sup>TM</sup> novel tells its own tale, many elements carry
forward and the novels are best enjoyed in sequence. The short story "Angel Flight"
is a bridge between the third and fourth novels and is included with the third novel,
DIVISIBLE MAN - THE SECOND GHOST.

DIVISIBLE MAN <sup>TM</sup> is available in print, digital and audio.

For a Cast of Characters, visit **HowardSeaborne.com**

For advance notice of new releases and exclusive material available only to Email
Members, join the DIVISIBLE MAN <sup>TM</sup> Email List at

**HowardSeaborne.com**.

Sign up today and get a FREE DOWNLOAD.

# ACKNOWLEDGMENTS

Every flight takes planning. And while pilots embrace the lone eagle image, the fact of the matter is that nothing leaves the ground without a host of good people contributing to the effort.

I'd like to thank my dispatcher, Stephen Parolini, for his editing expertise and the kind way he has of telling me something needs to be left on the ramp. Thank you to my first instructor, the late Victor Zilbert, for insisting that this machine belongs in the sky. Thanks to his business partner Arnie Freeman for a lifetime of ego refueling and friendship. Thanks to Denise Kohnke for navigation to all the best flight planning resources.

Those brave souls, the test pilots who took this thing into the air on faith, my beta readers and life-long co-pilots, Rich "Maddog" Sorensen and Robin "Polly Pureheart" Schlei, deserve special thanks for the initial airworthiness inspection.

Much gratitude goes to the ground crew at Trans World Data—to David, Carol, Claire, April and Rebecca for keeping the machine running—and to Kristie and Steve for taking over the reconnaissance so I can concentrate on flying.

I can't say enough about my sharp-eyed radar operators, Roberta and Steve Schlei, whose thorough copy-editing saw through the clouds and found every needless hyphen.

And thank you, Robin, for always knowing I need to fly.

*For Robin.*
*The many different people you are.*
*I love them all.*

# PART I

# 1

The first time I vanished, I figured it for a morphine hallucination.

*A hospital.*

People in scrubs hovered over me. Solicitous faces used sharp eyes and tender fingers to probe and examine me. I heard the beeps of relentless monitors. I heard the whisper of curtains pushed aside, then pulled back in place to shield the worried from the wounded.

I had no idea why I was here, or how I had been delivered here, or how long I'd been here. I had no anchor point in time, and I wasn't all that sure about time's traveling companion, space, either.

The room behind the hovering faces contained cabinets and stainless-steel medical fixtures. An IV stand stood near my head, dangling its plastic jelly fish bag and strands of clear tubing.

One of the faces, speaking to me as if I were a distracted toddler, said loudly, "We're going to give you morphine for the pain, Mr. Stewart."

*A hospital.*

*Morphine.*

In my head I sang out, *Yes!* Because the third in a trilogy of things I knew for certain was that I felt like I'd been kicked in the family jewels by an NFL place kicker.

Pain screamed from my groin, up through my guts, and grabbed my lungs with tongs dipped in hot coals. Pain made me pass out, made me want to puke when consciousness returned, made me want to claw the nerves out of my skin. When the morphine drip started dripping and a cool sea breeze blew through my screaming brain, I wanted to kiss someone. The cool sea breeze transformed into a series of sweet ocean swells, and the pain shriveled to become a nasty little man squalling at me from a tiny raft bobbing far, far away.

Logic suggested, then, that when I found myself floating six feet above a hospital bed lined with chromed steel rails, tethered by a thin plastic tube, it must be the morphine.

I rode the bliss, listening to Roy Orbison in my head singing *anything you want, you got it*. In the magical way of dreams, Roy Orbison became John Lennon urging me to turn off my mind, *relax and float downstream*.

I was indeed floating.

Somewhere in the distance the center of my body screamed profanities up the telegraph of my nervous system, yet thanks to Morphine with a Capital M, I didn't care.

Floating toward the acoustic tiles, I wondered how I was supposed to maneuver back for a landing in the bed. Fly a downwind, base and final? Or barrel straight in?

*No worries. You're a pilot. You got this.*

I wondered if anyone would judge the landing. Darkness shrouded the room. I saw windows covered by blinds, and beyond the blinds I saw parking lot lights against black.

Night.

A clock on the wall next to a flat screen pointed two hands up and into the dark small hours. Night in a hospital meant a busy, quiet nursing staff, which made catching anyone's eye unlikely, and made anyone catching me floating six feet over my bed equally unlikely.

I felt a little disappointed. Nobody to see me flying. Nobody to judge the landing. My mind wandered.

*I'm in a hospital. Floating. On morphine, because—*

*You have a broken pelvis.*

Someone said it. A boyish face, speaking emphatically. *You have a broken pelvis. We're going to give you something for the pain, Mr. Stewart.*

I had a broken pelvis. I had a broken pelvis because—

That's where my grasp ended, and my mind's fingers stretched out in vain, into black emptiness. I might have flailed and grabbed for an answer, were I not distracted by the situation at hand.

I floated six feet above a hospital bed, bumping into the ceiling like an escaped child's balloon, trailing an IV tube as my string.

Call it pilot's logic, or situational awareness, or call it being anal, but in

4

the midst of all this, I thought, *It's good to do this sort of thing in the middle of the night.*

If you're going to go floating, do it on the dark side of midnight, while the nurses catch up on Twitter and the visitors sleep at home, tucked in under their own sheets, perhaps a tiny bit thankful those sheets are not hospital sheets.

The dark hours in a hospital have a white noise all their own. I learned that when I was twenty-two and spent six nights in a hospital giving birth to a kidney stone (and having my first taste of Morphine). Hospitals at night whisper secret incantations in a language you think you understand, but it's a language meant only for magicians in scrubs. I heard voices from the nurse's station, tantalizingly close, sometimes carelessly loud, yet ever unintelligible. Harmonizing with those voices, an important-sounding machine hummed in the treble clef. I pictured a guy with a floor polisher. A wheeled cart squeaked, adding mechanical mouse sounds. An electric door latch released with a sharp *clack*, officiously granting entry or exit to guarded spaces.

It was the ideal time to go flying on Morphine.

I turned my head to see the bed below. It was a mess. Like someone had been wrestling trolls in it.

Morphine logic wanted to know why the hospital staff hadn't tied me down. We can't have people floating all over the ceiling now, can we? They could have at least tucked me in beneath the bleached sheet and that pilled blanket. Morphine counter-logic immediately answered.

*Because, you have a broken pelvis, dummy. Why would they assume you're going anywhere with a broken pelvis?*

During my kidney stone episode, I learned that morphine doesn't extinguish pain. It allows you to make friends with pain. It lets you chat it up without having to listen to it scream. I also learned that Morphine bears a special gift. Hallucinations. One night, while the kidney stone ran power sweeps down my right side, I found myself kneeling on that other hospital bed, doubled over with my fingers dug into my guts while giant crows pecked at my head. At the time, I wondered not so much what giant crows were doing in a private room at Essex County Memorial, but what they were hoping to find in my hair?

Morphine logic.

This floating—it had to be a hallucination. A pleasant hallucination. Conditions normal, everything a Go for a leisurely float above my bed. Relax, folks, we've got smooth air all the way to Des Moines.

The explanation made perfect sense until I got stabbed in the cheek by the sharp corner of the fluorescent light frame. One of those rectangular jobs, with a crosshatch insert like an upturned icetray, coated with cheap gold-colored film meant to add warmth to the colorless fluorescent bulbs. The damned thing jabbed me in the cheekbone below my left eye. It hurt, but I didn't care. Thank you, Mother Morphine. The coexistence of pain and the absolute indifference to it.

The other end of the light fixture jabbed my knee. I chose not to acknowledge it. I knew my knee hurt, the way it hurts when you kick a coffee table on the way to the kitchen in the middle of the night. But the pain was distant, someone else's pain.

Nudging up against the light fixture, I turned my head to avoid treating my nose to the same sharp corner. I looked across the white ceiling tiles, the Bonneville Salt Flats of ceiling. A filament of spider web drooped from one of the tiles, backlit by the wedge of light coming from the hallway.

Spider web. Dry tiles. Nurses outside my door talking about how "you can get that on Netflix." For a hallucination, it had the kind of rich detail you see in a Ridley Scott film.

I turned my head farther and looked down. The bed sheets lay crushed to one side, the blanket knotted where my feet had been. The room felt warm.

That's when I looked for my body and realized I wasn't there.

Gone.

Vanished.

*Nice touch*, I thought. I held my right hand, the one not attached to the IV, in front of my face. If I concentrated, I saw—or more likely, imagined—the shape of a hand, like something made of water within water. Just a shimmer of an outline to my eye. I looked for the rest of my body, still bumping languidly against the light fixture.

Gone.

I have vanished.

I'm floating.

I'm bumping into the ceiling.

This is not a hallucination.

*What the—?*

And that's when I reappeared, and gravity had her vicious way with me. I dropped from the ceiling to the empty hospital bed, broken pelvis and all.

The screaming that followed was not in my head.

. . .

FOUR THINGS HAPPENED, if not simultaneously, then in such rapid succession that four eyewitnesses would have given four different accounts to the police.

A monitor sitting stoically at the head of my bed issued a loud tattletale beeping.

The landing approach, far from stabilized and far from my best, caused my left arm to pinwheel wildly, like a cheerleader cranking up the home crowd, which caught the plastic IV tube on the safety bar running down the left side of the bed, which in turn yanked the IV bottle free, which then tipped the entire stand over with an alarming crash.

To my left, from a sofa nestled beneath the room's windows, a black cloud of blanket, pillow and wild dark hair rose up like God's own juggernaut of holy justice, and from this fierce apparition my wife's voice cut through the darkness.

*"Nurse! Need some help here!"*

And I passed out.

# 2

"Hey."

Andy's voice, soft and close. I felt her lips against my ear, on my cheek. I felt her hands on both sides of my head, her fingers threaded into my hair. Morphine was nice, but this…

"Hey, Pilot," she said. "You promised me you would never crash."

Was she talking about my six-foot drop onto the bed?

I considered opening my eyes but felt no need. Andy hovered so close it felt like she spoke inside my head. Her hair lay across my face, falling around us like a shroud. She held me in two worlds. The world of pain shrieking up my torso, ringing in my ears. And the serene world of her voice, her touch, and her scent.

"No, I didn't," I whispered.

"It was implied."

Something bad had happened. Bad enough to put me in the hospital. Whatever it was, it scared Andy. She held me tight.

"I suppose that makes it binding," I said hoarsely. My throat felt terribly dry. "Can you—"

"What, love?"

"Can you get me a beer?"

She laughed. Then she sobbed. The two mixed like wind swirling above me, and rain came. She sobbed, and her tears fell on my face. I tried to reach for her, but my arms had been bound tightly against my body, held in place by the blanket I kicked off when I went flying.

She'd been here. She'd been on the sofa, holding her vigil for me. I wondered if she'd seen me flying. Then I wondered how completely nuts I had gone to wonder that.

She cried over me for a minute. Then sniffled. She kissed me on the forehead, on the nose, on my lips.

"Don't ever do that again!" she commanded in a breaking voice that connected us like a vow. "Ever."

She kissed me on the cheek. It hurt.

She kissed me right where the light fixture had jabbed me.

# 3

My wife likes to tell people we met when she pulled me over for driving while full of myself. She insists such a law exists on the books in Essex County. That she pulled me over in full uniform while on patrol in a City of Essex squad car is not a lie, but she employs a bit of creative license in our origin story. With good reason.

The first time I saw her, the *actual* first time, she walked into the fixed base operation offices at Essex County Airport on the arm of a man named Carl Lofton. I was in my second year working as a pilot for Essex County Air Services, wearing the multiple hats of flight instructor, charter pilot, and sometimes as would-be mechanic wearing coveralls in the hangar, assisting with annual inspections and such repairs as Doc, our certified Airframe and Powerplant mechanic, would allow. Doc, thankfully, is about as good-natured a wrench-turner as the cold war Air Force ever minted, a fixture at Essex County Air Service since Bush Senior was president. I can follow directions and handle a set of tools, but I also ask a lot of questions, which Doc answers with endless patience. I think it has something to do with the fact that when I put on a set of coveralls, he hands off the dirtiest, most monotonous jobs to me.

The day Andrea Katherine Taylor walked through our tinted glass office doors, I was not, thankfully, wearing greasy coveralls. I stood looking my professional pilot best in a clean white shirt with a black tie and epaulets denoting my Captainly Authority, having just returned from an afternoon charter run to the upper peninsula of Michigan. I leaned on the counter, adding to my aura of great aviation prowess by holding a clipboard in one hand and a pen in the other.

Men are men, and when we see a woman like Andrea Taylor, we stop and look. Married men do it from behind sunglasses and with furtive glances. Single guys do it with tongues hanging out. We all do it. And we all run instant calculations, measuring ourselves against the dumb but lucky schmuck the woman is with. From those calculations, we project a flight path into a happily-ever-after future with such a woman. It's a fallacy that men don't want to commit. We do it all the time, all day long, with dozens of women we see on the street and in our minds.

Andrea Taylor could (and still can) stop a clock. Thick waves of auburn hair, taking and shooting back sheens of sunlight. A slender waist my hands instantly imagined gripping, blossoming into hips that signaled procreation to some lizard part of my brain. And legs. Oh, God bless the designer of that summer dress she wore, which shared most of her sculpted legs on one end and hung tastefully yet tantalizingly cut above the bosom at the other end, where she had just slightly more than most women her size and weight carry. Ever so slightly more.

Men stop and look, and some women collect those looks like Spanish gold, but a woman like Andrea will make you meet her at the eyes. They're too bright, too alert, too alive and they will hunt you down and demand direct contact. Once connected, she's the one doing the appraising, with little mercy. Her lips partnered with her eyes, pursed slightly, equally appraising. Their deep color seemed all her own and the smile they could conjure flashed like a magic spell. Her skin had just enough creamy caramel color to suggest what she took from the summer sun didn't burn and needed no enhancement.

She had the magazine looks, but it was immediately apparent she wasn't a two-dimensional beauty.

My first impression of Andrea Taylor was of a woman who knows when men are looking. When she chooses to look back, she will make you feel like the little boy you are.

My second impression was that she may have been on Carl Lofton's arm, but she flew in formation; she was nobody's cargo.

I didn't like Carl. Hadn't for as long as I'd known him.

Now I hated him.

Aviation is a family of like-minded people with a strong sense of dedication and purpose. The pilots I know, those I learned from, those I taught, and those I met along the way, are sharp, intelligent, precise, and humble before the forces of nature that we challenge. Then there are the Carl Loftons. They don't fly because a childhood passion sent balsa wood airplanes zooming around the back yard. They fly because an airplane is another notch in the belt, like the boat, the SL Mercedes or Corvette, or the place on the lake. They fly because money is no object, and yet it is the sole object. So, Carl Lofton, an arrogant ass who made his money being an arrogant ass in real estate or an arrogant ass practicing law or perhaps as an arrogant ass stealing social security checks, added a pilot's license to his hundred-dollar haircuts and single-malt scotch collection.

Carl had passed his Private Pilot Checkride a few months before, and we all knew he would be buying his own airplane too soon. It's an old saw, but a pilot who earns his license—who has passed a difficult written exam and flown a practical test under the severe eye of an FAA examiner—has only earned a license to learn. Except for the Carl Loftons of the world. They already know it all. Instead of continuing to learn, the Carl Loftons go out and buy more airplane than they should, usually a little too fast and a little too complex. And trouble follows.

Standing there, watching Carl and his new girlfriend sweep into the office, I faced a choice. Stay, and enjoy the view of the woman, or duck into the inner office and avoid Carl's smug, over-loud baritone. I caught a glance from Rosemary, the white-haired goddess of our front desk (ever since the Wright Brothers, she liked to claim). Her sharp look warned me not to run like the coward she knew I was, and she rolled her eyes when I did just that. Besides, I could still enjoy a view of the woman walking out to the flight line from the inner office, all the less obtrusively. A nice afternoon breeze swept the flight line, and that summer dress—lemonade and roses—looked delightfully light.

Carl rented one of the Cessna 172s he had trained in, and a short while later I watched the airplane wiggle a little in the crosswind as they climbed out into the late afternoon, summer-hot sky.

"THAT GIRL IS GOING to be sick," Rosemary announced a little over an hour later, looking out the office windows.

I leaned on the customer side of the counter, updating my logbook as a means of killing the last duty hour of the day. I had watched Carl's landing with clinical interest. We had a decent crosswind, ten to fifteen knots about forty degrees off the nose of the airplane. A Cessna 172 is a high-wing airplane, light in a wind, and a little slab sided. I grudgingly gave Carl points for holding a crab angle into the flare on landing yet kicking the rudder enough to line up the wheels on touchdown. He came in hot, though. I marked that against him. He rolled it off the runway and taxied to the gas pumps and shut down.

The woman let herself out of the passenger side without waiting for Carl to open the door. She stepped confidently onto the landing gear strut and down to the ramp. She moved with sharp intent. The way she left Carl behind and immediately headed for the office suggested trouble between the dating couple. But Rosemary read people well, and as this dark-haired beauty stepped purposefully up the sidewalk toward the office, I saw what Rosemary saw. The woman's hands extended at her side with her fingers stretched out, the way someone might reach for balance while walking on a beam. Her steps were measured and urgent. Her eyes hid behind a set of Ray Ban aviators—good pilot sunglasses though I later learned they were cop's sunglasses—but it was easy to see that her focus fixed on the next ten feet of pavement. She hurried.

"Here," Rosemary said. She handed me the plastic wastebasket from behind the counter. "She ain't gonna make it."

Already, the woman's right hand swept up to her lips. It was coming.

I pushed through the inner doors to the office, shoved open the outer doors and met her one pace beyond. She might have looked at me in horror, wishing no one was there to witness what was about to happen, but sharp appraisal kicked in; the wastebasket offered salvation.

I handed her the wastebasket. I took her by the elbow and pushed through the doors. Her pace doubled. With my hand on her elbow, I pulled her across the hall to the empty pilot's lounge. Her scent broke through the standard aviation cologne of grease, fuel, and what traces of tobacco lingered in the ceiling tiles from the days when everybody smoked. For a moment I caught a whiff of her perfume—something like fresh fruit at a summer breakfast. She rushed the last few paces to the leather couch and dropped in a flutter of summer dress, doubling over.

I had her hair in my hands as the first retching shook her shoulders. My own stomach announced its intentions to go aerobatic, but I barked back at it in my head. *Stand down.*

It came fast, in body-shaking heaves, then spits and coughs. I continued to hold her hair but extended one leg behind me and kicked the door shut.

She gulped some air and vomited again. The first round had been productive. This, not so much. A sheen of sweat broke out on her slender neck and the fine slope where it met her shoulders. A few errant strands of her rich hair curled in glossy moisture forming mysterious glyphs. God help me, the woman was vomiting into a wastebasket, yet for an instant I imagined that sheen of sweat and that dark hair against a pillow.

She tried to rise, but I bunched her hair in one hand and put the other on her shoulder.

"Eyes shut, stay still, just breathe," I said.

I got a nod. She pushed the basket away from her face to escape the smell before it induced another round. I took it from her and set it aside. She nodded again.

"'M okay," she whispered.

"No, you're not. This will take a while." I didn't want to let go of her hair, but she turned her head slightly, signaling that the moment was over. "You're going to want to lie down for a bit."

"No, I really—" She started to rise.

"Lasagna," I said.

She dropped sharply onto the leather cushions and her hands shot out, groping. I put the wastebasket in her fingers. She yanked it beneath her bowed head. Her body heaved. More coughing. More spitting. Then gulps of air.

"Bastard."

I had my hands wrapped around her hair again, figuring that gave me temporary immunity.

Her lungs settled into a rhythm of short, strong breaths.

"I'm Will," I said.

"I'm deeply embarrassed," she said into the top of the wastebasket, this time enduring the swill at the bottom, knowing how close she was to launching again.

"Nice to meet you, Deeply," I said. "Been there. Done that."

She didn't speak for a moment. She drew herself upright, and God help me again, but the view improved dramatically from where I stood above her. The light sheen of sweat condensed and traced glistening lines down the center of her chest. Her breathing continued in short, choppy in-outs, with a pause between each to see if the vomiting would be triggered again. After a cautious assessment, she pushed away the wastebasket once more. I took it.

"Lie down. Let the room stop spinning. I'll get rid of this."

Still not looking up, eyes still shut, breathing still quick, she slid across the leather sofa, feeling its dimensions, then she eased herself down.

I stole another long look before I left.

I dumped the wastebasket in the Men's Room toilet and gave it a quick rinse. I left it there.

Carl Lofton walked up the sidewalk toward the office. I took up a casual stance beside the office counter. A light electric sensation eased down the back of my neck. I felt the nerves in my arms answer. I flexed my fingers the way I do when I'm coming up on a final approach fix about to drop the landing gear and nail the glide slope needle. All focus. Everything clear and in its place. Something in the look on my face made Rosemary say, "Uh-oh." She departed her rolling office chair and found something to do in the inner office.

"Hey, Carl," I said flatly when he pushed through the doors.

"Will! My man!" The handshake was over-strong. Playing the alpha dog. I grinned at him, and he grinned back, too stupid to see that my grin didn't go any farther than my lips.

I said, "What a great day to fly! A little bumpy, but wow. Did you show her some stuff?" I flexed my eyebrows, like we were buddies, like I wanted to hear him boast. His shit-eating grin widened. Boasting is what he did best.

"You know it!"

"Yeah? Crankin' and bankin'? Makin' big holes in the sky?"

"If you know what you're doing, even a 172 can sing, am I right?"

*Except you don't know what you're doing, asshole.*

"You know it, man! You know it!" I punched his shoulder.

Carl glanced around and adopted a theatrical expression of conspiracy between brother aviators. "I showed her. Rolled that baby." He puffed himself up like I was supposed to give him a high five. I wanted to punch his greasy nose through the back of his skull, but I kept up the grin, and he bought it like cheap land.

"No shit three-sixty rolled it? Up and over?"

His head bobbed. Idiot. "You know it. She loved it, man."

I stared at him. Grin fixed. Eyes cold. I saw a flicker of dawning realization.

"Say, where is she?"

"You rolled it?"

More dawning. "Well, yeah. A nice barrel roll, you know. Pretty much just one gee."

"Carl, what category aircraft is a 172?"

"Huh? A 172?" He gestured down the hall. "Say, did you see where she went? Is she in the can? It was kinda bumpy out there today. I think she was getting a little green toward the end. Maybe I should check on her—"

"Carl, what category aircraft is a 172?"

I got a hesitant look from him. Somewhere in his smug self-confidence, a that's-not-right moment intruded on his lordly command of Carl's World. It's the moment when a pilot hears an engine misfire. When a landing gear light doesn't turn green. When the oil pressure needle wavers. Men like Carl generally don't recognize such moments. They don't listen when tiny voices whisper at them. But he looked at me now. My grin evaporated. Ice formed in my eyes.

"A 172 is not an aerobatic category aircraft, Carl."

"I know, but I can keep the gees well within limits. A barrel roll, that's just—that's easy, one gee if you do it ri—"

"You fucking barrel rolled one of our aircraft?"

"Look, I, uh—"

"Scared the shit out of some poor passenger?"

"C'mon, man, I know what—"

"You know what you're doing? Really?" My tone was smooth, even. Ice on a still pond. "You've had aerobatic training? You were in an aircraft rated for aerobatics?"

"Hey, I was careful."

"You're done here, Carl. You're never renting another aircraft from us. Do you understand me?"

"You can't—"

"Oh, yes I can. And I'm going to e-mail every other FBO in the state, so you can forget about taking your shit show on the road. You're an arrogant prick who doesn't belong in the cockpit."

"Fuck you!" Red streaks rose in his cheeks. Carl probably had twenty pounds on me, most of it billowing over his belt, but I had an inch of height. This wasn't going anywhere.

"Take your shit and go."

He was close to jittering, like an old car with a bad clutch trying to take a hill it shouldn't. Nobody talks to Carl Lofton like that.

"Fine," he said, like it was suddenly his idea. "Where's the broad?"

*'The broad?' Are you fucking kidding me?*

"She left," I lied. "She said to tell you never to call her again."

The red ran from his cheeks down into his neck. A vein throbbed above his right eye. I noticed for the first time that his hair was thinning badly. *Gonna need plugs soon, buddy.*

He still had the flight board in hand, with the aircraft key and the time-card showing how much rental time had been logged on the flight. He tossed it onto the counter. It slid across and dropped to the floor with a flat slap.

"I ain't fucking paying for this!" He started to turn.

My left hand clamped on his bicep, just above the elbow. He tried to jerk free, but I had it at the bone. With my right hand, I pulled my cell phone out of my pocket. I held it up in front of his face with the screen toward me.

"You're going to pull out your fucking Gold MasterCard and give it to Rosemary, and you're going to pay for this rental and anything else you have on your account. Because if you don't, the recording I just made of this conversation where you admitted violating several Federal Aviation Regulations and admitted to careless and reckless operation of an aircraft is going directly to the Feds, where it, and my testimony, and the testimony of that woman will guarantee your license is suspended, do you copy?"

Rosemary emerged from the inner office, her face aimed at the floor, probably to suppress a cheer. She picked up the flight board and began to work the keyboard on the front desk computer. I released my grip on Carl's arm.

Rosemary took her sweet time. She tallied up Carl's account. Today's rental. Two from earlier in the month. She ran his card while he stood staring, silent. His signature scratched through the slip. He threw down the pen.

"Fuck you," he muttered as he walked out of the office.

Rosemary squeezed her lips together, holding her tongue, watching him go.

After a moment, I jogged out the front doors after him. The sun hung low in the west, but a steady early-evening breeze pushed out the windsock. It may have been a beautiful summer day, but such days produce sharp thermals over the farmland and forests of Wisconsin, and the ride in a light plane can be rough, hot, and uncomfortable. Between that and Carl's bad judgment, I understood how the flight had spun the woman's head.

"Carl!" I called after him. He was on a march to his car, the inevitable Corvette. "Hey, man! Wait up a second!" I let a little softness ease into my tone, a little brother-to-brother.

He hesitated. He looked over his shoulder at me.

"Wait up a second, man," I said with a mild shrug, the kind he read as the signal that an apology would follow. He was wrong. I let my eyes fall to his shoes for a second. Let him be the alpha dog. He waited for me.

"Listen, I want to ask you one thing, okay?"

"Okay."

"Don't take anyone with you."

He stood still, ready for the apology, but those weren't the words he expected.

"What?"

"Don't take anyone with you."

"What's that supposed to mean?"

I heaved a sigh. "You're an arrogant prick. You think you know it all. That makes you a dangerous pilot. So, don't take anyone with you. When you fuck up and kill yourself. Don't take anyone with you. A girl. A wife. Kids. Don't kill them, too. Please."

Carl took a thousand miles off the tires of his Corvette when he peeled out of the parking lot.

ROSEMARY WAVED her keys at me when I walked back into the office. The wall clock said closing time. The door to the pilot lounge stood open.

"She come out?"

Rosemary nodded. "She went down to the Ladies. Are you going to take her home?"

I shrugged with all the Casual I was able to muster up, but it didn't fool her. Her cheeks balled up over a knowing smile that, unlike my grin for Carl, rode high into her pale eyes and lit them up like landing lights. She laughed and started to leave.

At the door, she stopped and looked at me.

"That girl is going to marry you."

I DIDN'T THINK SO after I drove the woman home.

Except for curt directions, she hardly spoke. She didn't tell me her name. It wasn't a cold ride, but it was solitary. She directed me to an apartment building on the west side of Essex. I considered asking how she was feeling, but decided the question invited too much review of what had happened.

For some reason, I felt acutely aware that my car was an eleven-year-old Toyota Corolla that hadn't seen a car wash, well, ever. I wanted to reach over and scoop up the litter on the passenger-side floor, but I didn't want her thinking I was reaching for those beautiful bare legs. Except for shifting, I kept my hands at ten and two on the wheel.

Pulling into the parking space she indicated, I let the engine run.

To my surprise, she turned and looked frankly at me, eyes squeezed down slightly, like someone searching for a landmark on a distant horizon.

"I heard what you said. To Carl. Outside."

I suddenly wondered if she'd also heard me lie to the bastard, telling him she'd gone and never to call her again. The pilot's lounge door was closed, but it's not soundproof. She probably thought I was an opportunistic ass.

"Did you mean it?"

"Mean what?"

"Will he kill someone?"

"I hope not."

She got out of the car without another word.

Rosemary was full of shit.

. . .

TWO WEEKS LATER, as I turned onto the narrow blacktop about a quarter mile from the driveway to the farmhouse I'd been renting, a City of Essex squad car rolled up behind me with its light bar exploding blue and red against a high summer twilight. I felt a cold anchor drop in my stomach, the one everyone feels when the blazing cop car lights fill up the rearview mirror. I pulled over and fished my wallet out of my back pocket and held it in my hand. No sense reaching for something in the near-dark, something a cop can't see. Shit, was I speeding? I hadn't paid attention, but the default answer to that is approximately twelve over the limit. *Shit.*

The officer strolled up, filling my side-view mirror with utility belt and a black semi-automatic service weapon. I already had the window open. The air conditioning on the Corolla died long before I bought it used.

I looked up at the face beneath the peaked cap and the anchor in my stomach turned to a cloud of butterflies, like some sappy Disney animation.

She wore her hair in an official-looking bun. I had a split second to feel disappointed that she wouldn't need me to hold it.

"Hello, Will Stewart," she said. Dummy that I am, I wondered how she knew my last name.

"Hello, Deeply Embarrassed," I said, instantly wishing I hadn't, and just as instantly feeling better when it brought a smile. She let the smile linger.

"Yes, well, do you blame me?"

"I told you. Been there, done that. And I was the pilot."

"You were airsick?"

"Blew my breakfast out the side window."

"That's not exactly reassuring to the passengers." The smile stayed. It seemed to dance on her face, lit like a party by the blue and red lights from her squad car.

"Is there a problem, officer?" Stupid, stupid question.

"It's Sergeant. Andrea Taylor," she said. Her hand came out. I took it. We shook warmly, curtly, professionally. I wanted to hold that hand. "And yes, there is a problem if you ever tell my chief why I stopped you."

"Okay. I won't tell. Why did you stop me?"

"I want you to take me flying."

She could have been speaking a foreign language, it was so utterly beyond what I expected her to say. I looked at her for a long moment, to see if some joke lay beneath the surface. She gave no hint of anything but sincerity.

I thought about it, and said, "No."

Surprise flashed in her eyes, then doubt, and maybe embarrassment, the genuine kind that follows when a sure-fire plan flops.

"No? You're the pilot."

"Why?"

"Because you have the license." Cute. The joke sparkled in her eyes. I liked those eyes.

"Why?" I repeated. "Why do you want me to take you flying?"

She hesitated.

"I don't like being defeated. I never flew in a small plane before, and I felt defeated afterward. I don't like that."

"Okay. Still No."

She rocked back on one foot. Her eyes darkened. "You won't take me flying?"

I shook my head. "You take me."

"Um, again...you're the pilot."

"Yes. But you do the flying. You take the controls. You'll be hands on. You'll be in control. You'll feel the aircraft and know what it's doing. I'll get you onto the runway, but you'll push the throttle up. You do the takeoff. You do the flying."

"Me? Takeoff?"

"Little known secret. Airplanes fly nicely without us. The airplane will take off practically by itself."

She drew a breath and considered the idea.

"I'll be there, right there, the whole time. But no stunts. No bullshit. Not like—"

"That asshole?"

"I didn't know if the two of you, um, were..."

"It was the second date. My mind was made up after the first date, but he offered to take me flying and it's something I always wanted to do. And I got sick and that took it away from me. I want it back."

This had nothing to do with saving face or showing me something. This was between her and her expectations, between her and the sky.

"Then take me flying," I said.

And she did.

I knew before I showed her how to start the engine I was in love.

# 4

"They found you in the pilot's seat, in a marsh about a half mile from the threshold," Pidge told me. She had a note of envy in her voice, like I'd done something she wanted to try. No surprise. She's crazy. "Fucking cockpit was gone. Just you and the fucking pilot seat."

"Pidge," Andy, my wife, the love of my life, fired a warning shot. "We're not supposed to talk about the accident. Maybe later, okay?"

Cassidy Evelyn Page, who we at the airport had dubbed Pidgeon after her first solo eight years ago, coughed out, "Fucking bullshit." She talks dirty and she flies. Hence, Pidgeon. Eventually, just Pidge.

I turned my head on the pillow. Andy sat close to me God love her. She held my hand. She had a good grip on it. She rubbed it, like she needed constant reaffirmation that it was neither cold nor dead. Her eyes glowed red and wet. Her long waving locks had been brushed through after last night's vigil on the in-room sofa. She'd been there the whole time. Which begged a question about what she had seen or not seen when I went flying among the light fixtures.

She let her gilded green eyes fall on me, and they were full of love and gratitude to such a depth I felt the air sucked from my lungs. It felt good, which helped, because I didn't. I hurt everywhere. The parts of my body that weren't screaming at me were muttering rudely, fomenting rebellion. I was running a little light on painkillers. The team kicking field goals into my nuts said so.

Since my night flight, I'd been in and out, awake, asleep, and in between on waves of pain and swells of bliss. Somebody cranked up the morphine and I must have slept. Now, the parking lot lights outside my window were out. The poles stood in silhouette against a blue sky.

"You're gonna have visitors," Pidge said dramatically. "The mother-fucking Feds."

My eyes felt gunky, so I blinked to clear them and get a better look at who was in the room. Andy held down the chair by my bed. Pidge, looking the blonde pixie she was, sat with her legs folded under her on the sofa where Andy had spent the night. It was the kind of couch you find in a hospital room that's trying hard to be both a chamber of pain, confusion and fear, and a three-and-a-half-star hotel room with wood paneling.

Pidge wore a grubby sweatshirt and cutoff jeans, so she was probably on her way to the airport where, like me, she worked for Essex County Air Service as a pilot. She kept her professional slacks and uniform shirt in a closet in the pilot's lounge.

"NTSB got there a few hours after they found you. Been out at the site ever since. Jesus Jumped Up H. Christ, Will. You spread Six Nine Tango all over Essex coun—"

"Pidge!" Andy cut her off. My girl can swing a word like a Viking swings a war axe. I got a hand squeeze and gave one back.

Pidge raised her palms in surrender, which is never that in a twenty-four-year-old pilot. I know. I'd been one a decade or so ago, and we of that ilk know two things: Everything. And nothing.

I deduced from what Pidge had let slip that I crashed one of the company's twin-engine Piper Navajos, which I flew regularly on charters. I could not remember a crash, or a recent flight, or waking up in a marsh. A giant empty hole obscured my memory.

A doctor identifying himself as Morrissey had been in several times. Morrissey owned the friendly face that told me they would give me something for the pain. Morrissey looked younger than me. That had never happened to me before in a doctor.

"Mr. Stewart, imaging confirms that you have a stable pelvic fracture. Just one, in the pelvic ring, and no serious internal bleeding. That's good news."

It didn't feel like good news. It felt like hearing that Hitler had invaded the Low Countries.

Dr. Morrissey seemed to want to bring home the point. He put his hand on my chest. "You're lucky. The fracture doesn't require surgery. It's a closed fracture. There's no skin break."

"Which means?" I managed to ask. A wave of pain ran up through my chest, under his hand and I nearly vomited.

"We're going to continue the morphine for the pain. We're going to keep you still. That's how it will heal." He pushed a nice, professional smile at me. "This could have been a lot worse."

In my ignorance, and deep in pain, I wasn't sure I agreed.

"There are no other overt injuries, but we're watching you closely." Something in his eyes said he was surprised not to have found more. "You had a period of being unconscious when you were brought in, so we're mindful of a possible concussion."

At some point, I think during daylight while waking from another cycle of pain-morphine-doze, I heard one of the nurses say to someone else in the room: This guy is a miracle. Plane crash. Broken pelvis. Classic seat belt injury. But not a scratch or contusion anywhere else. They found him sitting in his seat in a swamp.

I connected that comment to what Pidge said, grinning at me like I just flew under the Golden Gate Bridge and let her ride shotgun. She found way too much glee in this.

"Mwa—" my tongue stuck to the roof of my mouth. I reached for a cup with ice chips perched on a tray suspended over the bed.

"Let me!" Andy scooped it from my fingertips and pressed it to my lips. I probably could have managed, but I let her play Florence Nightingale. The ice did the trick.

"Nobody's telling me anything," I griped. "I wrecked Six Nine Tango? When?"

Andy shot Pidge a 40-millimeter anti-aircraft glance before she could open her mouth.

"Will, they only let us in to see you on condition that we not talk about the ... accident."

"Such bullshit!" Pidge opined.

"Otherwise!" Sergeant Andrea Stewart said, "Otherwise, they were going to keep you sequestered until the investigators got here." I didn't like the sound of that, and it must have shown on my face. Andy quickly added, "I think they just want to hear from you, you know, before you start hearing versions from everybody else."

"How long have you been here?" I asked my wife.

"Longer than you. Mike called me when they found you. I beat the ambulance here." She smiled a smile that revealed both her precocious underbite and a streak of mischief that paid bonuses in bed. She also used it to hide the terror I knew she must have felt driving through the night after getting the call. "I might have been speeding."

"Cops catch you?"

"The cop hasn't been born that can catch me."

Even if she wasn't a police officer, my wife was unlikely to ever receive a written citation. She had hinted to me that in the past she had slipped away more than a few times with a polite warning.

She looked at me sweetly and Mother Morphine met her match; Andy's gaze warmed me deeply.

"They're here," Pidge muttered out of the side of her mouth, unfurling her legs on the couch, squaring her shoulders as if the FAA and the NTSB intended to ramp check her on the spot.

Doctor Morrissey entered the room leading two newcomers.

A woman in a blue nylon windbreaker with NTSB on the breast, and a man in a blue hoodie, but without the yellow lettering, stepped into the room. The woman was short and carried the kind of weight that probably branded her with hurtful words in the schoolyard as a child. She used dark eyes like tools of her investigative trade to scan the room, its occupants, and most thoroughly me. Assessing. Recording. The man was younger than her, with an athlete's build. Rock climber. Or kayaker. His blondish hair and tanned face confessed to a love of sunshine.

Morrissey laid down the rules like a referee. "Mr. Stewart is receiving strong narcotic medication for pain, so you need to keep this short, and you need to keep this unofficial." I wondered if he knew something I didn't. I liked that he ran interference for me.

The newcomers introduced themselves. Connie Walsh of the National Transportation Safety Board and Joe Cyler from the Federal Aviation Administration Flight Standards District Office in Milwaukee, which pilots call Fisdo.

"Hi," Walsh said. "How are you feeling?" She didn't offer a hand, but I took that less as a snub than her thinking she might break something if she reached out and grabbed me.

"Like the scene of an accident."

"That bad, huh."

Cyler stood silent. He wore an expression that said this exchange struck him as only mildly interesting.

"You are, according to Dr. Morrissey, nowhere near as broken as you probably should be, Mr. Stewart," Walsh said. "In fact, I'm rather amazed to be standing here talking to you." The eyes, her tools, continued their investigation, paying no heed to the smile she applied to her lips. "When we got the call, we assumed it was fatal. When I saw the wreckage, I was sure."

Andy's grip on my hand tightened. I shrugged lightly. Then gritted my teeth. It hurt to shrug.

"Just so you know, this is not an official proceeding," she said. "We just want to get an initial idea from you about what happened."

My mouth remained dry. The words came slowly. "I might not be much help. In fact, I was hoping someone might fill me in."

"You don't remember the accident?"

"Nothing."

I expected her to think I was lying. Her eyes didn't leave me. She gave it a second to sink in, but she seemed to do so without judging.

"Do you remember flying a charter to Lansing? Dead-heading the return trip?"

I've been across Lake Michigan to Lansing with regularity for years. I remembered the approach clearances, the runway, the coffee in the FBO. None of those memories raised a hand to volunteer that they were connected to whatever put me in this hospital bed. I remembered a breakfast. Parking my car in the airport lot. Weather briefings. But were those memories for this trip or for any other day of my working pilot's life?

"Wha-happened?" I asked, a little put out with myself for slurring it.

"Well, initial indications are that your aircraft broke up. Possibly…" She glanced at Cyler. "Possibly because you hit something."

Cyler's expression said he didn't like her sharing.

"You mean the ground?" I had a sick feeling. I screwed up. Lost situational awareness. Vertigo? Flying an approach below minimums, slamming a perfectly flyable aircraft into the earth? Unforgivable aviation crimes that I, like every other pilot who has ever done it, felt sure I would never commit.

The NTSB report would classify it as CTIF; Controlled Flight Into Terrain.

I felt heartsick.

Walsh shook her head.

"No. Hit something. In the sky, not the ground." She looked at me for a reaction. I looked at her for meaning.

Neither of us found what we were looking for.

# 5

"How much trouble am I in?" I pointed the question at Cyler. I watched him make the catch, juggle the question, weigh it, fit it into the holes and slots of what he knew so far, and process an answer for himself that he wasn't ready to share. Surfer dude or not, his wheels turned fast.

"So far, we haven't found anything to indicate deviation from procedure." He replied. It was clear they weren't done looking. "You were cleared IFR out of Lansing. All comm was normal. Handed off to Chicago Center. Normal. Cleared for the RNAV 31 into Essex County. I haven't seen the radar track yet, but I talked with Center and they said it looks normal. You disappeared from radar at…" His eyes shot up to the ceiling to retrieve the information. "…twenty-one forty-seven. About a mile from the approach end of 31 at Essex."

"Altitude?"

"Say again?"

"What altitude? Last radar hit. What altitude?"

Cyler cracked a smile at one corner of his mouth.

"You were on the approach, on glideslope." Walsh answered when Cyler didn't.

The butterflies in my chest stopped beating their wings.

Walsh said, "After you cancelled, Center said you radioed, but were cut off. When they couldn't raise you, they called local PD to ask them to confirm your landing. Local PD reported no activity on the field. About the same time, they also got a report of a loud bang from a farmer."

I wondered if Walsh knew Andy was "local PD."

"John was on dispatch," Andy said. "Mike was in twenty-one and first on the scene." I got a hand squeeze as she said it, like a part of her had been out there looking for me.

"Mr. Stewart, you were found sitting in your seat in an area of soft ground," Walsh said, and something girlish glittered in her eyes, like she'd been winding up to say those words all day. Behind Walsh, Pidge grinned and nodded her head. Walsh let the statement hang, like I might fill in the blanks. It was a trick Andy used when questioning a witness or suspect—and sometimes me. I knew the trick and kept my mouth shut.

Walsh, defeated, eventually spoke. "The airplane is spread out over a quarter mile behind where you were, on the line of the approach."

"Collision? Somebody else on the approach?"

"So far, we haven't found any debris other than the Piper Navajo."

"What then?"

"We don't know."

"Was it a missile?" Pidge blurted.

"We're still investigating," Walsh said, but from her tone, I think missile was off the list.

"Wait," I said. "You don't know what I hit? How do you know I hit something?"

"Preliminary examination of the components we've been able to identify," Walsh said. "Very preliminary. Which brings me to questions. Do you mind if I record this part?"

"I'm not sure I'm comfortable with that," Sergeant Andrea Katherine Taylor Stewart leaned forward in her chair. My protector, putting herself between the threat and her loved one.

"I've already explained that Mr. Stewart is receiving strong doses of narcotics for pain," Dr. Morrisey added.

Walsh waved a friendly hand. "Duly noted, Doctor. And Mrs. Stewart, this will be noted as preliminary only. We're really not here to do anything except investigate the cause of the accident."

I wasn't sure Cyler had signed on to that.

"It's okay," I told Andy. "I don't think there's much I can tell anyone. I'm drawing a big blank. The day, the charter, the weather." I shook my head. "I got bits and pieces, but I think they're from other trips. Pidge, who was the charter?"

"Romain."

Romain Construction. Headquartered in Michigan, working a big highway project in Essex County. When they figured out our charter rates were lower than they had been paying out of Lansing, they became a regular customer, practically a scheduled run. Had been for several years now.

"Jackson? Bridley? Some of the crew?"

"Bridley and three crew. One way. I bet they're going to be fucking glad it wasn't the other way when they hear about this shit storm."

I had nothing. I could see Joe Bridley, with his red beard and sunburned nose. But not in connection with this trip. I could picture some of his crew guys but failed to come up with which ones were on the outbound leg to Lansing.

Hell, I could picture the climb out of Essex, the shore of Lake Michigan passing below and the span of blue wide enough to let you imagine it's the ocean for a few minutes before the other side appears on the horizon. I could picture low clouds, no clouds, cloud layers, moonlit night flights. Flights full of turbulence and ice and sweat. Flights on beautiful blue days hung like living dreams. I could fill in all kinds of blanks and the ATC voices to go with them, but none that anchored precisely to this flight.

*What the hell did I hit?*

"May I?" Walsh held out her phone, finger poised over a Record button.

I felt Andy coiled beside me, ready to object. She might hate lawyers, but she better than anyone would know when you should have one fronting the band. I squeezed her hand.

"Go ahead. But like I said…"

Walsh nodded and tapped her screen. She spoke a few preliminaries into the device, date, time, names of those present.

"Mr. Stewart, do you remember flying into Essex County Airport on the night of June fifteenth?"

"No."

"Do you have any memory of a collision while piloting a Piper Navajo?"

"No."

"Do you remember any details of a flight that originated in Essex County, with a stop in Lansing, Michigan and a return to Essex County?"

"No."

She tried a few more. And soon I got the impression she was doing it not to incriminate, but to keep me in the clear. I never met anyone from the NTSB, but I had heard stories. All of them painted the NTSB investigators as sharp professionals dedicated to the investigation, not to assigning blame. I sensed I was being helped.

My answers were as blank as my memory. It wasn't long before she nodded and pointedly stopped the recording.

"My turn," I said.

"Fair enough."

My voice was tight. My sentences were punctuated with short breaths. "What was the wreckage pattern? You said there was no contact with terrain."

"A nearly perfect straight line, starting with what we think was the left wing, engine and horizontal stabilizer. Then the rest of the tail. Then the right wing and center section along with most of the fuselage. Then parts of the nose and cockpit. Then you."

"How long? From the first piece to me."

"Almost five hundred yards. About a quarter of a mile."

That didn't make sense. Walsh could see it on my face.

"I know," she nodded. "CTIF would be more concentrated. A high-altitude breakup would have been much more spread out, and both linear and lateral. This was linear only. Like you kept flying and shedding pieces."

"The left wing." I said, wincing. The bones in my torso were pissed at all this chatter. I took a deep breath. "That was the initial impact point?"

Walsh tipped her head to one side, marking her answer as a guess. "We think so..."

"But?"

"But it's hard to tell.

"What about impact markings? Paint? What the hell did I hit?"

"We're looking at all that, but frankly..." she peeled off a glance at Cyler, who remained mute "...Mr. Stewart, I saw the left wing myself. It's barely recognizable. Same with the left engine, the nacelle. Parts of what we think was the left side of the fuselage. I've seen airplanes that made a crater that were more recognizable. Only this damage didn't appear to come from ground contact. The ground isn't scarred. Then there are parts of the rest of the fuselage that are split open. Farther on, the whole right wing, which looks nothing like the left. Practically intact. On that side, indications are that the blades were still turning when the prop hit the ground. And then, well, there's you."

"Me?"

"Doctor Morrissey here says you have a broken pelvis. Type—what did you call it?"

"Type A. Stable fracture. Not uncommon with a seat belt injury. The contusions across his midsection strongly support seat belt as the cause. No indication of the kind of rotational forces that produce a partial disruption of the posterior sacroiliac complex, or the kind of force that you might see in a motor accident or fall from a significant height. Those injuries would require surgery and a long, long recovery period. We talked about this, Will."

We did? Guessing at what I was thinking, Morrissey said, "Treatable with bed rest."

Bed rest. I wanted to ask when I would fly again.

Sitting in the pilot's seat in a marsh. Nearly intact, not counting the pelvic injury. What the hell? I usually fly the RNAV 31 Approach into Essex at 120 knots. The left side of the airplane gets torn off, my seat gets pulled out, and I wind up in a swamp—with a broken pelvis probably caused by the seat belt? Treatable by bed rest? With no other injuries? At 120 knots?

Those dots did not connect.

"I think you're seeing the mystery here, Mr. Stewart. For us at least." Walsh looked at me like I was a puzzle. "You are one lucky pilot. You were lucky to be deadheading. Had you been carrying any passengers we assume they would have all been fatalities. You probably should have been."

"Ejector seat!" Pidge offered, grinning.

Walsh said, "If the airplane had one, it would make a lot more sense."

# 6

By the end of the conversation, I decided I liked Walsh. I wasn't sure where Cyler was coming from, but most of the Feds I ever met like to cultivate that aura. They're not bad guys. They just like to stand behind their credentials. Walsh finished the conversation with a hearty handshake, having seen with her own eyes that I was an actual medical miracle and wasn't going to break if she took my right hand. She gave me a sincere thank you for being alive to talk to her. I told her the pleasure was all mine. Given what I figured she'd seen in her career, I think she would have argued the point.

After they left, Andy dispatched Pidge to the cafeteria for coffee.

"You're not going to heal properly if you pull another stunt like last night," Morrissey said, hands in his pockets, trying to be stern. He wasn't all that good at it. Morrissey looked the part of a fresh-hire prep school professor, with no-nonsense glasses and a slightly receding hairline. A young Michael Caine had the acting gig not worked out. Maybe not as tall. "The nurses said you were trying to get out of bed. Or standing up on it."

Not so much. I had a feeling, however, that explaining what I experienced would not hasten my release date.

"It's pretty fuzzy," I offered. "I think I was getting a little trippy on the morphine."

"We need to cut that back," he said, more to himself than to me.

*Dammit.*

"You have to remain stable. You're young but you're not a kid, Mr. Stewart. The bones will heal, but you need to give them the best possible chance of doing so. Jar them again like that, and we're looking at surgery, and extensive recovery time with extensive rehabilitation."

"You copy that, Pilot?" Andy said sharply.

"Roger."


THEY WEREN'T KIDDING about the bed rest. Either as punishment for my antics in the night, or to enforce their intent to immobilize me, they wrapped my midsection in an inflatable cast and secured it to the rails on the bed. A series of thin, air-filled ribs ran parallel to my body, starting just below my own ribs and ending about even with the family jewels. From this rig, an air hose ran to a compressor beneath the bed. Every half hour or so, the compressor started up, keeping the air pressure in the ribs set precisely at Fix This Guy's Pelvis, I assume. The compressor sang a low, muttering song, barely above a vibration. The first time I heard it, I thought of my cell phone. Which then made me wonder, where was my cell phone? And my pants? And for that matter, my wristwatch?

Andy told me my clothes had been cut off. She had my watch. She didn't know anything about my phone. My socks and shoes survived. She pointed at a closet.

She then helped me sort out a bigger question. Time and space.

We were alone in the room. Pidge had delivered coffee to Andy and gone back to her duties on the Essex County Air Service flight line, magnified now that we were one pilot short. The feds had gone back to supervise relocation of the wreckage to an empty corporate hangar at Essex County Airport.

"You were supposed to be back by ten," she told me. "Chicago Center called dispatch at ten-twenty. We got the noise call around the same time. Mike started at the airport, and when he didn't see anything or anyone, he headed out Highway C where the noise call came from. He started a grid search there. He should have called me. I could have checked the wind and told him which approach was in use, and to start on a line from the runway outward."

"That's my Co-Pilot," I said, "except why would he call you? He had no reason at that point to think it was me out there."

"Well, anyway he's the one that found the wreckage. He almost ran over part of it. There was a piece of it on the Old Bridge Road. That's when he called for help. They got the fire department out there and started walking through the fields. He said it was like stuff had fallen off a truck. Just a line of aluminum and airplane parts. As it turned out, entirely by chance, they started at the beginning, and you were at the other end. That's why it took so long to find you. They didn't find you until almost two a.m. That's when Mike called me. They … um, they…"

Her hand squeeze turned to concrete. Andy's voice went tight and high.

"They knew it was you. They thought, just looking at you…sitting there…that you were—"

"I've said it before. I'll say it again. Rumors of my demise have been greatly exaggerated."

She burst into a laugh and vented sobs that had been building.

"Do this again, Pilot, and I'll kill you myself," she said, wiping water from the corners of her eyes. "Anyway, that was around two. They couldn't believe it when one of the firemen got a pulse. They had to carry you to the road, about a quarter mile. I got here at around two-twenty. They rolled you in around ten minutes later."

Here. Essex County Memorial. That took care of space. Two-thirty a.m. arrival. That took care of time. Part of it.

"You were in the ER for a few hours. All they would tell me was that you were alive, and you were unconscious. I, um…"

Hand squeeze.

"I had to wait outside. They took you to Imaging. They wouldn't tell me what they were looking for, but I assumed it was head trauma, broken bones, or God forbid spinal. That's when they found the broken pelvis. I don't think it was what they were expecting. You woke up down there, they said."

"Did I tell them anything? About what happened?"

"You told them someone had shoved molten steel up your ass. Nice."

"It hurt."

"I guess. They said you were in and out of consciousness and in a lot of pain, and once they confirmed there was no head or spinal injury, they started worrying about internal injuries and bleeding. What?"

I stared at her. Questioning.

"Morrissey told me all this," she explained. "After the fact. I didn't know any of it at the time. I was out in the waiting room tearing the wallpaper off with my fingernails. So that's when they moved you up here and put you on morphine. They couldn't treat the pain until they were sure it was okay. That was yesterday morning. You went to sleep like a baby when I finally got in to see you. I thought—God, I thought so *many things!* And then I saw you there, sleeping like nothing happened. You were snoring a little."

"I don't snore."

"Right. Nobody does. You were sleeping and there were no bandages, and you had all your parts."

"You checked *all* my parts?" She ignored me.

"I was tearing my hair out the whole time."

"Please. Not the hair. That's the fourth reason I married you."

She ignored me some more.

"I guess I was a little worn out. I sat down on the couch there, and they brought me a blanket and pillow. Funny, but I remember telling them I didn't want to sleep. I don't remember lying down. But I do remember waking up. Will, you scared the living daylights out of me!"

She said nothing about me disappearing from the bed. Or re-appearing six feet above it. Thinking about this, I reached up with my free hand and rubbed my cheek.

Still sore to the touch.

"I guess you had some sort of nightmare. Were you thinking about—or dreaming about the crash?"

"I got nuthin' on the crash. Zip. I guess I woke up and the pain from this must have been a rude surprise. Sorry for all the noise."

Time and space. Now I had them both. Essex County Memorial, early Sunday morning. It might be a pilot thing, but few things agitate me more than uncertainty about time and space. I read the clock. Nearly eleven a.m. Sunday. Something about that gave me comfort. Like groping through a dark room and finally finding the light switch. The comfort lacked certainty, however. A big gap hung in my memory.

"You need to go home," I told Andy.

"No."

Her answer came with a head shake and a strand of hair fell across one eye. I'd seen this before. She left it there, a flag signaling the start of a stubborn, mortal stand.

"Dee." I used her pet name. Dee, as in D. E., as in Deeply Embarrassed. Also, a shortening of Andy, the shortening of Andrea Katherine, which I would invoke to press the point if I had to.

"I'm staying."

"I'm being pumped full of drugs. Can barely feel them welding down there in my pelvis. I'm going to fall asleep in mid-sentence here and start drooling all over the pillows. I don't want you to see me like that. You'll never want to get near me and a pillow again."

"You're lucky I don't jump you right now, Pilot."

Yeah, that wasn't a help, because things started stirring down under the magic inflatable cast that definitely should not be stirring at that moment.

"Go home. Get some rest. Let me rest. Come back tonight and I'll share my Jell-O with you."

The strand of hair hung defiant.

"Come back rested and I'll let you jump me." More stirring. I moved, or tried to, and a jolt of pain pushed through the morphine. That helped with the stirring thing, but it also painted the pain on my face. She abruptly pushed the strand aside and kissed my cheek. (Still sore.) "Andrea Katherine, go home! Seriously, let me zonk out."

Oh, if I could bottle the gaze that fell on me at that moment. Love. Pity. Warmth. Gratitude. I felt like such an ass, scaring her so badly. We share a life together with certain walls that go up when we're apart. When she's armed and in a patrol car at night, stopping who-knows-what kind of shitbird. When I'm on a charter and the American Midwest is producing thunderstorms like popcorn in a pan. The wall goes up and we lock down the part of our minds where the worst happens in Technicolor. This accident knocked down one of those walls and put her through hell. I was such an ass.

"A few hours," she surrendered.

"Take a nap. I'll ask for green Jell-O."

"You do know how to show a girl a good time."

I got another kiss, this one on the lips, long and firm and trading love between us the way power lines deliver lightning. More damned stirring. For the first time, I wondered how long it really took to heal a pelvis. I had plans for mine. Something I would ask Morrissey next time he appeared.

She worked her way reluctantly out of the room, giving me one more damp-eyed look at the door.

I scared that poor girl.

I wondered how in holy hell an airplane had been ripped apart under me and I wound up sitting in a marsh in the pilot's seat as if I had dropped in for some birdwatching. How does *that* happen?

# 7

"I saw your wife on the way out. She said she'd shoot me in the head if I stay more than five minutes. I believe that woman would."

Earl Jackson appeared in the doorway where I had been clinging to an afterimage of Andy. Earl is somewhere at the other end of the scale when it comes to human design. He looks like a live model for a gargoyle, a combination of squat, bald, and scarred with questionable proportioning. His face has bulges that suggest anger, his arms and shoulders have muscles that suggest murder, and his clothes suggest a rummage sale from 1960. Earl is also the model for one of aviation's oldest clichés. How do you make a small fortune in aviation? Start with a large fortune.

Earl Jackson made a large fortune either inventing or perfecting some sort of machine that bores holes in the ground for cables and pipes. And while I'm sure he did that with the single-mindedness of Genghis Khan conquering Asia, he also suffers from the same lifelong affliction that I do: he loves airplanes. While he was boring holes in the ground all over the world, he was boring holes in the sky with an amazing variety of aircraft. He also crop-dusted, flew checks through the night, flew package express, did a short stint for an airline called North Central (the one with the blue goose on the tail), and even did some flying in Central America for a diamond prospecting enterprise. I imagined him dropping out of a beat up round-engine twin-tail Beech Model 18 on some dirt strip, two bandoliers across his chest and a pair of .45s on his hips. Eventually Earl sold his hole-boring-machine company for a few dozen million and he bought Essex County Air

Service. And even though he could be sipping iced tea on a veranda in Monaco, he prefers to spend his days sitting in a tiny office crammed with maintenance manuals and pondering fuel purchases, or out in the shop arguing torque tolerances with Doc. Slowly turning his large fortune into a small fortune. I have no complaints about that. He pays me better than any airline offers fresh hires these days. He keeps better equipment than most charter operations. And he loves the miracle of flight more than the bottom line. He is an amazing, sometimes terrifying man. Now he stood in the space where the image of my wife had been. It was jarring.

Earl loves Andy, and she loves him. He often says she is my best quality. He also likes to look at her when he thinks no one is paying attention. I don't hold it against him.

"Hi boss."

"Don't 'Hi boss' me. What the hell did you do to my airplane?"

Someone pushed Earl into the room and said, "Earl! Language!"

A woman with skin the color of melted milk chocolate, striking facial bone structure and a gleaming smile appeared. She did what no other human on the planet would dare. She pushed Earl Jackson aside. She cast that smile onto me above a cloud of bright flowers I had no hope of identifying because they weren't red roses. The smile surpassed the flowers.

"There you are—now I feel better," I said, looking at Rosemary II. She marched into the room, and planted the flowers, conveyed in their own vase, on a shelf near the closet. A moment later she stood over me and put a kiss on my head.

"Oh, thank Heaven." She uttered the words as a prayer, her eyes squeezed shut. Earl rolled his.

"Hi Mr. Stewart!" Another bright voice joined the room. Lane, Rosemary II's daughter, all of fourteen going on twenty-five and already every bit the heartbreaker, stepped hesitantly to my bedside. She stood beside—and as a reflection of—her mother, whose real name is Amanda Franklin. Lane tipped a chipper salute in my direction.

Two years ago, the original Rosemary, the icon and authority at Essex County Air Service, the beloved insulation between Earl Jackson The Terror and our cash-paying students, renters, and charter customers—the woman who claimed to have had an affair with Jimmy Doolittle—marched into Earl's office and announced her intention to retire.

"Again?" (That's what Earl is rumored to have said. The story is shrouded in doubt, which we who work for Earl happily fill in with speculation.) "How many times does that make this week?"

"I'm moving to Mexico," Rosemary announced. I knew from experience that Rosemary, the woman who told me Andy would be my wife at a time when I was pretty sure Andrea Taylor associated my face with vomit, had moments when her pronouncements were marble-carved. If she said Mexico, she meant Mexico.

"You don't speak Spanish," Earl supposedly told her. Like that mattered. More to the point, he said, "You can't retire. Who's going to make the coffee?"

"I have just hired my replacement," Rosemary said. And she had.

That's how Rosemary II came to work for Essex County Air Service. It took two days before Earl realized Rosemary had been serious. It was another day before he came out of his office to meet his newest employee, whom he dubbed Rosemary II. Two weeks later, Rosemary, who would had to have been in her hundreds to have flown with Wilbur and Orville and was probably an infant when Jimmy Doolittle was rampaging through the air race circuit, died peacefully in her sleep at the blessed age of eighty-nine. She was in the home where she'd been born, in Essex, far from the Mexican sun. It happened one day before the first anniversary of my wedding to Andy, the wedding Rosemary predicted. In honor of that wild prediction, Andy and I had planned to remind Rosemary of her prescience with a toast. The unopened bottle of champagne we intended to share with her that summer sits on a shelf at home, mourning still.

"Hey, Lane," I said to the girl. "Who're you gonna fly for?"

"British Airways," she said affecting an accent and hitting the t in "British" like a native.

I gave her a thumbs-up and she gave back her mother's smile.

"What the hell—" Earl caught a sharp glance from Rosemary II, the same anti-aircraft weapon my own wife had used on Pidge, "—*heck* did you do to my airplane?"

"Broke it, so they tell me," I said.

"'S coming out of your paycheck," he declared. It was all for show. His threat was the equal of Rosemary II's kiss on my head, an Earl Jackson expression of gratitude for my survival. His retired prize-fighter's face rippled weirdly as that gratitude ran beneath the scarred landscape like one of his hole-boring machines. He coughed suddenly and shook it off.

It was a stark moment for me. I realized there were people who, upon hearing I'd gone down, had been frightened nearly as much as Andy. People who were now trying to draw a breath after discovering there would not be a funeral. The hard, sour knot it caused in my throat caught me a little by surprise, and I suddenly felt tired, tired beyond all expressions of fatigue.

The little man on the raft was screaming again, too. I think the pain showed on my face.

"I'll give you a couple days off, but then you get your ass back to work. We gotta find a new airplane," Earl said, reassuming his standard linebacker personality. "Hopefully one you won't spread all over the county."

"Oh, baloney," Rosemary II waved him off. "Now you rest, and get better, and thank the Lord for every heartbeat. And we are going to stop bothering you, aren't we, Earl."

"'Bye, Lane!" I gave another thumbs-up to the girl by way of apology. I was sure she had better things to do on a Sunday than visit hospitals. She returned the gesture happily, apparently not the least put out that she'd been dragged in for a thirty-second visit. I liked Lane, and I think she liked me, and I think she, too, was glad I wasn't dead. Her mother turned her by the shoulders and aimed her at the door, shooting Earl a gesture that said Get Out as she passed him.

"In a minute," he said. He turned to me. "There's goddamned TV crew out front."

From the hall: "Earl! Language!"

"They think you're a fucking miracle. Shit, I think you're a fucking miracle." Earl came a little closer to the bed. His eyes were sharp, penetrating, like he was looking at me for the secret. One I didn't have. "I saw the pieces. Talked to Walsh."

"I don't—"

He cut me off with a wave. Then he just stood there. Earl only does two emotions. Pissed and angry. But this was something different, and I was not entirely sure I wanted to witness it.

Earl surprised me with something I never knew.

"I flew Phantoms," he said. "Out of Thailand. Got my ass shot down."

I had never heard of this, and I have heard a lot of Earl Jackson stories, half of them from Earl Jackson himself.

Earl held his eyes on me, but I think he was seeing something else. Or looking for something else.

"Pretty close to home, I was. In fact, I landed among friendlies. Never wound up a prisoner, thank the gods and all the cheap beer at Udorn Air Base. Some kinda round, I don't know what, came up through the belly. Hit my fuckin' ejector seat and the damned thing blew me out before the whole airplane blew up."

"Jesus, Earl, I had no idea."

He waved me off again.

"Neither do I." He shrugged. "I talked to Walsh. Cyler, too. He's an ass hat. Walsh, I like. She told me what you told her. That you don't remember. So, this is what I want to tell you: I don't remember it. All I know is what was in the report put together by the I-team they sent out to find the scrap metal. I don't remember any of it. The mission, the hit, the ejection. Lost my back-seater. Tommy Day. They never found him. Nothing. Put his name on the wall, but that's all. To this day, I don't remember it. I don't remember losing Tommy D."

I saw pain in the way he clenched his jaw.

Now he looked at me. If he had grabbed me with the claws he calls hands and pulled me up into his face, it would have been the same thing as the look he aimed at me. He *looked* at me.

"I'm gonna go to my grave not remembering. Just how it is. An itch I can't scratch. I had to learn to live with it. Had to."

I tried to say something, but had neither the words, nor the saliva to make words work.

"I thought you should know. It happens that way sometimes. You learn to live with it. If it doesn't come to you on its own, don't try too hard to dig for it. Copy?"

"Copy."

Earl issued a sharp nod and the book closed. I had a feeling I would never hear another word about it. I sure as hell wouldn't ask.

"I want you back soon. Pidge will fucking drive me batshit if you're not around. Don't let those goddamned TV people in here." He turned and marched out, knowing Rosemary II would return to drag him away any second now.

An itch you can't scratch. Forever. I didn't like the sound of that at all. I wondered if the sore spot on my cheek would end up being an itch I couldn't scratch. My eyes hung heavy, but I took a last look at the ceiling before closing them.

At the tiny spider web hanging from the acoustic tiles.

# 8

I rode sleep into Monday. Andy sat on post again when I woke, with the sun shining through the blinds behind her. The wall clock said nine-twenty. It messed with me, because when Earl left it had been around eleven. I thought in addition to disappearing, I might be going backward in time. That seemed funny to me.

"What?" Andy stood over the bed, looking fresh and combed and wearing different clothes.

"Huh?" My mouth was dry.

"You're smiling," she said. She stroked my hair.

"Mwma…" I pointed at the water cup with the bendy straw. She provided. It was cold and fresh. More confusion on the timeline, as the last sip had been closer to room temperature.

I limbered up my tongue and said, "Happy to see you. Did you take a nap?"

Now she smiled, laughed a little. "I got some rest. You did, too."

"I'm getting that impression. Why is it earlier than when I saw you last?"

"It's Monday, love. You slept nearly twenty-four hours."

"Oh. Well, they're working me pretty hard in here. What about you?" My eyes cleared. I spotted the folded blanket and pillow on the sofa.

"I'm fine. How are you feeling?"

I took a quick inventory. I never lie to Andy. Ever. I might get away with omission, but she has a built-in lie-detector that the CIA would love to get their hands on. It serves her well on the job.

"Hurts again. And what am I feeling … down there?"

"You're still wearing the air girdle."

"Um, no, that's not it."

She smirked. "Well, you're a bit immobile…"

"Kinda know that."

"Um, it's not like you can get up and go to the bathroom."

Horror dawned on me. First, because I realized I needed to go. Second, because I began to realize what caused her smirk.

"They didn't."

"Had to."

"I'm wearing a—"

"An adult undergarment. It was that or a bed pan, and a bed pan means having to raise up your pelvis. Oh, my God, I've never seen you so red. Oh, love!" She kissed me on the cheek like a child. I felt my whole face burning. "Seriously, it's okay!"

"I'm wearing a diaper in front of my girlfriend. The romance is over!"

She fought back a giggle.

"Go ahead. Laugh at me. Please tell me you didn't, you know..."

She shook her head vigorously and said, "Oh, no! It wasn't me. A couple big male nurses came in and did all that." And then she broke into a giggle that grew until it shook her shoulders and made her gasp for air. "Oh, love! You should see your face!"

"Guys?"

"Stop! I'm teasing you. The nurses set you up. And they were very complimentary."

"*What?!*"

"Oh, my God, you are so easy."

"And you are in so much trouble. Stop giggling."

It was nice to see her laugh. It helped me, too. Because that NFL place kicker was loosening up his leg again. Low waves of pain rolled in, pushing up into my chest.

Andy told me the TV crews had returned. They positioned outside the front entrance to the hospital so that their setups would catch the sign in the background. The Fox affiliate called me a "Survival Miracle." The local NBC affiliate said I fell from the sky after my plane "exploded." I wondered what Walsh thought of all this. The Fox guys got the scoop with a mobile unit in front of the hospital yesterday. Andy said she saw Earl, Rosemary II and Lane on TV, trying to slip out the front door in the background of a report aired on the 10 o'clock news. Not to be outdone, the NBC guys joined them this morning and both did live reports, saying I was still in "serious" condition. I concurred with their assessment. It hurt.

"Earl said they're getting calls at the airport, asking about the accident, asking about you. I coached Amanda on how to handle the press." Andy refused to call her Rosemary II, even though I got the distinct impression Rosemary II felt honored by the nickname. "And a few nut balls, too. One guy claimed it was the hand of Jesus and asked for a lock of your hair."

"Has Morrissey been in?" I asked.

She read the grimace correctly. "What's wrong? Is it the pain?"

I blew out a breath, not wanting to complain, but … "I just wondered if he cut back on the meds. He said he was going to. Things … are getting just a little sore." I had to squeeze out the last few words.

Andy hit the call button before I could stop her.

"Hi, we were wondering if Dr. Morrissey is coming around."

The tin voice in the tiny speaker said, "He is on rounds this morning, so he should be seeing you. I can't say for certain when. Is there something you need?"

My head was shaking to which Andy paid zero attention.

"My husband is having a lot of pain. Do you know if there's been a change in his medication?"

"I'll send someone in to check."

Her lips pursed, accenting the slight underbite I found so sexy when she got steam up in a conversation. It extended slightly. I knew it as her I-don't-buy-this-bullshit look, but she held her tongue.

"We have another problem," I said.

"What?"

I rolled my eyes and made a face at her.

"Oh!" The giggle tugged at the corners of her mouth, trying to escape. "Oh, well, go ahead."

"Take a walk."

"Don't be silly. Just go. That's what it's for." She tipped her head at my waist and tried for all she was worth to hold a straight face. Utter failure. "I can't—I'm sorry! You're too funny!"

"Out!"

"Alright alright alright!"

I heard her laughter sparkle in the hall.

Try it sometime. Try just peeing in your pants. Or your bed. It took me almost ten minutes to go, as bad as I needed to.

This was going to be a bad week.

# 9

"Yes, we stopped the morphine last night, while you were sleeping," Morrissey said. "You'll be in less pain if you can keep yourself stabilized. So, you'll need less. No more trying to escape, of course."

"Not that I'm looking to become a junkie, Doctor, but I'm pretty uncomfortable right now. Are we going cold turkey?"

"Oh, no, no, no. I prescribed Oxycodone. It's a narcotic, an opioid."

"Pretty sure I've heard of it," I said. "It's all over the news. Epidemic."

"Yes, well," Morrissey shoved his hands in his pockets, "abuse may condemn it, but it does not mitigate its medical benefit when called for or under the right supervision. Sorry. I get a little soap boxy on this subject. People have an infinite capacity to turn any beneficial advance into something destructive. If you prefer, we can skip it."

"Morphine to heroin. In a way, I prefer to do without," I said. I was thinking about hallucinations. "But I don't think the brush fire in my gut agrees, and I trust your judgment. And—right now—this is killing me."

"We're going to use the extended-release form, ten milligrams every 12 hours. I brought your first pill now and I'd like to stick to a nine a.m. and nine p.m. regimen. That stands the best chance of making you comfortable during the day, and helping you sleep at night. I think after a few days we may be able to back off this, too."

He fished in his coat for a small packet, extracted a pill and handed it to me. The cop sitting next to me gave it a stony look. She'd seen too many of these in backpacks and plastic sandwich bags. I popped it in and chased it down with bendy-straw water. It left a metallic aftertaste.

"Don't operate heavy machinery. And no alcohol." Morrissey's delivery was so laconic I almost missed the crease at the corner of his mouth. "We're going to keep you on liquids for a while, partly to reduce the need to move your bowels."

"Praise Jesus," I said.

"But you might get an upset stomach. Also, shout out if you feel short-ness of breath, confusion. Other side effects include a reduced sex drive. Possibly impotence."

"This just keeps getting better. I don't think my chances of getting laid here are all that good."

"An interruption in menstrual periods," he went on.

Andy's hand shot up to stifle a laugh.

"Other than that, it should make you comfortable. A nursing assistant will bring your next pill at nine this evening. Think you can hold out until then?"

"Depends how well this works. Is this some really good shit? Primo?"

"Oh, we only peddle the best here, Will. Andy, any questions?"

"Can I bust him for possession?"

"Yes, bring out the handcuffs, officer," I challenged her.

"It's sergeant, and he already told you, no sex drive. Possible impotence."

"Care to test that theory?"

Morrissey logged out of the in-room workstation that contained all my secrets along with a catalog of his notes. "I'll leave you two to work that out on your own. But I sincerely doubt what I gave you is enough to knock down the pain you would feel if you do indeed test that theory. Call me if you need me. Otherwise, the happy fairy comes back at nine tonight."

The happy fairy's name was Nick.

# 10

Andy had a court appearance in the afternoon. I persuaded her not to cancel it by claiming I needed downtime for a nap. She insisted she would return for dinner, arguing she never got her Jell-O. I countered with a demand that she sleep in our own bed tonight, at home. She keeps a little-girl-pout in her repertoire for special occasions, and she pulled it out, but I bull-rushed her with the argument that it was hard enough sleeping in this place as it is, and how it would keep me up all night worrying about her. Besides, I knew she'd been told by the Chief of Police that she could take whatever time she needed, and that she'd be back in the morning. I begged her to get the rest.

She returned to see me picking over a dinner consisting of, well, not much of anything, at least not solid. She carried in a roast beef sandwich for herself from the hospital cafeteria but then apologized for eating real food in my presence. I called it nonsense and told her I lacked an appetite. The pill fought its fight against the pain for the better part of the day, treating me to a touch of nausea along the way. I wouldn't have called myself comfortable, but I had also made up my mind to do a little fighting of my own. Nevertheless, the returning high tide of pain contributed to my lack of appetite and made me poor company that evening. Andy turned on the TV and we caught the evening news. I think she was relieved to see that the only mention of the crash appeared in a crawl, in which they misspelled explosion. *Pilot survives aircraft explosoin, miraculously found alive in swamp after aircraft destroyed near Essex County Airport.* No live coverage, at least that we saw.

She channel-surfed until we settled on an Indiana Jones movie. I lowered my eyelids around the time Indy was lowering himself into the snake pit. Before the big finish, I reached over and hit the remote.

"Go home."

I got the pout. "Please let me stay."

We did another dance. In the end, I got kisses, deep ones, and made her go.

The drowsiness had been an act. The little man on the raft had come in on the tide and he was in my head screaming out the national anthem accompanied by Jimi Hendrix at Woodstock. I checked the clock. It was eight-ten.

Then eight-eleven.

Then eight-twelve.

I was afraid I would start grinding the enamel off my teeth when the night nursing assistant showed up at nine-fifteen. Nine hundred seconds late, if you must know.

"Hiya, Mr. Stewart! I'm Nick!" he said bouncing into the room behind a cart covered in tiny paper cups. He was tall, thin, and had a narrow Ichabod Crane face under a shock of white-blonde hair. His nose looked like it had been broken more than once. "How are we feeling tonight?"

"Five by five," I said, aware that my voice was just a little we-just-lost-an-engine tight.

"That's awesome, man!" He bobbed his head vigorously to show me how truly awesome that was. "You were all over the news, man! You're a miracle! Awesome! Coming out of something like that, wow. I saw some pictures. Holy cow. Don't know how you did it, man."

He parked his cart and checked in on the in-room terminal. He tapped out a busy little cadence on the keys, regarded his work, added a few more riffs, then pronounced his composition good with an extravagant poke of his right index finger.

"On a scale of one to ten, can you describe any pain you may be having right now?" He stood over me with a big grin.

*Sure I can. Count the holes in the ceiling. Multiply by infinity.*

"Maybe a seven. A little sore."

"Seven. That's awesome." A raging hippo crashing through the window probably would have struck him as *awesome*. "Okay, we're going to give you a pill to make you comfortable for the night. Did Dr. Morrissey go over all this with you?"

'In detail. Gave me a quiz and everything."

"A quiz! That's awesome! Okay, let me get that for you."

He went to his cart and, with his back to me, made a note on a clipboard.

He studied his collection of medications, and I presume picked the one that had my name on it. I got the impression of a magician in scrubs, hiding the deck from the crowd while he pushed aces up his sleeve. I wasn't far off. He turned around and extended a little paper cup to me, pill on board. I took it, popped it in, and did the water chaser again. Metallic with a hint of—what was that? Clove? He held out his hand for the little cup.

For a second, I had a feeling he was looking at me for a reaction. Like the effect of the pill would be instantaneous. Or that Mr. Hyde would suddenly appear. Then he abruptly crushed the cup and launched it into the wastebasket.

"Score! That should do you, Mr. Stewart. Is there anything else I can get for you? Ice chips? A hot blanket? I can heat one up for you."

I shook my head.

"If you could kill the lights and call it a night, I'm good."

"It's a night then. I'm gonna close this door so when we start playing field hockey in the hallway around midnight, it won't disturb you. You have yourself a *goooood* night, sir!"

With one hand in his pocket and the other on his rolling pharmacy, he slid out the door.

# 11

The itch began immediately.

There's no such thing as darkness in a hospital room. There are LED lights everywhere, bars of light above and below the door, and of course the parking lot mercury vapor lamps bleeding through the window blinds. It might be night, but no one would mistake it for darkness.

In that phony moonlight, I lay thinking, possibly for the first time. Since regaining my place in the third and fourth dimensions, between sleep and the ministrations of modern health care, I had no chance to deal with the itch. I had no time to find out if it could be scratched, or if, as Earl warned, it could not.

I started with The Crash. In my world, the word 'crash' carries the weight of a boulder and the depth of a Russian novel. I read accident reports regularly. It may seem morbid, but in every one of them I can find the 'there-but-for-the-grace-of-God' message. Many of the NTSB briefs I read contain stories of pilots doing things I would reject out of hand. That's why I read them. To confirm that I would have rejected the action out of hand. But there are also reports that give me pause and make me think of times and places where I came close. Where I might have pushed aside a warning or adopted an 'it's not that bad' assumption—about the weather, about the drop in RPM on the left engine, about whatever. Those are the reports I read carefully. The public sees the one-sentence crawl on the television news. Family of four dies in airplane crash. There is no such thing as just a 'crash.' Speed, altitude, weather, pilot proficiency, maintenance and a dozen other factors make up the equation. I see a multitude of missed cues, failed judgments and ultimately a broken promise between a pilot and his or her passengers. It's not a single explosive event, over in an instant. It's a chain that begins in training, or with attitudes developed over a lifetime, and continues through a convergence of people's schedules and decisions, machinery and its failings, and giant weather systems that span a continent. That's how I see it. That's how Walsh sees it.

So how was Walsh seeing my accident? I needed to talk to her. That was one itch I could scratch. The one I couldn't scratch went back to last week and hung like a black hole between then and now. I remembered trips I flew on Wednesday and Thursday. I remembered the dome of severe clear high pressure that made those trips comfortable and stress-free, weather-wise. I remembered a briefing for a trip to Minneapolis, but not for a trip to Lansing. Was there a weather briefing? Of course, there was. There had to be. It would be in the trip manifest, and it would be on record with Flight Service, and it would be something Walsh would have confirmed. Which meant everybody had it except me.

I pictured the approach leading up to The Crash. Flying westbound over the lake in clear skies meant that the horizon would hold a shimmering line of red light long into the summer evening, long after the earthbound thought night had fallen. I would have flown headlong into that soft glow, and maybe given myself a minute or two to enjoy the gradient of red to blue to black rising above the dark earth. It never gets old. It would have been a beautiful flight.

If the approach had ended in a landing.

If I hadn't ended up unconscious in a marsh.

After landing, I would have popped the side window for a little fresh air and taxied to the hangar. I'd be alone at that time of night. It's a rural airport. There's no twenty-four-hour service. Shut down the engines in front of the big hangar and start the rituals that comprise the end of a charter flight conducted under part 135 of the Federal Aviation Administration regulations. Generate the paperwork demanded by the feds, and which Rosemary II compiles for accounting and billing. An hour later I would be on the road and on my way home.

That's how it should have gone. That's how I should have remembered it. I imagined it easily, down to the smell of the propane gas-powered tractor used to push the Navajo, Six Nine Tango, into the main hangar, engines still ticking as they cooled. But that's not how it ended. And I couldn't remember. Instead, I had a maddening itch that could not and might never be scratched.

Tomorrow I would ask to see Walsh. I needed to know more. I felt a raging urge to unplug the air girdle, slide out of the you-know-what, find my clothes and escape to the hangar where the pieces of Six Nine Tango had been collected and catalogued. Maybe sight of the wreck would trigger the small cerebral explosion I needed to blow this black hole into fragments and let the memories flood back in. I needed to get out of this room.

*So, float out.*

It was time to touch the cheek again.

My hand ran across the bone beneath my left eye. Ever so secretively, a bruise whispered to me, *I'm still here*. I pressed. It hurt. Just in that one spot, just where the light fixture in my dream or hallucination (this bruise isn't a dream or hallucination) had jabbed me.

But that's not possible.

*What about your knee?*

Not possible.

I reached down. I stretched to get to the knee. Just as a lava flow of pain shot up from my pelvis, I felt it—a sensitive spot on the cartilage of the kneecap, a bruise like the kind you get when—

Catching a coffee table on the way to the kitchen in the night.

That, I remembered. Clearly. Vividly. It happened right up there, over my head, bumbling against the light fixture. No, there was no itch to be scratched in this. I remembered a kind of whoosh or whump sound in my head when my body reappeared, and gravity took me back again and slammed me down into this bed.

I had been defying gravity.

But wasn't this just a hallucination? A product of the morphine and—

*Oh, to hell with that. You jabbed your cheek. You stung your knee. That spider web is still there. You've been looking at it all day, dumbass.*

It happened.

It happened? Really?

Yes, it happened.

Okay, so what if it really did happen?

Forget the morphine rationalization and consider the possibility that what happened, really happened. Accept it. What's the next question? There's always a next question. What is it?

In that semi-dark hospital room, the next question was clear as day.

Can you do it again?

I lay on the bed and took stock of my body. The head of the bed was raised. I had a commanding view of myself. A thin hospital blanket, tucked in at the foot and sides of the mattress, ran up to mid chest. The outline of the air girdle made me look six months pregnant, but only if the baby was going to be born a rectangular cube. My legs extended my full six-foot-one-inch length. I wiggled my toes to confirm. Yup. Mine.

Running up the center of all this, I had pain. I was getting tired of noticing it, tired of wishing it would just go away already. The nine-o-clock pill was taking its sweet time to do its job. I might have to go back to Morrissey and challenge his claim that I was getting primo goods. A steady throb radiated up from my groin, into my guts, into my diaphragm.

The clock said eleven-o-eight, and goddamn, it still hurt.

*It will kick in soon*, I thought. *Has to. Focus on something else.*

Back to the question at hand.

I concentrated.

I closed my eyes and studied the blank canvas of darkness inside my eyelids. Painting with my imagination, I formed the cockpit of Six Nine Tango, a once-loved Piper Navajo that would never again see sky. The broad, high instrument panel took shape. Directly in front of me, the six-pack of primary instruments. In the center, the stack of radios. Below that, the throttles, prop controls, mixture controls. To the side of that, the round gear handle, shaped like a wheel so we throttle jockeys know it's the landing gear handle in our fingers. Opposite that, the flap handle, flat like a flap, again to lend tactile confirmation. Engine gauges to the right. Everything in place where it belongs.

Better. This was my world.

I put my right hand on the throttles and felt the reassurance of power. I put my left hand on the control yoke and felt command over the airplane.

The throttles aren't throttles, they're pain. Pull them back.

I pulled. I felt the smooth, measured friction as they retracted. In my mind, I heard the twin engines change their note, seeking a lower octave. I felt the pain in my chest move down, away from my diaphragm. I pulled the throttles farther aft, and a frosty sensation replaced pain. The absence of pain isn't nothingness, it's condensation dripping from a margarita in summer, it's a Corona shedding ice chunks as you pull it from a cooler.

*This is working.*

I wiggled my feet on the rudders in this imaginary cockpit. I used my toes to grip the blanket and push by push, removed it from the full length of my body. I kept my eyes closed but could see that blanket as I'd seen it two nights ago, bunched up at the bottom of the bed. I felt air on my legs.

Better. I felt better. Maybe the Oxy was finally kicking in.

*What if you made it happen?*

Eyes locked shut, I scanned my vision of my cockpit. I saw it in warm red, with night falling, illuminated by the glow of cockpit and instrument lights. My hands slid to the right on the throttle quadrant, past the mixture controls, to a new set of levers. These had no color, only shape. I felt them, but I couldn't see them. They existed in no known aircraft. They were fully retracted, like the throttles I'd just used to reduce the pain.

Try it. Push them forward. Full forward.

I pushed. I felt smooth resistance again, the resistance set by the friction lock on the throttle quadrant, the lock that ensures that these controls stay where the pilot sets them.

The full length of my body came alive. Like acquiring a sheen of sweat, but not wet. Like a fresh breeze that hits you when you walk up out of a lake in summer, but not cold. Like a hundred million goose bumps forming, but not shivering. I pushed these new, unnamed control levers all the way forward.

*Fwooomp!*

It startled me. This new sound came from inside my head, but not from my imagination.

My hair tingled. My toes felt cool water passing between them.

I felt negative gees. Weightless. With that, the pain stopped entirely. The pressure on my fractured pelvic bones, brought on by the simple fact that my body had weight, was gone.

I opened my eyes.

I was gone.

The bed lay empty. Between my eyes and the blanket bunched up at the foot of the bed there was nothing. The air girdle, holding its shape and tethered to the side rails by Velcro straps, hung just a fraction of an inch above the sheet that still bore an impression of my backside. My broken pelvis remained snug in the device, yet I saw through it.

*Holy Shit!*

I forced myself to breathe evenly. I remembered the way the realization that I had vanished had abruptly killed the effect last time, and I wasn't remotely interested in crashing down onto the bed again, even from a quarter of an inch in the air. Breathe in. Breathe out. Float.

My hands hung in mid-air, but I couldn't see them. They held their position, the left gripping an imaginary control yoke, the right resting on power levers controlling something never engineered by the Piper Aircraft Corporation. I closed my eyes to reaffirm the vision of my constructed cockpit, then opened them again to reaffirm the effect.

*Vanished.*

It felt like flying for the first time. You know it's happening. You can see the earth falling away. But part of your petulant mind wants to fold its arms across its chest and refuse to go along. This can't be happening.

*This is happening!* Gone. I was gone. My body, the flimsy gown they had me in, and the stupid you-know-what were all gone.

I eased my left hand down to where my chest should have been. I touched myself. My hand didn't pass through my body. The gown was there. My skin was there beneath it. I pressed and felt chest muscle, and beneath that, ribs. I reached over and felt the chromed steel side rail of the bed. Just as solid as I was. I looked around the room. Monitor lights blinked. A bar of light glowed beneath the hospital door. Parking lot light seeped through the blinds. There was no way this was a dream—or hallucination!

I held my hand up to the window.

Nothing.

Feeling adrift, tethered by the air girdle, I grabbed the side rail. My whole body gained purchase, relative to the railing now. I pulled myself toward it. I pushed myself away. Like an astronaut showing children in a classroom on Earth what it's like to be weightless in the International Space Station.

*Except we can't see you, Major Tom.*

I pressed my knees together and they touched. I rubbed one foot with the other and felt the callouses on my heel.

Easy. Easy. Take it easy and hold it. Don't let it get away from you. My instructor voice spoke in my head, as if teaching a student how to land. *Feel it, hold it, stay in command of it.*

A harsh realization exploded in my mind. What if I can't turn it off? What if I can't get back!

*Fwooomp!* The sound broke again inside my head, like something played on headphones, heard between the ears.

I dropped the quarter inch onto the bed. Pain bloomed, but nothing like the last time when I crashed from the ceiling.

Feet. Knees. Legs. Arms. Everything reappeared at once. The gown. The you-know-what. I felt myself pressing into the mattress, more aware of gravity than usual. I threw my hands onto my chest and saw them pressing where I had touched before. I pulled the gown up before my eyes. All here.

*Son of a bitch!*

# 12

The night went downhill from there.

What if I'm dead? What if these few days turn out to be some sort of in-between state? Between life and whatever follows? Nobody, at least no one I'd ever heard of, survives an in-flight breakup without a parachute. What if the body they found sitting in the pilot's seat was cold and breathless and this is all some stage play designed to ease me between Before and After?

I had repeated the effect. I wanted to feel joy in that, but I found only panic.

*What if you do that again and you can't come back from it? What if you get stuck there, wherever there is and no one can hear you, and no one can see you?* I wanted to laugh, and not in a good way. I wanted to cackle in a crazy what-the-hell-is-happening way. What if this is the process of becoming a ghost, doomed to haunt this never-dark hospital room in my adult undergarment forever? A panicked squeak broke from my lips because the thought struck as both horrifying and hilarious. Christ, what if the next time I see Andy she's in black, tears painting streaks of mascara and the smile gone from both her face and her heart forever? And I'm gone. What if I've been gone all along?

My chest tightened again. A tilt-a-whirl wave of nausea pushed up my throat. More panic, as I looked around frantically for something, anything, into which I was sure I was about to vomit. I twisted to see if my arm could reach the wastebasket beside the bed. The bones that should have been mending ground together and white-hot agony ripped up through my body.

I yanked back my arm, too late. I clenched my jaw to stifle the scream. I pressed my head back into the pillow and pushed my eyelids down hard.

My breathing sounded like a steam locomotive in full stride.

*Get a damned grip!*

I don't know how long I lay there, forcing myself to chuff air out and wisp air in. Minutes? An hour? The breathing, like a woman battling natural childbirth, was all I had. My hands clamped the sides of the mattress, fingers dug in to the first joint. The blanket remained at my feet. I shivered as the sweat poured off me and evaporated. I told myself over and over that there was no pain, there was no lava flowing up through my abdomen, there was no field goal kicker. I repeated the outright lie over and over until it gained purchase and my body slowly began to believe. The pain receded, but only by degrees. The hair trigger to vomiting slowly relaxed. I found darkness inside my own eyelids and stayed there, holding on.

Holding on.

I pushed aside all thoughts of vanishing and floating. I concentrated on fighting the pain, fighting the panic. I don't know how long that battle lasted.

Pill or no pill, sometime before dawn, I either passed out or fell asleep.

# 13

They had to wake me for the nine a.m. Happy Fairy. I took the pill. It snagged in my throat, dry and metallic. Someone poked a straw in my mouth, and I gulped. Then I slept again.

"Hi, sleeping beauty," Andy said.

My eyes felt caked.

She sat on the sofa with a paperback cradled on her knees. Different clothes. Different light through the window behind her head. I didn't want to be awake because I didn't want to hurt. It took me a few minutes to realize that I wasn't hurting. Spinning a little. Tingling slightly. Not hurting. The panic wanted to bubble up, but I pushed back. I desperately wanted to wrap myself in Normal. In this light, Normal seemed, well, normal again. Andy smiling at me. The sun high. Did they put me back on morphine? No. This felt different. Then I remembered the pill, the taste of it.

I recalled my experiment in the night and the stark terror that followed it. Now it seemed less terrifying, although the idea of repeating the experiment carried no appeal.

I got my hands around the cup and pulled long and hard from the water. It cleared away the gunk in my mouth and throat. After a few more minutes of booting up the systems, I spoke.

"What time is it?"

"Three-thirty." Of course. It was right there on the clock.

"God, I need a shower," I said. The bed felt like a damp piece of cardboard under a bridge in Chicago. A shower seemed like the very foundation of Normal. "I want to talk to Morrissey."

Andy folded her book and put it aside.

"I want to know how long I have to be stuck in this rig."

She stood up and came to the bedside, delicate fingers automatically stroking my damp, dirty hair. I wanted her to stop but didn't say so.

"I talked to the doctor this morning. He wants to keep you immobile one more day, then do a scan to see how things are healing. He said it may be faster than you think if you can behave yourself."

"And how long is faster than I think?"

"He said the bones are already fusing. But this part is delicate. They need to hold together to gain strength. You and I are not going running again any time soon."

I wasn't sure that qualified as bad news. Andy runs circles around me.

"*How long?*" I instantly regretted the anger creeping into that question. Andy let it slide.

"You might get that shower tomorrow. Maybe. After that, maybe another day in bed here, then *maybe* a discharge on Friday, but that's if we can keep you very, very immobile at home. Bed rest. Crutches to and from the bathroom. A week or so of solid rest, then crutches to get around. The idea is to keep weight off your pelvic bones as much as possible."

Honestly, that all sounded amazing. I feared it would take much longer.

"But you need to behave."

That, I decided, I would do. Because I wanted out of here more than anything. Well, I wanted a shower more than anything. Then out.

# 14

After the horror show that had been my night, and the better part of a day sleeping, I enjoyed a good afternoon. Not much pain. Dinner was best described as "damp." Andy tortured me by carrying in a Southwest Chicken Salad from the cafeteria, which seemed capable of serving decent food. They just weren't sharing with me.

I chased Andy out again that night.

Nick the Happy Fairy showed up with his cart again, this time a minute before nine. I gave him a "five" on the pain scale and it wasn't all bravado. I felt better. This came as *awesome* news to him, and he dispensed the nine-o-clock pill with a flourish.

I don't know why, but I let the little pill nest on my tongue for a moment. Metal again. And that hint of clove. Maybe spearmint.

He watched me. I suppose it's procedure, to ensure the patients take their meds. But again, I got the feeling he looked for something. I started to tell myself it was an unreliable impression—something generated by a deceitful cocktail of circumstance and paranoia. All in my head. Except I wasn't falling for that old con anymore. I had permanently moved to you-better-believe-crazy-shit-when-it-happens territory.

After watching me a split second longer than necessary, Nick declared my pill-taking *awesome* and bounced out the door, rolling his cart to the next room down the hall.

I decided I didn't like Nick and looked forward to being removed from his care.

I fought through another bad night. The spinning, tingling feeling I had felt during the day eluded me in the semi-dark. Eventually, sleep came, but in fits and starts, and I wasn't sure when I was awake and when I was asleep. The hospital soundtrack played in my dreams.

I dropped off before dawn. I woke up to sunlight, tired and sore and wondering why the nights were so bad. The thing is, I already had an idea why, but the answer lay buried beneath other headlines like You Fell Out Of The Sky But You're Not Dead and Your Body Disappears And You Defy Gravity. My hypothesis on why the nights were bad didn't raise its hand to be called upon until the Happy Fairy arrived that morning.

# 15

She was cute. Janice. She wrote 'Janice' on a white board by the door below a permanent label that said, "Your nurse is…" I hadn't noticed this customer service touch before. The white board had flower stickers on it.

"How was your night?" she asked, attending to the in-room workstation.

"I was visited by three spirits."

She looked at me blankly. She had a nice round face and friendly eyes. It made me think of her night counterpart, Nick. Not because of any similarity, but because of the contrast. Her eyes. She had honest eyes.

"Christmas Past, Christmas Present and Christmas Future."

"Oh!" She laughed and went back to the workstation. She typed something rapidly. I wondered if she recorded the visits by Dickens' ghosts.

We traded questions and answers. She checked and replaced my you-know-what and that's all I care to say on the subject. She hustled around the room and adjusted the blinds, scooped away the bendy-straw cup and replaced it with a new one. She produced a pill cup and handed it to me.

"On a scale of one to—"

"Six point three seven five. Ish."

"I will put that in your chart. Very precise-ish."

I popped the pill in my mouth and poked the straw in after it. I very nearly shot it down my throat with water, but again was struck by her honest eyes, and how it made me think of Nick, and how different they were. Just for a moment, I let the pill nest on my tongue. The taste was unpleasant. It was not a coated pill. It most certainly was not a pill you would crush and chew. I don't have a wine expert's palate, and I cannot tell you if a Merlot has an oak finish or a turpentine finish, but I know what a penny tastes like. I know the taste of a nail. This pill had hints of both, along with chalk. But no clove. No spearmint.

I hosed it down my throat.

In short order, I sailed pain-free on Oxy. I began to appreciate how someone could chain themselves to this feeling. My nights would be a whole lot better wrapped in this feeling.

Andy showed up. She wore a sunny smile on her face.

"I just saw Morrissey. You're going to have your picture taken!"

"Got a comb?"

"THERE'S BEEN GOOD PROGRESS, amazing really," Morrissey announced when he cruised in after reviewing the images. "The fracture has begun to fuse."

Andy squeezed my hand.

"Praise Jesus," I said. "When can I get out of here? More importantly, when can I take a shower and pee like a man?"

"The shower part, I'd like to wait. I can have them give you a sponge bath today if that helps. I'd like to enforce one more day of immobility. This is a delicate process, and you don't want to set it back. You're doing better than I expected. Being patient will pay dividends."

I hate it when I see the logic of something I vehemently disagree with.

"He will stay still," Sergeant Stewart, the enforcer, promised.

"The law has spoken," I sighed. "Fine. Another day. But then what? Andy mentioned crutches?"

"The key is not to put stress on the pelvis. Walking. Standing. Putting your weight on one leg over the other will put stress on the mending fracture. So, we stick with the bed rest for now. We follow that with some physical therapy, getting you to work with crutches so that you can keep the weight off as much as possible. And we're not talking about mobility with crutches. We're talking about using them to get to and from the bathroom. That's it. You really need to give this another week, maybe two, if you want to be certain it mends properly. If you screw up, and there is a new break, all that discomfort you've been dealing with starts over again. And I'm not as generous with medication as some of my colleagues. There's no long-term prescription in your future."

I conducted a quick assessment. It had been a little over three hours since taking the morning pill. I rode a nice wave, cool and smooth. If this kind of wave could keep away the pain, it would be easy to beg for another hit. And another after that. I also knew what Andy thought of people who begged for another hit, and sold their homes, their possessions and everything they could steal for another hit.

"The last thing I want," I said.

"There's something else," Morrissey said. "I've been asked by the administration if you might be in a condition in which you might give a statement, I presume they mean to the media."

Andy stiffened, "I talked to them about this!"

Morrissey waved his hand. "Yes, I'm aware. Frankly, so did I. And everyone here is on board with your wishes. But this came from the parent company public relations office. I'm afraid they see you as something of a celebrity. I expressed to them your position, but they put it to me as a medical question. Are you medically capable of giving a statement? I can easily tell them you are not, that you are still on strong pain medication, which is true."

I got the feeling there was a "but" coming, and not from Morrissey, whose first name I learned was Sam. Sam Morrissey did not appear at all comfortable with what he was being asked to ask me. I hated to see him in that position. I headed him off.

"Tell them this: There is an on-going NTSB investigation into the matter of my emergency landing. Until that investigation has obtained all the information relevant to the case, I will not be issuing any statement to any persons or organization."

"Wow," Andy said. "Nice. I like how you called it an emergency landing."

Morrissey smiled. "I like it, too."

"Tell them I give them five stars for the service and one for the food."

"I will do no such thing. But I appreciate the compliment."

"I mean it."

I didn't include the nighttime Happy Fairy in my thinking.

# 16

My day went well. I felt the Oxy, smooth and creamy, though mildly nausea-inducing. I worked hard not to move, and my pelvis gave back an appreciative note of silence. I sensed that Andy allowed herself to grow a little tired of attending to me, a sign she had become certain of my survival, so I pressed her to take the evening off and go home. She gave the *pro forma* argument but departed peacefully. My sponge bath never did show up, but I clung to hope that a real shower loomed in my future.

Dinner remained a liquid mystery, and perhaps it was the pill talking but I found myself not really caring. It had been a better day.

I watched the same Indiana Jones movie after dinner. Somebody on cable lacked scheduling imagination. The end credits had just begun to roll when the Happy Fairy arrived.

She was not Nick. Being a woman stood out as the first clue, and never once saying "Awesome" cinched it. She handed me the pill. I popped it in.

Metallic. No cloves. No spearmint.

I slept like the dead.

# 17

If there was a moment when I regretted not continuing to experiment with the vanishing act, it came when I finally got my trip to the shower. Things would have gone a whole lot better had I been both weightless and unseen.

"You need to leave," I said to Andy.

"I can help," she protested.

"I've got help. Janice here and, I'm sorry—what's your name?"

"Marie," the second nurse said.

"The A-team," I said. "They've got this."

"But I want to see you naked," Andy said.

"If I had a dollar for every time I heard that. Go." I got the pout again, which made me want to see her naked. I quickly thought about pre-landing checklists and engine manifold pressures and anything else that would head off the hint of arousal I felt. Because the A-team was about to see me naked.

"Fine," she smiled. I got a chaste kiss on the forehead. "I'll be in the coffee shop."

"We'll come get you when we're done," Marie said sweetly. She was old enough to be my mother. I'm not sure whether that helped or horrified me, but I fixed my mind firmly on how grubby I felt and how wonderful it was going to feel under a shower.

I paid for that shower. Blessed cleanliness, may it ever nudge godliness, but I gave that cleaning my pound of flesh. They parked me under the stream. I asked them to crank up the hot and leave me to simmer. The motion of my arms, raised to scrub shampoo into my hair, poured fuel on the pain, but I rinsed and repeated. Clean, somewhat damp, and hurting all over again, they eventually put me back in a gown, the adult diaper thing, and the bed, made up with fresh sheets and a new pillow.

I don't remember them leaving the room. My eyes were locked on the TV screen, fighting back the howling pain. That the TV wasn't on made no difference.

The Great Shower, as I came to call it, took place late in the afternoon, on the tail end of the morning medication cycle, so I never did recover from it completely. I feared, deeply, that we may have disrupted the delicate bone fusing that Morrissey worried about. I sought consolation in the fact that he had approved the procedure.

I didn't touch dinner.

Nick rolled in at nine, and I feared another bad night lay ahead. In fact, I expected it.

"Hey, Mister S, howzitgoin'?"

"Sucks," I said through clenched teeth.

"I got an awesome fix for that right here," he said cheerily, throwing a Vanna White gesture across his cart. "The miracle of American Big Pharmaceutical. They rake in the money on this little puppy." He turned his back to me and again I got the impression of a cheap magician trying to hide his hands while he stuffed a reluctant rabbit into a hat.

Instead of a hat, he produced a tiny, pleated paper cup. Instead of a white rabbit, it held a tiny white pill. "Open wide."

I caught his hand as he pushed the cup toward my face.

"Really? I'm a big boy. I got this." I took the cup from him. "Let's see what we've got here."

"Only the very best. A magic carpet ride to the comfort suite in the Hotel Essex, Mister S." He stood there, beaming at me.

Instead of pouring the cup into my mouth, I dumped the pill into the palm of my hand. I held it up and examined it. Without looking up at Nick, I felt his beaming smile fade.

The pill looked like a small aspirin. White. Creased on one side with an R over a P. On the other side, the number 10. Ten milligrams, as advertised. What wasn't advertised was that my nights were dark valleys of pain while my days were smooth and creamy. Now, why was that Nick? Why did my day pill taste like nails while my night pill had that hint of clove and spearmint? Why did your delivery always seem to put you between me and your little cart, while the morning nurse just pushed the cart up beside the bed? Why do you always go out of here with your hand in your pocket, jackass?

"Problem?" he asked, showing teeth. A lot of teeth.

"Nope." I popped the pill in my mouth. He watched me, like I was an experiment being repeated over and over and he was the scientist looking for any change in results. As he watched, I looked at him. I flexed my fingertips.

I bit down on the pill and chewed.

"Oh, you don' wanna chew these suckers, Mister S. Taste awful. Here. Drink some water."

I had Nick pegged for a liar, but no truer words were ever spoken. The sensation in my mouth almost made me gag. Still, I chewed, then swallowed.

"I'm good," I said.

"Wow, no shit. You really are some kinda miracle, Mister S. I gotta hand it to you."

He put the water back on my tray, tapped a few lines into the in-room workstation, then pushed his cart toward the door, fist thrust in one pocket. That's where he overplayed his hand. That's where he stopped and turned to me, and with a slow gesture, he pulled his clenched hand out of his pocket, unfurled it, and ran it through his white blonde hair.

"You have a *gooooooood* night, Mister S. Fly high."

Then he rolled out the door.

I waited until I heard him greet the next patient in the next room, then I grabbed the water. It took several huge gulps to suppress the metallic taste in my mouth.

Metallic. No hint of clove or spearmint.

Within an hour, smooth and creamy, I slipped away into sleep and didn't wake until dawn.

Bastard.

# 18

A ndy sat on the side of the bed, listening intently. I spoke softly.
"He's swapping pills, administering counterfeits." I explained the
taste test. "The difference is—no pun intended—night and day. You know
how bad my nights were. The day nurses are giving me the real pill, and my
days have been okay. Night—he gives me fakes. I wanted to gnaw my way
outta here."

"And last night was better?"

"Oh, hell yes. He knew I suspected, so he gave me the real deal."

Andy wore her cop face. In it, I saw a hint of darkness. I wanted to
attribute it to someone messing with her man. More likely, it was her default
setting for dealing with assholes.

"Opioids. We've talked about this. The AG is all over this epidemic. The
whole eastern corridor of the state, it's a drug highway, running up I-43 from
Chicago to Green Bay and the UP. Ever since Homeland opened the candy
store, departments our size have been asked to put together task forces on
oxy. We're getting intel from a dozen different agencies."

She sank her teeth into my theory. Andy or not, I expected the standard
playbook response. Are you sure? Maybe you just had a couple bad nights.
How could you possibly know what tastes like the real pill and what
doesn't? Instead, she offered no push back. She listened thoughtfully. She
took my observations as accurate. If she'd had her police notebook, she
would have jotted notes.

"The thing is," I said, "does this really make sense? I mean, a few pills here and there—is that worth it? Why not raid the pill cabinet?"

"Good luck with that. Hospitals have been working with law enforcement for years, upping their security, enforcing access protocols. It's not just a crime issue, for them it's a liability issue. After a few high-profile theft cases were connected to overdoses, families started signing on lawyers. That's when hospitals got serious about pill security. Today, trying to steal meds out of a place like this—I don't know—I'd have to see the protocols here, but I bet they're locked up tight."

"Maybe I'm way off on the street values, but I can't believe stealing ones and twos is worth the risk. He got two lousy pills from me, and I doubt he'll try again."

"Okay. On the other hand, multiply that by the number of patients on this floor who have been prescribed pain killers, and the number of floors, and so on and so on."

"But subtract for caution. I caught on after two nights. He can't steal them all, or patients would be howling up and down the halls."

"Did you get a good look at the fakes?"

"Not really. I mean, I thought I was looking at a fake last night, but it wasn't. I expect the fakes look the same, though. Wouldn't they have to?"

Andy plucked at the seam on her white summer slacks. She had one knee folded, up on the bed. Her feet were clad in white sandals and her toenails were painted a violet-tinted red. I liked the look, but more than that, I liked that she had taken the time. This hint of vanity suggested that she had taken a breath for herself.

"Hmmm…"

"How much would he need to pilfer in order to make money?"

She gave a calculating shrug. "The people playing seriously at this are dealing in baggies full."

"So, is he just collecting a stash for a weekend of partying?"

Another headshake. "You're missing a key point. The counterfeits."

"I know about the counterfeits. I'm the one who told you that."

"Yes," she patted my hand. "But how easy do you think it is to get or make fakes?"

I sank back in the pillow, seeing her point.

"Not easy?"

"No. Not easy. We took down some equipment last winter, some guy in a basement trying to make phony Viagra. Strictly amateur hour. The fakes were bad, which is why we were notified about him in the first place. He had a very unhappy customer who tipped us off. It was a cheesy setup, but even at that, the equipment we hauled away cost the guy thousands."

"Then this makes even less sense. If so much is involved in making fakes, using them to steal a few originals seems hardly worth the effort. And it goes back to my question: what good is such a small quantity of originals? I gotta go with personal recreational use," I said.

"If it is recreational, he'd be better off going to a pill-mill doctor and complaining of back pain. There's still too much of that going on. Plus, hospital staff is subject to random drug testing, although most of these losers know how to beat the tests. He's risking his job, his career, assuming he cares about either. Get caught doing this, and you're finished in medicine."

"So, do I palm the next one he gives me? Evidence?"

Andy hesitated. She didn't like the idea. Cops don't like civilians playing cop. "It sounds like you're off his list. I think you're going to get originals from now on."

"What then? Speaking as someone who suffered through a couple bad nights, thanks to him, I'd like to see you guys do a Bad Boys takedown right here in the hall. Get him shirtless and in cuffs, like you do it on TV."

Andy squinted and made a screw-you face. She didn't think much of the cable TV staple of rerun reality cop shows.

"If nothing else, the guy shouldn't be a nursing assistant, here or anywhere."

"No," she said. "Let me think about this. If he's pulling the swap right here, in the room, then he'll be in possession of both, and that would be hard to explain. Let me work on it. But look at you! Junior detective!" She beamed at me.

"Guy pissed me off."

"Well, I'm guessing you're also a little pissed that he stayed one step ahead of you. Admit it."

"I'll do no such thing. No matter how true."

"But don't expect a big bust. It's hard to make something of this. I don't even know if I can get resources on it, or interest from the DA. More likely the hospital will fire him, quietly, and leave it at that. Especially since prosecution means potential negative publicity. And we already know what hounds they are when it comes to publicity."

Following Morrissey's hesitant inquiry, Andy had been approached by a suit from the public relations office of the hospital's parent company. After a little glad-handing, the suit wanted to know if they could invite news coverage for my discharge. I wished I had been there to see her answer. She shrugged it off when she told me about it, but I bet she channeled a little of the past week's emotions into her response.

Andy was right to guess the hospital wouldn't want the public aware that a nursing assistant handed out fake pills.

"I have some other news that I think you will like."

"My liquid diet can now include beer?"

"No. Not if you insist on taking the real meds. No, I saw Morrissey on the way in. He wants to take your picture again. And if it looks good, I get to take you home."

"Oh, woman, do not tease me!"

"No teasing. Cross my heart."

"Let me." I reached.

"Stop it!"

# 19

Andy's surprise announcement triggered a whirlwind of expectation in me, which ended up in stark contrast to the Absolutely Nothing that followed.

Breakfast juices came and went. Andy and I watched the local news without much interest, beyond noting that I wasn't mentioned. Gang bangers continued to shoot each other in Milwaukee. Earnest reporters gave live reports in front of police tape. Police, they said, were investigating—the same thing they said about the shooting reported yesterday, and the one the day before. I decided the local news coverage of shootings was a lot like basketball highlights. You could play a tape from a year ago, and the average viewer wouldn't know the difference. Eventually, we turned off the tube and chatted about life's little busy work. Her car needed an oil change. The guy we had called to take down a dead ash tree still hadn't shown up.

When the 9 a.m. pill came around, I debated taking it. I had pain, but nothing like the nightmare roller coasters I'd been riding. A dull simmer. A three and a half out of ten. I seriously considered taking a pass on the pill. Andy didn't intervene as I debated the question in my head. She pointedly pulled her paperback from her purse and pretended to read.

"Oh, what the hell. How often do you get to get stoned on doctor's orders?" I asked aloud, just to see if she was listening.

I took the pill from Janice and regarded it. Same design as the one Nick had produced last night. It went down without being chewed, thank you very much.

It was a mistake to get my hopes up. Neither Morrissey, nor someone from Imaging, showed up all morning. When we finally asked, we were told Morrissey had an emergency. Nobody seemed to know anything about a fresh scan.

Lunch appeared in liquid form. The you-know-what served its purpose. A little while after finishing a yogurt and a few carrots, Andy announced she had to run over to the station for a few hours. Would I be okay? I had a feeling she planned to investigate Nick the Drug Dealing Nursing Assistant but didn't ask.

"Go. It's coming up on nap time."

"Don't leave without me," Andy planted a kiss.

"I'll try not to be here when you get back."

No such luck.

A nap dragged me under. I can't remember ever having slept so much. It had to have been the pain, sapping energy insidiously. Yet, with each sleep session, I felt stronger. Hope springs.

"Still no sign of rescue?" I asked Andy when I woke. She had magically reappeared on the sofa while I slept. The clock showed a few minutes before four. I had no idea how long she'd been gone or had been back in the room.

"Oh, hi!" She snapped her book shut. "Welcome back!"

"Morrissey? Pictures?"

"Patience, love. I did see the good doctor."

"And?"

"And you will be spending one more night at the Hotel Essex." It reminded me of Nick, her calling it that. The disappointment must have been written large on my face, because she added quickly, "He promised pictures first thing in the morning."

"Might be too late. I might tunnel out in the night."

"Maybe I better stay," she said. That meant she wasn't planning on staying. Which was good, I supposed. Although, feeling a little petulant, I think it bothered me that she'd be sleeping at home and I wouldn't.

"We could try to catch Pablo Escobar in the act tonight," I offered.

"What?"

"Nick?"

"Nope." She dismissed the idea firmly. She poked around in her purse and pulled out a prescription bottle. "I got you your own stash. Morrissey wrote up a scrip for me and took it off your orders. No more Nick." She rattled the bottle.

"Why? Why not try to nail the bastard?"

"Love, he wasn't going to play with you anymore."

"How about if you just shoot him?"

"Bullets are expensive." She rattled the bottle again. "You get one after dinner, before I go home. Get a good night's sleep and we do pictures in the morning. He put in an order for physical therapy, and you'll meet the PT specialist in the morning, too. They're going to give you some dual instruction on using crutches. Maybe let you solo."

"Listen to you, picking up the pilot talk. I would take flying solo to the bathroom."

"Bright side?"

"What?"

"There's solid food in your future!" She gave a perky smile. "Tomorrow, that is. Tonight, well…"

"Dammit!"

# 20

The nightmare rode in secretly, piggybacked on the white noise of the hospital room, like a computer virus hidden in a photo or sound file. Sleep ran deep, then shallow, and when it swam close to the surface, the sounds of the hospital intruded, joining the loose flow of dreams. Oxy isn't good for dreaming. The chemicals play mean-spirited games, twisting and distorting images, and counterfeiting dreamed events as memory.

I heard voices from the nurses' station, and soon they were streaming through my pilot's headset, joining the soft, minimal conversation of air traffic control. The controller chatted back and forth with a FedEx pilot about catheters before telling him to contact Chicago Center on 119.4, which the FedEx pilot repeated back flawlessly. My engines, the Navajo's engines, hummed steadily and the great glistening surface of Lake Michigan flowed below. I reached down beside the pilot's seat, past the checklists and extra pens in elastic pouches, and dragged my fingers through the smooth surface of the lake at one hundred eighty miles per hour. The water felt cold. I reminded myself that I would die if I had to spend more than three minutes in the water, so I pulled my fingers back up—all the way back up to ten thousand feet—and shook off the drops. Now the controller told me that Mr. Simon in room three eighteen vomited and I was cleared for the visual approach to runway 31 at Essex County Airport. I repeated the clearance and reached for the throttles. My fingers closed on the familiar knobs and I eased back the power, then rolled the trim wheel to lighten the load on the control yoke. The controller, sounding testy now, said to bring the *other* tray, and call maintenance. I rested my right hand on the throttles, pulling, pulling, drawing them toward me together. They stuck to the instrument panel, which glowed red—not the soft night-vision red I love, but a red that said heat—a terrible, unstoppable heat on the other side of the panel. I pulled harder and the altitude unwound, and the black earth of the shoreline passed under me now. No more dragging my fingers in the water. Ahead, I saw the airport beacon, but the itch I couldn't scratch loomed to one side, dark and empty. A black hole, into which memories were sucked as if by irresistible gravitational force. I tried breaking hard right to steer around it. The yoke turned but the airplane remained on course. My hands slid on the controls, wet, shaking. The emptiness, the thing I couldn't remember hit the left wing. Sudden. Explosive. The left wing vanished along with the side of the cockpit. I flew on with the wind ripping at my clothes. Pieces of the airplane dropped off, cast down into the countryside like discarded litter. The wind wrapped itself around me now, penetrating my clothes, my skin. It became a living sheath, cool and fresh-feeling, and it lifted me against the seat belt. And now I knew that the seat belt would tear me in half because the airplane was falling away around me.

My arms swept the air above my head, but nothing was there. Nothing but the empty, never-dark hospital room, filled with my ragged breathing.

I lay awake. No discarded, crushed airplane parts fell away from my body. Only sweat.

The clock told me I'd been visited by this nightmare just before midnight. Many hours of darkness lay ahead, each minute of each hour inviting the nightmare back for a return engagement. I didn't think there was a chance in hell of falling asleep again, nor did I try. I pushed up slightly in the bed, opened my eyes wide and fixed them on the black television screen.

I have no idea when my eyelids betrayed me and dropped the curtain on my determination. Show's over, folks. I slept dreamlessly until dawn.

# 21

Andy double-crossed the double-crossing publicity hack from the hospital's corporate headquarters. After Morrissey saw pictures of my mending bones and pronounced my progress satisfactory, he approved my release. I got a short course on the best way to use crutches to prevent my legs from putting stress on my pelvis, with ample warnings about falling on my face. The physical therapist, a young woman who looked all of twelve, had me do a round trip to the bathroom, with a little too much instruction on how to take care of business. I felt pain, but I would have taken bamboo shoots under the fingernails before saying so. On the return trip, she showed me how to slide myself back in bed, where I was apparently expected to spend another week. More pain. I think Andy knew it, but God bless her, she kept my secret, although she gave me a disapproving look when I turned away the morning pill.

When the PT ended, Andy arranged for a pair of EMTs from the Essex Fire Department to transfer me to a gurney. They rolled me out through the ER and into a waiting Essex FD rescue wagon, which had been signed out on a training exercise. The EMTs seemed only too happy to have a live transport to play with.

I had a limited view out the back windows of the rescue wagon. Andy watched from the jump seat. I saw her smile as she looked at the two television remote trucks parked at the front of the hospital.

I've never been so happy to put a place in the rearview mirror.

· · ·

"ON THREE. ONE, TWO, THREE!" The two EMTs effortlessly swung me from the gurney to the mattress. I guess they've had practice. Smooth and easy, and while I expected a deep pain for the effort, and had determined I would show none, I admit, it wasn't bad.

"Nice man cave," Thorson, the lead EMT said. He was young, muscular, and played softball with the fire department team like it was a death match, which seemed only fair because Andy and her colleagues on the police department team took no prisoners. "Look at that. Sixty-inch satellite TV. Gotcher remotes all lined up. Man, if I'm you, I milk this for all I can. Does the little lady bring you cold beer?"

"Hey, toad," Andy said, "I carry a gun."

"And I've got a big hose."

I eased myself up a little higher on the nearly table-height platform that made up the bed. Andy propped pillows behind me.

"How did you get the mattress down here?" I recognized our queen-size mattress, purloined from our upstairs bedroom. Now it sat atop the fold-out sofa-bed in our living room.

"What? It was easy," she said.

Eggert, the other EMT pretended to sneeze, "*Ahhbullshit!*" Apparently, fire department training exercises included squeezing a queen-sized pillow-top mattress down our farm-house stairs. No easy task.

"Thanks, guys," I said.

Andy threw a light blanket over me. She had scrounged up a clean pair of ultra-light work-out pants and a t-shirt for me to wear out of the hospital, and now they served as sleepwear. "You can't do stairs, and the mattress on this sofa bed was originally designed as a torture device. But stacking our mattress on top works out nicely. You're close to the downstairs bathroom. Close to the kitchen. TV. It's the only way I'm going to get you to behave."

"Be a good boy, and maybe she'll bring you that beer," Thorson said. He stuck out a meaty hand and we shook.

"You take care," Eggert seconded. "Glad you're alive."

I shook his hand on that.

They made their way out. Andy followed, and I'm sure proffered her thanks to the fire department. This was a strictly unauthorized transport but managed quite nicely as a training exercise.

Eggert wasn't being glib. Most of the fire department, I had been told, had spread out in a line that night, trudging through the marshes and fields, knowing they weren't going to find anything good. God doesn't give back from a wreck like that.

I watched out the front door as the rescue wagon pulled out of the driveway. Our rented farmhouse sits on a forgotten one-and-a-half lane blacktop that slices between corn fields and junctions against county roads barely much wider. The view through French doors and a screened porch shows a patch of lawn shaded by mature maple trees. Across the road, a corn field spreads to the southern horizon. The farm was sold long ago to a bigger farm, and the land is worked with magnificent efficiency. The owner, James Rankin, drops by from time to time in his oversized, annually new pickup truck, never for any particular reason. His empire stretches across the southern third of Essex county, and he sits on the County Board. He rents the house to us for a ridiculously small monthly check and treats my wife like a daughter. From this hundred and twenty-year-old monument to creaking floors, we look in all directions at American agriculture. The next nearest home is half a mile away. Peace surrounds us.

If there existed a better place to be at that moment, I couldn't think of it. Andy had the front doors, dual French windowed affairs, thrown open to the screened porch. A summer breeze whispered through the maples and skimmed through the porch. It kissed my skin with cool air that flowed into the living-room-turned-bedroom. Yes, I had a giant TV and a couple hundred channels at my fingertips, but nothing lured me into powering up the unit.

I had no idea how sterile the air in the hospital could be until fresh corn-scented breeze washed my lungs.

Andy would be going back to work, taking her station on the three-to-eleven shift. I expected to have the place to myself, although I needed to make sure Andy hadn't arranged for Pidge or Rosemary II to check up on me. And I knew Andy would swing by in the squad car.

Still, I anticipated time alone. I planned to use it.

# 22

Skipping the morning pill wasn't my brightest idea. By midafternoon, my guts throbbed. The absence of the air girdle offered the illusion of freedom, but in fact rolling to either side sent a saber of pain up the center of my body. I found myself sipping but not drinking the ice water Andy provided just to postpone a full bladder. My newfound ability to pee like a man restored my manhood, but I was a clumsy toddler mounting the crutches and trekking to the toilet.

Around three-forty-five I surrendered and took a pill. Relief came quickly. I reminded myself to curse Nick the Drug Dealing Nurse for denying me that relief through two hard nights.

Medicated, with the soft breeze stirring the room, I never had a chance. I dozed like an old man.

I woke to the same soft kiss of summer wind, but the room was dark and the yard outside the screened porch had a twilight effect as the features of the earth turned black against a blue-black sky. I did the usual assessment of the pain and deemed it distant. I checked my watch, blinking film out of my eyes to read the luminous dial.

"It's one-thirty," Andy said softly. I searched the room for her voice. I found her sitting in a bamboo rocker near the head of the make-shift bed. She wore a light summer robe. Her skin glowed in the receding light.

"Wow," I said. "I'm sorry. I didn't mean to—" I almost said disappear.

"You needed it. Can I get you anything?"

"Broken record, but that cold beer would really make my day. Unless you think it messes with the medication."

"Oh, I think one won't put you in arrest. Be right back."

She padded out of the room on bare feet. The light from the refrigerator door accented the gathering darkness. Night outside seemed brighter, though, or else my eyes had adjusted. The maples cast shadows, telling me the moon rode across a clear sky. I would have liked taking a stroll outside to see it. Crickets carried on a contentious debate beyond the screened-in porch.

Andy returned and put the open Corona in my hand. "Sorry, no lime. Haven't had a chance to get to the store." We did our grocery shopping on Sunday mornings, while the faithful sang in church and the store aisles were empty.

I took a sweet, sweet pull from the long-neck bottle.

"Oh, lord."

"I know you," she said, like she was saying it to herself, mildly surprised.

I looked up at her, silhouetted against the moonlight. "I hope so."

"Here." She touched her chest. "I know you here. I think maybe you've always been there. And I've always known you. I feel like, if I think back to when I was a girl, you were there somehow."

Her words sounded melodic. It wasn't music, though. It was release. She stood in the dark. She stared at me, and I felt it, I felt her letting go. Like she'd been in an argument, and now understood she'd been arguing the wrong side. "You can't imagine, Will. It wasn't just the idea of losing you. It was the monstrosity of traveling through life to this point, having you always there ahead of me, and finally finding you, and *then* losing you."

"Dee—" I didn't know what to say. How could I? She spoke of monstrosities. I didn't know the words to challenge such horrors.

"I need to know you're still here. In me."

"I—"

"Shhh."

Now she stepped away from the side of the bed. She seemed to glide toward the center of the room, framed against the moon glow outside. She turned to me and moved her hands across her waist. She slipped one shoulder, then the other, out of the robe and it fell to the floor.

She wore something shear. Little more than a film, clinging to contours and skin. Lace at the edges. It ended high at her thighs. It showed me everything. The rise and fall of her breasts. The deep taper of her waist. The secrets she kept only for me. She stood there for a moment, and she may have been all but naked and exposed, but it was she who did the looking. She studied me intensely. She took everything in.

"Dee, I don't think I can..."

"Oh, I think a part of you disagrees."

She had that right.

"I'll be gentle."

She came at me from the foot of the bed. Working her way up. Slowly. She took her time. She took a long, long time.

I have no idea how she managed it, but I scarcely moved. She had me, and I had her.

After, she lay beside me. I pulled her close and she cried. The tears glittered, tiny reflections of the moonlight in the windows, wet diamonds on my chest.

# 23

F *wooomp!*
    I must have been sleeping, because it was more the memory of a sound than a sound.

The room hung still and dark around me. The yard glowed with moonlight. The windows threw great rectangles of light and mutton-bar shadows across the floor. My breathing ran shallow and even, still rich with satisfaction. Andy dozed beside me. I felt her pinning my left arm, which surrounded her and hung so that my hand stroked the mysterious contours where her left breast swept into her side. The scent of her hair mingled with the scent of what we had done—or more precisely what she had done to me with a lithe skill I had not imagined possible. Honestly, if my pelvis had split open like a walnut shell while she'd been poised above me, I wouldn't have noticed. She worked magic on me without inflicting pain.

I understood her needs. I don't mean physical, although she had needed something intense and physical to mend the shock to her system. I understood that she needed to know, in a way that mere touch or conversation could never satisfy, that I was still inside her. Not in *that* way, although that had been key to securing her faith. I mean inside her being. She had reached her limit. For a week she had been pretending, thankful, loving. Worried about my pain. Managing my needs. She had been my medicine, without medicine for her own pain. Tonight, she took what she needed, and I worried, as I always did when the truth of loving this woman became too frightening to bear, that I might not be enough.

I looked down the length of her body and—

*Holy shit! I'm gone!*

Andy, naked against me, breathing the deep cadence of the soundly sleeping, lay pressed against nothing. Her breasts were pushed softly out of shape. Her left leg hung in the air where it rested on mine. She had substance and light and shadow. I was gone!

I felt it now. That sensation of a cool sheath. Water all around me. I had mistaken it for the night breeze, but the whisper of light wind against the screens had gone silent. This was *the other thing* again. Gravity and I had broken off our on-again-off-again relationship.

I imagined Andy waking, feeling me close, maybe running her fingers down my chest the way she sometimes does, slipping in and out of sleep wrapped in satisfaction. Then opening her eyes and having that cartoon moment when expectation and reality don't match. Then what? Screams?

And what would I do? Talk to her? I hadn't tested that yet. Could I talk? What if I slipped into this disappeared state and could not be seen or heard?

I held my breath. Then I let it out, listening, catching a faint sigh. Then I pushed it out harder and heard a soft hiss. I pursed my lips and whispered a shallow "*tsssss.*"

I heard it! I decided not to risk plucking at my vocal cords.

*Don't panic.*

*Relax. Assume control. And then, for God's sake turn it off!*

I closed my eyes. Opened them. I saw the sheets pushed aside and realized that, if not for Andy, I might have floated up to the ceiling. I closed my eyes. This time I pictured my body, still naked, silver streaks of sweat in the moonlight. I opened my eyes.

Nothing. A tiny vibration of sheer, absolute panic shivered deep inside.

Andy moaned softly, suddenly. She moved against me. I knew this pattern. There is a point, after we make love, after we hold each other to telegraph new vows that we are more than raw physical passion, when she feels safe and loved and she rolls away from me, and with a nesting wiggle she curls into a new, deep sleep.

She did that now. She released my arm and rolled away from me. I reached down for the blanket she had pulled away during her deeply erotic journey up the length of my body. I drew it up over her shoulders. I was rewarded with a light hum of appreciation. I stroked her back.

I forced myself to remember to breathe.

Without weight, I had no sensation of the fitted sheet beneath me. Action and opposite reaction rule. My action to tuck the blanket over Andy had launched me upward.

I twisted and tried to reach behind me. My fingers found the sheet. I tried and failed to close a grip on the fabric. I continued to rise. Now eighteen inches. Now nearly two feet, with my arm extended fully my fingers reached out.

Panic became more than a low vibration. It morphed into a shaking, rattling machine about to burn its bearings, shear its bolts and break loose.

*If you pop back out now, you'll drop like a rock and all hell will follow. Just go with it!*

I snagged a fold in the top sheet with my fingertips. The ascent stopped. A new thought came to me. What if my fingers slip, and I drift just far enough that I can't reach anything? It's the nightmare scenario of an astronaut with a broken tether. What if I wind up floating here, buck naked, disappeared, out of reach of anything? Not moving.

Suddenly the naked part struck me as funny. On top of everything else, I had it all hanging out. Maybe there was a bright side to being *gone.*

I pulled gently on the sheet, praying my fingers wouldn't slip. It worked. I floated downward, steady, holding course, keeping my body at attention so that my legs and arms wouldn't splay out and flop all over Andy.

There's nothing to grab on a bed except bed sheet. And that's not much. As I touched down in the same spot where the journey had begun, I eased my hands down along my sides and lightly plucked the top sheet away from the pillow top mattress. With enough fabric in hand, I closed my grip. Anchored at last, I stayed still. I steadied my breathing. I closed my eyes.

Across the inside of my dark eyelids, I painted the instrument panel, the controls and the bells, whistles, and buttons of my lost Navajo cockpit. It was a rough draft with blank spots. The image seemed to flash and flicker at me, a sign of my surging panic.

*Easy. Take it easy. Now find the throttles.*

I couldn't use my hand, like I had in the hospital. I didn't dare release my grip. I had to imagine my hands, one on the yoke, one on the throttles. The image didn't take.

Try again.

Instruments, good. Lights, good. Throttles … there they are. In hand. Now move to the right. Past the prop controls, past the mixture controls. Find the two levers that you need, the ones that were never there. Feel the nice round knobs at the top. Good. Now ease them back. Like flaring over the runway for a landing. Slowly, bring them back slowly. Control. Not too abrupt. Almost there—

*Fwooomp!*

So much like touchdown on a runway, I thought. The moment when the miracle of flight ceases.

I opened my eyes.

I lay naked and shining in the moonlight. Two thoughts raged in my head.

*You have GOT to get this under control!*

And

*You just controlled this!*

# 24

Sunday split between bliss and agony. Neither had to do with pills or pain. The bliss came from the genuine sweet comfort of home. Andy took full advantage of superb summer weather and opened the house to breezes and bird song. She ended my personal famine by producing blessedly solid food. She found time to slip out to the grocery store and return with supplies, including limes we wedged into cold Coronas in the midafternoon and again after dinner. She stayed close but didn't cling. Her desperation to reconnect seemed soothed. I peed and did other things like a man, and while it was a production on crutches, I didn't plant my face on the hardwood floors, and the pain hovered just below tolerable.

The agony came from my inability to experiment. With Andy close at hand, I wasn't about to try and turn on—and I hoped off—the vanishing act. It scared me that it had now happened twice while I was either sleeping or unconscious. I pictured sipping a beer with my girl, maybe with a ball game on the television, and hearing that *Fwooomp* sound in my head, followed by the sound of my wife screaming *What the hell?!* as she observed my beer bottle floating in the empty air.

This all goes on faith that what was happening to me was *really* happening. That I hadn't gone mad. Try as I might to dismiss the hallucination or insanity arguments, they hung in like those nut jobs who believe in chemtrails. Give them the facts all day long, and they still won't go away.

Andy's phone rang occasionally. When she would answer in her cop voice, I knew someone from the station needed her. Other calls prompted bright greetings, and she expressed thanks to friends for calling, and yes, he's doing fine.

For one call, I saw her check the caller ID and then take it out on the porch. She spoke in short, terse sentences and ended the call quickly.

"My mother," she said, reappearing in the open doors. "I guess they saw something on the news."

I didn't ask. We refer to Andy's relationship with her parents as The Shitstorm.

"She wishes you well," Andy said. She stalked off to the kitchen, signaling that there would be no discussion. Having an IQ above room temperature, I didn't ask.

I did make an unrelated mistake, however. On Sunday morning, out of the blue, I asked, "Is there any chance you could swing by the airport and see if they have my phone? For that matter, see if they have my iPad and headset. That's a thousand dollars-worth of Bose headset."

Andy stiffened. Sometimes, and I don't mean to suggest this is character-istic of all women, but sometimes she plays that most dreaded of all femi-nine games: Guess What's Wrong Now. Seeing her reaction, I thought we might be headed into one. The game typically starts with me saying some-thing that I (stupidly) think is perfectly innocuous.

"No," she said sharply. Okay. I guessed we were skipping the game and going right to the post-game press conference.

"Uhhh, okay…"

"You don't need them. You have at least a week of rest ahead."

"Right, no argument. I just thought it would be nice to have them back."

"No! I'm not going—" She stopped herself. She looked down at her feet and took a breath, every bit the image of a woman patiently counting to ten. "I'm not going there, Will."

"To the airport?"

"Not the airport. There. That hangar. I don't ever want to see it. Ever."

The wreck. If any of my personal belongings had been found they would be in the hangar, laid out with the wreckage for the NTSB to sift through. I got it now.

"Dee, no, I'm sorry. Forget it. You don't ever have to go there. It's okay."

She minced her feet. "I'll ask Pidge to ask around," she said. It was no small concession.

"You don't have to. Really. It's no problem."

Andy called Pidge, and Pidge told her that the NTSB team had gone, and that the hangar was sealed and locked, but that she would call them to see if they cataloged any of my personal effects.

I wanted to ask Andy to ask Pidge to reach out to Walsh but decided going through Andy wasn't wise. I needed to see Walsh again. The itch was still itching and unlike my wife, I very much wanted to visit the wreck, and very much wanted to know every detail. Clearly, I wouldn't be leaving home any time soon. The itch would just keep on itching until I came up with a plan.

On Sunday afternoon, Earl stopped in.

"Nice roadblock," he greeted Andy at the steps to the front porch. She ushered him in.

"Roadblock?" I asked.

"Your wife has this entire road barricaded and posted as Closed by Order of the Police."

I looked at Andy.

"It was that or have those television trucks parked out front. And we're the only house on this part of the road, so it's not putting anyone out."

"How did you get through, Boss?" I asked Earl.

"I got connections with the cops." He winked at Andy as she swept out of the room. When she returned, she handed him an ice water. Earl doesn't drink. I'm told he did once.

"If you boys are going to talk shop, I'm going outside to water the gardens."

I appreciated her intuition. The moment I had seen Earl's truck swing into the driveway, I tried to think of ways to occupy Andy elsewhere.

"You're king of the castle here, buddy," he said, looking around. "If I were you, I'd put in for disability and live like this for the rest of my days."

"Is that a hint? Are you firing me?"

"Oh, hell no! I need you back. Pidge is going to turn me into a murder/suicide headline. Maybe that will finally push you off the front pages."

"You can't be serious."

"I am. That girl will drive me to do it."

"No, the news. They can't still be going on about this, can they?"

"Christ, Will. It's gotten out that you fell out of an airplane that broke up —or as one bunch of morons put it, exploded—in mid-air. You fell out of the sky and lived. Like that girl in South America, remember her? The one who fell about twenty-thousand feet after that airliner broke up?"

I didn't.

"The damned thing broke up in a storm or some such, a goddamned airliner, Lockheed Electra, I think. She came down in the jungle in her seat. The only survivor. Broken arm or collar bone or something like that. She walked out. Something like ten days. Found a river and found some fishermen. Nobody could believe it, but she did it. Something like fourteen or sixteen years old."

"Never heard of it."

"Well you're the new miracle man. We've had the news people crawling up our asses at the airport. Somebody got pictures of the wreck. I'd love to know how that happened. Got a picture of the pilot's seat. It's been in the local and state papers off and on all week, but it's been picked up by the cable news, too. At least for as long as those monkeys pay attention to a shiny object."

"I had no idea."

"That's Andy's doing. She was a bulldog at the hospital. I talked to Joe Boetcher at breakfast yesterday. She engineered that whole business of having the fire department sneak you out of the hospital." Earl ate breakfast at the Silver Spoon diner every Saturday morning with local celebrities like Joe Boetcher, the fire chief, and Andy's boss, Tom Ceeves. And Armin Kirk, who recently made the papers after collecting his one hundredth John Deere tractor. Celebrity comes in all flavors in Essex County, although I wasn't prepared to count myself among them.

"No shit, a roadblock? That's one way to keep it quiet. I thought traffic was pretty light."

"Light, hell. I called Andy, you know, to make sure she wouldn't shoot if she heard me coming. I gotta be honest, I wasn't really sure she wanted to let me come." He looked at me, probing. "Is she okay?"

"This whole thing scared her. Badly."

"I hear that. Scared us all."

"She doesn't want to see the wreck. I guess I don't blame her."

"Don't ever let her see it. Or pictures, if you can avoid it. You can't unsee that shit."

"Well, I want to know what happened. And so far, it's like you said."

"An itch."

"Yup."

He rubbed his claws together. The callouses made a scratching sound in a silence that lingered just a little too long.

"How's everything else? Pidge notwithstanding."

Earl shifted gears and gave me some down-to-earth work talk to change the subject. Charter demands. Flight schedule problems. Maintenance issues with a couple of the airplanes. He said he was thinking about replacing the

Navajo with a King Air. Be still my heart, I'd been pushing for one of those glorious turboprops for years. I enjoyed hearing that the world still turned, and the sun still rose and set on aviation at Essex County Air Service. Fuel flowed. Airplanes flew.

He dropped the bomb on me unexpectedly.

"They're gonna pull your ticket."

I blinked.

"What?"

"Cyler told me. Asshole. They're gonna pull your ticket. He says it's temporary, just a formality while they wait for the NTSB report. And that they'll make a final disposition after the board report is completed. He said they're also going to issue a letter on your medical."

"For a broken pelvis? What the hell!" I felt a swirling mix of anger and helplessness. It can take months, sometimes years, to plow through the FAA bureaucracy to get a medical back.

"They wouldn't tell me anything. I called all over creation, and even chased down Cyler. Nobody's talking. But I think Cyler wants to hang it on pilot incapacitation."

"Horseshit!"

Earl nodded and shook his head at the same time. "Tell me about it."

"Walsh said I hit something! Or something hit me. That there wasn't any sign of controlled flight into terrain! This is such bullshit!"

"Walsh told me the same thing, off the record. She said they can't figure out what you hit. And that means trouble. She won't sign off on it, and she doesn't agree with Cyler, but down the road somebody is going to point a finger at the pilot. If they can't fill in the blanks with something else, they write your name in."

"Who do I have to talk to?!"

Earl tried for reassuring, but he's not what you would call touchy-feely. It came off angry. "You'll get your chance. Goddammit, they can't call it controlled flight into terrain, because it ain't. And they can't call it an in-flight breakup due to pilot incapacitation because it ain't. You were right where you were supposed to be, on glideslope, on speed. Them's the facts. Period."

"I need to remember," I said.

"Maybe you will, maybe you won't. What did the doc say about your head?" he pointed at his polished dome with a thick finger.

Morrissey had said there was no indication of head trauma. I wasn't sure his assessment helped my case. At least a bop on the head could be attributed to the crash. Memory loss without head trauma might be the reason the feds were looking at pilot incapacitation. Some sort of seizure. This was not good.

"No head trauma. Look, Boss," I said and glanced at the kitchen. I tried to listen for Andy, to see if she was still outside watering the gardens. "If I'm going to remember, I need to get in that hangar, and I need it to be without Andy knowing. You need to get me in there."

"Oh, son, don't drag me into something like that. The woman knows how to dispose of a body and leave no evidence."

"She's going back to work tomorrow. How about you come and get me?"

"There's a police roadblock."

"Gimme a break. Andy dug out some old barricades from the city shed. They can't be keeping a cruiser out there, can they?"

"Well, no. But you're in no shape to go anywhere."

I pointed at the crutches. "I'm a big boy now. Potty trained and everything."

"The way I hear it, you ain't supposed to move."

"I need to see it."

Earl shook his head, which I took as a Yes. A real No, with Earl, leaves no doubt.

# 25

On Monday, Andy turned out in full uniform, hair in a bun and sidearm strapped. Her shift didn't start until three, but she was gone right after lunch at twelve-thirty. No surprise.

Andy loves me, but if forced to choose between me and being a cop, or breathing oxygen and being a cop, I think she'd give me her blessing to marry again and try holding her breath. There's a picture of her at four years old, wearing a frilly party dress, standing in front of a birthday cake with burning candles, looking expectantly at the camera for the signal to blow out the four flames and get her wish. No one looking at that photo could fail to guess her secret wish. On the breast of that little dress is a sheriff's star and sagging around her middle hangs a holstered plastic six-shooter. Straight out of high school, she enrolled in the criminal justice program at the University of Wisconsin. With the ink on her diploma still wet, she entered the Waukesha County Technical Institute police academy program. She topped her class and had offers to join half a dozen departments. Tom Ceeves, the present Essex PD chief, had been a part-time instructor at WCTC, had her in several of his classes, and knew a rising star when he saw one. Even though he expected she would rapidly grow beyond the bounds of a small city department, he wanted her, and he got her. Two and a half years later, at twenty-three, she had her sergeant's stripes, and she had a bead on the rank of Detective.

I'm proud of her for all that. Andy pursues career goals like Sherman touring Georgia. Hers would seem the perfect story of a four-year-old getting her birthday wish. You would think her family took great pride in her.

Not so. Andy's passion for and success in law enforcement is the cause of The Shitstorm.

Andy comes from a family with money. Her father is CEO of one of the tentacles of Bank of America Corp. and her path had been pre-ordained. When she opted to study criminal justice at the University of Wisconsin, she left behind a stack of acceptance letters from the Ivy League, and parents who might have been happier had they been told their daughter ran away to become a mime. According to her parents, police work is for immigrants. When Andy graduated from high school, her older brother was already at Harvard Law, following in her father's footsteps. She was considered a legacy shoe-in. Andy's older sister was making babies for a lobbyist who hires out at five figures for an hour of his time and connections in Washington, D.C. Even with those acts to follow, Andy was the golden girl who scored one point short of a perfect ACT and had been beaten out for valedictorian of her prep school class by a boy who now heads a division of NASA.

When the girl with the plastic sheriff's badge announced her plans to attend a *technical college police academy*, the family door slammed behind her. None of her family attended our wedding. When I asked, oh so carefully, about their reaction to our marriage, Andy told me her mother called the fact that she was marrying a pilot who flies those "little" planes a twist of the knife. I sometimes wonder if a part of her choosing me was the twist of her own knife. I can't afford to think that way, but those little voices like to taunt.

I know it hurts her, but Andy never wavered. Her connection to the rest of the Taylor family is an icy road. Her father waits for her to call and apologize for ruining her life. She waits for him to call and apologize, period. Her mother pretends to be cordial with infrequent phone calls, but most end with bitter words. That her mother called to ask about me came as a surprise. Until I realized that if her son-in-law was making the cable news cycle, it counted as fame and earned status points in her circle of friends. She could hardly say she hadn't asked after me, now could she?

None of this wore on Andy's mind in the least as she put on her blues, kissed me, and went to work at a job she loved. I also suspected having her mind on her work suppressed thoughts of me falling out of the sky.

I love her dearly.

I couldn't have been more excited to see her go.

I had flight testing plans and now I had the house all to myself.

# 26

I expected frustration. I had stripped away the medication (I swapped the oxy for aspirin Monday morning), the hospital setting, the dark of night, and even the white-hot pain (as long as I didn't move too ambitiously). Who knew if any one of those variables played a role or held the key? Yes, it was possible to replicate the conditions that existed during each of my disappearances. I planned, however, to start with a clean slate. It might take hours, maybe days, to make it happen, if it was going to happen at all. I would be patient, methodical. I expected to focus intensely, concentrate absolutely, and maybe even squeeze myself like a toddler on a potty. I expected flickers and flashes and tantalizing near misses.

*Fwooomp!*

It happened on the first try.

I had centered myself on the mattress, removed the light blanket, stretched my legs out straight and propped my head up slightly on the pair of pillows I use at night. I took a deep breath, let it out, and flexed my fingers. I closed my eyes and meticulously painted the image of the Navajo's cockpit in my mind. No slapped-together picture this time, not like the night I had slipped out of Andy's embrace. I put detail into the construct, taking it slowly and considering each instrument, each cockpit control. I focused on the sensation of the control yoke, with its smooth plastic grip worn down over tens of hundreds of hours of flying. I felt the throttles, mixture, and prop controls, then slid my hand to one side the way a lover slides his hand toward a magic place on a partner's body. There, I found the new levers, and closed my hand on them. I invested in imagining the sensation of those controls in my palm. The knobs were round and warm. I pushed them forward.

As soon as the sound broke in the center of my head, I opened my eyes. Gone!

Yet still there. I knew if I touched myself, I would find myself, but I preferred hanging my hands in mid-air, gripping imaginary controls. Slow and easy, I breathed, not wanting to disturb the moment. I noticed the cool sensation, perhaps more acutely than before. Not cold or uncomfortable. A dip in a summer pond. A breeze on exposed skin. It seemed to ooze out of me.

My clothes vanished, too. I wondered about that. Not that I had a precedent for any of this, but didn't the guy in the old movies wear bandages over his naked body to simulate human form? Wasn't there always the famous moment of unanticipated reappearance, naked, in the most inconvenient of places? I liked that the light sweats and t-shirt I had been wearing were not visible, shaped like a person but with empty space where arms and legs belonged. Make a note. This affects clothing, too.

The weightless sensation took effect immediately. I saw the wrinkles in the bed sheet lose their shape as my body ceased to put pressure on the mattress. I floated upward. I made another note. I was weightless, but not made of helium. I floated upward because the mattress springs I had been compressing with my 183 pounds pushed me upward. That may have accounted for my trip to the ceiling in the hospital.

I didn't want to rise. I closed my eyes, found my image, found my control levers, and pulled them smoothly back to the stops. Smoothly. You never do anything abruptly in the cockpit.

*Fwooomp!*

My body reappeared.

I dropped slightly into the mattress, picking up a reminder of pain from my pelvis in the process, and a reminder that a fall from any higher would result in screaming.

"*Whooooohoooooo!*" I howled. "Yes! Yes, you sonofabitch! Yes! Yes! Yes! Let's do that again!"

Eyes closed. Levers forward.

*Fwooomp!* Gone!

Eyes closed. Levers back again.

*Fwooomp!* Solid again.

"Hooooooooly shit! Holy mother of all shit! *What the hell is this?*"

. . .

I SETTLED myself down and cycled the process several times. I wanted reassurance that *this thing* employed an On/Off switch. That *this thing* was not a trap into which I would fall and never return, although I guessed the only way to discover that would be to fall into the trap and be stuck. I had to take it on faith that the Off switch would work each time the On switch worked. I kept the duration short and stayed close to the mattress to prevent a fall. My mind made notes and asked questions. How long could this last? How many times can I do it before I can't? I considered the effect this might have on me. Was it fatiguing? Was it disorienting? The guy in the movies goes mad. Was I going mad?

"Well, bucko, this *is* fairly insane," I spoke aloud. "Not to mention you're talking to yourself."

I turned it on. I turned it off. I felt breathless amazement that it had worked so quickly, so effortlessly.

I noticed I'd begun to skimp on the vision of the cockpit I used to work this magic. In my excitement, when I closed my eyes, I allowed the virtual cockpit I'd created to fade, even wisp away like ground fog breaking up in sunshine. I had dropped my left hand from the control yoke, simply working the effect with my right hand on the levers I envisioned.

Now I dropped my right hand to the mattress. I closed my eyes and imagined my right hand on the levers, imagined the balls on top of the levers in my palm, and the smooth stroke as I pushed them forward.

*Fwooomp!*

Eyes open. Gone. Eyes closed and feeling my hand resting on the mattress at my side. Now I imagined pulling the levers back again.

*Fwooomp!*

"Oh, holy mother of God! This is incredible!"

I had expected this to require focus. Deep Kung Fu Master focus and superhuman concentration. Instead, it seemed light and comfortable. The transformation required nothing more than a gentle push in my head.

"Okay, let's try something new."

This time, hands at my sides, eyes cast comfortably down my body, not focused on anything, but relaxed in a sort of middle-distance stare at my toes, I imagined the levers. Hands on the knobs, smooth push forward.

*Fwooomp!*

My heart nearly stopped. I saw it happen! It looked like water suddenly flowed out from my skin, soaking through my clothing, and in uneven puddles, made me disappear.

"Whoa!" I said. And then I realized I had spoken. My voice sounded no different than had I been fully in sight. "Hey! Hey! Can you hear me? Testing, one, two, three strikes you're out *at the oooooold baaaall gaaaaame!"* I sang out the last part in the empty living room.

Check one more item off the flight test card.

I watched the empty space occupied by my body and imagined pulling the levers back.

*Fwooomp!*

I reappeared as if the spilled puddles evaporated, as if magic fluid that had come out of my pores to make me vanish now flowed back in.

I laughed. I broke into an utterly uncontrollable laugh. For one thing, it just looked funny. Bits and pieces of me reappeared in no apparent order. But it was more than that. The laugh rang with pure joy. Anyone watching me might have thought I'd gone insane. I didn't feel that way at all. I felt joy in its purest form. First solo flight joy. First time popping up through the clouds joy. First love joy.

I laughed and slapped my hands on the mattress. I laughed until tears streamed and my breath went ragged.

# 27

"Okay, let's try this."

*Fwooomp!* (I made a note: *I need to know if that sound is in my head, or if this process makes a noise.*)

Gone again. Starting the slow rise from the mattress, I pushed lightly with my left hand. I moved to my right. Movement without a body for reference felt mildly disorienting. I did a slow glide toward the side of the bed. I grabbed the crutches leaning against the mattress.

"Good thing nobody can see this," I said as I bumbled crutches and legs, trying to get the latter over the edge of the mattress. I dropped the left crutch, and it clattered to the floor.

"Idiot."

I leaned the right crutch against the bed again, gripped the mattress, and pulled myself into a seated position. I felt my feet flatten on the hardwood, but without weight. Keeping a grip with my right hand, I leaned down and pulled the errant crutch upright, then gathered the other. Hands on the handles, I eased myself vertical. My feet lightly kissed the floor. The crutches remained visible and became my anchor.

The way to the bathroom had been thoughtfully cleared, so I leaned and performed a two-legged swing forward, then pivoted on both legs and brought the crutches through. When lifting the crutches, I felt their weight, a few pounds, and it translated through my body to the floor. I planted them again, and repeated. It worked. It worked far better than when I had the full weight of my body on the armpit pads of the crutches. They were light, of course, compared to my full body weight, so I had to be careful not to use too much power in my movements. As I passed into the dining room, I looked in the mirror above the china cabinet and saw two enchanted crutches dance across the room on their own. Very cool.

At the bathroom door I stopped, put my feet on the floor, and lifted the crutches slightly. The weight of the crutches held me down. I leaned them against the wall. At once I lost contact with the floor and began to float. I grabbed the door jamb with both hands. I eased myself around the jamb through the open door and flicked on the light.

"This will be a neat trick."

My plan was to pee. I suddenly laughed. What if I stood, or rather floated, in front of the toilet and began to urinate, and took off across the room like a balloon leaking air, spraying the place.

"Okay, that's not going to happen."

I found a grip on the towel bar above the toilet with my left hand. With my right hand I gripped the essential plumbing, aimed and waited.

"Okay, no pressure. Nobody's watching and even if they were, they couldn't see me."

It took me a moment to get a stream going, and I have to say my aim was good. Call me a twelve-year-old, but the sight of a stream of pee coming out of thin air cracked me up.

Another flight test item checked off.

From the bathroom, I swung myself around the corner, re-mounted the crutches, and headed for the kitchen. Andy kept a jar of peanuts in a cabinet. I retrieved it and popped the top. I dumped a few in the palm of one hand. They floated in the empty air.

"This might be gross."

I put my palm to my mouth and chewed and swallowed. I looked down at my chest.

Nothing.

"Whew. I think I would have hurled if I saw them going down."

I worked my way back to the bed in the living room and secured the crutches. I made a minor mistake and un-vanished myself while sitting on the edge of the bed. My weight returned, and I sagged in a sitting position, igniting a sharp jolt of pelvic pain.

"Ow!"

I flopped backward, flat, to ease the weight.

"Okay, note to self. Don't do that."

I stayed flat on my back for a moment, then disappeared, floated back into position on the bed, pulled myself down against the sheets, and reappeared.

Unbelievable.

I checked the clock. A few minutes before two in the afternoon. I'd been screwing around at this for over an hour. I felt a little tired. There was no way to tell whether the fatigue came from simple exertion or whether *the other thing* sapped my strength. I didn't have a benchmark. Under ordinary circumstances pain along with several days of intense medication and immobility can make any exertion a high-energy-consumption act. Add a new variable and it was impossible to tell what caused what.

I relaxed for a moment and contemplated the plaster ceiling. No light fixture. No ceiling fan. Oh, what the hell.

*Fwooomp!*

I put both palms on the mattress and gave a gentle shove. Up. I floated effortlessly, silently upward. As the ceiling approached, I put out both hands and cushioned the collision with my fingertips. I had a split second of disorientation before my fingers touched the plaster, because I couldn't see them. Then they made contact and my body stopped. The room spread out below me. I considered the effect of weightlessness. My legs extended straight away from my hips. There was nothing dragging my arms downward. If anything, I folded a little at the middle, just because staying at attention is work. My knees bumped the ceiling. I considered trying to scamper around but being above anything other than the bed made me nervous. A drop onto the bed from this height would be bad enough. A drop onto the hardwood floor might put me back in the hospital. Instead, I decided to try a simple push-off to send me back down to the mattress. I thought about the force vector. I wanted to push from my center of gravity, or mass, or whatever state defined my missing body. Pushing off near my head might send me rotating backward.

I moved my hands down to approximately where my hips were and prepared to push when—

"Hey, Crash Corrigan! Let's do this!"

It was Earl! I heard his heavy feet on the porch steps.

*Oh, shit!*

I froze. What if he sees me up here?

*Idiot! What's he going to see?*

How could I have missed his truck pulling in? I looked at the screened in porch and saw his legs through the French doors.

He opened the screen door and entered the room, looking around.

*Now what?*

My path back down to the mattress was direct and clear, and with a simple push easily reached in a few seconds. But I couldn't just reappear on the mattress right before his eyes.

I turned my head toward the dining room and put my hands over my mouth. "In a minute! I'm in the bathroom!" It sounded stupid—just like someone speaking with their hands over their mouth.

"Don't take all day!" Earl called out. Loudly. Like he thought I was in the bathroom.

I looked at the path between me and the bathroom. The living room joined the dining room, like any good farmhouse. A wide archway separated the two. Seen upside-down, the arch was like a low wall rising from the ceiling. Our first-floor bathroom connected to the dining room, adjacent to the kitchen. A straight shot through to the dining room, then a hard right (if you are subject to gravity and your feet are planted on the floor).

I needed to get to the bathroom and reappear. That's assuming Earl stayed in the living room and didn't notice that the bathroom door hung open with the light off.

Earl didn't make a move.

I had a plan, but now I had another issue. I had nothing to grip on the ceiling. The simple plaster ceiling featured a nice decorative border on all sides. I had nothing to use as a launch point to send my weightless body toward the dining room.

I gingerly touched my fingers to the plaster ceiling, locating it. Then I made my hands as flat as possible. I swiped them against the plaster and in the direction of the dining room. I tried to put a little pool-hall English on it, to vector toward the center of the arch.

I moved. A little too rapidly. I began descending. I headed in the right direction, but I dropped fast. I looked at Earl, worried he had heard something, or sensed something. He stood waiting, impatient at the delay. He turned around to watch the corn growing across the road.

The dining room divider approached quickly. I grabbed and altered my trajectory, but I overdid the downward vector. I sank into the archway between the dining room and living room.

It became clear I would hit the hardwood floor. Probably with the back of my head. I went fetal, curling into a ball. My knees came up in counterbalance to my head and shoulders rising. I wouldn't hit my head, but now I took the shape of a cannonball, still headed for a furniture collision. This struck me as funny. I wondered what Earl would think of disembodied laughter.

Before annihilating the dining set, I extended my arms behind my back.

My hands contacted the floor. My palms served as brakes on the hardwood, reducing my speed to almost nothing—except now the force applied to the floor launched me for the ceiling. I pictured a blimp trying to land without a ground crew to grab the ropes.

I stretched. My fingers brushed one of the dining room chairs and then gained purchase.

I stopped.

"Tick tock, buddy!" Earl called out.

I used the grip to unfurl my cannonball body and leverage myself into a nearly normal, vertical position. If I reappeared where I now stood, nothing would appear amiss, except for one thing.

Earl had turned around again and had a perfect line of sight to me. He stood staring directly at me.

Our eyes met. Or at least mine met his. Then I realized he gazed straight through me at the wedding pictures hung on the far wall. I stared at him. He stared through me.

He suddenly broke contact and looked down at his watch.

"We don't have all day, buddy!"

I pushed, just slightly, against the chair, careful not to make the chair do a poltergeist wiggle. Perfectly upright, my toes brushing the floor, I glided to the bathroom door, looking in my mind like a ghost floating through a room. I passed from Earl's line of sight. I stabilized myself on the bathroom door jamb.

*Fwooomp!* I wondered if he heard it.

I dropped a bit, about a quarter inch, onto the floor, but it was a jolt to my body. I had to grab the bathroom door frame to stay steady. I realized this was the first time since the accident that I'd put the full weight of my body on my broken pelvis without crutches. It produced a sharp, intense pain.

"Don't tell Andy, but I decided to try this without the crutches. Not a good idea. Would you mind bringing them to me?"

Earl popped around the corner and handed them to me.

"Let's go, before her highness the high commissioner of police catches us." He looked at me as I winced and put one crutch under each armpit. "You sure you're gonna be okay?"

"Positive."

"Yeah? Cuz if I do this and mess you up, she will kill me slowly."

I believed that to be true.

"Let's do this," I said through clenched teeth.

# 28

The ride to the airport wasn't bad until Earl went off-road.

"We're going in through the service gate. I don't want anybody seeing us."

He turned off the highway and headed down a rough gravel driveway. He stopped at a locked gate, part of the anti-terrorist chain link fence nearly all airports acquired after 911. It never ceased to amaze me that terrorists hadn't heard of bolt cutters. However, in addition to thwarting would-be terrorists, the fence did a nice job of keeping the deer off the runways, so I gave a little credit to the brilliant minds at Homeland Security.

Earl rolled down his window and entered an access code into a keypad. The keypad beeped electronic approval and the gate slid slowly open. A few minutes later, via the access road that looped around Runway 06/24, Earl pulled up against the back side of a large hangar. He parked out of the line of sight of the Essex County Air Services offices. Rosemary II misses nothing.

At the hangar door, Earl used another code to open the door to a nicely appointed but empty corporate flight department lounge. This hangar had been empty for years. Dates on dusty magazines littering the coffee table told when the operation shut down. We passed through the empty lounge. A glass wall separated the main hangar from the lounge; the glass offered an unimpeded view of the hangar.

My heart went cold.

Six Nine Tango lay in a horrifying state of ruin on the bright, polished concrete floor. Her once white aluminum body, trimmed with gold and red stripes, looked as if it had been chewed up and spit out. The NTSB investigators had arranged the pieces in the shape of the airplane they represented, but that seemed cold treatment for a once-beautiful flying machine.

I don't know if all pilots feel the way I do, but to me airplanes are a higher form of machinery, as close to a living being as we small gods can create outside our own species. Shaping aluminum into a form that, with the bending of wind around its wings, can perform the magical act of flight is one of humankind's highest achievements. It means something to me, deeply, each time I roll one of these machines onto a runway and push the throttles forward, surging into the sky. Even as an airline passenger, or human cargo as I once heard an old airline pilot put it, I can't fathom how people in a busy aircraft terminal can sit staring into phone screens when the windows are filled with beautifully sculpted airplanes, rising to and descending from the clouds. The wonder never abandons me. I love aviation museums, yet I feel sad for the flying machines locked inside them, knowing they will never again touch the blue that waits above the clouds.

Seeing the wreck, shredded, dirty and cast onto a floor filled my throat with a sour, choking lump. Maybe I should appreciate the huge hole in my memory. How much worse would it be to have a memory of the moment when this machine was torn apart?

Earl stood silently beside me.

"Why am I alive?" I finally asked.

"Beats the shit outta me, buddy. Honest to Christ."

I studied the pieces. The right wing appeared undamaged, except for the obvious torture it endured when hitting the ground. It had come down nearly intact, engine attached. The propeller blades were bent back, indicating rotational damage when the pieces hit the ground.

The tail, or rather the pieces of the tail, were partially recognizable. The vertical stabilizer had separated from the fuselage and lay flat on the floor. The horizontal stabilizers spread themselves on the left and right of a rough centerline. The right side had identifiable shape. The left side might have been the crumpled, discarded gum wrapper of some giant.

If it had been a giant, swatting me down like an annoying insect, it would account for the crushed, torn and shredded mess that composed the left wing. The largest piece appeared to be the engine block. Few pieces were identifiable. The main spar, the wing skin, the fuel tanks—all were twisted and torn apart. Some pieces had been smashed flat.

*You hit something.*

Whole parts were gone. I couldn't see anything resembling an aileron or flap. I wondered if they had been able to find everything.

Whatever had happened to the left wing, had also happened to the left side of the fuselage. The body of the airplane resembled an opened eggshell, with most of the left side torn away. Three of the four passenger seats were still inside, attached to the floor. The fourth lay in a ball of steel frame and upholstery on the concrete floor. Except for the right wing, this section of the fuselage comprised the largest piece of wreckage. It ended, however, at the back of the cockpit, where the back of my seat would have been.

I walked around the perimeter of this mayhem, looking for the cockpit. I found the instrument panel, which lay face down on the floor. Wires streamed in every direction, ending in shiny, torn sparkles. Ahead of that, forming the front of this modern-art junk sculpture of an airplane, the nose had shape, but it too looked as if it had been clawed open on the left side.

Alone, to one side, I saw the pilot's seat. Almost intact.

I crutched my way to it and stood staring.

I could not connect with it. I could not relate to having been in it, to having been seated when this kinetic horror took place. I'd flown this airplane hundreds of hours, comfortable in this chair, joined through it to the airplane. Take this worn seat—or any piece of the whole—out of the machine and it loses all meaning.

Connie Walsh's voice broke the silence.

"They found you in that."

She emerged from shadow in one corner of the hangar. Earl had not turned on the lights in the hangar, a mercy. Like many such hangars, this one had windows high along the walls on two sides. Though coated with dust, the glass cast just enough light to make the interior look like a black and white photo.

I considered her comment.

"Where's the seat belt?"

"Still attached to the floorboards, over there. It broke at the buckle. Must have taken quite a bit of force. Enough to break your pelvic bones, it seems." She stood next to me. "The seat legs are sheared off—almost as if they were cut. Like the seat and the floor separated violently. To answer the question that you asked when you walked in here, I don't know why you're alive, Mr. Stewart."

"Nice to see you, too."

"No! No! I mean that with the deepest sense of wonder, Mr. Stewart. I am delighted to be talking to you in person. No matter how often I try, with these investigations, a Ouija Board just never works."

I turned to her and put out a hand. She shook it, heartily.

"Call me Will. Nobody's happier to be here than me," I said. "But it's still like I told you in the hospital. I have nothing. I can't come up with a single memory about what happened, or the flight, or the whole damned day. I'm glad you're here. I was really hoping you might help me with that."

"I'm sorry. I get the puzzle after the fact. I only have the pieces. Not sure if that helps."

"Tell me about the pieces, then."

"She's not supposed to," Earl said.

I looked at him, at her, questioning. She formed a pained expression on her face.

"Um, technically that's correct. It's an on-going investigation and you're a principle in the investigation—" I started to blurt out a protest when she waved her hand between us "—which is why I'm not here right now."

"Neither are we!" Earl said, grinning.

"And ... since I'm not here right now, well, I guess anything you imagine you might hear in this empty hangar would have to be chalked up to a dream. And I must warn you, Mr. Stewart, going around telling people that you dreamed a conversation between us will not help your case."

"My case?"

Earl said to Walsh, "I already told him Cyler is out for his ticket."

"Yeah, what about that? Isn't there supposed to be some due process? A hearing? Or at least a report?"

"Yes, and yes, and yes."

"So why the railroading? They're gonna yank my ticket!"

Walsh nodded, a little sadly, a little resigned. "Cyler is pushing pilot incapacitation."

"Complete bullshit!"

"Yes, but he thinks it's actionable, something he can do right now. He's also the one advocating to pull your medical, pending re-authorization. The pelvic injury could easily prevent you from performing your duties as pilot in command."

"That's crap!" I declared. She cocked an eyebrow at me.

"Really? Let's go fly a twin and I'll pull an engine on you. How long do you think you can keep one leg on the floorboards holding full rudder?"

I didn't answer. I don't like to answer when it makes me look like a complete idiot.

"Look, I don't know your medical diagnosis, but I do know you've been on strong narcotics. So, there's that. I know you've had a terrible injury and will undergo rehab of some sort. It might be a few weeks before you're even close to being ready to fly again. With or without administrative action, you're grounded for a while."

I thought about my flight testing less than an hour ago. Not as grounded as she thought.

"By then, maybe all this will be sorted out. Or maybe not. The physical stuff, I'm sure you'll manage that. Here's what you need to worry about: Cyler is pushing incapacitation because you have a blackout period. If he can make a case for some sort of seizure or TIA or stroke or any of that career-ending shit, well—that's what you're going to have to deal with."

"So, to state the friggin' obvious, I need to get my memory back."

"Well, it might help, but recovering traumatic memory loss isn't a gimme. Even if you do, it's not like a soap opera where every other week someone has convenient amnesia and then pops out of it in time for the Friday cliff-hanger."

I looked at her. She blushed a little.

"Okay, so I watch *General Hospital*. Sue me. The point is, you may or may not get back your memory, or even pieces of your memory of what happened. And if you do, I'm not sure you can hang your hat on that alone."

"What else have I got?"

She smiled.

"Well, you've got me. And I've got my teeth sunk into this one, Will. Come. Let's take a look."

For the next forty minutes she walked me through the wreckage. She pointed out tear patterns on the aluminum skin. She showed me how pieces of the left wing were compressed. She showed me the cylinders of the engine, which I had been looking for earlier, unrecognizable, torn off the engine block. She lifted up the pilot's seat and showed me how the legs securing the seat to the rails in the floorboards were sheared off as if sliced with a fine surgical instrument. She described the way a career's worth of dust and grime gathered in the bulkheads of the fuselage had sprayed out suddenly, indicating a massive deceleration. She talked about rivet shearing, metal fatigue, fissure patterns and a host of other things compiled from a professional life of picking up pieces. She offered no opinions. Instead, she provided enough facts to fill an investigative book. Finally, she picked her phone out of the pocket of her gray slacks and held it up. I listened to a recording of Chicago Center, issuing instructions to me to change to Essex County advisory frequency at my discretion and report cancelling my instrument flight plan either airborne or on the ground. Then my voice, calm and clipped through the aircraft transmitter, said, "Six Nine Tango, I have the field in sight, cancel IFR, have a good evening."

"Six Nine Tango, roger your cancellation, change to advisory approved, squawk VFR. Good night."

Walsh held up her phone and let the recording continue. A long count, eight or ten seconds went by, then my voice said, "Chicago, six ni—"

A sharp burst of static cut me off. Then silence.

"Navajo Six Nine Tango, Chicago."

No response.

"Navajo Six Nine Tango, Chicago Center."

Walsh touched her phone and stopped the recording.

"That's when you disappeared from radar contact. Right before you made that call, your transponder changed to the VFR squawk code. Do you understand the significance of that?"

Changing the transponder code is as routine as anything you can do in the cockpit. I would have been assigned a discrete code when under the care of air traffic control on my instrument flight plan. Upon cancelling that flight plan, with the field in sight, the discrete code was taken back by ATC and I was told to turn my transponder to the standard visual flight rules code of 1200. Just like any other VFR aircraft in the air. I wasn't sure I saw that as significant.

"Will, you did that! You were on glide slope, field in sight. You were lucid and in communication with ATC, and in command of the aircraft. Twelve seconds before your radar signature was lost, *you* changed the transponder code. That's the act of a pilot in command of the aircraft. Don't you see? That, in my book, is not pilot incapacitation."

"So, tell Cyler!"

Walsh nodded. "You called ATC back. Did you hear that?"

"Yes."

"Why?"

"Same answer. No memory of it."

"There's a burst of noise cutting you off." She looked intently at me. "I think that's the impact."

"Can you be sure?"

"I sent the recording to our lab in Washington, D.C. If it is, they'll know. I'm including it in my report, and that's worth a lot to you. Look, they make their own moves at FAA, and Cyler seems to want to play this one his way. But that's why I'm pointing all this out to you. All this! This is your case. The recording, *the call you made*, the radar track, and all this mess! Nothing, and I mean *nothing* here says pilot incapacitation."

"So why? Why is he doing this?"

Walsh put her hands in her pockets, and her head down, and she minced her feet to stall for a moment.

"Bottom line, Will? I think it's because there's no answer to this one.

You asked the million-dollar question when you walked in the door. Why am I alive? There's no answer we can come up with. We have no idea how the pilot's seat landed upright with you sitting on it. You weren't even strapped in! The seat belts are still attached to the floorboards! How does that happen? Unless you wake up with a memory of hanging on to that chair for dear life and flipping through the air to land perfectly, I'm not sure we're ever going to know."

I suddenly thought that there's no way, physically, someone could fall like that and survive—

*But what if they floated?*

"There's one more thing," she said. "Nobody has the answer to this one either."

"What?"

She stood back a step and regarded the sculpture of metal wreckage, the death scene of an airplane.

"I've been telling you that you hit something."

"Which seems obvious to me."

"Not my point," she said. "You were cleared to change frequency, but you came back to call center and that's when it happened. Why? Why were you calling center?"

I had nothing and showed her with a shrug.

"I think you saw whatever it was you hit."

# 29

Earl hustled me home as if he expected Andy to be waiting in her squad car with the lights blazing and backup squads lining the road in front of the house. Connie Walsh's technical monologue cycled through my head, over and over. I tried to attach the fact of my disappearances and weightless floating to the wreckage I'd seen, and to her just-the-facts-man analysis, but all that did was launch an array of questions like distress flares. How did the seat clear the wreckage? When did the airplane come apart? What did you hit? How did you come down?

*Why aren't you dead? What did you see?*

The questions gave me a headache, but that was nothing to the pain I had awakened in my mid-section while standing on the crutches and riding in Earl's truck. Earl and I had good reason to behave like little boys stealing the old man's girlie magazines from the garage, praying we wouldn't get caught. Because Andy would be furious at my leaving the house. With good reason. Running around with Earl had done me no good whatsoever in the healing department. Sadly, it had done me no good whatsoever in the memory department, either. The closest I came to a memory existed as a drug- and pain-induced nightmare from my last night in the hospital, and I worried that those dreamed images would become indelibly confused with actual memory.

By the time Earl pulled into my driveway, I ached and felt a deep sense of loss for having seen the wreck of Six Nine Tango. Like Earl said, you can't unsee that. Earl offered to help me into the house, but I wanted him gone as fast as possible. Not just because Andy might drop by to help me get supper or check up on her patient.

As soon as his truck drove out of sight, I pushed the levers in my head, and disappeared. Clinging to the crutches, the sensation of weightlessness took the killing pressure off my pelvis. With Earl gone, the magic crutches did their jig across the front lawn and up the front steps. I nearly dropped myself onto the old lounge chair on the porch, surrendering to exhaustion and pain. Instead, I clenched my jaw and pushed into the living room and onto the mattress. The crutches clattered to the floor. Sprawling across the mattress gave sweet relief, and I closed my eyes and almost didn't notice when I started to float again. I had forgotten to reappear. I resolved the error with a small drop to the mattress, which hurt. It prompted me to consider, for just a moment, taking a pill. Andy, wisely, had placed the oxy bottle in the medicine chest in the bathroom. You're a big boy, she had said. Take it if you need it. I needed it. But I was grateful they were out of reach. Instead, I reached to the side table where she had left a bottle of ordinary aspirin. I took three, chased them with water from a glass on the same table, and flopped on my back.

"You've got a lot to think about, bucko," I said to myself, closing my eyes again and settling in for a good long think session.

At which point I promptly fell sound asleep.

# 30

"Wake up, buttercup."

Andy stroked my unruly hair away from my forehead. I became aware of her sitting on the mattress beside me. Black night filled the French doors. The lights glowed soft and low in the living room, and the fixture in the kitchen cast a big square of light on the dining room floor. Andy had her hair down and wore boxers and a t-shirt, her favorite night gear. She must have let me sleep while she changed out of her uniform.

"Mmmm. What time?"

"Eleven-forty-five. How long have you been sleeping?"

I worked some moisture around in my mouth to improve my speaking ability. "Couple hours, I guess. Can you hand me the aspirin?"

She did. I took two this time, with water. My stomach protested, reminding me I hadn't eaten since lunch. Andy and I often eat a near-midnight snack after her shift ends unless I'm scheduled for an early charter flight. Not much chance of that for a while.

"You hungry?" she asked.

"You're a mind-reader."

"Good! I'm pre-heating for nachos!" She patted me on the chest and hopped off the bed. I found it hard to relate to her high energy. She bounced lightly out of the room, injecting a little extra swing in her step as she went. "I have news!" she called back at me from the kitchen.

"I have a full bladder, so give me an hour or so to maneuver on these crutches. Nachos sounds fabulous."

I looked old man slow getting off the bed and onto the crutches, and wobbly crossing the room. I managed to drop one of the crutches while lining up for the toilet. Andy tried to charge in to see if I was okay, but I persuaded her that nothing broke. By the time I finished, washed, and found my way back out, she had completed assembly of a tray with a big platter of heated tortilla chips topped with melted cheddar, and a bowl of salsa.

"How about nachos in bed?" I asked. I headed for the mattress in the living room, hoping she wouldn't suggest sitting at the dining room table. Sitting in Earl's truck had ended my sitting aspirations for the day.

"Sure!" she said brightly. I blinked. Miss-Don't-Eat-In-Bed threw her rules to the wind tonight. Something was most certainly up.

I slid onto the mattress, organized the crutches, and let her work everything else around me. Blessed angel that she is, she brought along two cold Coronas.

"You look like you're going to burst, girl. Tell me."

She couldn't help it. She wore a triumphant expression.

"I got him!"

"Dillinger?"

"Your drug-stealing nurse. Nick. I got him! Well, I didn't get him, and I'll get to that, but I nailed the bastard." She dipped a chip, bit, chewed and beamed at me.

"Give it up, Sergeant."

"Usual disclaimer?"

"Usual disclaimer." Andy lives by the rules, and one of the rules is not to share police business with civilians. However, our rule is that we supersede all rules, and a secret shared with Andy is a secret shared with me, and vice versa.

I reminded myself that I had a secret I wasn't sharing, which sparked a pang of guilt.

She bounded into her story.

"Okay, so what do we know about most criminals?" Before letting me answer, she said, "They're stupid. And this one is no exception. He has his moments, I will admit, but he's still a dumbass. When I got to work today, I dove into Nurse Nick's social media. It's the usual BS. Pictures of himself on a boat, pictures with some girl, at some car show—pictures in a bar in Milwaukee." On this last item, she added emphasis.

"What bar?" I asked, thinking I had been queued up to pose the question.

"It's a night club called Faze, on Water Street. It's become a banger hangout, a bit to the consternation of the local businesses, I imagine. But the club doesn't matter. What matters is who he was all chummy with in the photo. His home boys, the caption said. A couple of guys showing a lot of gang ink. I mean—seriously, if you're going to play master criminal you don't go posting this stuff all over Facebook!"

She paused. My cue to prompt with a question. "So, what's a nurse from Essex County Memorial doing with inner city gang members?"

"We already know, of course. The oxy. Oh, and he's not a nurse, by the way, but I'll get to that. He posted pictures of himself hanging all over these guys, so I ran the lot of them through facial recognition."

"You can do that? I thought that was high-level FBI crime-stopping technology."

"Oh, please. You can practically download the software off the internet now. We got it from DOJ. Part of the package of toys they're handing out from Homeland."

"On TV that takes special priority and at least two commercial breaks before you get results. You did all this today?"

"I did all this before my first coffee break. It's practically instantaneous. I got hits on one of them, a gang banger from Milwaukee, with a bunch of different gang affiliations. The flavor of the month is some outfit called Pan D."

"Panda? Sounds cuddly."

"Pan D. Don't ask me. Anyway, I also got a hit on our boy, Nick. Only he's not. He's Nathan Lyman, three convictions for possession with intent, with a record going back to middle school. The most recent conviction was four years ago for cannabis and cocaine. Served twenty-four months of a four-year sentence. Currently out on Supervision."

She stopped to munch a salsa-loaded nacho and wash it down with cold beer.

"Some supervision," I said. "I gotta ask, how does an ex-con with a drug history get a job as a nurse handing out narcotics?"

Andy hurried down another chip.

"A very good question, Doctor Watson. Nathan Lyman doesn't. Nicholas Lee does. Nicholas Lee was created by Lyman as a new identity, which is a little bit impressive. And by the way, he wasn't a nurse, he was a nursing assistant at Essex. Before that, he was a nursing assistant at a hospital in Fond Du Lac, and before that a nursing assistant at clinic in New Holstein—according to the resume they kept on file at Essex Memorial. This guy is a con artist, probably a sociopath, which for him makes lying as easy as breathing. He's smart enough to build a new identity with a work history in a medical profession, but stupid in that Nurse Lee's social media pages had photos with gang bangers. Dumb, because those photos led me to Nathan Lyman."

"True, but not everybody has access to facial recognition software tied to a known-criminal database. The hospital HR people certainly don't."

"*Grmphtd*," she said through a mouthful of nacho. "Granted. Anyway, once I made the connection to Nathan Lyman, I found *his* social media pages, which go way back, full of all kinds of connections to gang bangers. For heaven's sake, he's got one photo of himself with big wads of cash in both hands! He also promotes one of those pyramid schemes, lists himself as head of some health supplement company—"

"I can imagine what kind."

"He calls himself a venture capitalist, only he doesn't know what that means because in the same breath he says he's looking for investors in 'new real estate concepts.' It goes on and on. One scam after another. But the one item that matters is where he promotes himself as an IT consultant specializing in medical administrative systems. I think he might have some semi-legit computer skills, and that's how he invented Nicholas Lee."

"Oh, come on! He can't have gotten anywhere with that! Hospitals run huge networked systems full of security and firewalls. You saw the workstation in my room. That's a big-bucks system. Even if he could pose as an IT consultant, the hospital isn't going to hire him. They'll rely on vendor reps from the company that developed and sold the system."

"You're right. A hospital like Essex County uses a big-time proprietary system. But go back to that clinic in New Holstein. Or some doctor's office before that. Some little office running a PC network, having trouble hooking up printers. He had a web page for his IT services. Looked as professional as anybody else. I don't know how he did it, but he got into somebody's system, probably by being hired to come in and replace a hard drive or something. He got access and that was the key to creating Nicholas Lee and getting the next job up the line. Plus, he was smart to make himself a nursing assistant, not an RN. RN credentials would be tough to counterfeit, and easy for someone hiring to confirm."

"So, he built Nicholas Lee with a combination of phony ID, phony references and job history--"

"*Counterfeit* references within legitimate records, and then a fake job history followed by actual jobs. Moving from one to the next until the trail is deep enough that someone checking a resume doesn't go back far enough to see the disconnect. He listed his associate degree as having come from one of those for-profit on-line universities, one that has since gone belly-up. Someone being lazy about checking references didn't question it. This isn't hacking the Pentagon. This is all low-level stuff—the stuff people get away with because the clutter is so huge, and the consequences of shoddy background checking are minimal. He was smart enough to lay the foundation for the lie at the lowest possible level. If he had tried that at Essex Memorial, he would have been caught. This way, after the first small lie, everything up the line is relatively true."

Considering how often it has seemed insurmountable to correct even simple errors with banks, insurance companies, or the government, it was easy to see how the clogged arteries of a digital bureaucracy offered a place to hide.

"So, you have him dead to rights. Did you pick him up?"

Andy's grin spread again.

"Oh, this gets better and better. Guess who got busted going nineteen over the limit down I-43 in Manitowoc County last Saturday morning at oh-nine-thirty-five?"

"Let's see ... who do we know with a lead foot, besides you?"

"Nurse Nick!" As she said it, she grabbed both of my shoulders, nearly upending the salsa on the tray between us. She beamed.

"Uh, okay," I said, mildly bewildered, dipping a chip and munching.

"And guess who had a duffle bag in the back seat of his car full of empty Ziploc sandwich bags with little slips of paper with peoples' names?"

"Our boy?"

She nodded, delighted. "And four burner phones. And a half bag of marijuana. And a tin full of what appeared to be Oxycodone...!"

Now I was smiling. It was infectious.

"Nurse Nick was making a run!"

"He got pulled over in a rental car."

I recognized the prompt, so I asked, "Why a rental?"

"Okay!" she wiggled into the mattress a bit. "So, you've got a guy—Nathan Lyman—with a record for possession with intent arrests and convictions—supposed to be on supervision. Now he's running pills up I-43 into Green Bay and beyond—at least that's where he said he was all night—in a bar in Green Bay. Clearly, he's delivering. Nathan Lyman can't use a car registered to Nathan Lyman—and there is one, by the way—because everything going up that highway is subject to plate readers. *Everything.* If a plate reader picks up a known drug felon, it's going to draw attention. He doesn't have a car registered to Nicholas Lee. I checked. Maybe because the phony identity wouldn't survive a credit check for a car loan. What does he do? What do these guys do because they know we're reading plates? They come up with the genius idea of using rental cars, right? Thinking that we're not going to stop some tourist or businessman who's renting. Even if we know they're using rentals, we can't pull over all of them. He got away with the run up, and he might have gotten away with the return trip, except the dumbass comes screaming down the highway at nineteen over the speed limit. Of course, he gets pulled over."

"What an idiot."

"Right? As soon as they run his license, his record pops up. And they can see the duffel bag in the back seat. They find the Ziploc bags, some oxy, the weed, the phones."

"How? What was probable cause?"

"Officially? The trooper reported an overwhelming smell of raw marijuana in the vehicle. But at that point they already knew who he was. And at this very moment, Nurse Nick is enjoying the hospitality of the Manitowoc County Sheriff's department jail."

She raised her beer bottle and clinked with mine. We drank a toast to justice.

"I hope his nights are every bit as comfortable and quiet as he made mine," I said. "What about the pills? Were they real or fakes?"

"We don't know. Remember, he got grabbed up on the rebound. The delivery was already made. It sounds like the pills they found were his own stash."

"Does that mean no case?"

"On, no! My bet is they're going to find everything they need on those phones. To prove intent to deliver. I already talked to the troopers and let them know what we're working on. They got a warrant for the phones this morning and everything is on the way to the state lab."

"Nice work, detective."

"Tom let me run with this," she said. It meant the chief let his patrol sergeant play detective, no doubt with the blessing of the senior detective, Jeff Parridy. Jeff is a good guy who wouldn't let ego pull rank and deny Andy an opportunity. I made a mental note to thank him when I see him next. "Tomorrow I start pulling all the background intelligence. Oh! And guess what they found balled up in his clothes when they checked him into the Hotel Manitowoc! Seventy-seven hundred dollars in cash!"

"How did he explain that?"

"He said it was from his computer consulting business, and that he doesn't trust banks!" She laughed.

I pinched my nose and tried my best old-time radio announcer imitation. *"Like President Hoover says, keep your money in your mattress!"*

"What a dumbass!"

Andy talked for a while about her plan to shore up the false identity investigation. She thought it might be necessary for me to give a statement about my medication experience, not because it would lead to any charges, but because it would have to be brought to the attention of the hospital. A full inventory of their narcotics would be necessary. Patients who were served by Nurse Nick would have to be interviewed. Issues of confidentiality were sure to loom. I tried to imagine the PR hack that had been pressuring Andy to make me a public spectacle. I wondered how much fun this would be for him.

She talked until we scraped the nacho plate clean, finished the beers, and the high wind of this day finally slipped from her sails. It was after one a.m. before we cleared the bed and killed the lights. She slipped in under my arm in the darkness and I stroked her bare back under her t-shirt until her breathing settled into shallow repetition of sleep.

*Usual disclaimer*, I thought. No secrets between us.

I withheld something monumental from Andy. Omission might work for a while, but only until she asked. Then I was screwed.

On cue, she slipped out from under my arm and turned her back to me, muttering a quiet, "Good night, Pilot."

"G'night," I said.

Her voice came softly out of the darkness.

"Oh ... I forgot to ask. How was your play date with Earl? Never mind, you can tell me in the morning."

So screwed.

# 31

Andy didn't bring up the subject of my excursion with Earl. Letting me know that she knew, and not telling me how, served as punishment enough. That, and a good dose of pain the following day, paid my debt to society. Andy hurried out of the house with a kiss and a smile, buoyed by the excitement of her detective work and the prospect of doing more.

I spent the afternoon using the faux grandfather clock in the corner of the room to time ever longer periods of vanishing and floating. By late afternoon, I was up to half an hour. I occupied the time reading a backlog of aviation magazines. They also served the purpose of weighing me down. I effortlessly assumed the posture of someone seated, and then propped the magazine on my thighs. My butt and heels touched the top of the mattress, and without wind in the room, there I stayed. The absence of weight or pressure on my pelvis helped. I think I healed faster, overall, thanks to the time spent floating.

I had my ambitious moments. I had already observed that my clothing vanished along with me. The magazine resting on my lap remained visible. Mostly. The page edges resting on my body seemed fuzzy to my eye. I decided to conduct a test. Before the next cycle, I picked up the aspirin bottle and shoved it in the flimsy pocket of my workout pants.

*Fwooomp!* Gone. Me, my pants, and the aspirin bottle. I dug into the pocket for the bottle and pulled it out. Gone. I felt the cylinder shape in my hand and when I shook it, the pills inside rattled. But it stayed as gone as me. I held it out over the mattress and let go. For a split second, I thought it

might float, but in that instant, I felt a cool kiss on my fingers where I'd been holding the bottle, and the bottle reappeared, resumed its natural connection with the Earth's gravity, and dropped to the sheet.

Interesting.

I picked it up again. It remained visible in my fingers. Like the magazine. I closed my hand around it, felt fresh coolness spread across my palm, and watched it disappear.

"Abra-freaking-kadabra!"

*This will come in handy if I'm ever floating through a bank vault!*

I let it go. It reappeared. I picked it up and slipped it into my pocket, and it vanished, and remained gone when I extracted it from my pocket and dropped it again.

Whatever this was, it had a certain consistency.

My efforts for the day were like that. Low key. My longest test ran to a full hour, between 5 and 6 p.m. The duration seemed to have no effect on me. Returning to normal after a long period seemed to take no more effort than I applied to perform a quick flip back and forth.

Except for a couple trips to the bathroom and kitchen, I stayed on the bed. I worried about becoming untethered and floating out of reach of anything. Granted, here in the living room, it would be a simple matter of reappearing. Gravity would take over and do her thing. Doing that six feet in the air, with my body out of position, however, would not end well.

I extended that thought beyond the French doors to the open yard. Coming untethered outdoors ignited a whole new set of worries. I might float up high enough to be badly hurt—or worse—coming down.

Tuesday started sore and slow, but the day ended with a sense of progress made and healing within. Andy returned after her shift carrying news of progress of her own as she buttressed law enforcement's case against Nick or Nathan or whoever he fashioned himself to be. I listened, happy to see her flexing her skills as a detective.

I had something to ask her but waited until we finished a late supper.

"I got a lot of rest today," I said. "I behaved myself."

"Awww. You're so cute when you're being a good boy." She pinched my cheek.

"Yeah, well idle hands are the devil's workshop. I'm getting seriously bored here. Daytime television sucks. I want to do something with my hands. And since you're not here to play with…"

She ignored my suggestive leer.

"I want to use the credit card to order a hobby project, a radio-controlled aircraft. Something I can build while I'm immobile, and maybe fly around the yard. Just a little electric. Nothing expensive."

"You don't need my permission."

"I know, but I feel like I've already made a mess of the house, and I didn't want to start spreading airplane parts all over the place and creating an irritation."

"Sounds like a fine idea."

And that's how I started down the road to nearly killing myself in the barn.

# 32

Pidge dropped by on Wednesday to complain about Earl. Earl dropped in on Thursday to complain about Pidge. Two other Essex Air pilots tagged along with Pidge. Harvey Keith, a retired Midwest Express airline pilot, instructed part time for Earl. Jim Gunderson was a kid like Pidge. He was a short timer. He had already been accepted by American Eagle and waited to be assigned to a training class. It might have been my imagination, but both pilots acted as if I were contagious, as if crashing an airplane could rub off. They made the standard jokes about how it's better to have the same number of landings as takeoffs, but the humor felt strained. Doc tagged along with Earl, which surprised me, because nothing gets Doc out of the shop. He looked at me with bald reproach and said, "Goddammit, I oughta lock you in that hangar and make you stay there until you put my airplane back together!" I think he got a little choked up. I told him I felt the love.

Earl wanted to know how the hell Andy found out about my jail break on Monday.

"I have no idea," I said. "Did she say something to you?"

"No!"

I didn't get it. I asked Earl, "How did you find out that she knew?"

"All of a sudden, I got a cold shiver down my spine, like I was in some sniper's telescopic sight. I'm thinking of taking a long vacation in Belize."

I swore to him that I didn't rat us out.

Rosemary II and Lane came to visit on Friday, bearing supper, and in a ballet of perfect timing, Andy turned her squad car into the driveway less than two minutes later, clocked out for a dinner break. We ate on the porch in tribute to a beautiful late July afternoon, breathing fresh air from a western high-pressure system and sitting in sight of blue skies laced with mare's tail clouds.

"Who are you going to fly for, Lane?" I asked the girl, who I swear looked even prettier and older than the last time I'd seen her.

"Lufthansa, *mine Herr*!" she replied. "747's! Queen of the skies!"

I looked at her mother expecting to see disapproval, since Rosemary II had a daily firsthand look at the lifestyle and character of aviators, but I saw nothing but a mother's boundless pride.

Most of the visits left me feeling anxious. They were interruptions to my solitude, and my chances to experiment (let's face it, play with) *the other thing.* In contrast, supper with Rosemary II and Lane felt light and relaxed. The conversation sparkled and flowed around us like dancing spirits lost in the music of our voices. We laughed, made bad puns, picked on Earl, gossiped about Pidge, and deftly avoided all reference to The Accident. We talked of movies, of sweet corn becoming ripe, and how quickly this summer seemed to be flying past us. Rosemary II asked about Andy's studies for the detective rank, and Andy asked about Lane's coming freshman year in high school.

"She's signed up for the advanced math," Rosemary II said proudly.

"Mom," Lane protested, "do we have to talk about school? It's summer!"

"Math?" I asked. "Favorite subject?"

Lane nodded shyly. "I like math. I really like physics."

"Okay, Miss Einstein, I have a question. What's the difference between weight and mass?"

She gave me a *Seriously*? look. *Like, ask me something hard.*

"Weight is a measure of the force exerted on an object by gravity. Weight requires another body exerting gravitational force to exist." My blank expression prompted her to go on. "Like, we require the Earth, and its gravity, to have weight. Weight varies depending on how much gravity is present. Did you know that the astronauts in the International Space Station aren't weightless?"

"Given that we see them floating around all the time, this sounds like a trick question," I said.

"The force of gravity at the altitude of the International Space Station is approximately nine tenths the force of the earth's gravity. Each astronaut actually weighs around ninety percent of their earth weight."

"And that floaty thing they do?"

Lane squared her shoulders. Her hands came up, full of energy. I caught both Rosemary II and Andy smiling at the girl's spirited demeanor.

"Ah! They're falling," she pantomimed the point. "They're in free fall toward the earth!"

"Okay…" I knew where she was going, but I let her run with it.

"But they're also moving forward at the same time. They're moving at the perfect speed—like, seventeen *thousand* miles per hour! Their speed takes them around the curve of the Earth fast enough so that as they fall, the Earth falls away below them. Every celestial body in every orbit around every other body is falling toward that body, but by traveling in orbit at exactly the right speed, they never—um, *get there!*"

She showed me with her hands. One fist forming the Earth, the other, the orbiting body.

"So, what's mass?"

"Well, lots of people think mass is the same as weight, but it isn't. You know how weight is, um, defined by gravity? Mass is defined by inertia. Okay! Like, you can have a giant asteroid weighing millions of tons, just floating weightless in space, but if you go up to it in your space suit and push on it, it's not going to move—only that's not because it's heavy, it's because your mass is puny compared to its mass. You're the one that's going to move. Its inertia is vastly greater than yours. Inertia is the resistance of an object to being accelerated when acted on by an external force!"

"Tah-dah!" I exclaimed, and she blushed. "Impressive! Now let me ask you this: Can an object have substance—er, mass, but not be subject to gravity?"

"Impossible."

"Can such an object have no inertia? No resistance to being accelerated?"

"Impossible."

"But what if it could? A solid object, made of molecules and whatever, but not subject to gravitational pull from other bodies, and no inertia? No resistance to acceleration? Did I say that right?"

She pulled at her lower lip, thinking.

"As an inherent property of the object? Like it's made of something weird?"

"Something not yet discovered?" Andy asked, lobbing one in from the sidelines.

"No, just a regular object. A rock. Or a spaceship. Anything."

"Well, if you could make a spaceship like that, you would re-write the laws of physics," Lane said. "You could probably accelerate to faster than light or decelerate instantly without wrecking it or killing everyone inside. We could get to Mars, you know, like *really fast*. Or beyond. Interstellar travel might even be possible."

"Hmmm," I sat back. "Invent that, and you'd be humankind's biggest hero. After Wilbur and Orville, of course."

"It's totally impossible," she said with the absolute authority of the young.

"So was human flight, once."

From there we wandered to the subject of flying lessons. Lane hoped to start next summer, and she chattered about the path that intersected her birthday with the ability to solo at sixteen and obtain her private license at seventeen. Rosemary II stayed quiet, and I knew why. Dreams like that take money. Money is the cruel border patrol that separates wishes from what is, especially for a single mom.

I found myself listening to two conversations. The voices around our small table, and the voices in my head, asking questions about mass and weight and floating into light fixtures.

Or falling out of airplanes.


"WHAT'S THIS?" Lane asked. She stood at the dining room table with her back to me.

"Something to keep me from going insane lying around here," I said. I had been exiled to the living room mattress while Andy and Rosemary II packed and refrigerated leftovers. Against three women who seemed intent on mothering me, I had no chance. "I figure I can stay current flying it around the yard."

Lane ignored the joke and extracted the lightweight electric model airplane from a tangle of plans, tools, and parts.

"Why is the motor missing?"

"It's there. I just need to mount it."

"Why do you have two?"

I lied. "They made a mistake in shipping. They thought I ordered two. I was going to send one back, but then I figured there was a good chance I'd need spare parts. My track record for landings lately isn't great."

"Can I try it? When you get it all done, I mean? Would you teach me?"

"Sure."

And now I saw the kid, the fourteen-year-old. I saw past the façade of accelerated maturity. Legs a little too long and coltish. Elbows not knowing where they belonged all the time. She studied the kit.

"You have both motors out."

"I wanted to compare them." Another lie.

"Lane, honey, would you get the blue bag from the porch?" Rosemary II called out from the kitchen.

"Okay, Mama." She returned the parts to precisely where she had found them.

In short order, the party broke up. Andy, gun-belted and vested again, planted a kiss on me and escorted Rosemary II and Lane out into the summer evening, and then departed to finish her patrol shift. I settled on the mattress, television remote in hand as if I intended to use it, until both cars were on the road.

It would be five hours before Andy returned. Time to fly.

# 33

The barn behind our house stands empty. I would have expected our landlord, the barn's owner, James Rankin, to store something in it. Hay. Or machinery. Or a boat. The kind of things you find in barns. He explained to me that if he started storing junk it would, first, increase the amount of junk he has, and second, require insurance. Barns like that, built by veterans of the Civil War, are big red fire hazards. He had even taken pains to disconnect the old electrical wiring, and have piles of old chaff removed, leaving an empty gymnasium-sized space made of hand-hewn beams and walls full of sunlight pin-holes.

I liked the place. I grew up around barns and farms. I earned my first dollar-an-hour wage on an uncle's farm when I was barely nine. I felt comfortable with its uneven wood floor and the spider population in its corners.

Tonight, I saw it as space. Safe open space for testing *the other thing*.

Standing in the barn, examining the dimensions of the hay loft with a new eye, I declared it perfect. The construction offered ample inner support beams and cross beams to grip and use as pivot points. Open space spread between the beams, and between the floor and the roof. More than enough space to really *fly!*

I brought along the model airplane parts but set them aside. I closed the big barn door behind me, propped up my crutches, and claimed the barn loft airspace as my own.

"This Restricted Area is now active," I called out for the benefit of any other pilots planning to navigate under the same roof. "Let's start with something simple."

A large, hand-cut, squared-off beam rose out of the floor. It ended at a junction with a cross beam running from one side of the barn to the other, even with the point where the barn walls ended, and the roof sloped upward. Someone had nailed a rough ladder to the vertical beam. From the look of the worn wooden rungs, the ladder had been part of the original construction. Thousands of boot steps rubbed the rungs smooth.

I put both hands on the ladder.

*Fwooomp!*

Gone. I danced my fingertips lightly along the sides of the ladder and pushed off the floor with my toes. Nice and easy. I rose immediately, straight up. My fingertips brushed the sides of the ladder. The ascent was effortless. When I arrived at the top of the ladder and the cross beam, I grabbed the ladder and stopped. I have no fear of heights, but I will admit to a wiggle in my chest as I looked down from twenty-five feet up.

I moved my hands along the cross beam, and my weightless body followed, still upright. This induced another chest wiggle as I moved away from the security of the ladder.

"Houston, we have liftoff..." I grinned.

I eased along the cross beam, keeping it roughly even with my chest, until I reached the wall.

"Okay. Ready for something more exciting?"

With one hand on the beam, I rotated my body on its vertical axis until I faced outward, toward the center of the barn space. A duplicate cross beam stood approximately thirty feet away.

"Here goes nuthin'!"

I pushed off the cross beam.

Twenty-five feet up, silent, over empty space, *I flew!* The dimensions of the barn spread out before me, below me, above me—*and moved.* Like a camera shot taken from a helicopter. Like a first flight. Like nothing I ever felt before.

The silence struck me. I realized I had stopped breathing. My hands spread out at my sides. My legs hung somewhere under me. I drifted a lazy line diagonally across the empty center section of the barn, straight toward a duplicate of the ladder I had followed. I felt like a zeppelin easing toward a mooring mast.

In a moment, the flight ended. My trajectory, perfect. My hands closed on the top of the ladder. I stopped.

"*Whoo-hooo!*" I cried out. The sound filled the empty loft. "That is the coolest thing I have *ever, EVER done!*"

A stab of fear struck me at that moment, maybe in counterpoint to the celebration. If this thing turned itself off on me, the way it had the first night, I was screwed. Twenty feet stretched beneath the soles of my shoes and the barn floor. A fall from that height or anything higher would likely finish me. And all this hinged on an imaginary set of levers—

*Don't think about them! Don't touch them!*

—in my head.

I fixed my attention on the ladder, got a grip, and exerted light thrust on a downward vector. The rungs of the ladder passed upward in front of my face until my feet touched the floor.

*Fwooomp!*

Back again. Solid. Feeling the floor and my full weight. I lifted my arms and flexed them. I gently rose and fell on my toes. I reacquainted myself with gravity.

"You know, gravity is a bit annoying," I said, noting the ache in my pelvis reawakened by the weight it carried.

For the next hour, I toured every beam and interior dimension of the barn, from the naked wood floor to the peaked roof. If I had been visible, I would have looked like a spider, working my way up and down beams, down the angled roof, and eventually on long glides across the open expanses. I moored myself at the dusty windows at the peak of each end. I steered myself the full length of the top of the barn along a steel conveyor that had once been used to send bales of hay across the top of the barn to be flipped off as each section of the hay mow was filled. I found bird nests, spider nests, and a few bats, who interestingly wiggled nervously when I approached, but did not flutter away.

I grew more comfortable with the space beneath my feet and suppressed my fear of accidently flipping the switch to the Off position and dying at the hands of gravity.

Deepening twilight seeped into the barn, barely noticed by me, until the shadows in the corners turned all but black. It had grown late. I had one more task on my checklist.

I steered myself to a landing not far from the barn door where I had dropped the model airplane parts. I picked up the two electric motors Lane had studied. What Lane hadn't noticed is that I not only removed the motors from the airplanes but had built new mounts for the motors and their batteries in compact balsa wood boxes. The new mounts fit neatly in my hands, and I positioned the on/off switch under each thumb, allowing me to point the small motors with their attached propellers in any direction.

It was one thing to float myself around like an astronaut in the International Space Station, vectoring from one grip to another. It was something entirely different to be able to control myself in *flight*.

"Ready, Wilbur?"

"Ready, Orville!"

I squared myself in the center of the largest section of the hay mow, gathering the greatest possible volume of open space above and around me. I held the devices, one in each hand, pointed up. My thumbs hovered above each switch.

"On three."

*Fwooomp!* Gone.

"One."

"Two."

"*Three!*" I hit both switches. The electric motors, tiny little devices barely able to lift a light balsa wood aircraft, both whirred to full speed. I had been expecting next to nothing to happen.

I shot directly up as if I had kicked myself off the floor with both legs. The shock of the acceleration made me throw my arms out in counterbalance. It was a mistake. Unevenly pointed in relation to my body, the asymmetrical thrust of the motors and propellers rotated me wildly to the left. My legs flew out in a futile attempt to stop the motion. I caught sight of the cross-beam shooting past, then glanced up to see the approaching steel frame of the conveyor running across the barn ceiling. I ducked just in time to take the blow from one steel tube on the crown of my head instead of my face.

*Fwoo—*

"NO!" I threw open both hands, ejected the motors, and swung wildly for the conveyor.

*—oomp!* I saw my hands, my arms. Gravity grabbed me forty feet above the floor.

One hand clamped on the steel tube of the conveyor. The other missed and stung itself on the sharp conveyor chain hanging along the center line of the device. Gravity yanked me down. My fully visible arm extended with a jolt and my fingers clenched the steel tube.

I heard both motors hit the floor and chatter as the spinning propellers broke.

I swung my free arm upward. Missed. Swung again and found a grip. The grip felt slippery. The conveyor chain had gouged the flesh inside my thumb. Blood smeared my palm.

My heart thundered. My legs kicked the open space above the spot where I expected Andy would find my dead body. And boy, would she be pissed! Suddenly my eyes stung. My vision reddened and blurred. The thought that I was about to pass out joined my general panic until I realized blood streamed down my forehead into my eyes. The blow to my head announced itself as throbbing, white hot pain.

*Breathe, dummy!* I sucked in air, held it, then blew it out. My fingers screamed at me. I felt an instinct—a desperate need—to kick my legs up and hook them on the open framework of the conveyor. But my right hand, the bloodied hand, might as well have been greased. Any movement or stress on it would cost me its grip.

*The way out of this is NOT upward.*

Air in. Air out. Calm down. Hold on.

I settled myself on my dangling weight, closed my eyes, and focused.

*Fwooomp!*

Relief came instantly. Weight and gravity, which had conspired to kill me, vanished along with my body. Still, for a long moment, I refused to release my grip. The blood that stung my eyes continued to run down my face. I tasted it. I felt it on my neck. But it no longer obscured my vision. Hanging there, considering the gash in my scalp, the most serious thought of all hit me.

"How the hell are you going to explain *that* to Andy?"

I slowly eased my fingers loose. My breathing settled. My heart rate dropped somewhere back in the range of a buffalo stampede. I pushed. I was a little too anxious, because I pushed harder than I wanted to, and hit the floor a little more aggressively than I wished. But Lane's assessment of mass and inertia paid off. The sudden stop seemed to have little effect on my mending bones.

Stabilized on my feet, I found the levers in my mind and switched off again. Gravity and tremors in my legs brought me to my knees.

Blood dribbled down my face and from my palm.

The electric motors lay dead on the floor, the propellers shattered.

I had nearly killed myself.

I laughed out loud.

"Holy shit! *It worked!*"

# PART II

# 34

Y ou have days when everything goes right. The world seems to spin on an axis that runs through your wishes and whims. The most important thing about days like that is to remember that the universe will always counterbalance, and the shit will eventually hit the fan.

Friday, near-death experience notwithstanding, felt like one of those golden days. The dinner with Rosemary II, Lane and Andy stayed warm in my memory, and I came away from the barn flight test wounded but elated. My earliest days of flying lessons filled me with the same feeling, a combination of discovery and heady disconnection from everything ordinary. Nothing outside of dreams came close to the feeling I experienced gliding through the beams and spaces of the barn. I knew at some point I needed to sit down and think, really think, about what was happening. But for the moment, I was a kid in a candy store, enjoying the treats.

The gash on my head stopped bleeding in the shower. I showered fully clothed, and fully visible. It hurt, putting weight on my mending bones, but I needed to see the bleeding stop, and see my clothes to wash the blood out of them. Both my t-shirt and warm-up pants were black, so the blood didn't leave obvious stains. The gash on the fleshy part of my thumb took a Band-Aid. An ER doctor might have given it a stitch or two, but I'd done worse to myself in the maintenance shop at Essex Air. I vanished and floated my way to the laundry room where I threw everything in the dryer. Andy's shift wouldn't end for another two hours, so I spent the forty minutes while the clothes dried floating around the house, not bothering to get dressed. I considered clearing away the model airplane parts on the dining room table. Both kits were useless now without motors and propellers. However, I wasn't finished exploring the concept of propulsion. Keeping a vague project-in-progress spread all over the table served a purpose. Andy would ask questions if everything went to the trash and a new supply appeared.

I mentally drew up plans for the next excursion. Clearly, two motors proved unwieldy and too powerful. I shot up like a fighter in full afterburner. Impossible or not, inertia wasn't an issue. Speed and power might seem like a good idea, but I needed control, and I needed to be able to stop. I needed a single motor with a speed controller. Something reversible. Time for a trip to a hobby store.

When the dryer buzzed, I dressed and grabbed a snack. To keep the weight off my pelvis, I floated over the mattress with the television on, sketching ideas on a note pad until Andy's headlights flashed across the yard. She entered wearing a smile. It had been another good day playing detective, digging into Nick the Drug Dealing Nurse.

We each had a good Friday.

# 35

Saturday morning, I knew something had gone south when I saw Andy at the mailbox, fanning through the morning mail. She stood rooted to a spot on the empty road. She stared at one letter, then another, then a third. The third, she opened. Multiple pages unfolded in her hands. She locked her concentration on each one in succession. It was not good news.

I sat on the old lounge chair on the porch doodling sketches of handheld, directable propulsion units, or HHDPU's, an acronym I invented that was not going to survive the sketch phase. Andy wore an unmistakable expression as she climbed the porch steps and sat at the foot of the lounge chair.

"What?"

She shook her head grimly. I reached out for the letter she had opened, but she held on to it. "It's the hospital bill."

I winced. "Through the roof?"

"We'd have to sell the roof if it were ours to sell. It's twenty-six thousand dollars."

"Are you kidding me? For what? I was flat on my back for seven days, living on Jell-O. What the hell?"

Andy unfolded the pages. "Ambulance. ER. Imaging. Testing. A lot of stuff here I don't recognize. The medications. It's four pages long."

"We have insurance," I said. Andy had a family plan through the police department. "That's what it's for."

"We have a five-thousand-dollar deductible."

Now I knew where this dagger had pierced my wife. Neither of us makes

137

much, and she still carries a few thousand in student loan debt, which takes a bite every month. But even with that, we put away a little every paycheck. Once or twice a month, over a fish fry or burgers somewhere, we kick around the idea of a home of our own, and we volley back and forth the question of having children. Last I checked, we had a little over forty-two hundred in a savings account.

"I'm so sorry," I said. "This is on me. I never meant…"

"Hey!" She clamped a sharp grip on my leg. "Stop it! This isn't on you. God, how could you ever think that? Do you think they could ever come up with a price higher than losing you? *Fuck that*."

Andy never, and I mean *never* uses the f-word. When she does, you better pay attention.

"We'll figure it out. We'll find a way." She frowned, making her lower lip prominent.

I wasn't so sure. I had no idea what my future held. Earl Jackson will walk through hell and plant daisies for spite in the name of loyalty. But how long he could keep writing paychecks with my name on them, without me being able to fly his airplanes, I couldn't say. Nor did I expect it from him.

As if dark gods had written the script, on that thought Andy lowered her eyes and said, "There's more."

She handed me the other two envelopes. I didn't need to open them. One was from the Federal Aviation Administration Certification Branch, and the other was from the Federal Aviation Administration Aeromedical Branch.

When I looked up at Andy, she had tears in her eyes.

# 36

Saturday wasn't finished with us. Technically, the worst came on Sunday, a little after one in the morning, but I would forever remember it as a single Bad Saturday.

Banging on our porch door blew us both out of a sound sleep. Andy, light and lithe, was off the mattress in an instant and had her service weapon in hand before I made it up on one elbow. Where she kept her gun when we slept, I had no idea.

"WILL! ANDY! PLEASE!"

I recognized the voice and the silhouette against the screen door.

"Amanda?" Andy called out.

*"Please, I need your help!"* Rosemary II appeared when Andy hit the porch light. Her wide eyes projected open terror. *"It's Lane! They've taken Lane!"*

Andy pulled open the door and swept Rosemary II through the porch and into the living room. I swung my legs off the mattress and groped for the crutches. The two women stood face to face. Rosemary II clutched Andy's left hand with both of her own hands like a lifeline. Andy had not yet holstered her weapon. She held it at her side, pointed at the floor, her trigger finger aligned with the barrel.

*"Oh, god! They have Lane! My baby! They took her!"* Tears streamed down the woman's face.

"Amanda, sit down, honey. Will, can you get water?"

I moved, not knowing how I was going to pull that off while on crutches, but with the certainty that it wasn't a request.

"Sit down, honey," Andy said, putting her left arm around Rosemary II and guiding her to the edge of the mattress.

"Oh, my God! Oh, dear God!" Rosemary II cried.

By the time I managed to get to the kitchen and back with a glass of water, Andy had secured her weapon somehow, somewhere. She held Rosemary II close as the woman cried, shaking. Andy took the water from me and pointed at a box of tissues. I handed them over.

"Who? Who took Lane?" Andy asked. I had no idea where she found the inner calm. I felt twisted tight inside.

"Those bastards!" A stark, wounded wail came out of Rosemary II and she threw her arms around Andy.

It took several minutes before Rosemary II steadied herself.

"Start at the beginning, honey," Andy instructed, holding Rosemary II's hands between hers.

"Street thugs. From where we lived before. They wanted her two years ago, and now they have her."

"Where? Where was Lane tonight?"

"She worked. She worked until eleven."

"Lane was working?"

Rosemary II nodded. "She wanted to help earn money. She asked Leo Willis from church to let her help with stocking at Farm and Fleet. Just on Saturdays. They're doing inventory, so they worked until eleven tonight, for extra pay. She had a ride home with one of her, um—one of the other kids, an older girl. But she didn't come home. I called Lane, but she didn't answer, so I called older girl, Donna—I called her, and she said she thought I picked up Lane, because when it was time to leave, Lane was gone—and I didn't know what to do! I got my keys and I was going to drive over to the store—and when I got to my car, one of them was there. He put a gun in my face!"

"Who was there?"

"A boy we knew, a boy from the neighborhood. He's older now. He was always bad, always hanging with the ones who were ganged-up. He put a gun in my face, and he said, 'She's with us now, bitch. Go back inside and if you leave, we're gonna cut her up. If you call the cops, we're gonna cut her up.' He—he—he said that about my baby! We have to find her!"

"We will. I promise you, we will."

"He said they would be watching. He told me to go inside and to leave the lights on, and if I called anyone they would—"

"They're still there now?"

"I think so."

Andy glanced at me and pointed with her eyes at her phone on the table by the bed. I maneuvered around the two women and retrieved the phone.

"How did you get out without anyone seeing you? How did you get here?"

"I called Pidge. I called her, and told her to park two streets over, and to come in through the back yard, to the back door. She's there now. The curtains are closed, but the lights are on, and I told her to pace to make it look like I'm still there. And I took her car. I thought of you. Please—!"

"I need to make a call," Andy said, reaching toward me. I handed her the phone.

"NO! You can't! They said—!"

"Amanda," Andy took Rosemary II's face in her hands. "Listen to me. I love your daughter like she was my own, and I will *never* do anything to put her in danger. You have to trust me. You have to. You came to me and you did the right thing, but you have to let me do what I do."

"No no no no no…" Rosemary II shook her head, her voice tiny and pleading, but Andy held on.

"Listen to me. I can do things they will never know. Right now, I need to find out if they're still there. If they are, it may help us find her faster than if they are not. But we *have to know*. I can't do it alone. Please, let me do what I do. Let me do what you came here for."

Through tears and silent sobs, Rosemary II nodded reluctant agreement.

Andy pulled her phone up and touched the face. Her in-call volume was high enough, and the room silent enough that we could all hear it ringing. Mike Mackiejewski answered.

"'Sup, Andy?"

"Mike, where are you?"

"The Plaza."

"Okay, I have a situation. Serious. I need you to roll by an address, low key," Andy said. She held the phone up. Rosemary II recited her address. "Did you get that?"

"Got it. What's the deal?"

"Child abduction. The perpetrators might still be there, watching the address. Look for anyone sitting in a car, surveilling the address. But don't move on them, do you copy? Do NOT move on anyone or anything you see there. Keep it casual. And keep it off the frequency. Call me as soon as you clear."

"Copy that, Sarge." Andy broke the connection. Now she tapped open another call from her contacts list. The phone rang, rang, and finally Tom Ceeves picked up.

"Chief, it's me, Andy."

"I see that." Sleep quickly left his voice. No phone call at this hour is good.

"I need you here, at my place. We have a child abduction. Lane Franklin. Her mother is here with me, and we've got circumstances—we need to keep our moves under the radar. Somebody may be watching or listening. How soon can you get to my place, Chief?"

"Ten minutes." He clicked off. I marveled at his trust in Andy—that without details or questions, he could be pulled out of his bed in the middle of the night.

Andy handed me the phone.

I asked, "How does Lane know gang—?" Andy cut me off with a brisk wave.

She turned to Rosemary II.

"We're going to do this, Amanda. We're going to get her back. Now I need you to tell me everything. From the beginning. Slowly and clearly."

Rosemary II nodded, gathered herself. The terrified mother receded as the smooth, organized office manager of Essex Air fought to emerge.

"Isn't there something else you can do? Should we go and look for her?"

"I need reinforcements first. I can't stress this enough, Amanda, I need to know everything. Everything."

"I just—I don't know—"

"Mike will call us in a few minutes. The Chief is on his way. Talk to me."

Rosemary II took a deep drink of water.

"When we came here," she said, "to Essex, we were running away. We lived in Milwaukee, in the inner city, the 'hood,' folks around here would say. My—Lane's father—he was gone—"

She hesitated.

"I never told you this. I never told Rosemary. Or Earl. I—oh, Andy, I was so afraid of what you all would think of us!"

"It's okay," Andy said.

"He's in prison. Has been since before Lane was born and will be for a long time. Thank heaven. I made bad decisions. Lane, she came when I was nineteen. By that time, I was alone. After Lane came, I moved us in with my cousin. I tried to work when I could. I tried to raise her as best I could. She was so precious, so bright. I saw something better in her, something better for both of us. I wanted so much for her. You know her. She's a jewel. But where we were, it was bad. Drugs. Gangbangers. Kids with guns and knives. Some nights we slept on the floor in the back of the house, in a pantry, because of the shooting. Twice, bullets came through the walls. One street over, a little girl, she was just nine—she—she died."

Andy handed Rosemary II a tissue. Rosemary II blew into it, loudly.

"But in all that, Lane never lost her heart, her bright soul. She had school, she had friends, kids, little kids at that age when even the worst places in the world are still a playground to a child. I got a job working for the DNR, an office job. There was never any money, but I still had hope. Lane gave me hope. The neighborhood seemed to get better for a while. Like it was cleaning itself up, but that was a lie. Instead of wanna-be gang-bangers, a tougher, worse bunch came in. They forced out the ones they didn't need and recruited the rest. It became more organized, and more vicious. It was like being liberated by Nazis. Instead of hanging on the street corners, they roll up in their Escalades. Instead of half a dozen different losers selling crack out of their pants pockets, they set up houses, and recruited kids to be corner boys. They used kids with school backpacks to deliver drugs and money. And there was a lot of money. They all had big TVs and cars. And guns. So many guns.

"Then they came for Lane. She was just twelve! She developed, you know, early. And she's so beautiful. Boys came around, sniffing around. She knew. She's smart. She knew what they wanted, but I raised her right. But those animals came for her. This one, Mauser, all high-up in the gang, in his big black SUV. He came around, and he came to me, and told me she was *fine*. That's what he said. *Fine.* Like he could taste it. He said she was Princess material. He said she had been seen by somebody important, and she was his now. He—*he told me to get her ready!*"

She spit the words out.

Andy took her hands and held them.

"That's what they do with the girls. They recruit the boys for their corners and for runners. And they choose the girls. Lots of the girls want it, they preen for it. And they get passed around or turned out eventually. But this Mauser, he told me Lane was *selected* by someone big, someone on top. She would be a Princess, he said. Meant for someone special. *She was twelve, for God's sake!* He told me he would come for her. Sick bastard!

"The moment he drove off, I packed a bag and took my cousin's car keys. And we left. We left and drove as far as a half tank of gas would take us. I had forty-seven dollars and one nice dress. Lane," Rosemary burst out a laugh/sob, "I told Lane to pack and when I looked in her bag it was full of her favorite books! She didn't even have a change of underwear!"

"Of course," Andy said.

"We got this far, to Essex. I thought it was enough! *How did they find us?!*"

"We're going to find out. Keep going. I need to know it all."

"There isn't much more to it." Rosemary II drew a long breath. "It was hard. I knocked on doors, looking for a job. I don't know if you'd call it a plan, but I thought if I got a job, and got that first paycheck, we would be okay. I thought we could sleep in the car, and then find something, some-place. Anything would be better than, you know…

"And then the Lord took me by the hand," she said, casting her eyes upward. "It was the second day. The car was running on empty, and I guess we were, too, and we kept stopping and I kept asking. Waitress. Clerk. Anything. Lane would wait in the car, but I think people saw her, and it just didn't look right. Nobody had anything, they said. But I knew some of them just didn't want to do with a Black woman in a beat-up car. Lane, she never complained, but she needed a bathroom, and we were near the airport, and I thought it was an airport, you know, like a regular airport. I'd never seen a general aviation airport before. I didn't know what an FBO was. Lane, she had to go, so we walked in and it wasn't a regular terminal, it was just the office. And there was an angel there." Tears welled up in her eyes. "One of God's own angels was there."

She didn't mean Earl.

"Lane, she ran down the hall, practically holding herself, and she did her business, and when she came back, I wanted to go quickly because this wasn't any airport terminal like I'd ever seen. But Ro—Rosemary was there, and she had one of her banana breads on the counter."

I knew them well.

"Lane, God bless the poor child, she couldn't take her eyes off it. I wanted to take her away, quickly, but she was—she was hungry. She couldn't help herself. And Ro—"

She couldn't go on for a moment. The memory flooded her eyes. She pulled in hard, deep breaths. Her voice went high and thin.

"Rosemary, she said to Lane, 'Honey, would you mind tasting my banana bread? Nobody here seems to like it and I can't remember if I put in baking soda or ground up worms. Would you try it? Please?' And Lane almost didn't, but I guess that's how hungry she was. And of course, it was heavenly. And then Rosemary came out from behind the counter, oh, she was so tiny but so big at the same time! She came out and she picked up the plate and took me by the hand and she took me into the pilot lounge and put the plate down, and she told us to sit. Then she brought Lane a can of pop

and me a coffee, and she sat down and took my hands, and she said, 'Now, you tell me why this beautiful child and her mother have had nothing to eat today.' And I spilled it all. I broke open. I couldn't help it."

"She could do that," I said. Something stung my eyes and the back of my throat. I rubbed my eyes and coughed.

"She hired me that day. That was the day she told Earl she was retiring, and I was her replacement."

I had no idea.

"She gave me the keys to her house, and she sent us there to wait for her. Can you imagine! I tried to say no, but—"

"If you had, you might have been the first," Andy said.

"I didn't know how near the edge I was. I had been numb. And here was this angel. We went to her home, but I couldn't go in. We had the key, but we just couldn't. We waited for her outside. We were scared someone would see us and call the police, but no one did. When she got there, she had groceries and she took us in and made, oh my heavens! Such a meal! And she made us stay with her. She took me to work the next day and she told Lane to take good care of the place and trusted her to stay there alone. She had that cat, do you remember? I never saw a cat so fat. Lane fell in love with him. Buster. We have him now—oh, Andy, Lane loves that cat!"

Her hands went to her face. It took a moment before Rosemary II was able to speak again.

"Rosemary took me to work and she taught me. My head spun, but she was so patient. Like it was just another day. We stayed a week with her, and then she took us to the house—where we are now. It belongs to her nephew. She said the rent was paid for two months and the furniture was junk, but it would do. And then…"

We knew. Andy and I knew what happened next.

"And then she was gone. A week later, she was gone. It was like God sent us to her, and she did His work, and then He called her home."

We knew, yet we never knew. We never knew the other side of the story.

"And Earl, he called me Rosemary II. And I have never been so honored. And I thought we were free. Two years and I thought we were free. How could they find us here? We never went back! *We never saw any of them!*"

Andy looked at me. I saw in her eyes that she had an idea. I had my own guess.

"They're taking her to *him*, to whoever that Mauser said wanted her!"

"Then we know where to start looking, and we know they won't hurt her," Andy said. Just then her phone rang.

"Mike," she said.

145

"Nothing here. The street's clear. What's the story, Sarge?"

"Drive out to my place, Mike. Hurry, but quietly."

"On my way." They disconnected.

"Amanda, what was the name of the gang?"

"I will never forget. Pan D. I don't know what it means, but I will never forget."

Headlights swept through the windows. A minute later Chief Tom Ceeves climbed the porch steps and brought himself to a halt in the center of our living room. Tom Ceeves is six-foot-six and if he weighs less than two-seventy, he's been dieting. Approaching sixty-something, he is as much a force to be reckoned with now as he was when he served as a lineman for Notre Dame's football squad. I've never seen him carry a service weapon. A weapon would just look puny on his hip. He wore a flannel shirt over black jeans.

"Who do we know in the gang unit in Milwaukee?" Andy asked before he could utter a word.

"I know a guy," Tom said, his voice deep, the equal of his powerful frame. He turned to me and put out his hand. "Glad you're not dead, Will."

I shook hands and agreed with him.

"Lemme make a call. Got any coffee?"

## 37

The war council convened in the kitchen. I made coffee. Andy delivered a concise recap to her boss. Tom Ceeves issued rapid-fire orders to Mike Mackiejewski.

"I need you to reach out to the highway patrol. I want all their plate reader data for I-43 and I-41 between Milwaukee and Highway 34. Everything for the last 24 hours up to the minute. Both ways. Get it from them and then park your ass at the station and start going through it. Call in help if you need it. I'll be right behind you. Whatever looks like it might belong, compile it and start running them. Look for matches going both ways by time blocks. I think there's a filter for that."

"On it," Mike said. He stopped long enough to hug Rosemary II, then bolted for his cruiser.

"We need to get to Manitowoc," Andy said to the Chief.

"Lyman?"

"He's the one that tipped them. I'm sure of it. You know Bill Shears. You can call him. Get us in."

Tom considered it and nodded. Andy told me Bill Shears was Sheriff of Manitowoc County, and in charge of the Manitowoc County Jail. That's where Nick the Drug Dealing Nurse had begun what I hoped would be an extended vacation that would eventually land him in one of the state's fine prisons.

"I know Bill, but I wouldn't call us drinking buddies," he hedged, but then he glanced at Rosemary II, who wore hope in every pore in her face. "Yeah. I'll roll him outta bed."

Andy handed me the phone. "Call Pidge. She's still at Amanda's house. If she flies us, we can be there within the hour, and from there we can meet Tom's MPD guy in Milwaukee." Tom had called an assistant chief at the Milwaukee Police Department. From the tone of the conversation, they seemed close. Tom made it clear that this was personal. The guy agreed to meet us at General Mitchell International and grease the wheels with the gang unit. He said he would get the top people on this. He told Tom he would start making calls as soon as they hung up.

"I'm getting dressed," Andy said. We all looked at the clock. It read one-fifty. "Amanda, you do not get a vote. You stay here. There's absolutely nothing you can do in Manitowoc, and from there we're going to Milwaukee. This is about being police. You're not police. It's how it works, and it's how we're going to get her back."

Rosemary II closed her eyes in prayer. There was no mistaking it. In that moment, her faith was fully invested, in God and in my wife. She nodded.

"I need you in Manitowoc. Can you handle this?" Andy asked me, gesturing at my crutches.

"Easy. It's calling Pidge that has me scared."


"WHAT THE MOTHERFUCKING SHIT?!"

I held the phone away from my head.

"Pidge—"

"I'll kill the motherfuckers, Will. Swear to shit. I have a Smith and Wesson 40 caliber and I am a dead shot, and I will fucking shoot their tiny dicks off, you know I will! They will fucking die slow. I'll show them my tits and they'll get a hard on and bleed to death, motherfuckers!"

"Pidge—"

"Is Andy on this? Did she call out the fucking National Guard? Tell me she is going psycho fucking nuclear on their asses!"

"PIDGE!"

Tom Ceeves, working his own phone, turned my way and scowled, then went back to his call.

"What?"

"Get in your car and get out to the airport. Preflight One Nine Alpha. We need to get to Manitowoc, like an hour ago. You're P.I.C. Load enough fuel to get us down to Mitchell after that."

"Oh. Shit. Okay." She hung up.

"She's headed out to the airport now," I said when Rosemary II looked my way.

"Are you going to call Earl?" she asked.

"It's two in the morning. Hell, no."

## 38

P idge waited with the right engine running on One Nine Alpha, a virtual duplicate of the Piper Navajo I had destroyed. Tom Ceeves rolled through the airport gate and onto the ramp. Andy rode shotgun. She wore a dark pants suit with a white blouse instead of her uniform. She had her weapon and badge, the latter hooked over her waistband. When she came downstairs, Tom gave her a look, and she gave it right back. I watched him cave in on the subject of how she would handle her rank in Milwaukee. In the car, he made it official ... ish.

"When you get to Milwaukee, introduce yourself as Detective Stewart," he told her. "I'm appointing you temporarily. Don't let it go to your head."

From the back seat of Tom's cruiser, I couldn't see Andy's face, but I'm sure she was smart enough not to smile at having bullied her Chief by dressing in plain clothes.

"Don Schultz will pick you up at the airport. He'll get you in with the right people. With a little luck, you'll have something from Lyman that they can use, and Mike may have something from the readers."

"Right."

"And call me."

"Right."

"Andy," Ceeves said pointedly, "if Lyman's in on this at all, in any way, this thing with Lane, you go ahead and fuck him over. Clear? The same goes for their case in Manitowoc. Don't let Bill Shears buffalo you. Lane comes first."

"Clear."

Rosemary II and I rode in the prisoner cage in the back of the cruiser. She refused to stay at the farmhouse. She decided to establish camp at the office. In the morning, she would fill Earl in on his stolen airplane, and deal with the scheduling storm its absence would cause. She said it would help her, a little at least, to be busy. We promised to keep her up-to-date, and if anything happened, we would send Pidge back to get her. Parked behind the Navajo, clear of the prop blast from the right engine, Tom and Andy released us from the locked back seat. Andy jogged around the front of the car and took Rosemary II in a tight embrace. They spoke into each other's ears, words lost to me under the rumble of the big Lycoming engine, the message as clear as the starlit sky over our heads. I snapped a salute at the Chief and started for the airplane. Andy hurried into place beside me.

"After you, Detective," I said into her ear.

She smiled, grim and determined, and took it with her up the airstair into the cabin. I handed her my crutches and worked my way to the back-row seat by the door. It hurt to move in the tight cabin. I needed three tries to get the door closed, and broke a light sweat in the process.

"Light it up, Pidge!" I called up to the pixie in the pilot's seat.

"Fuckin' A!" she called back.

Andy looked at me, worried. I mustered a guess that she feared post-traumatic stress brought on by me being in an airplane for the first time since the crash. Maybe there would have been if I had any memory of crashing this Navajo's sister ship. But I still had nothing. If anything, I wanted to be up front, in Pidge's pilot seat, although I grudgingly admitted to myself that Connie Walsh had been right. I doubted very much that I could work the rudder pedals with the pain presently waking up in my pelvis. I gave Andy a shake of the head and a shrug.

"Nothing," I said. "Let's worry about Lane, okay?"

She returned a nod. Pidge fired up the left engine and we rolled forward.

# 39

A Manitowoc County deputy met us on the ramp at the airport. Five minutes later he pulled up to the County Court complex and into the Sheriff's Department sally port. Tom had shaken the Sheriff, Bill Shears, out of bed, but Shears had delegated the mission to the senior deputy on duty. His name was Wilson. He looked like he'd been riding a desk and interrogating Twinkies for some time.

"We've got your man in here, in the D2 interrogation room." Wilson led us through narrow cinder block hallways painted glossy institutional yellow and lighted with institutional fluorescent lights. "He's bitching about being hauled out in the middle of the night and demanding his lawyer."

"He has a lawyer?" I asked.

"Court-appointed. First thing he did was declare himself indigent, so the taxpayers have to cover his legal bills."

"His parents stopped paying for lawyers when he was still in high school," Andy said. "He's been using public defenders ever since. He knows the system."

"I don't know how indigent you are when you get picked up with eight Grand in your pants," Wilson commented, extracting a set of keys from his belt and opening a steel door into a new hallway, identical to the previous hallway. He waved us in, closed and locked the door behind us, then led us deeper into the building.

"Okay, he's in here. I've been told to wait outside, and that this meeting never happened. Check your weapon with me, Detective."

Andy slipped her Glock out of the pancake holster I bought her for Christmas. It was meant for plainclothes use. This was the first time she used it on duty.

Wilson looked at me. I put up both hands. "Strictly kung fu. And these crutches."

Wilson unlocked the door. "Knock when you want out. If you use the crutches on him, use the padded end. Won't leave a mark."


THE SHOCK of yellow-white hair pointed in all directions. His narrow face looked pale in the naked fluorescent light. Dark crescents hung below his eyes. Good, I thought. Short on sleep. Nathan Lyman, or Nicholas Lee, sat with his wrists in manacles. The chain slipped through a steel loop on a steel table bolted to the concrete floor, the same as the steel stool under his ass. He swung a look oozing contempt toward the sound of the opening door, but it flashed to surprise when he saw me.

I wanted to say, "Hello, asshole," but my wife had made my role clear. My mouth stayed shut.

"Mister S," Lyman said, hooking one side of his lip up in a lop-sided sneer. "On a scale of one to ten, how's the pain tonight?"

"Mr. Lyman, I'm Detective Stewart," Andy said, "and I suggest you shut your mouth."

"I want my lawyer," he snapped at Andy. "You can't fucking drag me outta bed in the middle of the night. This is harassment. This is torture."

"What? Rough night?" I asked. "On a scale of one to ten—"

Andy shot me a look. I shut up.

"You don't get a lawyer for this meeting, Mr. Lyman, because I am specifically advising you to shut your mouth and not speak to us. You have the right to remain silent and I strongly suggest you exercise that right."

"Doesn't matter, I'm not telling you shit."

"I'm not asking."

Andy sat down and folded her hands on the table. I tilted my crutches against the wall and took the only other chair in the tiny room. We sat with our backs to a mirrored window which, like the room itself, seemed much smaller than the ones on television cop shows. I guess they didn't need to get big cameras and lights behind this one.

"You fucking can't do this, you know. I'm going to file a complaint."

"There you go again," Andy said with a sigh. "Are you finished? Or would you like to sell me some health supplements? Or maybe explain how Big Pharmaceutical is poisoning us all with chemtrails from commercial jets, making us sick so we're forced to buy their drugs? I've seen your website. You are passionate about your ignorance."

"Talk to me when you get cancer, bitch, and they're charging you seven hundred dollars a pill for a cure they've had in their vaults since 1953." I watched Lyman's eyes. True Believer's eyes. Andy had explained to me that, the more she learned about him, the more he read like a classic psychopath. Not the movie shower-scene slasher type. The kind that can lie without a tell, and then fervently believe the lie they just heard coming out of their own mouth.

"Again, are you finished?" Andy asked. "Or do we have to run through a discourse on the Deep State, or the International Jewish Banking Conspiracy, or how NASA faked all six Apollo moon missions?"

"Fuck you."

"I think you'll find that we're here to fuck you, Mr. Lyman. So again, why don't you shut your mouth and let us explain to you how we plan to do that, royally, with a red-hot poker."

Lyman slipped a sulk onto his already long face.

"You switched my husband's medication at Essex County Memorial. You stole his Oxycodone and replaced it with counterfeit pills," Andy explained.

"Bullshit," he said. He just couldn't keep his mouth shut. I think Andy counted on that. "You can't prove any of that. I repeat, I want my lawyer. This is an illegal interrogation. You're violating my Constitutional Rights, bitch."

"I'm not interested in proving it in court, Mr. Lyman," Andy said airily. "I only need to pass the word along to Pan D."

Lyman's sulk rippled through a remarkable transformation into an expression of awakening fear.

"Oh, did I touch a nerve?" Andy asked sweetly.

Lyman slammed his fists down on the steel tabletop. I think he expected the blow to produce a commotion, but all he got was a dull thud. "Deputy! I want outta here! NOW!"

Andy folded her hands and gazed calmly at Lyman. He shouted several more times, then allowed the silence of the room settle around him.

"Feel better?"

"Fuck you, bitch!"

Andy waited a moment. Then she said, "I had to ask myself, why were you carrying close to eight thousand dollars in cash when you were arrested?"

"I told them, that's my—"

"Nuh! Nuh!" Andy waved an elegant finger at him. "I don't care. Again, Mr. Lyman, I really don't want to hear a word from you. Everything falling out of your mouth is a lie. I have no more interest in the lies you tell about yourself than I do the lies you harvest off the internet."

She tested him for a moment. He held his tongue.

"So, I asked myself, why would you be carrying nearly eight thousand dollars after making a drug run to Green Bay for Pan D?"

Lyman's posture telegraphed another tirade, but Andy raised a single finger and silenced him.

"That's not policy. They never mix the money and the drugs. Runners like you deliver. Other runners return the cash. You delivered the oxy after you got a signal that the cash was in hand. Whoever got the cash had the good sense to drive back to Milwaukee at the speed limit. What were you going? Nineteen over? Brilliant. Policy being policy, there's no way you were carrying Pan D's cash with you. Which made me think, you're either a very wealthy young fellow, who doesn't need to be selling drugs, or you've got a little side business going. And since you filed for Indigent status, I don't see you as the hedge fund type. That means, the eight grand is from your side business."

Andy let the point settle in.

"It's awfully nice of a vicious gang like Pan D to let you take a taste on the side. I would have thought it would cut into their business, and they're usually not very friendly about that sort of thing. Especially if someone is replacing their product with fakes. You must have special status with them, Mr. Lyman. You must be a real friend of the family."

"You don't know shit, lady."

"Oh, but I do. First, I have my husband here, who can testify that you were swapping his pills."

I gave him a mirthless grin.

"Then we have your source for the fakes."

I almost shot a look at Andy, thinking, *What? You do?* I held my grin on Lyman and registered his reaction. His composure flickered. He seemed to be torn between petulant denial and all-out panic. Andy plowed on, treating the point as insignificant.

"But the question we asked ourselves is this: With the number of fakes you had available to you, how could you possibly have made that much money by swapping ones and twos at the hospital? You gave yourself away with my husband after just two nights. Obviously, there's a limit to what you could obtain by switching pills. Until I realized what you were doing at the hospital was small change. You were pulling the real swap on your Pan D associates. You were pilfering from Pan D, replacing theirs with counter-feits, and running their oxy as your own product, to the tune of eight grand on this most recent trip. Who's going to complain? A bunch of junkies in Outagamie County? You probably rationalized that giving junkies fakes only made them want more, which would be good for Pan D's business, am I right? That pittance from the hospital, that was just you not being able to help yourself."

"Bullsh—"

"Shut! UP!" Andy snapped at him. The harsh contrast to her calm demeanor made an impression. "How many times do I have to tell you? We are not here to listen to anything you have to say."

Lyman tried to put on a look that could kill. It came off as misaligned pouting.

"Do you know why you're sitting here? Why you're looking at your fourth conviction for possession with intent? It's because you think you're the smartest person in the room—any room. Granted, you were smart enough to engineer a false identity with a multi-layered work history that landed you a job as a nursing assistant at a good-sized hospital. You have computer smarts. Con artist smarts. But you also have the one thing genuinely intelligent people do not."

Andy's compliments reignited a smug expression. "What?"

"You have an unshakable belief that everything coming out of your mouth is true. You believe your own lies. That's what makes you gullible to every loser with a conspiracy theory. That's what makes you think you can survive double-crossing Pan D. Which takes serious guts. I've heard these guys make the Crips and Bloods look like a social club. You were on a Pan D run, but you pilfered their product and substituted counterfeits, then took their product and sold it to your own list of clients. It's all in the phones we took out of your car. It's all in the baggies we found with the names in them. And it's obvious from the cash you were carrying. Pan D's cash went south with someone else, someone you probably don't know and never saw. Because that's how they do it. You're a one-man band. You had to carry the product up, and the cash home."

Andy stopped and let the silence punctuate her point. Then she leaned in and narrowed her eyes on Lyman.

"The question before you, Mr. Lyman, is ... what are you willing to give me to keep me from telling your friends at Pan D that you were swapping their pills?"

Lyman swallowed several times. I imagine the saliva in his mouth had

disappeared along with whatever remained of his bravado. He looked stricken.

"What do you want?" he demanded through his teeth.

Andy leaned back.

She said nothing.

She let the moment hang and the knife turn.

"Bitch, what do you want?!"

"What I want, Mr. Lyman, is to know about the girl you delivered to Pan D."

He blinked.

"Huh? *What girl?*" I may not be the judge that Andy is in this kind of situation, but I took his reaction as genuine bewilderment.

"The 'princess.' The girl they grabbed out of Essex tonight. You called them and told them about her. You knew they were looking for her and you saw her at the hospital."

"I don't have a fucking clue what you're talking about! I never—Oh!" A light came on for Lyman. I don't think Andy expected it, but Lyman made a connection in his head and broadcast it on his face. "That wasn't me! No! That wasn't me. I know the girl you're talking about! That wasn't me. They asked me about some girl, but I never saw her. I never saw any girl. That wasn't me!"

"Your lips are moving. We know what that means." Andy leaned forward. "When we prove you delivered a child into the hands of a street gang, you'll be an accessory to kidnapping. And if they do anything to her, you'll be an accessory to murder."

"NO!" He slammed his fists on the table again. "I didn't have anything to do with the girl!"

"You just said they asked you."

He shook his head wildly. "Right, right! But no! Right, they *did* ask me. But I worked second shift. I never saw her! I told them I never saw her."

"How did you know she was at the hospital?"

"I didn't. I just told you! They asked *me*. They saw her!"

This stopped Andy for a moment. She kept her eyes on Lyman, but her wheels turned behind the steady gaze.

"They saw her?" she asked, a delaying tactic, while she thought about it, tried to re-order the pieces.

"Right! They saw her! Then they asked me about her—if I'd seen her. But I never saw her. I told them I never saw her."

"When were they at the hospital?" Andy asked.

"You don't fucking know, do you!" Lyman switched on the smug again.

He couldn't help himself. He had to prove himself the smartest one in the room. "They were *never* there. They fucking saw her on TV! When the TV was reporting on *him*!"

He pointed at me. My blood went cold.

It had been because of me. The television crews outside the hospital— their "live" report caught Earl and Rosemary II and Lane on camera. Because of me. Lane had been taken because of me.

"I never had anything to do with any girl. Never," Lyman waved his hands to make the point.

Andy took a shot.

"Mauser is taking her to someone. Who?"

Lyman's head shook back and forth, frantically.

"Oh, no! No, no, no! I'm not saying a word about anybody or anything! That guy, he doesn't fuck around. Mauser, he's fucked up."

"You should have considered that when you started ripping them off for the oxy."

"Fuck you. I'm not telling you anything."

Andy acknowledged his stance with a thoughtful nod of the head. Then she said, "Mr. Lyman, I think it's in your best interest to tell me what I want to know. If you don't, I'm going to walk out of here. It will be the last you ever see me. But within 12 hours, one of the day shift deputies is going to trade information with one of your fellow lowlifes. Happens all the time. Some friendly gossip. A little tit for tat. Like maybe how you were swapping fakes for Pan D's product and selling it as your own."

"YOU CAN'T! THAT'S MURDER!"

"Now do you get why your lawyer isn't here, dumbass? We don't care about you, or your case. Tell me what I want to know, and this conversation never happened. None of this goes into the public record. Stonewall me, and if I were you, I wouldn't turn my back on anyone here … ever."

Lyman's head kept shaking, but his gaze fell to the table. His face, stricken, worked itself as if an argument raged under skin devoid of color.

"You gotta protect me! You gotta put me in Witness Protection!"

"You watch too much television," Andy said. "You're going to gamble just like you've been gambling. You're going to roll the dice that they don't find out. They won't hear it from me, if you tell me what I want to know, but beyond that, if they ever figure it out, that's all on you. Your choice is between a guarantee that I will tell them, and the chance they never find out. Decide."

"Mauser. He's the one who was looking for her."

"Was it him? Who took her? Did he do it himself?"

"Oh, hell no! Are you kidding?"

"Mauser. Is that a name or a handle?"

"It's some sort of German gun he used for his first. His initiation. His first kill. Some badass antique German gun, so he got the name. Mauser. And he drives a big Mercedes. He's got a thing for German shit."

"Is the girl for him? This princess thing they do, is that for him?"

"No." He laughed. "That's higher up. The top. That's Pan D."

"The gang?"

"No. The man. Pan D. Don't you know anything? He gets a princess when he wants one, because he's the fucking king. He picked this one out a couple years ago, but she took off. Then there she was, right on the evening news. Right there in Essex. He probably doesn't give a shit about her anymore, but somebody must'a told him and he can't let it slide."

"Where is he? Where will Mauser take the girl?"

"How the fuck do I know?!"

"You know him. Where does he like to party?"

"I don't know him. Never saw him. Never met him."

Andy sat back. She considered Lyman for a moment. Then she stood up and I took that as our cue to leave, so I reached for my crutches.

Andy moved fast. She leaned across the table and clamped her right hand around Lyman's throat. She jerked his head back until only the chain on his manacles, pulled tight, prevented him from going over backward. His knees banged on the underside of the table. His eyes bulged, ringed with white.

"Mauser," she said quietly.

Lyman words sounded like sandpaper on stone. "I swear! Please, I swear! I don't—"

Andy stretched him tighter against the manacles.

"Pray, asshole. Pray to whatever god you think gives a shit about you. *Pray that nothing happens to that girl.* If something does, I will go insane with grief, and when I do, I will sell you out just so I can frame a copy of the Sheriff's report on how they cut your balls off and stuffed them in your mouth!" She gave his head a jolt and released him.

She turned. Rapped twice on the door.


ANDY LEFT the room without looking back and steamed down the hallway leaving Wilson to lock up, and me to hobble after her. We heard Lyman tattling to Wilson about Andy grabbing his throat, choking him. Wilson said nothing. Slamming the door to the interrogation room put punctuation on Lyman's rant.

After letting us through the locked outer hallway door, Andy turned to Wilson and asked, "Could you give us a minute?"

Wilson handed back her weapon and shrugged. He cracked a smile that told us he had been listening at the door and had enjoyed himself, and then he waddled away. When his considerable back end finally disappeared around the next corner, Andy stepped up and threw a hug around me.

"I'm shaking," she said. "How dumb is that? I'm shaking. Some detective."

"Dee, that was—Christ, I hate to use the word—*awesome!*" I pulled her in.

"I've never done anything like that!"

"No one ever deserved it more. How did you find his supplier? The counterfeits?"

"We haven't yet." She pulled away and looked at me with a feline smile. "The biggest liars fall for the biggest lies."

"Wow. And all that about the money? About him pilfering?"

"I was guessing. But he had to be. It was the only thing that fit," she said. She looked at her watch. "We need to get moving. I want to call Rosemary II. I don't have much I can tell her, but I know she's dying to hear something. And I need to talk to Tom."

"Hey," I said. I pulled her back in. "Proud of you."

She squeezed me back. "We have to find her. We have to."

# 40

Pidge had us in the air in a matter of minutes after the Manitowoc deputy pulled up to the waiting airplane. Andy called her from the car and Pidge cranked the right engine as we arrived. Andy's call reminded me that I had no phone. I felt naked without one.

The Navajo made the forty-minute ride to General Mitchell International in smooth air. We didn't light the cabin and we didn't talk much. Red instrument lights warmed the cockpit. Andy and I sat in the dark with dark thoughts, thinking about Lane, or trying not to. Halfway down the shoreline to Milwaukee Andy reached across the narrow aisle and took my hand. She pulled it into her lap and threaded her fingers between mine. We stayed that way until the wheels touched down at MKE.

An MPD unmarked car waited on the Signature Aviation ramp as Pidge taxied in and killed the engines.

"Let me come with you," Pidge pleaded. "I want to seriously fuck somebody up."

"We're not kicking in doors, Pidge," Andy said. "We won't get anywhere without MPD, and they probably won't let us do anything but watch. And I'm sure they won't let a civilian like you or Will do *that* much."

"We *should* be kicking in doors and balls," Pidge said. "What do you want me to do?"

"Be ready," I said. "Gas up. Cross your fingers we find her."

"We'll call you," Andy said.

We left Pidge alone in the cockpit. She may have been a feral ball of rage, capable of castrating someone, but when I looked back and saw the hope and fear mingling on her face, she seemed small and young.

"DON SCHULTZ," he said, extending a hand as we walked up to his car.

"Deputy Chief," Andy shook it. "I'm Sergeant Stewart. This is my husband, Will."

"Tom told me to call you Detective Stewart, but I appreciate your honesty. Nice to meet you, Will. How come you're not dead?"

"Clean living." I shook his hand.

"Hop in. We can talk on the way."

Schultz drove like a maniac, slouched carelessly behind the wheel. The sun had broken the horizon. The eastern sky glowed, and the day warmed quickly. Thanks to the early hour, the highway lacked traffic for Schultz to ricochet off as he careened wildly up the interstate from the airport.

I guessed Schultz to be in his early sixties, like Tom Ceeves. Maybe they met in the military, or on some police department. Maybe they were rookies together. Schultz didn't have Tom's football lineman physique. He owned more of a beer-drinker's build. He had a square jaw and crew cut hair. A touch of John Wayne in his later years.

"Tom's processing some hits from the readers," he told us. Andy sat up front. I had the back seat, which wasn't set up as a prisoner cage in this vehicle. The car had no suspension. I spread my legs to resist the wallowing as he weaved. His driving wasn't doing my bones any good. "He sent us the raw data from the state troopers. We're running it against some databases we have that he doesn't. My guy said your guy did a nice job of first-filtering it, though."

"I'll pass that on," Andy said.

"We're giving this a full-court press, Detective, but I have to ask before we trip over our own dicks here. This girl. She didn't just decide to run off to the glamourous life of being some gangbanger's fuck toy, did she? This isn't some argument with mama, is it? Hooking up with an old boyfriend from the hood?"

I didn't like the suggestion, not about Lane. Andy took the questions in stride.

"No. I've personally known this girl for two years. She's an honor student. She's involved in school, involved with friends, not sulking at home on the internet. She's had no association with these people. Until tonight. They came to Essex for her. One of them put a gun in the mother's face. She recognized him from two years ago."

"She can pick him out?"

"I think so." Andy explained that Rosemary II was at Essex Air, waiting for word.

"She have internet access?"

"Yes."

"We'll do a remote with her. Show her some photos," Schultz said. "I love technology. So, what happened two years ago?"

"The girl. Somehow, she got picked out of a crowd by somebody high up in Pan D. She was just twelve, but they came and told the mother to get her ready. Her mother took the girl and ran."

"A princess?"

"You know about that? I need to ask you ... is that really a thing?"

Schultz shrugged. "We've heard rumors. We've never had a case. Not a reported case, I should say. A couple interviews with women who were suspected of using their daughters like that, for a payoff—and by payoff, I mean oxy or heroin. They weren't exactly cooperative. I'm going to be honest. We didn't think it was real. Some of the guys might grill you like I just did. They still don't think it's real."

"Do you think it's real?" I asked.

"If it is, they can call it whatever they want, it's pedophilia, pure and simple. And it's sick." Schultz drummed his fingers on the steering wheel as he nearly traded paint with the back end of an eighteen-wheeler.

"What about that?" Andy asked, "I thought these gangs went through all kinds of leadership changes. Why would they keep leadership that did something like that?"

"Once, they wouldn't. But it's all changed. There's less street leadership now. Less social grouping. It's more organized."

"The girl's mother," Andy said. "She told us it was like being liberated by the Nazis. Cleaning up the streets, and improving things, but then things getting worse."

Schultz nodded, inviting Andy to go on.

"Then I can't see them allowing someone, even their own leadership, to roll into a neighborhood and pick out a twelve-year-old."

"Uh-huh..."

"I mean, okay, these girls start young. But twelve? Picking out a twelve-year-old? That's a pedophile. The street culture is a strong reflection of the prison culture because most of these guys—that's where they get their training. And in the prison culture, the child molesters are scum. That's why some of the lock-ups segregate them."

"They do. Too bad."

"So, things changed. You're saying this is something different."

Schultz looked over at Andy. I wished he wouldn't. I wished he'd watch the road as we flew over the big bridge spanning Milwaukee's industrial valley.

"That's what I'm saying."

# 41

Andy stopped asking questions and I felt marginally safer. Schultz looked out the windshield instead of at my wife. He stopped talking while driving. We dove through a tunnel, ran a couple red lights, and pulled into the police garage below the Milwaukee Safety Building. Sunday morning, both the city and the garage felt deserted. Our car doors echoed off the concrete as Schultz led us across a span of greasy floor to the door. A short ride in a shabby elevator took us to a fluorescent-lit floor full of cluttered desks. We weaved through them to a glassed-in conference room where two men sat at a table working laptops.

"We got a hit," one of the men said. He had a medium athletic build and Marine Corps haircut. He had the rock-climber look, reminding me of Cyler enough that I told myself not to dislike him immediately. He started talking before we cleared the room's threshold. When he looked up from his laptop, he saw Andy and nodded a hello.

"Detective Martin, Detective LeMore, this is Detective Stewart of the Essex PD," Schultz pointed all around. "This is her husband, Will."

"Jim Martin," the athlete said, shaking hands.

"Greg," the other laptop operator said, barely looking up. He was short, wiry, and blessed with dark facial hair that probably needed mowing by an electric razor three times a day. "Two vehicles from the reader list were reported stolen about an hour ago. Like within five minutes of each other. Smartasses!"

"Were they on the readers going both ways?" Andy asked.

"Flying in formation," Martin said. "Going up and coming back down. They knew we would be watching, so they borrowed a couple civilian cars, then told the owners to call them in as stolen once they got back. Blue Toyota Camry and silver GMC Tahoe."

"You guys want coffee?" Schultz asked. "It's disgustingly good. Greg wants to be a barista when he grows up."

"Yes, please," Andy said. She moved into position behind Martin, who had returned to his laptop. I nodded affirmative on the coffee. I wanted to ask if they had any aspirin. My midsection was throbbing.

Andy asked, "Are you in Vantage?"

"Yup. That's our contract vendor for plate data. We ran them already and got hits all the way up, in Essex, and back down again. Looks like they got back here around 3 a.m. We've got hits here in town and narrowed the location down to a couple of grid squares. Patrol is already rolling on them. My guess, we'll find the vehicles sitting by the curb, keys in the ignition, ready for the owners to pick them up again."

Andy had told me about Vantage, a private company that sold and installed license plate reader cameras for police departments, private security, and just about anybody willing to put down twenty to thirty thousand dollars for the sophisticated cameras. The data fed to Vantage's servers. Clients paid a subscription to draw data and photos from the system. It, and dozens of systems like it, served as a boon to law enforcement, who could, as I just witnessed, identify vehicles involved in a crime and track them across a wide territory as each camera registered the vehicle going by. Sometimes the images made it possible to identify the driver. I asked Andy why the bad guys didn't just obscure their license plates, to which she replied a missing or obscured plate offers a great way to call attention to yourself and get stopped immediately. Better to use stolen plates, or stolen vehicles, or rental cars, in the case of the drug runners. In this case, they used plain civilian vehicles that gave no cause to be stopped. Once Lane had been taken, and delivered back to Milwaukee, the vehicles were reported stolen.

It gave me hope.

Schultz produced two cups of coffee from a sideboard at the end of the conference room. He handed one to Andy and one to me. The coffee tasted as good as advertised.

"Head's up," Schultz said, looking through the glass across the squad room. "We got incoming. Do me a favor. Drop the covers on those things."

I followed his eyes to where a tall Black man and proportionally short, heavy-set white woman worked their way across the room in the company of a senior officer in uniform. The senior officer, also Black, carried abundant gold on his collar. The tall man was strikingly neat. His hair trimmed to perfection, his face clean-shaved, his suit—and I'm no judge—probably worth more than my car. The white of his shirt collar, snug against a silk tie, was eclipsed by the white of his teeth, bared in a friendly smile that made me wary. The woman, again by contrast, looked rumpled and surprisingly at home in the cluttered police squad room. Her clothes suggested an imperfect fit and no allegiance to fashion. Her hair consisted of a tight, slightly frizzy collection of rings and curls, with strands of gray that said the color needed updating. She wore makeup, and I saw color on her nails, hinting at vanity sabotaged by the scowl on her face. Where the man radiated a confident warmth, the woman gave the impression of a walking land mine.

Martin and LeMore discretely closed their laptops and rose to a loose form of attention.

"Deputy Chief Schultz," the command officer said by way of greeting.

"Deputy Chief Stiller," Schultz replied. "Good morning, Councilman Andre. Councilwoman Denninger, you're up early."

"As if you weren't to blame, Chief Schultz," the woman said coldly. "Is that Detective LeMore's coffee?" She didn't wait for an answer but went straight for a cup.

Schultz extended a hand. The councilman shook it firmly, making practiced eye contact, frosting it with a politician's smile. "Don, good to see you. Gentlemen."

"'Morning, sir," Martin said. LeMore waved. "Ma'am."

Chief Stiller took over the introductions. "Detective Andrea Stewart of the Essex PD, this is City Councilman Miles Andre. His district sits at the heart of the area most actively affected by some of these criminal elements, and he works tirelessly to keep our people connected to the community. I called him as soon as we got word on this. He came to help."

Andre shook hands with my wife. "It is a community effort. We all work together. I'm aware of this situation with the young girl and am here to help in any way I can. I'll be seeing church leaders later this morning and we will reach out to everyone we can."

"Deeply appreciated, sir," Andy said.

Chief Stiller turned to the woman, now sipping LeMore's coffee from a mug with the name Porter and Don't Touch written on it in Sharpie.

"And this is Councilwoman Mary Denninger, she—"

"They call me The Ax behind my back," the woman said. "Deny it, John and I'll show you how I got the name when I review your budget next quarter." She switched the coffee cup from her right to her left hand and shook with Andy. "Detective, what makes you think this girl didn't just run off to play hide the salami with her gangbanger boyfriend?"

I blinked, but Andy held the Councilwoman's eye. "Lane Franklin is the kind of child we hope for. The kind that survives the worst a city can throw at her and still finds beauty in the world. But that aside, shortly after she was taken last night a Pan D gangbanger put a gun in her mother's face and told the mother that they had her daughter. We also have confirmation from an incarcerated Pan D drug courier that they were looking for this specific girl."

"Pan D looks for a lot of girls. I hate to think we're going to Defcon One and diverting resources from helping girls in our own community because our gang problem reached out and touched a white bread farm community."

Andy stiffened but held her tongue.

Andre said, "Don't be such a cynic, Mary. This is a child who needs our help."

"I don't doubt that, but you two want to pour expensive resources into a missing girl from Essex when we had—what's the count from last night, Don? How many shootings?" The woman shook her head. She caught sight of me. "And who are you supposed to be?"

*Someone looking for the nearest foxhole.*

Andy stepped in. "This is my husband, Will. He was instrumental in identifying a witness we interviewed several hours ago."

"I am familiar with your husband," Andre said. He took my hand. My eyes watered. His cologne probably cost a small fortune per ounce, but that didn't stop him from bathing in it. "A pleasure to meet you. According to what I've seen on television, you're something of a miracle."

"That's what my mother always said."

"How are you feeling? I thought you were in the hospital."

"I'm fine. We appreciate your help getting our girl back safely. She's special to us. All due respect Ma'am," I said to Denninger, "Lane Franklin is exactly as my wife said. She's what you wish for in a kid. If you had a city full of Lane Franklins, everyone in this building would be out of a job."

"There's an idea," Denninger muttered. "Alright, Don. Go ahead and run your fire drill, but unlike my esteemed colleague here, I won't be out in church this morning shaking the pews for votes. I'll be camped out here, keeping an eye on things so I can explain to the budget committee why our body count is going up nightly and our overtime reserve is going down. I'll be in my office and I expect you to keep me informed, Chief." She refilled her coffee and marched out.

Andre waited until he was certain she had exceeded earshot. "Council-woman Denninger doesn't mean to suggest that this is not an urgent situa-

tion. We all understand that this child is special. We'll do everything we can. This is a fight we're all invested in. These gangs have brought a pandemic to our country, to our neighborhoods, and to our children."

The deep voice, the smooth inflection and the polished words sounded well-rehearsed. It was easy to imagine him delivering the same speech in churches, community halls, and most importantly for cameras, over and over. No doubt, his political interests went far beyond fighting gang crime or a drug pandemic, but under the circumstances, I couldn't complain about the fact that those interests intersected ours. If a slick politician making self-serving moves put Rosemary II's arms around her unharmed daughter, hell, I'd vote for the guy as many times as possible.

"Have we made any progress?" Andre asked the room. "You said there was a witness?"

Schultz spoke up quickly. "In fact, we have made progress. The mother might be able to identify one of the kidnappers." Andy and I traded quick looks. We each caught Schultz's derailing and rerouting of Andre's question.

"Is she here? I would like to meet her and assure her of my full support," Andre said.

"She's still in Essex, but we're setting up a link to show her mug shots."

"Well, then. I think the best thing I can do to help right now is get out of your way," Andre said with a clipped laugh. "I have a personal commitment to attend to this morning. Please, carry on, and Godspeed. Let's bring the dear child home. Keep me posted!"

Chief Stiller took that as his cue and escorted the Councilman out. When they cleared the greater squad room everyone exhaled.

# 42

"What's their story?" I asked.

"City Council. Andre and Denninger are on the special over-sight task force. Our personal watchdogs," Schultz said. "She's exactly the ballbuster you just met. He has more money than God, with his fingers in development projects all over the city. He's been leading the charge on gangs and drugs for a few years now. Talks about it every chance he gets, to anyone who will listen."

"Is it working?" Andy asked.

"No," Martin and LeMore said in unison.

Schultz disagreed, or tried to. "He gets us some traction in the community, and that counts for something."

"It gets him votes," Martin said sourly. "And it gets him in here. A lot. He lobbied hard to get himself named to the drug task force. Stiller is his—"

"Detective!" Schultz interrupted. "Let's just say he's relentless on drugs, on oxy."

LeMore said softly, "That part's personal."

"How so?" I asked after nobody else did. LeMore and Martin traded glances.

"The story is he lost his son to gangs and drugs. Then, five, six years ago, a business partner of his—there was a home invasion. Addicts looking to hit a rich family in a big fat house. It went south. Father, mother, and teenaged daughter wound up dead. Don't ask."

"Andre's been on a crusade ever since," Schultz offered. "He spends a lot of time in the community, reaching out. When Pan D came in, a lot of our regular sources dried up."

"More like died up," Martin said.

"He's trying to help."

"BS—sir," Martin said. "He spends a lot of time kissing babies in churches to get votes, when he's not all up in our business, or in his penthouse at the top of Crystal Tower."

Schultz didn't argue.

"Just keep him outta my way," Martin muttered. LeMore didn't disagree.

"Should I even ask about Councilwoman Denninger?" I ventured.

"What you see is what we get, every damned day. She can squeeze the copper out of a quarter," Schultz muttered. "She means it, too. She's going to be in our hair all over this thing. Every detail. Let's have a look at Vantage, shall we?"

"Right."

Martin and LeMore opened their laptops again. Schultz turned to me.

"I'm afraid this is where you get off, Mr. Stewart. As a civilian, and as a witness, we can't have you involved in the investigation."

"Not an investigation, Chief. A rescue. And I would think all-hands-on-deck would be better."

"Point taken, yes. It is a rescue. But you still can't be here. Your wife is here in an official capacity as liaison with her department, and even that took some string pulling."

Andy read my disappointment. She laid her hand on my arm.

"We'll find her," she said. "They're putting a lot into this."

A phone rang. Martin reached in his pocket and picked up the call.

"Martin…Hold on, lemme put this on speaker. Chief Schultz is here. Hang on." He laid the phone down and touched the screen. "Chief, this is Sergeant Dunning, fifth district. He's got the vehicles."

"Morning, Sergeant."

"Morning, Chief. We got both vehicles. They parked them nose to trunk here on Locust, a couple blocks from the freeway. I already called for a flatbed so we can get them to the garage. No girl, of course. But we found blood in the back of the Tahoe."

Andy's hand, still on my arm, tightened its grip. I put my hand over hers.

"It's in the carpet. Painted in. The initials, LF."

Andy's hand shot up to her mouth to cover a burst of breathed relief. "Oh, my God!"

"Clever girl," Schultz said.

"Top of her class," I said, poking at his earlier doubts about Lane.

"We need a DNA match on this right away," Andy said. "We need a baseline. Something to test the blood against, to confirm."

"Can we get something from the mother? From Essex?" Schultz asked.

"I'll call Pidge," I said. "She's our pilot. She can fly back up to Essex and get the mother. The mother can bring whatever you need. We can have it back here in a couple hours."

"How fast is your lab?" Andy asked.

"If we light a fire under them, we can confirm a match in about four hours."

I looked at Andy. "Rosemary II should be here."

"Agreed."

"Sorry," I said to Schultz, "her name is Amanda, but we all call her Rosemary II. Long story."

"Bring her here. But let's try to do the mug shots now, remotely, while your pilot is on the way up to Essex. It'll save time. Detective Stewart, you handle it. If we put you to work on something, I can tell The Ax that having you involved saved the city money. You're done here, Mr. Stewart."

Andy turned to me and interrupted my protest.

"Let me walk out with you. I'll be right back," she said to the others.

At the elevator, Andy took my hands.

"You look tired, Pilot," she said. "Do me a favor and take a cab over to the Hyatt. Get a room and get some rest. I'll call Pidge."

"Let me help. There has to be something I could do. You could be out kicking in doors with the A-Team."

"You don't even have a phone. And as much as I want to kick in doors, we have no doors to kick in yet."

"They do," I pointed at the conference room.

"Yes, they do," Andy said, and I felt myself touching a line here, pushing her where she didn't want to be pushed. "And I need to work with them to get them to share with me, okay? I know this is hard—"

"It sucks."

"But you have no idea how much they're giving us by simply letting me play in their sandbox, Will. Let me take advantage of that my way, okay?"

"Dee, this is Lane! I can't just flop in a hotel room and watch courtroom comedy on daytime TV! C'mon!"

"Love," she pulled me closer. Apparently, she thought charm and sex appeal would work better than staging an argument in front of her colleagues. She was right, of course, but I hated that I was so easy. "You're no good to anyone if you break those bones apart again. I can see you're in pain, and I need you. I need you rested and ready. Because I don't know if you've considered it, but Amanda may need us both to be strong if this ends badly."

The thought, a dark one, had indeed crossed my mind.

"I can't believe you're benching me," I sulked, surrendering. Damned charm and sex appeal.

"Call me when you get a room," she said, "so I have a number. I promise to keep you up to date. They won't let Amanda stay here, so I'll send her to you after she delivers the DNA sample. I think it's a good idea if she's with someone. In case."

I minced my feet, but Andy made the point by pushing the elevator button. I wanted to take her in my arms, but at this moment she was a cop in front of other cops. I got a lousy peck on the cheek and, "Love you!"

She hurried back to the war room to make war.

While I waited for the elevator, I resolved to make my own war.

# 43

Andy and I spent a weekend at the Hyatt Milwaukee last year. A mixed bag of anniversary and birthday celebrations, and a general torching of big handfuls of cash. We obtained theater tickets, ate expensive dinners, danced at loud clubs full of people who looked too young to be there, and had delicious upscale-hotel sex all weekend. I couldn't help but think about the last part when the cab dropped me off.

I put a room on our credit card, thinking why not? With the hospital bill and my employment future in doubt, the hole seemed deep enough that a few hundred more wouldn't matter. Key in hand, I looked up at the huge empty atrium and the glass elevators. I had no intention of going to sit in a hotel room alone, although the idea of doing a little floating over the bed had some appeal. Andy wasn't wrong—my bones ached.

I briefly considered floating up to the ninth floor in the atrium. After the experiments in the barn, the massive open space looked inviting. But now was not the time.

Alone, possibly bound. I wondered if Lane had an idea of why she'd been taken, or what she was being taken to. I couldn't guess what could be running through the girl's mind. It cheered me enormously that she had painted her initials in her own blood on the SUV carpeting. It told me she wasn't paralyzed with fear. She found a way to fight. I prayed she could stay fixed on that idea, and not give in to despair.

*Who are you going to fly for, Lane?* Right now, fly for yourself. Scratch, kick, fight, run. Do whatever you can.

I needed to *do* something. I wanted to hit the streets and look for Lane, but that was utter nonsense. I couldn't very well jump in a car and cruise the gang territory. Even if I had a car, I wouldn't know where to start. I would be an alien on that landscape. I wouldn't know a crack house from a post office in an urban neighborhood.

I needed information and from the moment Andy pushed the elevator button, I felt something like a sunrise inside—the dawning of a brilliant, and possibly insane idea.

First things first. I power-crutched across the open atrium to the front desk and asked for a phone with an outside line for a local call. The clerk, a young woman, looked at me like I was a large bug. Who doesn't have a phone in their pocket? She pointed me at a house phone on the concierge desk, which sat empty at this morning hour.

"Dial 9 for an outside line," she instructed me.

It worked.

"Andrea Stewart," my wife said, not recognizing the number appearing on her cell phone screen.

"Dee, it's me."

"Hey. Are you at the hotel?"

"Checked in. Room 919. Or I will be. I'm in the atrium on a house phone, so don't bother keeping this number. I want to hit the gift shop and pick up some aspirin. Maybe something to eat. You should get something to eat, too."

"I will. Get some rest. Listen, I gotta go. They're waiting for me. Love you!"

"Love you, too."

The call ended. There was no mistaking Andy in full-on cop mode. Being allowed *in* by the MPD cops gave her an electric charge. Yes, this was about Lane, first and foremost, but Andy now pitched in a major league park. Heady stuff. I forced myself not to take the too-busy-for-you exchange personally.

I went to find aspirin in the gift shop, then a cab in front of the hotel.

# 44

The first part of my rough plan required ditching the crutches.

When the cab dropped me off at the Milwaukee Safety Building, I used the public entrance. Cameras made note of me as I worked my way through the metal detector at the security checkpoint. It didn't matter. Trying to look like I belonged, I purposefully moved to the elevators. The squad room and conference room took up the fourth floor. I got off on the first floor. The hallway offered me the usual two directions. I took right and tried to keep moving like someone who had business being there. On a Sunday morning, the building lay quiet but not dead. Doors were universally closed. Going from one to the next, wiggling doorknobs, would look suspicious. Sooner or later, someone would ask questions.

Halfway down the hall from the elevators, I found a short side hallway, and at the end of that, a Men's room. Opening off the S-turn entrance, I found a utility closet stocked with toilet paper, cleaners, and sporting a horribly rusted sink and a chlorine smell. I reached around behind the door and propped the crutches up against the wall. Unless you went completely into the closet and closed the door, you'd never see them.

Off the crutches, the pain immediately notified me of its intention to ruin my day. I took the weight off my legs.

*Fwooomp!*

Much better. The cool sensation kissed my skin. This being my first public disappearance, I double-checked to make sure I had completely vanished. It wouldn't look good to see a pair of shoes or a wristwatch floating down the hall.

I had a flight plan in mind. I kicked off the floor and rose. The nine-foot ceiling made it easy to fly well above the heads of anyone walking the halls. No sooner had I stretched out when a cop strolled into the bathroom directly below me. It reinforced the point.

I made the short glide to the Men's room doorway. Using the jamb as a grip, I pulled myself into the short hallway, and from there to the long hallway that bisected the building. The war room on the fourth floor sat at the end of the building opposite my present position, however it wasn't necessary to fly the full length of the hall. The elevator bank stood midway down the hall. A stairwell was located next to the elevators. I wanted the stairwell.

I startled when I noticed a camera mounted high in the corner at the end of the hall, and then marked its twin at the other end.

"Not a problem," I reminded myself.

The hallway had a string of light fixtures hanging in the center, globes suspended from chains. Bumping one or trying to use them as grips might send them swinging. Instead, I used the fire-suppression sprinkler system pipe running off center the length of the hall. It was easy to grip. I held on and rotated my body parallel to the pipe, belly up, back to the floor. I had to hang my head backward to see where I was going. Without gravity to suggest up or down, I simply imagined this pipe as vertical, running up a tall wall.

I paused for a moment to ensure that I was alone, then said aloud, "This is freaking amazing." My heart pounded out a marching band beat. I needed to calm down. "Alright. Enough acting like a tourist. You've got work to do."

I worked my way up—or forward—along the pipe. I started with a cautious hand-over-hand technique, like climbing a rope, but quickly realized all I needed was a pull to start moving. After that, I touched the pipe for minor adjustments. Once moving, I kept moving—a body in motion, according to Sir Isaac Newton.

The elevator bank arrived quickly. I stopped. The door to the stairwell hung adjacent to the elevator bank, but this presented a new problem. It was a door, and it was closed. This meant having to get down to normal-person position in the hallway and then gaining leverage to open the door.

I used my grip to orient myself to face the door, head up, body curled into a loose cannonball. Then with a combination of grip on the pipe for steering, and hand on the ceiling for thrust, I pushed myself on a vector designed to take me into position directly in front of the door, like any normal person approaching to grab the handle.

It worked. Then went bad.

*Shit!*

The elevator doors opened, and three police officers stepped off. Two of them turned their backs to me and moved away, chatting. The third turned directly toward me and started walking. I had no way to stop floating across his path. We were on a collision course, made worse by the feeling that the cop was looking right at me, even though his eyes scanned through me and down the long hallway.

The collision became a near miss at the last second. I flattened myself and extended my fingertips to touch the wall, then pancaked against the cold paint. The officer passed agonizingly close behind me. A second later, or a fraction of an inch closer, and we would have touched. And then what? I had no idea.

I moved my left hand to the door handle and waited. No sense taking a chance that the door would squeak and draw a glance back from the officer. He found his destination and disappeared into an office.

I had the hall to myself.

I looked through the small window in the door, cleared the space in the stairwell, pulled the door open and pulled myself through the door. I glided across the landing to the railing, gripped the railing and swung myself over it into the empty space at the center. The railing fell away geometrically below me and rose in a squared off spiral above me. A quick push up, and I climbed. I floated up past the second-floor landing, past the third, and then reached out and caught the railing for the fourth floor. I pulled myself over and checked the small window in the door.

The squad room had become busy. Not just with Andy and her colleagues. Others worked at their desks around the room. People came and went on the elevators. Opening the stairwell door and slipping through would be tricky. Also, the ceiling in the squad room hung lower, only eight feet. Acoustic tile with recessed light fixtures offered precious little to grip.

"One thing at a time, flyboy."

Andy stood behind LeMore, who sat at a desk working a computer terminal. Schultz hovered behind Andy. Martin worked at his laptop in the conference room, with his phone to his ear. Andy and the others fixed rapt attention on the terminal.

I gripped the door handle, then suddenly realized I had a new problem. I couldn't push the door open. I had no leverage. My feet floated inches above the floor. The wall around the door was smooth and offered no counter-grip. The railing was too far away to use as an anchor. Now what?

"Duh. Idiot."

I moved myself to one side, out of eyesight of everyone in the squad room, and scanned the stairwell. No cameras.

*Fwooomp!*

Visible again, my weight settled on my feet. Facing the wall, I used my left hand to push the door open. I slipped my fingers through the space. The door's pneumatic piston held it snug against my fingers.

*Fwooomp!*

Gone again, with my fingers hooked through the door, I moved back to look through the glass. All clear. I pushed the door open with one hand and pulled on the jamb with my fingers. I squeezed through the opening. The door closed silently behind me.

I kept one hand on the inside door handle and considered my options. Again, the ceiling won out. That's where this all started, bumping up against the ceiling in the hospital room. *Or did it start before that? And you just don't remember.*

I pushed off the floor, curled my legs, touched the ceiling and used the contact to extend my legs, belly to the ceiling. I held my hands at my sides, with my fingertips holding a grip on the narrow metal strips between acoustic tiles. A light breeze could break that grip, but a light breeze didn't seem likely.

Using not much more than the movement of my fingers, I set off across the room above the desks. Eventually I stopped one desk away from where Andy stood behind Martin, rotating my legs and my head to see the computer terminal they all faced.

"Amanda, I have you on speaker now, are you there?" Andy said to the phone on the desk.

Rosemary II replied, "I can hear you. Give me a minute, I'm logging in to my e-mail here. Hold on."

Schultz said to LeMore, "Go ahead and send it. Just that one."

LeMore hit send on an e-mail. I couldn't see any mug shots. He must have sent them as an attachment.

"Okay, I'm logged in," Rosemary II said. Her voice sounded steady but the strain was evident. "There's nothing from—wait a minute! Here it is. I'm opening—YES!"

Schultz and Andy exchanged glances.

"Yes! That's him. That's the one that pointed a gun at me!"

"Do you have any doubt, Amanda. Take a breath and be sure," Andy said grimly.

"I don't need a breath or a heartbeat or a millisecond! That's the boy that we knew back in the neighborhood. He has more tattoos in this picture, but that's him. Shellandre...? Shell—? Oh, I can't remember his name."

"Shillique Johnson," Schultz said. He didn't look happy.

"Yes! That's him! Can you find him? If you find him, he can tell you where Lane is!"

"Amanda, we're on it. This is good," Andy said. Something wasn't good, though. Her face said it was anything but good. "Hurry now. Go get a hairbrush and hurry back. Pidge will be there soon to bring you to us."

"God bless you, all of you! God bless you!"

LeMore reached over, lifted the receiver, and dropped it again, ending the call.

"Shit," he said.

"Where did they find the body?" Andy asked, and now I knew why this was not the good news it should have been.

"In front of his house, around four. Cock fight," LeMore said.

"I'm not familiar..." Andy said.

"'S what we call it. A cock fight. Feathers flying, somebody winds up dead," LeMore replied. "Yeah, I know. Double meaning because in the news it's always 'male, early twenties.' Witness said there was a 'group of people' and an argument. Nobody knows anything, nobody knows who fired. Could be an argument over a girl, or drugs or fantasy football. Nobody ever knows. Could be a drug deal shoot 'em up."

Schultz turned and called across the room to a detective sitting at another desk, working another terminal. "Doug! Did they find a gun on him?"

"One second," Doug called back. He worked the desktop mouse, scanned the screen, worked the mouse a little more, then called out, "Negative!"

LeMore started thinking out loud. "So, this kid is involved in a high-level tactical action, a gang kidnapping of a girl-child that has the potential to become a major headline. They don't like headlines. They don't like high-visibility violence. Yet they go for this. And this kid gets picked. Being picked for something like that, it takes some trust, right? That makes him more than just a foot soldier. How does he wind up shot a few hours later?"

"Maybe it really was a cock fight," Schultz offered.

"Yeah...no. That doesn't happen to these guys anymore. Not the trusted ones. It happens to wanna-bes. Or competition. It's how they eliminate competition, making it look like random street violence, just another unsolved."

"He wasn't supposed to show his face to Amanda," Andy said. "He made a mistake."

LeMore pointed his finger at Andy.

"Agreed," Schultz nodded.

"That's how these guys operate? One wrong move and you're dead?"

LeMore and Schultz exchanged glances.

Schultz said, "We need to change the game, here. Get word out to the detectives on scene that this is tied to us, and it is now shit-hit-the-fan time. This was supposed to look like another shooting-of-the-night, and if we had treated it that way, if not for the mother's eye-wit, we would have missed the connection. This is part of the kidnapping, so I'm bringing everybody in on this. Greg, more coffee! I have to make a call, then we pow wow."

Schultz went to another desk and picked up a phone. Andy went to the conference room. LeMore logged out of his terminal and followed her.

# 45

"Alright," Schultz sat down at the head of the conference table. LeMore sat down. Martin stowed his laptop. Everyone had availed themselves of LeMore's coffee. On one hand, I envied them. On the other, I didn't want to start thinking about needing a trip to the restroom.

I floated just inside the conference room doorway, belly flat just below the ceiling. Best seat in the house.

Andy took a chair near the head of the table on the far side. Martin and LeMore faced her, with their backs to me. Andy looked strikingly professional; they, less so.

"How did you know it was him?" Andy jumped in before Schultz could speak. "You pull one mug shot and it's a home run. How?"

LeMore answered. "We know he's a player. I saw him on the board twenty minutes ago. Last night's action board. We post anything related to gang activity in case it's something we're working. From there, call it a hunch."

"One heck of a hunch," Andy said.

"You, too," LeMore said to Andy. "I think you're dead nuts on. I think the kid wasn't supposed to show himself, let alone put a gun in the mother's face. I think he was supposed to watch, to see if the mother tipped to the girl not coming home. Think about it. A girl disappears. Even in a small town, how much time before it gets reported? How much time before everyone fumbles around checking with friends, looking to find out if she shacked up with a boyfriend, whatever? After that, there's still no immediate indication of imminent danger, so how much time before it gets reported, taken seriously, goes to an Amber Alert? Would the mother have put it together with the gang business from the past? That shit they were running from? If so, would anyone believe her? I think this whole thing broke open way before it was supposed to."

"If this had gone as planned," Schultz speculated, "she disappears. Maybe dead, more likely moved into the pipeline."

"Pipeline?" Andy asked.

"Trafficking. She becomes product. Either way, to the world she's just another kid on a milk carton. To her mother, a tragedy with no answers. Some sort of random psychopath on the loose, some unknown sex offender next door or driving around in a minivan."

Martin filled in the blanks. "Everybody thinks serial killer, meanwhile, Pan D has a couple days to … you know."

Andy looked around at all of them, face by face.

"So, what haven't you told me? This is not street gang normal."

"No, it's not," Schultz said. The detectives agreed. "The mother told you it all changed. That was about four years ago. Gang dealers and leaders became more violent. Shootings every night. Cock fights, we thought. But a pattern emerged. Greg, you tracked it first."

LeMore took the cue. "Gunfire after midnight is nothing new. But a surprising number of gangbangers, real players, were ending up shot. Dealers. People with long records. It almost read like a vigilante thing if you look only at the result. Otherwise, the scenarios fit the same old pattern. A group of people, an argument, a drive-by. Except in the old days, you spend a week or two asking questions, and sooner or later someone's ex-girlfriend tells us that someone's cousin had a thing with somebody's boyfriend and dot to dot to dot, we find out the shooter was the schmuck's best friend. In the old days, it was a big, violent soap opera. This wasn't. There were more unsolved. Nobody knew who did what, or where the shots came from. And they were deadlier. More assholes winding up on a slab than in the hospital. Kill shots. A few theatricals."

"Theatricals?" Andy wasn't afraid to ask questions.

"Movie shit. Some doodler taken to an empty house or garage and cut up, or burned, or hung up. Done in a way that makes a statement. Sadistic shit."

"At the same time," Martin chimed in, "the drug trade changed. Fewer independents. Fewer snitches. Fewer random busts with any kind of yield, yet lots more product on the market. They moved it off the street, too. We have hundreds of repossessed houses in the inner city, and they started using them as distribution houses."

"The neighbors are intimidated," LeMore said. "Our information sources dried up. People are more scared. And when we do isolate a house, it closes and the operation moves somewhere else. The next block. Four houses down. It's whack-a-mole." LeMore made a fist and pounded the table. He pointed at the wall. "That's a map of the ones we know about."

The map had dozens of pins clustered in an area north and west of the city center.

"The red pins are burnouts," LeMore pointed. "It's a trick they use when we hit a pill or product house. They keep mason jars of gasoline on hand. At the first sign of a raid, they drop the jar and toss a lighter. They come pouring out of the house like roaches, and the product, evidence, everything, goes up in flames. The house and a handful of product are disposable."

"And as all this changed, the name kept coming up. Pan D," Schultz said.

"What does it mean?" Andy asked.

"We're not sure," Martin shrugged.

"Pandemonium?" LeMore offered.

"If it is, it's the exact opposite, it's organized," Schultz said. "And spreading."

"Up the I-43 corridor," Andy said. "We know. We hear it from the AG's office all the time. Rural drug demand is outstripping urban."

Martin scoffed. "The AG's office, fuck! They couldn't find their own asses with radar. We've been trying for two years to get them and the feds and anyone who would listen to recognize this for what it is."

"Organized crime," Schultz said. "Someone got wise and found a way to mold street dealers into an organization. Not just a gang, not just tats and initiations and strutting around. Genuine organization, with rank, with strategy. And powerful internal discipline."

"Like this execution? Shillique Johnson?"

"Yeah," LeMore nodded. "Plus, there's a lot of money being spread around."

"That's what Amanda said. Cars. TVs. Lots of guns."

"Lots and lots of guns," LeMore said. "Not crappy street shit, either. Sigs, Berettas, even AR's are popping up. Tactical shit. Even silencers."

"These dipshits must have stayed sober long enough to watch 'Goodfellows' or 'The Godfather' because the model changed from gangbanger-centric to old-style mob," Schultz said.

"So, who is Pan D? Other than a pedophile?"

"That's the multi-million-dollar question, Detective. Some think he's home-grown. Some think he's outta Chicago, bringing a branch of their shit show here. Some think he doesn't exist, that he's some sort of composite constructed by new leadership. We just don't know."

"And Mauser. Who's Mauser?"

The three MPD officers shared quick glances of recognition.

"How do you know that name?"

"Lane's mother knew it. And the witness in Manitowoc I told you about." I thought Andy would say more, but she didn't.

"We think Mauser is the go-between. The link between Pan D at the top, and the street soldiers."

"Why don't you grab him up? Get to Pan D through him?"

"Not for lack of trying," Schultz said. "He's a nothing on our books. No known connections. No record. He's a ghost. Mauser is a street name."

"C'mon, there has to be somebody behind the name. People have seen him. Lane's mother has seen him."

Schultz shook his head. "We had three in-custody deaths, couple years ago. Pan D players, not real high up, but guys who wore it in the open. We picked 'em up on a variety of charges. Drugs. Gun charges. One was a viola-tion of supervision. Unrelated. All three wound up dead in custody."

"Mauser?"

"Probably, but here's the thing. We weren't trying to use them to leverage something higher up. These were routine arrests. But a few months later we actually tried that. We picked up a guy we thought had direct connections to Mauser. We went to work on him to give us something, and he told us the three in-custody deaths were guys killed as a warning. This is what happens if you think about talking to us. No, if *they* think you might think about it."

LeMore said, "That's how he does it. Hides in plain sight, connects to the business through a handful of lieutenants, talks to Pan D on top. He's not street. He's management. He doesn't care about street cred. There's no flash. But you want rumors? Mauser cut the head off a dealer skimming. Mauser killed the pre-school daughter of a guy who bragged about Pan D business. Mauser was special forces. Mauser was a cartel hit man. Mauser killed fucking Kennedy."

"But!" Martin interjected. "If you think about it, he's just middle management. And it's possible all this BS is propaganda. He could be made up entirely. Either way, it's insulation between the street operations and Pan D at the top."

"Up until now," Schultz said, "we had nothing even close to a shot at either Mauser or Pan D."

"Oh." Andy sat back in her chair. "I see."

Andy lowered her eyelashes and stared at her hands, folded on the table before her, much as she had done with Nick in Manitowoc. Her lower lip gained prominence. I knew the look. The first spark of anger shaded with disappointment.

"That's why I'm here, isn't it? That's why you let me in. My case, Lane, it's your first best shot at Pan D, isn't it?"

"Sure," Schultz said casually, dodging nothing. "No question. That girl is a serious move outside their playbook, and it opened a door, so yes, if you can get us through that door, then we're going through that door with everything we've got, Detective. Sure. That's why you're here. We're using you. Believe it. You're also here because you need all the help you can get, and we'll also take all the help we can get. This ain't some TV cop-opera where every department hates every other department."

"Second that," LeMore said. "I like your instincts, Detective."

Martin nodded. "We'd really like to nail this fuck."

"So, are you in?" Schultz wanted to know. "Because like you said, the clock is ticking, and we've got a shitload of work to do before dark."

"Never a question," Andy said.

# 46

S chultz laid out a plan which started with hitting every known Pan D distribution house. It would be a huge effort, the kind that usually takes days to organize, yet Schultz set the strike hour for 7 p.m. He told the detectives it meant going all the way to the top of the department, not just Stiller and Andre and Denninger, but the Chief of Police himself. The detectives moaned at that, but Schultz pointed out that the only way they would get approval for what he had in mind was to grease the political wheels and tell the brass what the payout would be. And because of the burnouts, they would have to alert the Fire Department, maybe even have units follow the raids and be at the ready a few blocks away. What he had in mind was a huge manpower draw. He warned that there would be push-back from other units, especially Narcotics, because it would show their hand; it would reveal that MPD knew the houses they were using. That could throw a wrench into the works for other investigations. He planned to roll over any objections like Patton, he said, using Lane as a banner. From the raids, they would make arrests. From the arrests, they would interrogate until they found someone involved in the kidnapping. And from there, find Mauser and find Lane, and from there, find Pan D.

Andy endorsed the idea. Martin and LeMore agreed.

The meeting broke up. Schultz assigned LeMore to the phones, to call in resources and set up briefings. He assigned Martin to begin target analysis, determining which houses to hit. Schultz said he would start calling the brass, then the unit commanders, including special tactical squads, the Fire

Department, plus the County Sheriff's department and the FBI and DEA liaisons. He pointed Andy at a thick binder and told her to get up to speed on Pan D. Maybe, he said, she would find something connected to the mother and girl, or to the witness in Manitowoc. I thought it mildly amusing, with computer technology oozing from every corner of this building, that an old-school three-ring binder probably had more value than all the bytes stored in the MPD servers.

Andy accepted the assignment but asked to meet Rosemary II when Pidge delivered her to Signature Aviation. Schultz said he would call downstairs to assign her a car.

The tempo of activity ramped up around the squad room. Martin and LeMore disappeared. Andy refreshed her coffee and spread out the binder at the big table. Schultz pulled out his phone and called Chief Stiller. Schultz queried him about finding Councilman Andre, obviously hoping he wouldn't have to sell his plan to Denninger alone. I think he saw the councilman as a buffer, an ally. Stiller told Schultz the Councilman had a personal engagement and couldn't be reached, but that he would leave word with his staff to check in as soon as possible. Stiller told Schultz he would alert the Chief, who was probably on his way to church.

When the call ended, I had two things on my mind. First, I needed a long look at the map on the wall.

Second, I needed a bathroom. The coffee I'd consumed earlier was ready for recycling, and all the recent talk of more coffee made it worse.

# 47

I took care of the bladder issue when I retrieved my crutches. Reappearing reminded me of my relationship with Gravity, and the pain it gave my pelvis. In turn, that gave me an idea.

Being a Sunday morning, it took me almost fifteen minutes of standing on the curb in front of the Safety Building to hail a cab. I shoved my crutches in first and slid onto the seat, issuing a theatrical moan in the process.

"You okay, mister?"

"Do I look okay? Sorry. Broken pelvis. It seriously hurts, and I'm out of meds." I tilted my head back and closed my eyes, painting on a grimace.

"Want me to take you to the hospital?" The driver was in his mid-thirties, brown skin, but not African. Possibly Asian. I felt bad for not being worldly enough to know. He didn't have an accent. The closest he came to ethnic garb was his Aaron Rodgers Packers jersey, common tribal garb in these parts. His eyes registered genuine concern through the rearview mirror.

"Not unless you just rewrote the healthcare laws. I'm on my own here. Listen," I leaned forward to the divider and lowered my tone through the holes in the Plexiglas. "I need some oxy. You gotta know where I can score. I'm from outta town and—"

"GET OUT OF MY CAB! GET OUT!"

The outburst pushed me back in the seat.

"NOW!"

"Okay, okay, okay," I said, holding up my hands in surrender. "No trouble, pal. No worries."

I barely pulled my crutches free of the cab before the driver roared off.

"Thanks a lot, buddy."

I considered the empty street again. The sun hung midmorning high and hot. I glanced at my watch. Almost ten-thirty. That hardly seemed possible. The day drained away fast. It frightened me to think of where Lane might be, and of how each hour lost felt like blood lost. Time for a different approach.

Watching for the next cab, I set off down the street. The Police Safety Building rests close to the part of downtown Milwaukee served by the old Auditorium, the old Arena, and the new playhouse the city and state built for the Milwaukee Bucks with my tax money. I have never been a basketball fan, so I harbored a bias on that one. My hope, in heading toward the sports venues, was that my chances of hailing another cab would increase.

Dumb idea.

Twenty minutes later I had almost reached the Hyatt again, when I finally pulled another cab to the curb. Crutches first, then me, I climbed in and closed the door. I didn't need any theater this time. The pain was genuine. A wave of fatigue hit me.

"Where to?" the driver asked.

I gave him an address. He automatically turned to his wheel and put his hand on the shift lever, but then stopped and looked back at me.

"Where?"

I repeated the address. He gave me a lingering look, glanced at the crutches, then decided a fare was a fare and threw the cab in gear.

He drove better than Schultz, but not by much, and only because he had no one in the front seat to distract him. I held on as he shot up Third Street, out of the sports district, and into diminishing layers of city decay. Up, over, up—we followed a stepped path to a narrow residential street. People stared at us from sagging porches as we rolled by. Unattended kids pedaled Big Wheels and bent bicycles on the frost-heaved sidewalks. I pictured Rosemary II, a dozen years ago, watching over a toddler in one of the tiny yards. Each street told a story of decline, yet I could imagine Lane as a toddler finding bright discovery in the colors and smells of a summer day in the only world she knew.

One or two of the houses we passed were boarded up. Another had sooty burn marks above windows without glass, and scorched furniture laying on bare dirt at the foot of the front steps. My cabbie pulled to a stop at a house in the center of a block. The number above the front door matched the address I had given.

The cabbie said nothing as I studied the building. It was one of hundreds of row houses built when this neighborhood had been filled with promise and immigrants who carried lunch pails to the booming breweries. The house sported a peaked roof, the usual porch, and had been built high above street level as if the builders expected a flood. The windows had glass but were covered on the inside. The front door was made of heavy steel, with a tiny window, also covered on the inside. A brass deadbolt lock sported a fresh shine. There was no mistaking its purpose.

This house was a pin on the map in Schultz's War Room.

"Is this what you're looking for?" the cabbie asked. I stared at the house, looking for signs.

"It's where I was told to go," I said.

"Who told you?"

"I'm not sure that's your concern, my friend," I said. Then I said, "Look, sorry. It's just, I've got this broken pelvis. Hurts like a sonofabitch, you know what I mean?"

"How come you're not in a cast?"

"Doesn't work for a broken pelvis. You just gut it out. They gave me pills but they're so stingy, I'm all out. A guy in a bar told me to come here. But it doesn't look like there's anyone home."

"No," he said, considering the house with its empty-eye windows. I sat and stared at the house, letting the silence weigh on him. People feel a need to fill silence. "Look," he said, "I might know another house. This one, right now, like you said, nobody home. They're like that sometimes. Sometimes here. Sometimes not."

I closed my eyes and blew out a long sigh. "Man, if you would do that for me, that would rock."

"For an extra fifty."

"What? C'mon!"

"Extra fifty."

"Twenty."

"Thirty."

I shook my head. "You're kicking a guy when he's down, man."

"We're all down."

I pulled out my wallet and located a twenty and a ten and waved them at the driver.

"When you get me there and I have what I need."

He pulled away.

Five minutes later, after zigzagging through the neighborhood, he pulled up to a house alongside an alley. It had the same tired look, the same vacant eyes, and a nearly identical fortress-like front door, with an identical lock. I wondered if the police had noted the pattern.

This house, and much of the block, looked deserted except for a single sign of life. A chunky boy, I would have guessed seven or eight, perched on the first step of the house with his arms dangling between his knees. His clothes were dirty and his hair lay matted against his skull. He looked at the cab blankly until I rolled down the window. On that cue, he rose and strolled down the weedy sidewalk.

He stopped at the window, saying nothing. His expression was blank, his gaze disinterested. Apparently, it wasn't his job to determine whether the customer was legitimate or not.

"Two," I said, holding up two fingers for clarity.

Nothing changed. I wiggled the fingers.

"Twenty," he said. He held out his hand. I found a bill and put it in his pudgy palm.

He turned and strolled up the walk and climbed the steps. He didn't knock or signal. He simply held his hand up to the tiny window and waited. A moment later, the window slid open, and the bill disappeared. His job done, he sat down again and dangled his arms between his knees.

"Seriously, man? Two?" The driver had an opinion.

"If this shit's any good, you'll be bringing me back again."

He shook his head like I was wasting his time, although the meter continued to run.

Five long minutes passed before an abrupt squeaking sound approached the car window. I turned and saw another kid, a girl with outraged pigtails aimed at the sky. She pulled up to the window on a rusted two-wheeler. She poked her fist in through the window. I cupped my hand under it, and she opened her fingers to drop two small pills into my palm. Her job done, she rolled away down the sidewalk. She looked even younger than the bored kid on the step.

I examined the pills. They had markings I couldn't make out, but I was sure they weren't the same as the ones Morrissey had prescribed.

"I don't suppose you've got a Coke up there, do you?"

The driver snorted. "Where d'you wanna go now?"

I dropped the pills from one hand into the other, then with the empty hand pretended to slap them into my mouth. I pantomimed chewing and made a face, then tilted my head back and closed my eyes.

"Nirvana."

"If you got the cash, I'll take you."

"Pull up to the corner and turn right, then right at the next corner, then stop."

The driver followed my instructions. I handed him the thirty bucks. "Fare's eleven dollars."

I gave him a ten and a one and got out. He looked at the cash like I'd spit in his hand.

"Dude, you shook me down for thirty bucks. There's no tip in this for you."

"You need a ride back?" he asked.

"Thanks. I just got my ride." I closed the door and he drove off, leaving me on the hot sidewalk.

A few faces along the street, sitting Sunday-morning guard duty on front porches and in lawn furniture, watched me warily. The crutches seemed to vouch for me, as if misfortune had come my way, as it had to many on this street. I wobbled my way down to the center of the block where an alley connected back to the street on which I'd done business with the Little Rascals. Badly used trash containers and contrasting shiny cars, a few surprisingly new, lined the alley. I glanced at the rooftops and saw satellite dishes. Cars, TVs and guns.

I made my way up the alley, trying to assess whether I was being watched or not. Once, I stopped, patted my butt as if I'd forgotten my wallet, looking back the way I'd come. Then, having reaffirmed that it remained in my jeans pocket, I ambled on. A few seconds later, I realized how stupid I had just been to call attention to the fact that a man on crutches was alone in an alley with a wallet in his back pocket. The glance back allowed me to scan of the houses around me. No obvious signs of watchers, but I had no illusions about who had amateur standing here.

The house I wanted, the one guarded by the bored boy, stood ahead on my left. A weedy back yard lay surrounded by a collapsing chicken-wire fence, rusty lace draped between short wooden poles. A frost-heaved walk joined the back door of the house to the alley. I wondered if this was where the girl came from. Then I remembered Andy's speech to Nick about policy, about separating the cash and the product. The more I thought about it, the more I believed that there were two houses in the neighborhood, one handling demand, the other handling supply, probably connected by cellular communication. God bless the modern age.

So where was the other house? The question was incidental. I wasn't looking for the product house. I wanted the cash house, the one with the fat boy working the front.

A slovenly garage stood off the alley to my right. The doors hung open, sagging into tall weeds. The condition looked permanent. In shadow beyond the doors, I saw rust, chrome, and canvas. A car sat under a loose, paint-stained tarp. Piles of boxes, cartons and junk hugged all sides of the car. There was no telling the make or model. The tires were dusty and flat.

I hobbled into the garage like I had business there and stacked my crutches against the inside of the sagging door and took a careful look back into the sunny alley. I saw no one.

*Fwooomp!*

In the shadows, I disappeared, wrapped in the familiar cool sensation. I blessed the relief of removing the weight from my pelvis. I was developing a strong preference for this condition. I wondered if I might end up doing so much of this that my muscles would atrophy like an astronaut's.

Free of observers, I took time to scan the alley seriously. I searched for lookouts and found two windows that offered a good view. One was in the cash house, above the back door. The open bottom half of a double-hung window looked over the back yard. No cardboard, no plywood. It was probably an upstairs hallway. The open window offered an unobstructed view of the alley. I had no doubt someone had seen me coming. It didn't matter.

The other lookout perch could be found several houses away, similarly above a back door, similarly open. This one had a faded shade drawn down to the sill. I watched it for a moment and saw the shade wrinkle. Someone peeked. I pegged it as the product house.

My destination was the cash house. The upstairs window, open like that, offered an entry point. The idea of getting there made me nervous. This would be the first time I used *the other thing* outdoors. I felt all too aware of the potential for floating away from grips and pivot points. I also noted power lines running above the alley. Gliding up into those would not end well.

The upstairs window might not be the best option if a lookout stood guard. I might not get past him. On the other hand, the back door had to be locked. The front door was certainly locked.

So, what was it to be? Window or back door?

I decided to try the door.

I worked my way to the edge of the sagging garage door, steadied myself, and pushed off. I lifted my knees and glided over the fence. My feet tickled and disturbed the tops of goldenrod and Queen Anne's lace. An observer would have seen the movement as an errant summer breeze on a breathlessly hot summer day. I glided straight to the back door and landed one hand on the handle. It didn't move. Worse, the back door opened on a small porch buried in stacked furniture, boxes, cartons, and debris. Nothing passed through this door; not lately.

I studied the window above, then pushed off and rose along the dry, chipped-paint siding of the house. As I ascended, I gained a sense of the window dimensions. The lower half was fully open. It looked more promising the closer I got. I made a rapid calculation and equally rapid decision. As my head cleared the sash, I gripped the bottom of the window and pulled myself in, face to face with a heavy, tattooed sentry sitting on a gaudy orange plastic chair, chewing on a candy bar and thumbing the screen of his phone. He had no clue I was less than three feet from him, snaking my way into the window. Too late to change course, I curled myself over the sill and into the hallway. Midway through, I arched my back and pushed upward. If I had been seen, I might have looked like a swimming mermaid, the way I flapped my feet behind me through the window. I miscalculated. Both feet bumped the sill coming through.

The sentry looked up. Blinked. Looked outside for the source of the sound. He leaned forward. I continued rising, headed for my new favorite refuge, the ceiling. The bump from my feet drew his interest, but after a cursory look through the window at an empty alley and empty yard, he returned to his phone. Onion smell hung in a cloud around him.

The hallway extended to a stairwell. I rolled onto my back and finger-crawled the length of the hallway. Open doors lined either side, once bedrooms for growing families. From my vantage point I spotted the corners of dirty mattresses, a litter of old magazines and dirty clothing. A smashed wristwatch lay in one doorway. A condom wrapper in another. Heat gathered in the high spaces of the hallway, but the strange cool sensation massaged my skin.

The stairway was narrow and steep. It opened into the first floor through a single doorway. It would be tight and serious trouble if someone came through that door and climbed the stairs while I worked my way down. A person of medium height wouldn't clear me. I floated to the angled ceiling and decided to finger-crawl down headfirst, using my hands on the narrow walls. Before starting, I paused and listened.

Music pounded through the walls. A television played somewhere. Muted voices carried on conversation. Counting the sentry and allowing for error, I put the occupancy of the house at somewhere between four and eight.

I initiated an inverted glide downward, fingers touching both walls. At the bottom, I hooked my hands on the top of the door jamb and pulled myself down for a look.

A girl in nothing but pink panties looked directly back up at me. Every muscle in my body tightened. She padded toward me, jiggling. I pushed myself back and spread my arms for purchase on the walls of the stairwell. Once I had a grip, I pushed up as hard as I could, pressing myself against the angled ceiling. She entered the stairwell and climbed the steps. Thankfully, she was petite. Her head cleared my body by a couple inches. She climbed the stairs and turned down the hallway, cooing a greeting at the sentry in the plastic chair. I checked again, then pulled myself into an open foyer. I rose to the safety of a tall ceiling.

The television played in a sitting room to the left of the front door. I saw the back of a shabby leather couch with someone sitting on it. Music came from what must be the kitchen, opposite the front door and to the right of the stairwell. I maneuvered for a look.

Two men sat at a scarred Formica table. Small piles of cash were spread between them. One of the two men counted from a wad of bills in one hand, slapping them onto the table. The other sat watching, sipping from a long straw driven into a tall brown bottle of beer. The first man finished counting, scooped up the pile and rolled it into a cylinder, binding it with a rubber band. It joined a stack of cash cylinders.

Exactly what I was looking for.

I worked up a vector into the kitchen and pushed off. A ceiling fan spun lazily over the table. It posed a problem. I couldn't get into position directly over the counting operation.

The men sat adjacent to each other, one facing the entrance to the kitchen, the other with his chair turned, facing his colleague with his back to the door. Two additional chairs remained vacant. I lowered my legs and prepared to push down from the ceiling to take up a standing position behind one of the empty chairs.

A phone rang. The man not counting fished it out of his shirt pocket. He poked it, held it to his ear, listened, and poked it off, then shoved it back in his pants pocket.

"He's here." He stood up abruptly and walked to the front door. After a moment, he opened it.

The one doing the counting hurried his process, produced another pile of bills, rolled them into a cylinder and put it with the others. I got the feeling he was supposed to have already finished this job. I also got a panicked feeling that if someone had come to collect, my idea would fail.

Two new actors entered the stage through the front door. Both were heavily tattooed. Neither looked friendly. One carried a satchel. They offered no chit-chat. The larger of the two, the one without the satchel, took up station by the front door. He observed the room from behind cheap sunglasses. Security. The other went straight for the table where Counting Man hurried to roll up another stack.

"Jus' double-checking!" he said. He grabbed a pen from the table and scribbled on a pad. He stripped away the top page and handed it to Satchel Man. Satchel Man took it, regarded it, and then dropped his bag on the table. It bore a sports logo and might have carried gym clothes. He unzipped it.

"Where's Tula?"

"Bitch is upstairs, giving JD a blowjob," Counting Man said. I sensed tension. He sat stiffly in the presence of command. I looked at Satchel Man and wondered if he was Mauser. "You wan' her? Got time?"

"Fuck no," Satchel Man said. "I wouldn't dip my dick in that."

"Don' be like that, Zee Zee! You'll hurt the bitch's feelings!"

Everyone laughed and the mood lightened.

Zee Zee, I thought. Not Mauser.

Zee Zee casually dropped the cash cylinders into the bag. Many more already occupied the bag. He didn't seem interested in counting them. He stuffed in the last two and zipped the bag closed.

"Wanna beer? In the fridge. Fuckin' hot today," the Counting Man offered eagerly.

Zee Zee shook his head and closed a grip on the bag, and I saw my chance slipping away. Then he paused.

"Fuckit. I'll take one." He called out to his companion with the sunglasses. "AJ! Beer?"

"I'll take two," Sunglasses said somberly.

Zee Zee released his grip on the bag and went to the refrigerator. Counting Man followed him with his eyes.

I pushed off from the ceiling. I dropped to the floor and grabbed the chair. I didn't stop to consider it. I grabbed the satchel. It had weight and it pressed me to the floor. On my feet again, I swung it over the chair. Counting Man saw the bag float. His eyes went wide. The bag moved magically through the air. He gawked, too stunned to move, afraid to touch it.

I dropped, curled into a ball, clutched the bag against my belly and pulled my shirt over the bag. The bag vanished, instantly losing its weight. I pushed with my toes and floated upward, keeping my body curled around the bag. My pulse thundered in my temples.

At the same instant, Counting Man said, "What the fuck?"

Zee Zee turned, beer in hand, startled.

"Where'd it go?" Counting Man demanded. "It was here!"

I bumped the ceiling but stayed in a cannonball curl with the bag pulled close to my belly under my shirt. My nerves rattled.

"'Da fuck?" Zee Zee's dark face clouded over. "Where's the fucking bag?"

"Where is it?" Counting Man also asked.

"That's what I ass't you, fucker. Where's the fucking bag?"

"It was right here! It—I don't know—it started flyin' all by isself—then I saw it disappear!"

"WHERE'S THE FUCKING BAG?!"

"I—I—I don' know, man! I swear, it was right here! I don't have it!"

The commotion brought Sunglasses—AJ—into the room behind a huge nickel-plated semi-automatic handgun aimed at Counting Man. He charged the table and put the barrel of the gun against Counting Man's left eye.

Counting Man stammered and waved his arms, pressed backward. His chair tipped.

"WHERE'S THE FUCKING BAG?!" Zee Zee glared at Counting Man, whose remaining eye bulged.

"*I—don—got—it!*" he sputtered.

"You're the only motherfucker here! Where did you put it?!"

BLAAAMM!

The gunshot slammed my ears. Counting Man went over backward. AJ stared at the smoking end of his gun. Blood and other material splayed in a vee-shape across the floor behind what was left of Counting Man's skull.

In a voice several octaves higher, Zee Zee demanded, "WHAT THE FUCK DID YOU DO THAT FOR?"

"It's this trigger, man. This trigger. Fucking thing."

The front door slammed open. Counting Man's companion vanished into the summer sun.

"YOU FUCKING KILLED HIM!"

"Yeah, I know. It's this trigger. It just goes sometimes." AJ kept staring at the gun, like he expected it to explain itself.

"Motherfucker! Where's the fucking bag? Look for the fucking bag!"

Someone else pounded out the front door.

The copper scent of spilled blood clouded the hot kitchen. My stomach turned over. A sheen of sweat broke on my skin. Nausea blossomed. It was almost impossible not to look at the body on the floor. A black, burned hole had replaced Counting Man's left eye. Thankfully, I couldn't see the back of his head, which had exploded all over the floor and wall behind him.

Zee Zee poked erratically around the small kitchen, looking for the bag. AJ studied his gun. He kept his fat finger on the trigger and carelessly swung

the big weapon sideways across Zee Zee, who didn't seem to notice. Neither seemed to understand or care about muzzle safety. As the idiot examined the weapon, it swung distressingly toward me.

I held the cannonball posture sideways against the ceiling. My left hand locked my shirt over the satchel and gripped both in place. With my free right hand, I gripped one corner of the refrigerator and pushed toward the kitchen door. When it came within reach, I closed a grip on the top of the door jamb and stopped, steadying myself.

I prepared to pull myself through when a high-pitched scream froze me.

The girl in the panties stood below me, hands thrown forward, screaming. AJ jumped and swung his big weapon around and for a moment I expected to see her shot by another unintended trigger pull. Her eyes blazed, wide open and white ringed, then miraculously grew wider when she switched her gaze from the body on the floor to the hole at the end of the big silver gun. She turned and ran screaming out the front door.

"MOTHERFUCKER! WILL YOU PUT THAT THING AWAY!" Zee Zee shrieked. AJ stuffed it down the front of his sweatpants. I expected the next explosion to spray his genitals onto his shoes.

I secured a grip on the top of the kitchen door jamb. Zee Zee and AJ moved around the table. Zee Zee tossed Counting Man's body back and forth, as if the satchel had been hidden under it.

I pulled myself toward the front door.

"It's not here! Fuck!" Zee Zee cried out, his voice rising to match his panic.

Behind me, JD the window sentry thundered down the stairs. I floated, committed to a glide toward the front door with the satchel under my shirt. I had nothing to grab, and no way to change course. I reached the door frame directly in JD's path.

JD, the grown-up version of the fat boy outside, pounded across the floor directly toward me.

I had no choice. My right leg kicked out. My heel connected with his nose. His head went back while his legs pounded forward. He dropped flat on his back with a yowl, less hurt than stunned.

The kick fired me through the open front door. I put an arm out and caught the jamb, which swung me around hard. My forward motion arrested. I hung with my right arm hooked on the front door. I pushed. A short glide took me across the porch to the roof overhang. I caught the edge and pulled myself up and over. From there, I aimed for the edge of the eaves. JD, with one hand cupping his bleeding nose, shot out the door and down the steps for points unknown.

Clinging to the eaves, I surveyed the steep roof of the house. I didn't like the look of it. The shingled surface offered nothing to grab. Instead of going over the house, I worked my way around it by gripping the flimsy, leaf-choked gutter. Reaching the back side of the house, I pushed down into the back yard and gripped the fence. From the fence, I vectored back to the garage and slipped around the edge of the sagging door. I pulled the bag out from under my shirt and fumbled for the unseen handle. It slipped free of my grip. My fingers felt cold electricity as the bag reappeared. I grabbed it before it hit the floor. The bag remained visible and weighed me down.

Given the dust and dirt in the garage, it was obvious no one had been here in a long time. I doubted anyone would be cleaning here soon. I found an old milk carton, turned it over, put the bag under it and piled on a mound of filthy clothing.

Not that I cared if I ever saw this bag again. Theft wasn't the plan.

As far as the plan went, I needed to get back to where the two stooges were no doubt still scouring the kitchen for their money. Zee Zee had been bubbling toward panic. The errant death of one of the cash house occupants might not create much of a stir, but lost cash would not sit well with management.

A few minutes later, retracing my route, using the eaves again to round the house, I slipped back inside and took up station in the high foyer. So far, nobody thought to close the front door.

Zee Zee held his phone to his head. Thin, with sharp facial bones, he looked mildly skeletal. A flat gray pallor draped his face. His companion, AJ, resumed a stoic guard pose outside the kitchen with the touchy hand-cannon tucked in his sweatpants.

"We got a problem," Zee Zee told his phone. He listened as someone on the other end explained how much they didn't care. "No, you gotta tell Mauser." The other person explained that telling Mauser was not going to happen. "I don't fucking care if he's busy! He needs to know. Fucking Comber and Boogie tried to rip us off. Pulled a gun on me and AJ when we came to collect. AJ got Comber, but Boogie got the money and took off." The response was harsh. Zee Zee closed his eyes, squeezed them hard. "I don't fucking know! Maybe forty. Tell Mauser we need him over here right away!" He lowered his phone and jabbed a finger at the screen, missed, jabbed it again, and again, and again. A scream grew in his throat and roared free. I ignored him.

Mauser.

Bingo.

# 48

"I ain't sitting in there with that shit," Zee Zee proclaimed. He paced the foyer below me, his skin glistening with sweat. AJ had wandered off to answer the beckoning call of the television screen still on in the sitting room. From a steady crunching sound, I surmised he found a bag of chips.

Zee Zee darted into the kitchen and brought out a chair. He moved quickly, as if the room were radioactive. He planted the chair near the sitting room entrance, as far from the kitchen as geometry would allow.

"Where the fuck izzee?" Zee Zee randomly shouted. AJ didn't venture an opinion, drawn as he was into a conflict unfolding in a daytime television courtroom. He seemed utterly unconcerned with, or unable to remember, the colleague he had just shot in the eye.

Zee Zee's phone rang. He yanked it out of his pocket.

I couldn't hear the other end of the exchange over the television. Zee Zee listened and cringed. "Mauser, man—I don't know whuh—Okay! Okay! Not on the phone, right!" More exchange. Zee Zee nodded obediently.

The call ended, leaving Zee Zee staring at the screen. He shoved the phone back in his pocket.

"He's coming!" Zee Zee called to AJ. He reached in a pocket and pulled out a pair of pills. He slapped them into his mouth and chewed hungrily, then sat, stood, paced, jittered, sat, and muttered for what felt to me like another hour.

. . .

I HAD no idea what time it was. I couldn't see my watch or the angle of the sun outside. Early afternoon? It seemed like ages had passed since Rosemary II banged on my front porch door. By now, Pidge would have made the round trip to Essex, and returned with Rosemary II and a sample of Lane's DNA for comparison to the bloody initials found in the Tahoe. I would have thought the initials were proof enough that Lane had written them, but it seemed important to Andy and to the others that they acquire forensic confirmation. Andy would have met them at the airport to hurry the process. I liked the idea that Rosemary II was joining us in Milwaukee, closer to Lane. Or that we would be closer to Rosemary II if the worst happened. The Worst, with a capital W, crawled around the edges of my thoughts. I pushed it away, but it lingered. The only sure way to banish it was to find Lane. Finding Lane required finding Mauser. That meant floating high in a hot, stinking cash house above a panicked gangbanger.

Framed that way, I resolved to hover all day, if that's what it took.

Zee Zee paced below me dripping sweat and fear. The combination followed him as a cloud of stink.

Another daytime television courtroom (how many ersatz judges are there?) gaveled into session for AJ. A few minutes later, during the opening commercial break, Zee Zee's phone chirped.

"He's here! Turn that fucking thing off!"

AJ found the TV remote and killed the device. Zee Zee jumped to the door and released the dead bolt. He didn't bother with the peep hole. He swung the door open and stepped back deferentially.

The Mauser that walked through the door bore no resemblance to my expectations. I had pictured the television gangbanger stereotype. Tattoos mapped over every inch of skin. Leather. Weapons. Someone oozing buffed up muscle and bad attitude. I'm a farm boy who spent his life at airports and in airplanes, interacting with respectful, friendly people. The closest I'd ever been to a street gang was being intercepted by high school dance squad girls selling pizza coupons at the Essex High homecoming parade.

Mauser would not get a callback from any movie auditioning for gang-banger extras.

He was smaller than me. I guessed five-seven or eight. He cut a trim figure. Not bony. Not buffed out. Trim. He wore expensive sports gear with demure logos on a crew neck collar. His gray shirt had a vague shine and no buttons. His trousers were dark and neatly creased over expensive-looking running shoes—not the brightly colored style currently in favor. There was nothing gaudy about the man. He might have been coming from a round of golf at his country club, which was reinforced by a small athletic bag he carried, like the cash bag I had stolen. I could not see a single tattoo. He looked like a politician, the kind that puts on a sporty look for a sports event, carefully considering every fiber of it in a full-length mirror before stepping into the spotlight. He looked more like the city councilman I had met than the top street dog in the Pan D gang.

The upscale look ended at the eyes. I had a clear view, having moved to where the stairs emptied into the foyer. I faced the front door. The eyes were cold and lifeless. His eyelids hung down as if it took effort to hold them fully open. No matter what the rest of the face did, I doubted those eyes ever changed expression. Entering the room, they swept it, cataloged the contents, judged, then moved on. He ignored Zee Zee, who had stepped aside to where AJ, still wearing his shades, now stood loosely on guard at the entrance to the silent sitting room. The two of them looked like prisoners awaiting sentencing.

Mauser didn't speak to them, nor they to him. He moved to where he could see the kitchen but didn't enter it. He lingered over the scene, longer, I think, than was necessary to assess it. I had the feeling Mauser took something from the tableau of death and gore. Took it and absorbed it.

Zee Zee couldn't hold his tongue any longer. "Mauser, man, it was Comber and Boogie. They grabbed the money. AJ got Comber, but Boogie, he took off. He took off with the money!"

Mauser stared at the body in cold silence.

"I had to shoot him," AJ offered. He nodded at Zee Zee to show solidarity. Zee Zee returned the nod like a bobblehead on a sports fan's dashboard. Between the pills and the panic, Zee Zee hovered on the edge of losing whatever grip he still possessed.

"It was him or you?" Mauser asked, his voice low and measured, his half-open eyes still fixed on the scene in the kitchen.

"Yeah!" AJ said, liking the idea.

"Where's his gun?"

AJ looked at Zee Zee, who looked back at his bodyguard, wide-eyed, but he was quick. "Didn't Boogie have a gun? Waving it around all gangsta!"

"Yeah! Boogie had a gun! Wavin' it and shit," AJ agreed.

"So. You pulled on the one without the gun and shot his ass."

This confused the two Pan D soldiers into silence. Mauser lifted the sports bag with one hand and unzipped it with his other hand. He pulled out a pair of leather driving gloves and worked them onto his fingers, adjusting each digit in turn.

"Show me."

This immobilized the two conspirators. Mauser put his gloved right hand into the bag and withdrew a dull black semiautomatic pistol. Andy carried one like it, a Glock 17. He turned now and aimed it at AJ, who threw both hands up as a shield and uttered a single, "Whoa!"

"Zee Zee, take that stupid gun out of his pants and come over here and show me. AJ, you stand very still, do you understand?" Mauser's diction was practiced and perfect. He could have been a sports announcer or television newscaster, if not for the lifeless chill in his delivery.

Zee Zee bobbed his head, visibly relieved. He reached carefully and pulled the weapon out of AJ's waistband with two fingers. Once free of the pants, Zee Zee wrapped his hand around the grip. He was loath to put his finger through the trigger guard. He skittered over to Mauser's side of the room.

"So. AJ was at the door, like I taught him to do when you collect, right?" Mauser asked.

"Right, right! Watching the door!"

"Show me."

Zee Zee took up a position where AJ had been when they had come to collect.

"Right here, man! Right here."

"And that's where he was when he shot Comber, right?"

"Uh-huh. Right here!" Zee Zee jittered, all in on the lie.

I didn't like where this was going. I pushed myself farther away from any geometry that connected the three corners of the tense triangle below me.

"Zee Zee, point that thing at the floor," Mauser said calmly. Zee Zee complied.

Music erupted, tinny and small. Mauser raised one finger on his free hand, calling a pause to the proceedings. Left-handed, he reached in his pocket and extracted a phone. He read the incoming number and regarded it suspiciously. He touched the screen, held up the phone, but did not speak.

He listened. His expression remained unchanged, but he slowly lowered his face until his half-lidded eyes fixed on the floor. I felt my heart pick up speed. Maybe he would say something about Lane.

"How many?"

He listened.

"What time?"

He listened.

"We should give them one or two."

He listened.

"What about the pink house?"

He listened. He shook his head, the tiniest side-to-side motion. Something he didn't agree with. Something he chose not to express. The call ended and the phone disappeared into his pocket again.

Mauser swung the Glock over and pointed it at Zee Zee's face.

"Where's the money, Zee Zee? Because this idiot isn't smart enough to take it. And Comber didn't have a gun. And Boogie is an ignorant fool. That leaves you. And I don't have time for this shit today. I am having a bad day, and you are imposing a deleterious effect on it. Do you know the word? Deleterious?"

"Mauser, I swe—"

The two shots went off so close together I felt the shock wave as one. For the second time today, pressure clapped my eyes and ears. Mauser shot Zee Zee in the face. The bullets struck his nose and upper lip.

A third shot went off, hitting Zee Zee in the groin before his body crumpled to the floor, twitching once like an animal struck on a roadside.

Mauser took a step forward, holding the pistol on its victim, yet turning ninety degrees to stare at AJ, eyes still hooded as if nothing had happened.

"AJ, do you know why you're not dead?"

"Uh-uh."

"Because you're too stupid to have engineered any of this tragic bullshit."

"Uh-huh."

"I intend to alter that paradigm tomorrow at …" Mauser looked at his watch "… three-forty p.m. Twenty-four hours from now. At that hour, I will stand before you and ask you to drop your pants and bend over. I will then shove the largest weapon I can find up your rectum and empty a clip into your sorry guts. Unless, of course, you return the money to me. Do you think you can do that?"

"Uh-huh."

"I do not for one second believe a word I've heard here. I do not care, either. Put the money in my hands, or I will put a gun up your ass. Do you understand?"

"Uh-huh."

"Get the fuck out of my sight."

AJ didn't hesitate. He bolted for the door, stopping only to reach for his weapon.

"DON'T TOUCH THAT!" Mauser barked. "Idiot!"

AJ jerked his hand back as if scalded, pulled open the front door and pounded across the porch and down the steps. A black SUV sat at the curb.

AJ veered away as if it were the Devil's own carriage and passing too close might pull him screaming into darkness.

I had expected an SUV and Mauser met the expectation with Mercedes-Benz luxury. I made note of the luggage rack.

Mauser stepped between me and the door and kicked it closed.

Mauser turned to business. He collected the three ejected nine-millimeter casings and went to the kitchen where he dropped the casings, then knelt beside Comber. He rubbed the barrel of the weapon on Comber's wrist and forearm, then worked the weapon into his limp hand, carefully wrapping dead fingers first across the slide, then around the grip and into the trigger guard. Satisfied with his work, he stood up and studied the scene, then studied the kitchen. Snack food litter, empty beer bottles, and the general debris of poor living decorated every surface. None of that mattered. He picked up the pen and pad of paper sitting on the table, the one on which Comber had written his tally, and pressed them into his sports bag. No other sign of business conducted in this house attracted Mauser's attention.

Mauser left the kitchen and hooked into the stairwell. He took the steps two at a time.

I needed to get out. Now. *The pink house.* Could that mean Lane?

I pushed across the foyer and grabbed the doorknob. I swung myself into position and put one hand on the frame for leverage. Mauser's footsteps moved across the second-floor hallway, checking room by room. Using the counter-pressure of my left hand on the frame, I pulled the door open far enough to slip through, then pulled it closed behind me. The heavy latch made an annoyingly loud snap as it fell into place. Too loud. I heard the drum of Mauser's feet on the stairs inside.

Mildly panicked, I rotated and reached out for the porch rail. Too far. I reached back and pushed, then floated over the railing. Grabbing it, I swung my body over like a gymnast. The front door opened. Mauser filled the frame, sports bag in hand, eyes scanning, searching for the source of the noise. The street lay silent in summer heat. The boy guarding the front steps was gone. There were no children cycling on the sidewalk. No one sat on a porch seeking the comfort of a cooling breeze.

Mauser snapped the door shut behind him and produced a key from his pocket. He locked the deadbolt and turned to leave. That was my cue.

I took stock of the angles, the obstacles, and the options. My target was the roof rack of the SUV parked at the curb behind what I assumed was Zee Zee's car, a low-slung black BMW. A silver roof rack on top of the SUV offered a perfect grip.

As a plan, it sucked. But if Pan D, the pedophile, had yet to take delivery of his prize, then delivery would likely be handled by the one person he trusted. Mauser. I planned to stick to him until he either got me to Lane, or I decided to beat it out of him, which was an absurd notion for someone requiring crutches.

I crouched against the porch railing, gripping the wood with my hands, knees bent, legs coiled. I looked across the yard at the SUV, roughly thirty feet away. Tall old trees lined the street on both sides. The trunks lined up as dark pillars beneath crowns that spread at roof-top height. The SUV sat neatly between two trunks. The flight path was free of signs, wires, and mailboxes. Clear sailing.

Mauser descended the porch steps and strolled to his urban truck, sports bag in hand. He pulled his phone from his pocket and worked the screen as he walked. From a distance, he might have been just another member of the new city gentry, in on the ground floor in a neighborhood about to convert to upscale condos. Looking fit and trim on the way to the gym.

I waited for him to clear the sidewalk and round the rear quarter panel on his way to the driver's side, then kicked off.

My right foot cracked through the rotted porch railing and hooked itself. My left gave me propulsion, but with the right foot snagged, I swung around and flopped against the porch steps. I managed to get my hands down to prevent scraping my face across the wood. Something stung the skin on my left forearm.

*Shit!*

I righted myself and yanked my right foot free of the broken railing. Hanging onto the porch steps, I re-positioned.

*Shit-shit-shit-shit!* I heard the driver door open and close. The vehicle's engine started.

Crouched against the porch steps, I pushed hard. I flew forward and upward.

*No! No-no-no-no-no!* Too much up angle! Too high!

The sidewalk fell away. I knew instantly my trajectory was too high. I tried to roll forward, jack-knifing my legs as counterbalance. I reached as far downward as possible. The sidewalk and curb passed under me.

Too high! Too high!

The Mercedes began to roll. I stretched my arms, hands and fingers for all I was worth, for all Lane was worth. The silver roof rack swept under me, inches away. It might as well have been miles.

I missed.

The black SUV pulled away. I sailed over the street.

"NO!" I cried out. *No! No! No! NO!*

Mauser accelerated away.

I thought about dropping out of the vanished state, but a fall to the street would finish me. I should have crashed down onto the roof of the SUV. He might have stopped and looked, but so what? Nothing to see.

*Stupid!* I overestimated my ability. I became overconfident. All this effort to attach myself to the one link that could get us to Lane, and I had blown it.

A wave of despair flooded me, reminding me it was my fault Lane had been taken in the first place. I felt my will wash away, draining my strength with it. I hung limp in the air, gliding across the street, the sidewalk and the yard opposite the cash house with my helpless fingers still outstretched after the diminishing Mercedes.

I hit the outside wall of the house on the other side of the street, directly above a porch roof. The impact took my concentration and—

*Fwooomp!* I reappeared. Gravity grabbed me.

I dropped onto the porch roof in an awkward tangle of my own arms and legs. Pain shot through my abdomen and I welcomed it. I deserved it.

I lay on my side against the burning asphalt shingles. I let the burn penetrate my skin, punishing myself for letting this chance slip away. For letting Lane slip away.

I failed.

*Please, God,* I begged. *Let Andy find her.*

I looked up at the midafternoon sun, but it offered only heat.

# 49

I needed a phone. I needed to call Andy and confess my sins. Maybe not everything, but she should know about "the pink house." It might mean something to her, or to Martin and LeMore. Something that could take them to Lane. The police needed to know about the dead men in the locked cash house, although I had no idea how to explain that to my wife.

Phone. Cab. Hotel. What to tell Andy. Logistics jangled in my mind like pieces of something broken. Darkness brought on by my spectacular failure clouded my thoughts.

I sat up and looked for a flight path to take me back to the alley beside the cash house, back to my crutches. Then from there—

A head-splitting scream sliced the air behind me.

I jumped. I nearly dove off the porch roof in full gravity. My balance held only by planting both hands and my butt firmly on the scalding asphalt shingles. I jerked my head around to confront the source of the scream.

Two wide eyes glared at me behind the screen in a window just above the porch, not far from where I had smacked into the side of the house. A tiny girl stood framed in the window.

*Christ! That scream could be used as a weapon.*

"MOMMY!"

I did the only thing I could think of.

*Fwooomp!* I vanished.

I didn't think it possible, but her eyes grew even wider. She screamed again and turned and ran.

"MOMMY! DIVISIBLE MAN IS ON THE ROOF!"

She darted into the depths of the house, repeating the cry over and over. I decided not to wait around for Mommy. I turned and looked across the street for something easily grasped, something that would start me on a path to the crutches.

The black BMW sitting at the cash house curb obstructed the direct line to a tree trunk I might have used. I didn't like going high but decided to cross above the car and catch the tree higher up. From there, working around the house to the garage seemed viable.

Too bad Zee Zee couldn't have parked—

*Zee Zee!*

That's when I realized I had a whole new set of options.

I dropped all consideration of the tree and drew a bead on the porch of the cash house. With screams of "DIVISIBLE MAN!" chasing me, I launched across the open street.

# 50

Zee Zee provided the answer. As soon as I realized it, I made the flight across the street, back to the top of the cash house porch where I hooked the eaves. I worked hand over hand around the house and dropped into the thick atmosphere of the cash house through my reliable upstairs window. JD's orange plastic chair lay on its back halfway down the hall. The stink in the house grew oppressive as I traversed the upstairs hall and made the glide down the stairwell. I nearly gagged when I emerged into the foyer to search Zee Zee's corpse.

*Fwooomp!*

I crouched next to him, fully visible so I wouldn't have to deal with floating untethered, careful not to step in the slowly spreading blood. I pulled his phone, thankfully blood free, from his left hip pocket. I gingerly tapped each pocket, hoping to strike the shape of a BMW key fob. The fob remained missing.

The phone would do. The phone could bring a cab. I abandoned the search for the car key because I wasn't about to lift his body to check his blood-soaked back pockets. Then I remembered something.

Beer.

Comber offered Zee Zee a beer. Zee Zee first rejected the offer, then changed his mind. If he hadn't, the opportunity to grab the bag would not have materialized.

I poked my head into the kitchen. I looked over the table. Nothing. No keys. I looked at the counter beside the refrigerator.

A BMW fob lay on the Formica countertop beside an unopened beer bottle.

I grabbed the fob and ducked out of the kitchen.

I took one last look at Zee Zee.

"See what drinking on the job gets you, asshole."

The front door remained dead-bolted and required a key on the inside. I gave no thought to searching Zee Zee's pockets for another key. I vanished myself again, welcoming the cool sensation and the release of pressure on my pelvic bones.

With the phone and car key pocketed, I hurried out of the house via the upstairs back window, hoping never to see its kind again.

I followed a familiar route back to the shabby garage. There, I uncovered the carton holding the empty cash bag. I removed the bag and dumped the cash rolls into the carton. There must have been fifty or sixty. I shoved the carton into the shadows and piled on the old clothing again. Chances were excellent I'd never visit this garage again. Somebody was in for the find of a lifetime if they ever cleaned the place out.

I took the empty bag and crutches, figuring I'd make the short hike out to Zee Zee's car and be on my way.

I stopped and gave it a little more thought.

So far there had been four gunshots and one screaming girl child in the neighborhood on this quiet Sunday afternoon, yet there were no sirens, no patrol cars rushing to the scene. The street appeared empty. The neighbors had all but barricaded themselves in their homes, but I felt certain they were watching. White guy on crutches seen leaving the scene of a double-homicide. I had no doubt I would be seen. And I happened to have just met some MPD detectives who knew me as a white guy on crutches. What were the odds?

Except for my initial buy, and the stroll up the alley, my movements had gone unseen. Now wasn't the time to make an appearance.

I altered the plan, leaving the crutches and the empty bag.

*Fwooomp!* Gone again, I struck out for the car. I followed a tortured path, zigzagging from one grip to another, finding vectors that assured me of short flights. Having fouled up so badly with Mauser's Mercedes haunted me. Eventually, I caromed off the tree trunk next to the BMW and floated over the hood to grab the side-view mirror. I found the fob in my pocket and pressed with my thumb, releasing the car door locks.

I jackknifed myself inside. Zee Zee was shorter than me. The car smelled new. The push-button start fired it up quickly.

I didn't care if people reported the car driving away "all by itself." That would be a whole lot harder to get a cop's attention than a description of a white male, mid-thirties, with dark hair and crutches.

I found the seat controls and gave myself some space. I snapped the seatbelt to keep from floating off the leather. Squared away, I pulled the gearshift into Drive and wheeled into the street.

A short trip around the block took me into the alley from the back, the same way I had walked it. I pulled up to the garage and put the car in Park. Following the same routine in reverse, using the driver side mirror, I pulled myself across the hood of the car and into the garage. I stowed the crutches and the empty bag on the passenger seat, repeated the short flight across the hood, and rearranged myself behind the wheel.

I drove four blocks before reappearing.

ANDY ANSWERED on the sixth ring.

"Andrea Stewart." I heard caution in her voice, not recognizing the number.

"It's me."

"Will? Where have you been?"

"Dee, I cannot begin to explain, but I will. Everything. Just not now."

"We've been calling the Hyatt and—"

"Dee! Listen to me!"

I got silence. I sensed a simmering anger.

"What do those guys, Martin and LeMore, know about a 'pink house'?"

"A what?"

"Pink house. Do they know anything about a pink house?"

"Where did you get this? Will, what are you doing?"

"Dee! See what you can find out about a pink house. I'll call you back in a little while."

"Will, wait!" she said. "Look, I can't give you the details, but they have a map here, of all the known locations Pan D uses, distribution houses."

I knew the map well.

"Pan D uses color names. Green. Blue. Like that. How do you know about a pink house?"

"Is there a pink house? On the map?"

"I have no idea. It hasn't been mentioned," Andy said. "I'll find out. They're gearing up to hit sixteen of these places in the next couple hours. I'll find out right away!"

"Make it quick. Because that may be where they have Lane!"

"How do you—?"

"I gotta go," I said.

"Wait! How do I reach you? What phone are you using?"

"Borrowed," I said.

"Will, what are you doing?!"

"I—will—call—you! Love you! Gotta go!"

I clicked off before she could protest and before I dug myself into deeper shit.

I looked at the phone. Thankfully, Zee Zee didn't believe in password protection. I touched Recents and found what I was looking for. I touched the call button.

It rang. Once. Twice. Three, four, five times.

*C'mon, asshole! Pick up!*

It stopped ringing. I heard nothing. No sound, no breathing. I pictured Mauser's lifeless expression. He had to have recognized the caller ID. I felt him through the connection, the lidded eyes staring into a distance, looking for Zee Zee across that distance—Zee Zee calling Mauser with nine-millimeter holes in his face. I spoke first.

"I've got your money, asshole."

"You've also got Zee Zee's phone. Should I be impressed?"

"You might be impressed by the video I have of you shooting the dumb bastard in the face, twice. That shot to the groin, was that a homophobic thing? Because that's not cool."

Silence.

"Twenty minutes. Behind Faze. The alley."

"I'm going to shoot you in the balls first. Maybe then—"

I touched the screen and killed the connection. I set the ringer to mute. For what I had in mind, I couldn't afford to have it suddenly ringing in my pocket. Andy doesn't give up easily. She would try a callback.

I examined the alley where I had parked the BMW behind the Faze nightclub on Water Street. The club rose three stories and took up most of the first third of the block. The alley felt like a canyon between buildings, but not so narrow that you couldn't get two vehicles side-by-side. I didn't much care about the approach angles, or the exit. I cared about getting Mauser into the alley. I assumed he wouldn't feel comfortable pulling in if he couldn't see a way out.

Twenty minutes. I hoped it gave him just enough time to get here, but not so much that it would allow him to do anything else, specifically anything to Lane.

Evening approached quickly; a perverse date night for the pedophile who called himself Pan D. If the scenario suggested by Andy and the two cops played out, it seemed likely Mauser had a role. Setting it up. Delivering her. Ensuring privacy. Providing the location. Security. I counted on it, for Lane's sake. I prayed it hadn't happened yet. I prayed that the Pink House was just the name of a secure location for holding her, and that the Pink House clue would lead Andy and the finest tactical warriors of the MPD to Lane before anything happened. If not, I prayed I would get there first—a cut-rate cavalry to the rescue.

I disappeared, picked up the empty cash bag and eased out of the car. The bag hovered magically in the air and helped hold me down until I set it on the hood of Zee Zee's car. Gripping the wheel well, then the grille, I worked my way around to the passenger side. I pulled the crutches out, and again using them as a weight, hopped over to a dumpster sitting tight against the back of the building. I tossed them in.

Back to the front of the car, I reached down to the cracked and broken pavement and found a handful of loose dust and dirt. I threw it onto the black hood, then another, then another.

I surveyed the bag and the dust-covered hood. Satisfied with my work, I wrote with my finger in the dust. The letters appeared magically.

MEET ME AT THE PINK HOUSE

It looked good, but it needed something…

NOW ASSHOLE

Perfect.

I had already worked out a perch for this trap. A metal fire-escape hung from the side of the building overhead. I pushed with my toes and floated up to grip the iron railing. The soles of my feet dangled fifteen feet above the pavement. The alley ran east-west. The setting sun sank toward the buildings of the next block, elongating shadows. The hot afternoon promised a warm evening under a cloudless sky. On the other side of the Faze building, traffic noise rose from Water Street, an avenue lined with clubs, restaurants, and shops.

Mauser responded faster than I expected.

The door to the back of the club opened abruptly below me. A silver semi-automatic like the one AJ favored poked through the open space. The gun swept left, then right. Corded and tattooed arms followed, with a shaved and tattooed head close behind. The head searched the scene using rapid choppy glances. Satisfied, the gun's owner moved into the alley and looked over the car. He walked around it, checked inside, then spent a moment studying the alley and the buildings. He squinted directly at the fire escape where I floated. Looking directly at me, he gave me a start. His arms and chest bulged. He wore an expression of permanent anger. The weapon fit his hand. He did not wield it like a totem or a toy, but with the seriousness of death itself.

He pulled a phone from his pocket and walked back to the front of the car.

I suddenly saw my scheme fall apart. The message on the car had been a means of luring Mauser into taking me to Lane. Delivering the message by phone would destroy my chances of getting to her through him.

The muscle man moved to a position almost directly under me He poked the phone screen, then lifted it against his shiny head. Options flashed through my mind. Drop down on him. Kick him in the head. Find something to club him with. The idea of combat with anyone terrified me. Kicking JD, the cash house sentry, in the nose may have bloodied his nose, but it also launched me out the front door. This guy hauled far more muscle than JD. On my side, I had no weight, no inertia.

I hesitated, frozen by indecision. By hesitating, I got lucky.

His voice growled, deep and thick. "Zee Zee's car is here. The bag is on the hood of the car. There's something here you should see."

*Yes!*

As big and mean-looking and well-armed as this guy was, I guessed that he had no stomach for reading the message over the phone and calling Mauser an Asshole. Score one for creative writing!

"Yeah, it's clear."

He ended the call and took up station at the BMW's driver-side door.

A few minutes later the black Mercedes SUV pulled into the alley entrance and drove half its length, parking almost headlight to headlight with the BMW. Mauser slid out. He did not acknowledge his underling, whose posture had become rigid and alert. Muscle Man knew to stay on his toes and keep his distance.

Mauser stood at the grille of the BMW for a long minute. I rotated my body until my legs extended away from the Mercedes. I aimed myself at the top of the SUV and pushed silently off with my arms outstretched. I floated briefly, then caught a grip on the rack. I pulled myself hand over hand to the back of the vehicle and swung my legs down until my toes touched the back bumpers.

*Got you, you bastard!*

Mauser didn't move.

"Did you check the bag?"

Muscle Man shook his head.

"Do it."

Muscle Man tucked his weapon in his waistband and leaned over the fender. He picked up the bag, hesitantly shaking it up and down.

"It's empty."

"Open it."

He did.

Mauser examined the empty bag, then jerked his head toward the club's back door.

"Give me a minute, then get rid of this fucking car."

Muscle Man closed the club door in his wake. His departing body language said he was glad to be clear of the scene.

Mauser reached in his pocket and pulled out his phone. He touched a button on the screen. He stood with the phone to his ear, staring at the message in the dust, not moving. Whoever he called seemed in no hurry to pick up. When it went to voice mail, he lowered the phone and disconnected the call. He waited a moment. Touched the screen again. Held the phone to his ear again. He waited. Still no answer. He repeated the routine patiently, moving nothing but his hands.

Third time, someone answered.

"Because it's a fucking emergency, that's why. Who did you tell about the Pink House?"

He listened.

"Well, somebody knows."

He listened.

"I don't have time to explain. Are they moving?"

He listened.

"When?"

He listened and looked at his wristwatch.

"That should give me enough time."

He listened.

"Burned? You're sure?"

He listened and swung his head back and forth, a silent gesture that he either disagreed or saw folly in the path ahead. If he felt that way, he kept it to himself.

"Yes."

More instructions.

"Yes, I'll take care of it. This phone is done."

There were more instructions. Then the call ended without another word from Mauser. He stepped to the dumpster. He pulled the back off the phone and pulled out the sim card. He put it in his mouth and crunched down on it. Chewing, he smashed the phone against the edge of the dumpster and tossed it in. Then he walked to the opposite side of the alley to spit a spray of plastic chips. Finally, he walked back to the front of the BMW and ran his fingers through the dirty message until it resembled a child's finger painting.

He climbed into his expensive off-road limousine and drove out of the alley with me hanging from the luggage rack.

# 51

Mauser drove like an old woman. He sat idling at stop signs, allowing abundant gaps in the traffic to pass him by without pulling out. He rolled down the street below the speed limit. People tailgated him, making me exceedingly uncomfortable, perched on the back of the SUV. At one point, he idled at a green light while an angry driver immediately behind us in a Dodge Challenger shouted obscenities. I expected to witness another shooting. When the Challenger roared around Mauser, cutting close to his fender, it occurred to me that the driver had no idea how near to death he had danced.

It all made sense when Mauser eased around the same block twice. I dropped below the roofline of the SUV and looked forward at him. Chillingly, he stared straight back at me through the rearview mirror. He watched his mirrors more than he watched the road ahead.

Checking to see if anyone followed.

Having no weight, and without inertia to pull me from side to side on the turns, I found it surprisingly easy to hold on. The wind hit me and flowed around me, just as it would if I had been fully visible. I had time to find that interesting. Except for wind, my means of following Mauser worked surprisingly well.

I thought about Mauser's phone calls and drew a frightening conclusion. He, and whoever he talked to, knew as much about MPD's planned assaults on Pan D houses as the detectives in the squad room with Andy. If that wasn't bad enough, it sounded like the Pink House was not on the police map or on the list of houses about to be hit.

Mauser acknowledged that the Pink House had been burned by me and my message in the dust. He would have to assume I was someone within his own organization, making a bold or stupid move against him. He would know he was walking into a trap. He would be wary, and damned dangerous. I knew I couldn't count on upstairs windows or doors being left open. This time, I might need to force my way in.

Mauser drove. I held on.

# 52

Mauser's meandering path to avoid surveillance approached the ridiculous. Instead of angling back to the near north side of down-town, and the rows of decaying homes and foreclosures, he turned east. He took a series of turns that put him on Lincoln Memorial Drive, where he drove north along the lake. Cars lined parking spaces along the boulevard. The Sunday afternoon sun brought people to the beach by the hundreds. Sunbathers crowded the sand. Lake Michigan's blue water stretched east to infinity.

Mauser followed the Sunday traffic up a hill to Lake Drive, where his black Mercedes-Benz was just another family car. Antiquated mansions dominated the bluffs overlooking Lake Michigan. Women, fit and showing it off in expensive sports gear, followed tiny dogs on the sidewalks. Old money oozed past us on both sides of the vehicle.

After cruising a few blocks, Mauser slowed. I ducked down to see where he aimed his eyes. They scanned the street and then fixed on a property approaching on our right, on the lake side. A low stone wall divided by an open wrought iron gate protected a stucco Spanish-style mansion.

Pink stucco.

Mauser abruptly accelerated and cruised on. He drove several blocks, turned left, turned left again, and turned left a third time to re-join Lake Drive. He idled at the stop sign, letting the Sunday afternoon flow of traffic roll past in both directions. His methodical movements chilled me. In theory, he was keeping someone waiting—me. I had called him to a meeting at the

Pink House. He had to assume I waited in ambush for him, yet he displayed no urgency. I considered the possibility that his slow response served as a negotiating tactic. But what about Lane? If he held her at this Pink House wouldn't that have pushed him to hurry?

Not for the first time today, I recognized the possibility that I had this all wrong.

Riding aimlessly on the back of the SUV gave me too much time to think, too much time to doubt. I wanted to reach in my pocket and pull out the phone and call Andy to sound the alarm. I couldn't. It wasn't just my grip on the luggage rack that prevented me from using the phone. I couldn't see the phone. It had disappeared when I put it in my pocket. I would have to take it out and release it to have it pop back into the visible spectrum. Attempting to release the phone while surfing on the bumper of an SUV invited disaster.

A new worry surfaced. What if Mauser took a tactical approach to the Pink House? What if he parked several blocks away and skulked his way to the building? On the drive-by, I noted that ravines separated the Pink House from its neighbors on either side. The ravines were packed with vegetation and trees, offering ample cover for an approach. I would have no way of keeping up with him through something like that. Even shooting from tree to tree, I would end up shaking branches and leaves along the way. Or being blocked entirely while he slipped through some thicket or hedge.

Mauser put that fear to rest as we approached the property a second time. He slowed down and lit up the left directional signal. After letting a couple cars pass, he turned into the mansion's driveway.

The turn immediately raised my hopes of finding Lane. A sign had been posted along the cobblestone driveway. KEEP OUT. CONDEMNED. A sheaf of papers, some pink carbonless copies, hung stapled to the sign. Below that, block letters said, DEMOLITION AREA.

The mansion hardly seemed like a derelict waiting for demolition. I'd heard of this. Big money built and owned these homes. Bigger money came along and bought them, destroyed the old, and erected newer and grander monuments to capitalism. It had become a common, if controversial, practice around the lakes in Essex County.

Mauser rolled past the sign. He drove onto a cobblestone circle in front of the house. If he feared ambush, he wasn't showing it. I began to realize Mauser carried one weapon against which I had no chance: a ruthless will, unburdened by moral restraint or remorse. I had witnessed, firsthand, how effortlessly he flipped the switch from conversation to shooting a man in the face.

He stopped in front of the house. He allowed the motor to run while he studied the front door, the windows, and remnants of gardens lining either side of a walkway. Close up, this house showed neglect. Leafy debris cluttered the sidewalk. Weeds surged through layers of mulch in the gardens. The lawn had been mowed, but the clippings hadn't been blown off the walks or the driveway.

The last owner or occupant had departed some time ago. My stock in finding Lane rose.

I had no intention of releasing my grip on the luggage rack while he remained behind the wheel with the motor running. I watched Mauser through the tinted rear window. He dug his hands in his sports bag. I could not see what he was doing. After rummaging for a moment, he reached behind the front passenger seat and pulled something from the footwell— something rectangular and flat.

He turned off the motor and opened the door.

Instead of going to the front door, he stepped to the front of the SUV and crouched below my line of sight. I didn't want to work myself into an awkward position trying see what he was doing. If he made a move to enter the building, I needed to be ready. I wanted to enter with him.

Finished with the front of the vehicle, he walked around to the back. I feared he planned to open the rear hatch. I pulled myself up and swung my legs clear.

He didn't open the rear hatch. Instead, he held a license plate up and fixed it over the one already on the car. It must have been rigged with magnets for rapid deployment. Clever. I guessed that the plate was legitimate, perhaps stolen from someone with the same vehicle. It explained in part how Mauser maintained his ghost status, while the police all around him spied on vehicles with plate-reader systems. But why now? This didn't seem like the time or place for a routine security protocol prompting a plate change. Not when he had just arrived at what was almost certainly an ambush. Why the change?

Mauser extracted a black semi-automatic pistol from his waistband. I recognized the Berretta forty-caliber from visits to the range with Andy and some of the other Essex PD officers. Nine-millimeter will kill you. Forty-caliber guarantees you will not rise from the dead. He extracted a suppressor from a pocket and twisted it on the barrel, then held the weapon close at his side, finger inside the trigger guard, hammer pulled back for single-action firing. I didn't see or hear him rack the slide back, so I assumed he already had a round in the chamber.

He turned and regarded the house. Spans of geometrically divided windows lined the first floor, offering a view over trellised gardens and the cobblestone turnaround. Without curtains, the descending sun in the west invaded the windows and revealed empty rooms. Full-length windows and French doors on the second floor opened out onto stubby balconies, spaced along the front of the house. Mauser examined each window. He spent several minutes rooted to one spot, making an excellent target, apparently holding faith that whoever had challenged him by stealing Pan D's money wanted something other than his life.

I expected him to walk the perimeter of the house, and I prepared for it by making note of what had become a reliable means of movement—the gutters below the roof. From the top of the SUV, a flight to the gutter would be easy.

He didn't meet my expectation. Finished with his study of the front windows, he stepped up the walk toward the front door like he owned the place.

The front doors were tall, arched at the top, and regally constructed of heavy, dark, reddish wood. The Spanish style made the doors look like they'd been taken from some fortress Zorro planned to attack. I liked the doors. They were tall and wide. As Mauser approached, he fished in his pocket for a key. I pushed off the luggage rack and eased up the walk above and behind him.

He worked the key in the lock as my hands touched the stucco above his head. Bits of pink plaster fell, dusting Mauser's hands. He shot a look upward, directly at me, giving me a jolt. He brought the Berretta up fast. I froze, not just in answer to the instinctive fear that he'd seen me, but because my hands remained flat against the flaky plaster. Moving them would cause a cascade. I couldn't hold the position for long. Nothing gave me leverage to put pressure on the wall. I felt myself starting to float free.

Mauser's half-lidded eyes locked on the space I occupied. After a moment, he lowered the weapon and finished inserting the key. A heavy bolt clapped free. He pulled the door open. Mauser stood to one side with the gun at the ready, letting the door swing wide. I pulled myself in. More bits of plaster fell, but he didn't seem to care. His attention drilled the space inside the doors. He searched for threats in the shadows and angles of the interior.

I floated into a large foyer. Blue tiles spread like a pool beneath a waterfall of curled marble stairs. Matched sets of steps curved upward on the left and right. A huge wood and iron chandelier hung directly ahead of me. I drifted to the chandelier and grabbed it.

Mauser closed the door behind him. He strolled to the center of the foyer, taking a position beneath the chandelier. For a moment, I considered the mechanics of dropping the iron monster on his head, Errol Flynn style. Heavy bolts anchoring the fixture to a blue and white ceiling put the fantasy notion to rest.

"Where's my fucking money?" Mauser asked, affecting a flat, hostile drawl.

I cupped my hands over my mouth. A grade-school trick, trying to send my voice. It had worked with Earl.

"Who's the girl?"

Mauser looked sharply left and right. Then up. Then over his shoulder at me. Seeing nothing, he moved toward an expansive parlor to the left of the door. The complex inlaid wood floor gleamed, heavily waxed and contrasting the tile in the foyer. He stepped to the borderline between the two spaces and stood still, listening, looking.

"Party favor," he replied.

# 53

M y heart hammered. *She's here!*
Mauser moved back into the foyer. "Why? You want her? You can have her. Soon as I get my money back."

I repositioned myself on the assumption that if she was here, she was in an upstairs room.

"Keep your party favor," I said. "Two million, or we keep hitting you. We keep taking from you."

Mauser laughed. It echoed in the empty space, hollow and cold. "Good fucking luck with that." Even as he said it, he hurried across the foyer to the opposite entrance of a front room. He held the gun out in firing position. Not some TV gangsta stance with the weapon turned flat on its side. He used a two-handed grip, shoulders squared, knees bent, the product of serious firearms training.

"You got balls, motherfucker," Mauser swung the weapon high then low, head cocked, reading the sound. "I don't know how you hit Zee Zee today. I'll find out. Whatever you did, it won't happen again. Whatever you did, you had help. I'll find out who. I'll take them apart slowly. They'll give you up. Then I'll take you apart bone by bone."

"I intend to alter the paradigm, Mauser." His body language tensed, hearing his own words turned on him. He swung the pistol back and forth, straining to find the sound's source. I worried he might start shooting out of sheer rage. I cupped my hands in another direction. "You have twenty-four hours. Two million. The same spot behind Faze. Leave Cro-Magnon Man in his cave this time."

I made my move. I pushed off the chandelier aiming for the left-side stairs where blemishes in the plaster suggested family portraits or fine art had once graced the curve above the marble steps.

I approached the wall with my arms extended, made contact, and used my momentum to vector toward the upstairs landing. Mauser scanned back and forth between the rooms at the front of the house. Abruptly, he dashed between the sweeping staircases toward the back of the house.

I had bet Lane was in an upstairs bedroom. Was I wrong?

I uttered the Test Pilot's Prayer—*Please, God, don't let me screw up!*

I reached the upstairs landing area. Hallways spread out left and right forming a junction with a third hallway extending deep into the house. I gripped the railing at the top of the stairs and swung over into a nearly normal posture on the landing.

I gambled again. It seemed unlikely they would keep her at the front of the house. The windows for all the front rooms, seen from the outside, had no curtains, no sheets of cardboard or plywood, to shield what was inside from outside eyes. They wouldn't take that chance. I ruled out the rooms to my right and left.

Below me, I heard a door slam somewhere in the back of the house.

I needed leverage and speed of movement.

*Fwooomp!* I came back from *gone* and hurried down the hall under my own weight and on my feet again, instantly stabbed with pain in my midsection. It quickly became apparent that the home's façade, facing the front lawn and road beyond, was not the greater dimension of the building which stretched farther toward the lake than I expected. Midway down the hallway, it suddenly split into two balconies circumnavigating a round, open atrium. I was about to break right when Mauser darted into view returning from the back of the house.

Whether he saw movement or heard my footsteps, he reacted by dropping into a firing stance. I dropped to the floor. I heard *Snap-snick! Snap-snick! Snap-snick!* Holes appeared in the wall above me. Plaster bits dropped onto the naked wood floor around me.

*Shit!*

Mauser's expensive running shoes squeaked on the floor as he dashed out of sight again, retreating to the back of the house. There had to be a rear stairwell. He would climb the stairs in a moment. I didn't need to be told the difference between a target you can see, and one you can't.

*Fwooomp!* Gone again, I had an awkward moment on the floor of the hallway. I pushed myself upright and shoved off the wall to gain a grip on the balcony rail. Then I pulled hard to soar over the balcony on a straight shot through the atrium toward the remainder of the upstairs hallway.

Flying down the hallway, I hooked the first doorway, pulled myself into position, and twisted the knob. Using my fingers to grip the frame, I pushed the door open. An empty room.

I twisted and shot myself across the hall to the next door, glancing in both directions to see if Mauser ascended the stairs. So far, no. Using the same motion and geometry, I opened the second door. Nothing.

As I reached the third door, on the left, something happened that threw me into near panic.

*FWOOOOMP!* The sound broke louder, sharper, and stronger than I had ever heard in my head. I looked down expecting to see I had fallen out of the disappeared state, expecting that *the other thing* had failed. In an instant, my mind ran through the disaster that would follow. Not now! Not this moment of all moments!

I remained *gone.*

*Then what was—?*

I smelled it. First, the fragrant chemical cocktail of gasoline, then the scent of something burning. I looked to the rear of the house. At the end of the hallway a stairway dropped to the first floor. I couldn't see the stairway, but I saw the smoke rising from it.

Fire! Mauser had lit the rear of the home on fire! He cut me off.

I counted. Four more doors to check. I turned back to the one at hand, turned the knob, pushed it open.

A darkened room spread before me as the door opened, exposing empty space like a curtain sweeping aside to reveal a stage.

Earl's words came unbidden to mind. *Some things you can't unsee.*

Lane.

In a starkly empty room, a naked Lane curled tightly into herself at the foot of the wall immediately to my right. Her dark skin gleamed with sweat. Small light seeped around the edges of plywood that had been nailed to the windows. The thin light outlined her shape and dimension. She looked tiny and alone. She heard the door open and tightened her arms around her knees. Something looked wrong, and it took me a moment to recognize it.

A dull gunmetal collar circled her neck, and a heavy chain hung from it, curving up to a heavy metal plate in the wall. The plate and chain looked capable of holding a dump truck. More than that, they had her head encased in what looked like a close-fitting leather helmet. It had a breathing hole, but otherwise covered her entire head.

At that instant I knew murder existed in my heart.

I took one last glance at the hallway. Smoke curled at the far end, near the back of the house, a short forty feet away. He wouldn't come that way. Looking the other way, I expected to see Mauser charging toward me behind his handgun. Not seeing him—

*Fwooomp!*

—I reappeared.

I ducked in the room and closed the door behind me. At the sound, Lane jolted, shoving herself back against the wall defensively.

"Lane!" I called to her. I crossed the room and put a hand on her shoulder.

The shot she gave me came out of nowhere. She transformed into a storm of flailing arms and legs. A blow caught me on the side of the head and took my balance, driving me into the wall. Blows rained down on me. She kicked and caught me on the knees, in the ribs. For a split second, I feared she might smash into my pelvic bones and split them again, assuming I hadn't already done so today.

"Lane! It's—!" A flat-hand slap landed on my face. I threw up my hands, first in defense, then to try and restrain her. Each time I closed a hand on one arm, the other would pound it free. Her muscles coiled, rigid. Her fingernails raked me. Under the mask, muted, she screamed.

*Christ, we don't have time for this!* I thought. At any second, Mauser would burst through the door and finish us both.

I did the only thing I could think of. I dove on her and wrapped my arms around her, pinning her arms at her sides. Her legs kicked, but I was too close. She struggled and slipped on her own sweat. She screamed under the mask.

"LANE!" I shouted into the side of the mask. "IT'S WILL!"

She didn't stop. She twisted away from me, trying to break free.

"WHO YOU GONNA FLY FOR?"

She froze.

"It's Will, honey," I said, catching my breath. "Who you gonna fly for?"

The fight evaporated. She went limp. She pulled her hands away and pressed them to my chest, my chin, my face, reading with her fingers. I eased my grip on her and let her touch, search, and verify.

"Who you gonna fly for, honey?"

She made a sound through the horrible mask, but I couldn't understand. I pushed back and found a strap drawn tight under her chin. The strap circled her neck. At the back, the two ends were joined by a small padlock. I pulled a pocketknife from my jeans and sawed through the strap. The instant it came loose, her hands shot up and she clawed the hood off. She threw it across the room where it landed with a sick slap on the floor. Sweat plastered her hair to her head and face.

She took long enough to look at me, to absorb that it was really me, before her eyes flooded and she shook uncontrollably, quaking as her body erupted in sobs. She threw her arms around me and pulled tight.

"Am-Amer-American Airlines!" she cried.

I pulled her close. She drove herself into me, seeking refuge.

In that instant, so close, I knew—*knew*—without question or doubt who had done this to her. Fury boiled up inside me.

"Lane, we have to get out of here," I whispered directly into her ear. "There's someone here and he's got a gun, and we have to get out."

Her head nodded, but I still had to work myself free. We parted. She curled tightly into a ball.

I looked at the door. Mauser had to know I was here. He had to be coming. Any second now.

I turned back and scooped up the chain connected to her collar. My hopes crashed when I saw the collar construction. Steel, with the chain bolted tightly to the back of the collar. I saw blood on the nut and bolt. I followed the chain up the wall where it was bolted to a steel plate. More blood. I looked at Lane's fingers and understood.

I grabbed the chain and put my weight into it, but the plate on the wall didn't quiver. Four heavy bolts held the plate to the wall, driven into structure that would not give. A lightspeed assessment told me I needed a tool or a weapon.

"Lane, I gotta get something to break you free, a tool."

Still sobbing, she bobbed her head. Her hand shot out and closed on my arm, giving a squeeze. I put a hand over hers and squeezed back.

"Just a few minutes. I'll only be a few minutes."

I hurried to the door and gingerly opened it expecting to find Mauser standing in the frame with his half-open eyes and the devil's grin.

I found something worse.

Black smoke clouded the far end of the hall, bubbling like inverted flood waters along the ceiling, pushing toward me. I made an instant decision and ducked back into the room.

I pulled out the phone, balanced the odds of getting the fastest result, and instead of calling Andy, dialed 9-1-1.

"Nine-one-one, what is your emergency?" The voice sounded irritatingly calm.

"Fire. House on fire. Man with a gun. This location. Pink mansion on

Lake Drive. Send cops and fire trucks," I said. Without answering her next question, I laid the phone on the floor and shoved it across the room to Lane, leaving the line open, praying the operator could determine the location from the call, because I had no idea of the address.

"Be right back!" I called out to Lane. "Stay on the line with them!"

She picked up the phone. I slipped into the hall.

The smoke hadn't reached the door yet. I limped in the opposite direction, looking for something to use to free Lane, a lever or tool, anything that might twist the chain, or break through the wall.

Mauser's car!

His car had to have a jack, and the tools to work it.

I wanted to run, but my body would have none of it. After a few hard steps, the pain shooting up my center brought a veil of darkness to my eyes.

*Fwooomp!* I disappeared.

I grabbed the nearest door jamb and pushed as hard as I could. I shot up the center of the hallway. If Mauser came this way now, we would collide, and I would do my best to snap the bastard's neck on impact.

I shot across the open atrium at the center of the house, up the short hallway to the landing at the top of the stairs. I reached out to grab the railing and vector myself downward to the front door.

I closed a grip on the railing and started to alter course—then grabbed with all I had to stop myself.

*Mauser!*

My body swung over the railing. I threw out an arm to stop before my head hit the edge of the second-floor landing.

He stood in the foyer.

I righted myself. Mauser stood beside a plastic milk crate. He reached into it and pulled out a Mason jar. He unscrewed the lid and sent half the contents left, and half the contents right, across the polished tile floor. The thick petroleum perfume of high-octane gasoline clouded the room.

Two more open jars sat open on the floor, at the foot of each set of stairs, where the spreading fuel now touched them. Two more sat on the stairs, one on each set, halfway up.

*Burned.* He wasn't talking about the location being found out, and 'burned' in the clandestine sense. He had been told to burn the location. To burn Lane alive. There was no hiding that this was arson. He didn't care. That's why he had changed his license plates. If someone saw him driving away, and someone surely would, with the smoke now rising from the back of the house, it wouldn't matter. Two blocks away, he would toss those license plates into the street and be gone.

The back of the house burned. In seconds, he would ignite the front of the house. Eliminating Lane. And maybe in the bargain, eliminating whoever he thought had stolen from him, whoever challenged him.

Satisfied with his work, he pulled the weapon from his waistband and removed the suppressor. One shot, the muzzle flash hitting the fuel on the floor, and the vapor now rising from it, and the entire foyer would light up. He would have enough time to escape out the front door before the flame ignited the open jars. After that, the entire space would fill with rolling fire.

Gasoline does not burn. There would be no dramatic rivulet of flame racing across the floor, no race to beat it. Gasoline explodes. This would be over in a literal flash.

I'd never make it to the car. I would die in the first explosion and Lane would die slowly.

Mauser opened the front door behind him. Securing his exit path, he crouched and aimed the weapon where the spilled gasoline had spread on the expensive Spanish tiles.

I jerked myself over the railing and pushed hard for the left side stairs.

"Hey asshole!" I shouted.

Mauser looked up sharply.

"The price just went up. Three million, or we send the cops your boss's identity!"

I shot across the open foyer space, grabbed the descending handrail and swung over it.

"Burn in hell, motherfucker!" Mauser said, lowering the barrel of the gun to the floor.

"Oh, you don't think I'm actually there with you, dumbass?" I pulled myself down to where the mason jar sat on one of the marble steps. Too high! I needed to reposition to reach the jar, and then reposition again to be able to use it. It would take too long.

"As a matter of fact, I do," Mauser said coldly.

I had no choice.

*Fwooomp!* I reappeared as a full figure, hovering above the steps. Gravity pulled me down abruptly. I threw my legs forward and landed on my butt with the open jar between my knees. The pain was murderous.

Mauser gaped at me, his face showing the first true emotion I'd seen, genuine astonishment. It bought me a moment. I picked up the jar with both hands and launched it toward the chandelier. Gasoline sprayed an arc of amber sparkles, caught in the remnants of setting sun that angled through the foyer windows. The jar hit the iron rim of the chandelier and shattered.

"What the fuck!" Mauser's eyes, fully open for first time I'd seen, tried to take in what he had just seen, and grasp the shower falling on him. Time expanded. I saw the glass shards of the jar spreading in the spray. I saw his eyes. I saw the gun swing up from the floor.

I planted my feet on the step where the jar had been and launched, not standing, not even trying to find balance or attempt to run. I kicked as hard as I could and—

*Fwooomp!*

—disappeared, shedding weight and shooting back up the stairs.

Mauser, reacting like the animal he was—

BANNNGGG!

—he fired a shot at where I had been. I'll never know how close it came or where his bullet hit. To him, I was an apparition, impossible to comprehend, but not impossible to shoot. Shooting followed on instinct.

His worst and last.

Mauser fired into the descending shower of gasoline. The muzzle blast from a Berretta forty-caliber handgun extended only a few inches, but it was enough. The shower spreading around him ignited, wrapping him in living fire.

I shot up the stairs, hit the railing with one shoulder and bounced off it. When the fireball ignited, I was nearly centered on the upstairs hallway. The pressure wave hit me like a truck made of heat and light and unimaginable power. I had no chance. The blast launched me down the hallway, tumbling. Doorways blew past me. The atrium swept under me. I got one hand up and caught the edge of the entrance to the second hallway. It slowed me but didn't stop me. I clawed at door frames. Each bite I got altered my trajectory, slamming me into the walls.

I slowed but couldn't gain control. Billowing smoke from the first fire came at me from the back of the house. If I continued, I would shoot into it like an airplane entering a cloud. Death curled and roiled in that black cloud.

*Fwooomp!* I dropped out of the disappeared state and gravity yanked me to the carpeted floor. I skidded to a stop. It hurt, but the pain was a distant concern compared to what I saw coming.

Black smoke boiled from the back of the house. The smoke reached Lane's door. I rolled to my feet and grabbed the doorknob. I let myself in and slammed the door behind me. Hungry black smoke curled in with me. The black smoke would kill us. Not just the smoke and its toxins. Inside the smoke pouring along the hallway ceiling like an ugly inverted river, was heat. Hundreds of degrees of heat. The firefighters Andy and I knew in Essex explained it to me in grim detail. People caught in black rolling smoke breathe in heat that sears the throat and the inside of lungs like meat on a grille. Even if they survive long enough to be carried out of the building, there's little hope.

Lane startled. She looked at me with wide eyes, filled first with tears and second with brimming, growing terror. She held the phone to her ear.

"They're coming. I couldn't tell them where, but the lady thinks she knows." She held the phone toward me. "She wants to talk to you."

"Not now!" I ran across the room to the windows. They had been covered with plywood sheets nailed to the window frames. Whoever had done it, had counted on the chain and collar to restrain Lane, because each sheet was held in place by a single nail at the corners.

I found room between the wall and the plywood for my fingers. I planted a foot against the wall and yanked the corner. The first nail screamed and came out, releasing the lower right corner. I repositioned my foot and my grip and yanked out the lower left nail. Now the whole sheet could be lifted upward like a hatch. Leverage drew out the remaining nails which protested with metallic howls.

I started to toss the plywood aside, then changed my mind. Grabbing it near the center, I stepped back and charged the window. The plywood shattered the glass above and below the center sash. The frame cracked. I hauled back and hit it again. The center of the frame snapped. Pieces fell out into the evening light. I stepped back and used the plywood sheet to smash the remaining pieces out, clearing the frame. Then I threw the plywood out. I pulled the broken frames away from the window, throwing out wood and glass shards until the opening was clear except for fragments of shattered glass on the sill and the floor.

"Will!" Lane shrieked.

I turned around. She pointed at the door.

The door had turned black. Smoke boiled up from the space at the bottom of the door. It climbed to the ceiling. Black death spread above us. I instantly regretted throwing the plywood sheet out the window. It might have been used to block the bottom of the door.

"Lane, scoot up against the wall!" I gestured with my hands. She did as I ordered. The chain hung limp.

I gathered the chain in my hands then doubled it near the plate on the wall, creating a loop about twelve inches long. It drew the rest of the chain and Lane's neck, tight. She stared up at me wide-eyed, but if it hurt, she said nothing.

Now with the loop in hand, I twisted it. As it twisted, it shortened and stiffened. Eventually, it would turn no more. It formed a short lever in my hands. I worked the lever around until it found resistance against the loop and bolt on the wall plate. I threw my weight onto it.

The chain-lever moved slowly. I felt metal bend. I pushed harder.

"C'mon! You motherfucker!" I uttered through gritted teeth. The lever gave a little, then a little more. "C'MON!"

"WILL!" Lane cried. I followed her eyes. The smoke monster filled the ceiling above us. It descended, rolling closer and closer to my head.

I heaved, jerked, and jammed the chain-lever. It gave a little, then remained rigid. I shouted at it as I pushed harder, then harder still. It gave a little, then stopped. Heat touched my head. My eyes burned. Smoke filled in around me.

I pushed harder still. Somewhere in my midsection, my pelvis screamed back at me as my legs added all they had to the fight.

The chain gave, then held.

The smoke pushed past my head and the heat and burning became unbearable.

I let go.

I fell to the floor beside Lane. She looked at me with open terror on her face.

"Please, I don't want to die!" she cried.

In falling to the floor, the chain-lever I had created had released, and now the chain hung loose, mocking me. I grabbed it and howled at it. I leaned back and jerked against the wall plate. I slammed myself against rigid resistance.

*Nothing!*

The smoke dropped below the wall plate. The wall plate disappeared. The heat bore down on us. Lane ducked farther and farther down to the floor. I lost my grip on the chain. It had become wet. I had no idea my hands were bleeding.

Lane grabbed my arm. "You have to go!"

"No!" I tried again to find a grip on the chain, but the smoke pressed down from above. The window that had taunted us with salvation disappeared in the black. Wisps of smoke swept into the night. The remaining air between the smoke and the floor thinned to almost nothing and we both fell flat against the floor.

"Will, please! Tell Mommy I love her, please GO!" Lane cried and pushing at me with her hands.

Heat attacked us from above. Black smoke sank around us. I knew it wasn't just smoke. I knew it was filled with combustible gases. With one spark, would ignite everything in this room.

I couldn't leave her.

She cried, and in her sobs and tears she repeated one word over and over.

"Mommy!"

Just a child. Just a child, alone, crying and I had nothing to give her. The chain would never let go. I felt a despair blacker than the smoke falling upon us.

I did the only thing I had left, not knowing if it would mean anything against the searing death that owned us.

I threw my arms around her so that she would not die alone. She threw her arms and legs around me and held on tight. She cried for her Mommy. As the heat built up, moments away from burning our throats and lungs with the few breaths we had left, I tried to give her a cool barrier.

*FWOOOMP!*

I pushed everything I had in my mind into those imaginary levers. Balls to the wall. The cool spread across my skin and became an electric cool where it touched Lane. With the last light thinning to blackness in the space below the smoke, I saw through her. She vanished. The collar around her neck, the collar that would kill her, vanished. Half the length of the chain vanished. Where the other half hung in the air, the end looked faded, almost frayed.

The window.

*The window.*

It wasn't rational thought. It didn't come as words in my head. It came as instinct. My mind fixed on the window and on the air beyond where we would live.

Here we die.

There we live.

The sensation came as a tug at the center of my body, a shift in momentum where there had been no momentum. Inertia when I had no inertia. We had gone weightless. The floor suddenly shifted below us, and it took me a second to realize we were moving, not the floor.

After that, everything blurred. Motion. A tug and snap. The chain whipped past us.

We shot through the smoke, through the window, into clear night air. Whatever moved us came from something at our center. A directional pressure, a propulsion I couldn't describe.

Lane held me tightly. I held her against my chest with a grip that must have hurt, thinking I would never let go.

Behind us, the window belched smoke. A blast of flame burst into the night and lit up the yard as the flashover ignited anything and everything that had been combustible in that room.

We didn't float. We flew. We flew across open lawn. Surrounding trees reflected the conflagration glow. We crossed a driveway leading to a carriage house and shot into a stand of trees bordering the ravine at the edge of the property.

Branches brushed us, then bit into us. A stiff bough caught me on one shoulder. I threw out my free arm and closed a grip on a branch. The branch bent but held. We stopped.

We floated, free of the fire and heat, twenty feet above the lawn.

I felt Lane moving, breathing. She cried—then she stopped crying. It was stranger than strange, feeling her body wrapped around me, clinging to me, unseen. I wanted to move my hands, to be sure of holding her, but remembered she had no clothing. Groping around her skin struck me as a bad idea. I kept one hand on the branch, the other firmly around her back and on her shoulder. She had no weight. Holding her required no effort, yet I held tightly.

Lane gave no sign of releasing her own desperate embrace, her arms around my waist, her legs around my hips.

Which hurt. I thanked God for the pain.

She spoke. Her voice sounded small against the now roaring fire.

"Are we dead?"

"People keep asking me that." We burst into a helpless, heat-releasing, life-affirming laugh. We laughed until we gasped for air. Then she cried, and I felt her sobs as tremors through her body.

Finally, her body and her breathing steadied. She sniffled and coughed. I felt her lift her head and look around. Hesitantly, she said, "Mr. Stewart, is there something you need to tell me?"

"Kiddo, you have no idea. I swear on my pilot's license, I will tell you all about it. Later. Right now, let's just—um, hang out?"

This brought another tension-releasing laugh.

Approaching sirens wailed. We hung from a tree branch twenty feet up on the perimeter of the property and watched the Pink House engulf itself in flame. Window after window blew out, pouring smoke into the sky like an inverted black waterfall. At the front of the house Mauser's Mercedes-Benz SUV glittered with reflections. The SUV wasn't burning, but something on the cobblestones near it swirled with flames. An indistinguishable heap, parts angled in all directions.

Mauser.

Asshole.

# 54

"Lane, I have to ask you some questions."

"Okay."

"When they took you, they put you in an SUV."

"They put me under a really stinky blanket."

"And you cut yourself and wrote your initials—" I stopped. Son of a bitch. I choked up. I felt so proud of her, so awed by her courage. I coughed to clear it away. "You wrote your initials in the carpet."

"Uh-huh. I wanted Mama to know I was there."

"Did you come here, directly here, to this place? Were there any stops?"

"They took me out of one car and put me in another car. Then we came here, but when they took me out of the first car, they put that mask on me. It had something stuck in my mouth. I couldn't see, and I couldn't talk."

"Okay."

Fire trucks reached the driveway. Led by a command vehicle, they streamed onto the property. I counted five fire vehicles, then two police cars. Then an ambulance. They rolled onto the lawn, through gardens, taking up advantageous positions to battle the blaze.

"One more question, and then we have to move. They took you to that room. Did someone come to you? I know you don't have any way of knowing time, but it would have been hours and hours ago."

"Yes."

"I need to know this. Did he touch you?"

"He didn't rape me!" She said it firmly. It wasn't shame. It wasn't denial.

238

It was Lane, being specific, being clear. "I can't see you, but you're blushing now, Mr. Stewart, because you blush all the time when Andy says things."

"You got me there."

"He didn't rape me. But he took my clothes away from me and he tried to touch me. I fought with him. I thought he was going to—you know. But he didn't."

"Good. Good, honey. I'm so glad." She was a fighter. I had the bruises to prove it.

"He took pictures."

I felt her tuck her head into my shoulder.

"He took pictures of me, with one of those cameras that shoots the picture out right away, the kind that sort-of fades into a picture?"

"Polaroid."

"I guess. I heard it every time he took a picture."

She didn't speak for a moment.

"He touched me—while he was doing that. But he didn't touch me after that."

I hugged her firmly.

"One more thing. I'm going to take you down there and get you taken care of. But you can't say anything about—well, about this. They'd never believe you anyway. You can't say anything about me."

"They asked me who you were."

"Who did?"

"The operator. The 9-1-1 operator. They asked who was with me."

I forgot about that.

"Okay. Then you can tell them I came and got you out, but don't tell them about—*this*." That would mean Andy would know by now that I was in the burning building. I couldn't leave her wondering, Christ, not again. "When you see Andy, you tell her I was with you, and tell her we got out the window and went for the trees, okay? Tell her I'm fine, okay? She worries."

"Okay."

"It's not a lie because it's true."

"Okay."

"Just leave out the fun part. Promise?"

"Promise."

"Good. We gotta go."

# 55

The ambulance parked on the lawn with the rear doors spread open. Firefighters deployed portable extinguishers and doused what was left of Mauser. The ambulance crew looked him over. The best EMTs in the world weren't going to do him any good.

The 9-1-1 operator knew a child had been in the building. They knew about me because I made the call, and Lane told them who I was. They would be looking for a child and an adult. With the building engulfed, I don't think anyone held out much hope. Mauser had been thorough, and the gasoline had been efficient.

The sooner the firefighters knew we weren't inside, the less chance someone would get hurt looking for us.

The EMTs stood near the back of the unit, watching the big house burn. The driver's side of the unit faced the tree line and offered us cover from the dozens of firefighters working around the burning building.

I pushed off and descended toward lower branches. It should have been awkward with Lane holding me tightly, but she had no weight or inertia. I felt the chain from the collar around her neck. It floated along with us, once or twice tangling with small branches. I wanted to coil it, but feared releasing my grip on Lane, in case it released her from *the other thing*.

When we reached the lowest branches, I halted. My feet nearly touched the ground. The ambulance sat on the grass thirty yards away. I worked up an angle and moved into position, then pushed off the last branch. We floated across the grass.

Lane, still hitching aftershock sobs, now giggled. I shushed her.

At the ambulance, I caught the large side mirror. I repositioned, then pushed. We floated to the open rear door. I grabbed the edge of the door.

"Hang on," I whispered to Lane.

*Fwooomp!*

I dropped onto the grass. Lane became a weight in my arms, and a terrible pressure on my body. The chain slapped down against her back. I let out a sudden, involuntary groan and she released herself quickly. She looked up at me, her face streaked with tears and soot, her eyes wet, her hair matted. I've seen few things more beautiful.

"Are you okay?"

"Fine," I lied, but my face told the truth. She pulled me down and kissed me on the cheek.

"Your mom will come for you," I said. "Make sure you tell those EMTs that I got out. Tell Andy I'm fine. Tell her I had something I needed to do right away. Couldn't wait. Tell her I will call her as soon as I can get to a phone."

"That's all true, right?"

"All true. You won't be lying."

She nodded solemnly. Such things carried weight with Lane.

I poked my head around the ambulance door. Two EMTs stood absorbed by sight of the fire. I ducked back and did one more thing. I lifted the end of the chain in my hand and examined it. The chain simply ended on an intact link.

I dropped it and guided Lane around the edge of the door so that the EMTs could see us.

"Hey!" They turned, startled, then registered that a young girl stood with me, wearing nothing but the steel collar. "Get a bolt cutter and get this fucking thing off of her! And get a blanket around her! Now!"

My face was sooty, my clothes a wreck. They had no idea who I was, or why I had tears running down my cheeks, or why I had pain etched in every muscle of my face, but they knew "Victim" when they saw it and authority when they heard it, and they jumped. I pushed Lane gently in their direction and slipped behind the geometry of the door hanging open, to where they couldn't see me.

*Fwooomp!*

Gone.

# 56

I returned to the tree line to avoid being hit by moving vehicles and running firefighters. I watched as the EMTs, full of purpose, rushed to attend to Lane. One swept a blanket around her and seated her on the cot inside the truck. He fussed over her while the other jogged to a toolbox on a nearby truck. He returned with a large bolt cutter and snapped the collar free.

The murder in my heart solidified, becoming something hard, impervious. I knew where I had to go and what I would do when I got there.

More trucks arrived. Heat from the gigantic fire reached across the lawn. Some of the first trucks to arrive pulled back.

Andy and Rosemary II arrived in an unmarked car. I heard her coming long before I saw her. She made that V8 engine scream on Lake Drive. She took miles and miles off the tires when she skidded to a halt and bounced the sedan into the driveway, bottoming the suspension violently, scattering cops at the perimeter. The headlights swept across the back of the ambulance, illuminating Lane where she huddled in the back of the rescue unit. For a second, I thought Andy hadn't even put the car in Park before she and Rosemary II jumped out the doors, but the old Crown Vic stayed put, humming.

Lane saw them and leaped out of the EMTs care.

Rosemary II swept up her daughter. They fell to their knees and cried in each other's arms.

Andy gave them a moment then dropped to a crouch and took Lane's face in her hands. I couldn't hear Andy over the roaring fire, but I knew what she asked, the words coming urgently. Lane spoke quickly, earnestly.

Andy asked something else. Lane shook her head. No, she didn't know where I had gone.

Andy stood and darted to the side of the ambulance where the full fury of the conflagration lit up the night and turned the twilight sky black in contrast. She pushed her hands through her thick hair, looking in vain for me. After a moment, she returned to kneel beside the reunited mother and daughter. She spoke to Lane again. Lane took her hand and pointedly told Andy I was fine. Good girl. She and her mother pulled Andy into their embrace. Looking at the three of them, my throat constricted again. My damned eyes became wet and blurry.

To shake off the emotion, I stole the police car.

# 57

I had murder in mind.

I backed Andy's Crown Vic out of the driveway and hooked the wheel around sharply. A cop waved for me to Get The Hell Out Of The Way, so I did. More rubber gone from the abused tires.

I wove through a cordon of patrol cars deployed on Lake Drive. Once free and clear, I accelerated south against the now blocked and stopped northbound traffic. In the car's mirrors, flames rose above the trees.

I have a reasonable knowledge of the streets of Milwaukee. Andy and I have dined on Water Street. We've parked on and walked the lakefront on Lincoln Memorial Drive. I don't think I've ever been up Lake Drive before, and after tonight I didn't think I would be invited back. I had a general idea I wanted to be downtown, where Wisconsin Avenue runs east and west. I guessed my destination to be north of Wisconsin Avenue, more than likely on the east side of the river, nestling in the land of high-priced real estate.

Racing up a narrow street lined with rich old homes mingled with what I took to be upscale restaurants, I spotted a valet parking station. I slammed on the brakes and dove the Crown Vic on its wallowing suspension into a short driveway. Two attendants jumped back, startled that I had bombed into their perimeter so violently, and that anyone looking like I did would show up at this restaurant in a car like this. They answered the question I asked by pointing over the hood of the car.

There, against the remnants of twilight, stood a high residential tower sheathed in blue and silver glass, lined vertically with balconies.

I thanked the boys for their guidance, disappointed them on the question of a tip, threw the car in reverse and launched into the street again. There are good reasons why Crown Vic cop cars have no hubcaps.

A few minutes later, I parked beside a fire hydrant beneath the glass tower. I killed the car engine and threw the keys under the front seat.

I took a moment to breathe and take stock.

The shining condo tower rose twenty or so stories above a reasonably quiet street, three or four blocks north of Cathedral Square, a green space where Andy and I had once stumbled on a summer evening of jazz played for hundreds of listeners spread out on the grass. Restaurants lined the west perimeter of the park, and from them a maddeningly delicious-smelling scent hung in the solemn evening air. I realized that I hadn't eaten today, and probably hovered on the edge of dehydration. On top of hunger, I realized I had badly abused my healing bones. I found crusted blood on the outside of my left forearm and had no idea what had gouged me. Working the chain at the Pink House reopened the gouge in my thumb. Blood coated my palm. I had a howling bruise on the back of my right shoulder. I felt stinging on my neck. In the rearview mirror, I saw three lines of broken skin running into my shirt collar. It made me smile. Lane's fingernails. My face had soot between my nostrils and upper lip, and at the corners of my eyes. Paths of soot ran down my cheeks, the mark of tears. My hair had been matted ever since Rosemary II jolted Andy and me out of a sound sleep about a million hours ago, so that didn't count. In all, I thought I might make a good candidate for a role in a zombie film. I certainly felt dead enough.

I realized as I took inventory that my muscles were stiffening. I needed to move. If I sat much longer, I might not be able to move at all.

I had no guarantee that Pan D, the man, the monster, would be in residence. If not, then there would be time to lick my wounds and restore my strength while I waited for him.

I would wait all night if I had to.

I stepped out of the car. I immediately missed my crutches. A jolt of pain shot up my guts and I faltered. If not for a grip on the car door, I would have dropped to the street.

Two men walking a tiny hairless dog cast judgmental glances at me but chose not to intervene with someone so obviously drunk. I considered simply vanishing before their eyes, in part to take the weight off my legs, and in part to give something back to the deeply disapproving looks they painted on me and my stolen car, and the fire hydrant against which I parked. I didn't. They passed and took their disapproval with them.

I worked my way to the trunk of the car, then crouched. Whether anyone watched at that point or not, I didn't give a rat's—

*Fwooomp!*

Relief lifted me and flooded my skin. *The other thing* wrapped itself around me and lent a thick, cool sensation to my entire body. I wondered, suddenly, how much this had shielded Lane and me from the hot gases we passed through as we shot toward the window.

*And how did that happen, exactly? How did we move?*

*How did that chain snap?*

I pushed the questions aside.

I had a murder to commit.

Rising now, with a grip on the Crown Vic, I surveyed the street and the building.

Cars lined the curb, filling all available parking spaces. Milwaukee uses electronic parking, which gets paid at kiosks set on random corners. Instead of meters, spaces are delineated by posts with numbered plaques. The posts offered handy grips, and I used them to float to the corner for a better look at the building.

The entrance extended from the structure as a glass cube. Two sets of glass doors had to be negotiated to enter the building. Between the two doors stood a styled pedestal with a glowing LCD touchscreen. Entry required possession of a passcode. Reaffirming the security features no doubt coveted by the rich residents of this glass tower, I counted four cameras fixed on the front of the building and in the entry cube. Inside, sitting behind a desk in a marble lobby, a security guard watched the world go by through layers of glass.

I could try to squeeze in with someone, or possibly create a commotion that would draw the security guard out, creating an opening, but the game would have to be played for both doors.

Even if I managed to get into the lobby, and into the elevator, it might require another layer of security codes or keys to get the elevator to open on the penthouse.

I looked up. The building seemed to sway against the darkening sky and the stars that had begun their silent nightly sparkle. A symmetrical row of balconies ran up the side of the glass tower. Lights cast signs of life through full-length windows. Urban living at its finest.

From one parking post to the next, I worked into position near the front of the building. The security guard seemed to stare directly at me. Cameras recorded the empty space I occupied. I chose a conservative line that would take me across the sidewalk, up the side of the cube. I cleared my airspace, left and right, and pushed off. I reached out and gained a grip on the top edge of the clear, waist-height balcony wall. These were not balconies for people with high anxiety. The clear half wall gave the impression of no wall at all. It explained in part why these balconies had no furniture. More than likely, a rule published in the condo bylaws prohibited cheap aluminum or plastic lawn furniture from cluttering the outside of the building. The old lounge chair on my porch would never pass muster here. I doubted I would either.

I looked up. Twenty stories. Cruising around the roof and gutters of the cash house today had been mildly gut clenching. Twenty floors up in the open air promised to be terrifying.

"Maybe you'll get the chance to send someone down the same way you came up," I said to myself, mustering both courage and incentive. I pushed myself upward, floated between floors, and caught the next balcony wall. So far so good.

They were all the same. A push, a float, a grip, and a breath of mild relief as I reset myself on each floor. I kept my attention either directly ahead, or upward. In my peripheral vision, the city around me fell away.

Most of the windows and sliding glass doors I passed were unlit. A few lighted condos contained people. Some sat. Some wore expressions dictated by whatever they watched on glowing television screens. A few moved in and out of the rooms I passed. Everything looked expensive. The people I saw were a perfect television casting mix of races. I saw no tattooed, t-shirted gangbangers with rubber heroin hoses wrapped around their arms. No shiny nickel-plated semi-automatics or dead-flat-black Glocks laying around on coffee tables. Not in this neighborhood. Pan D the man apparently didn't hang with his underlings in Pan D the gang.

I should have noticed the architecture of the last balcony when I started. It circled the entire top floor of the building like the brim of a glass hat. The gap I had been flying through didn't exist. It meant my last leg of the vertical journey had to angle away from the building, like a rock-climber hitting an overhanging cliff. Worse, the underside of the balcony wasn't some hunk of steel, with edges and places to grip. It was a smooth slab of composite material. I needed to touch it, work my hands around it, and get hold of a tiny edge where the glass wall rested on the floor of the balcony. The lip was less than a quarter of an inch. That lip was all I had to change from an outward trajectory to an upward trajectory.

I didn't think about it—or the consequences of missing a grip. I took it slowly, floating up and under the overhang. I reached up, gently touching the surface, careful not to push. I brushed my palm along the bottom, then around the edge, then up. My fingers found the narrow ledge. With both hands on it and my body floating free of the bottom, I pulled myself up.

I eased up the glass half wall and got my first look at Councilman Miles Andre's luxury condo.

It appeared empty.

# 58

C lear of the balcony wall, I realized my mistake. I had come unarmed. For the second time in as many hours I found myself lacking a weapon or a tool. The balcony twenty stories up offered little access to intruders, but the Councilman still locked his balcony door. He also obeyed the no furniture doctrine. The balcony contained nothing with which to break a window. Charging the glass wasn't an option. It works in the movies because movie glass is made of sugar and breaks into thousands of harmless little gems. Glass like this probably wouldn't break. If I were lucky enough to smash through, I would probably bleed to death from multiple plate glass amputations.

I stood in the quiet evening air, feeling a simmering, volcanic anger threatening to erupt. Andy tells me I don't get angry often, but when I do, it's worth being in another county.

I should have brought along the collar and chain to beat the man to death. It might have served to breach the glass door. Maybe. Studying it closely, the glass looked a bit beyond average glass. It was a single pane, but thick, strong and undoubtedly well insulated. Wisconsin winters, especially along the lake, call for more than ordinary single pane glass.

In my fatigue and the warm evening air, my mind wandered back to the idea of the collar. It would have been poetic to bolt it around Andre's neck, hook the chain to something, and then toss him over the balcony. Of course, I would need a bolt, some wrenches, and I would need a plate to secure the chain—

249

The chain.

I thought about it.

The chain.

When I examined the chain, I saw that it ended with an untouched link. No break. No bend. But where was the next link? The chain dangling from Lane's neck when we reached the EMTs extended only twelve or fourteen inches, a third of the original length. It had snapped when we shot out the window. How was that possible? How could she have put that kind of force on a steel chain without snapping her neck?

The portion still attached to her had been the length of chain that had disappeared. When I wrapped myself around her, I had no idea whether she would be consumed by *the other thing* or not. But I had pushed hard, with everything I had. In addition to Lane, the collar and one third of the chain vanished. The first visible link looked faded, fuzzy.

*Frayed.*

At the dividing line between visible and not visible, the chain had broken.

Just like the frame of the pilot's seat belonging to my crashed Navajo.

Less than an hour ago, *the other thing* wrapped itself around me and made me vanish and made me weightless and broke all the rules of physics —it had saved my life and Lane's life by developing a powerful, directional propulsion. It sent Lane and me out the only opening in the room, an opening I couldn't see—

*Except in my mind! I saw the window. I saw life beyond the window!* Without words, I fixed on a destination that promised life, and it took us there.

And at the border between visible and not visible, the chain broke.

*Holy shit.*

I still had no memory of the crash. But I now knew why I was alive. This thing, this *other thing*, didn't happen because of the crash. It saved me from the crash. I went out the side of the airplane the same way Lane and I went through that window.

The chain broke where *the other thing* ended.

Just like the seat frame.

*Son of a bitch.*

"Okay. Let's test the theory."

I pivoted and pushed myself to the metal handle for the locked patio door. A good, sturdy, you-paid-a-butt-load-of-money-for-this-condo latch and lock. I closed my hand around the handle. At first, the handle remained visible, but I *pushed* and as my hand covered it, it disappeared. Just like the aspirin bottle. I gripped tighter and concentrated. I pictured my imaginary levers. They weren't quite at full power. I shoved them forward.

The handle vanished. The effect spread to the baseplate, then to the whole mechanism. I saw through it into the condo. The edges were faded and frayed. *Frayed.*

I jerked the handle and felt a tug and snap, like a tendon letting go. The door slid open. Half of a broken metal latch hook tumbled onto the balcony floor.

"Holy shit! This just keeps getting better and better."

I pushed the door open and stepped through. For good measure, I turned around and closed the balcony door. Silence hung over me.

"Hey!" I shouted. Not exactly police procedure, or even a very bright idea.

Nothing, not even a faint echo, replied.

# 59

I reappeared. The penthouse had been built around a central alcove containing the elevator. A ring, sometimes a hallway, sometimes a great room, worked its way around the alcove. The penthouse occupied the entire top floor of the building. It felt even larger with what must be a twelve-foot ceiling. Schultz said Andre was a developer, with his fingers in deals all over the city. I guessed this was one of them, a pet project, and he saved the best for himself. On all sides, the cityscape shimmered as night fell.

Following the ring, I found what looked like a master bedroom on the east side of the layout. The head of a king-sized bed butted against the inner wall. The foot aimed at floor-to-ceiling glass where the sun rose every morning no doubt as an act of Miles Andre's will.

From the master bedroom, I found the master bathroom and a giant, walk-in closet. After lighting it up, I found what I was looking for, glittering in a black box with a red velvet lining.

Clive Christian No. 1 Pure Perfume for Men.

The instant I opened the jewel-like bottle and tested the scent, I knew it had been Andre in the room with Lane. Andre stripping her naked. Andre shooting Polaroid photos of a girl chained to a wall. His princess. Andre touching her.

I smelled him on her.

Andy gives me credit for a good sense of smell. I don't know how it compares to other people, but she relies on me to check the milk in the fridge to see if it's gone over. I can smell a smoker when they enter a room. I can smell burning cigarettes in the car in front of me on the highway at 70 miles per hour.

I smelled Andre on Lane the moment she stopped fighting me. He left his scent on her skin, the same scent that had watered my eyes in the MPD squad room. What was it he told Chief Stiller? That he had to go—something about a personal commitment. From the squad room, he had gone to the Pink House for a taste. He couldn't wait. He went to shoot photos of his prize. Photos to whet his appetite, or maybe make himself hard for the main event. When I smelled his perfume on Lane I recognized it instantly. I wondered if Andre knew about the trail he left. If he knew, perhaps he simply didn't care. Perhaps his plan included disposing of Lane when he finished with her.

"So where are the Polaroids?" I asked myself aloud. I looked around. They had to be here, somewhere in the penthouse. I didn't think he'd carry them around.

The closet sprawled. One wall contained a rotating device that exchanged rows of shirts hung on hangars. A similar device on another wall traded rows of suits. Another looked like a library of shoes and ties, with the bottom half divided into drawers like oversized safe deposit boxes. If I had forever, I knew I would not find his private collection of pedophile art. First, there were too many places to search. Second, I strongly suspected he wouldn't keep incriminating Polaroids anywhere that could be easily searched.

I wandered back through the closet and through the master bedroom. I had another idea.

Rich people favor panic rooms. If he had a panic room, it would be at the center of the floor, likely adjacent to the elevator, part of a solid structure. The surrounding rooms, some broad and open, some smaller, didn't allow for anything like that. I saw no walls with unaccounted-for space behind them.

The ring-like hallway that channeled around the central alcove didn't offer any clues. I found no keypads, fingerprint readers, retinal scanners. One room, an office, had a wall of security monitors, including views from the four cameras I'd seen at the front door. I didn't see any views of the penthouse interior, for which I was grateful, since I'd been wandering around fully visible, and the system undoubtedly had a record function. The office contained a desk surrounded by walls with bookshelves. I tried to figure out if any of the bookshelves might be rigged as moving panels, exposing doorways to a private room. But again, the spaces behind the walls I examined could be accounted for. I saw no scrapes in the carpet suggesting a door, or gaps in the moldings, or errant breezes blowing from cracks in a wall.

Nothing.

I had no way of knowing how much time I had before Andre showed up. Minutes? Hours? I made several circuits of the entire floor. Giving credit where credit was due, I acknowledged if there were a panic room or secret vault, it was easily hidden from an amateur B&E artist like me.

Returning to the kitchen, I raided his refrigerator. The act of opening the refrigerator caused my stomach to roll over and remind me I was hungry. I ignored the reminder.

I found a bottle of barbecue sauce. It was a brand I'd never seen, but so were most of the brand names in the refrigerator. I chalked that up to a slight difference in our paychecks.

The bottle featured a squeeze top. Perfect for my needs. I took it back to the central alcove where the elevator doors occupied one wall. The doors were finished in a brushed gold. The wall opposite the elevator wore white wallpaper with gold fibers running vertically through it. In the center of the wall hung an oil painting. Having no artistic talent or appreciation for art of any kind, I had no idea whether the painting carried a high price tag or not. It simply looked nice to my eye. A landscape, with vague purple mountains describing a jagged horizon, and broad, soft fields in the foreground. A girl played in the foreground, showing blossoms of petticoat.

A young girl.

I removed the painting. Given what I now knew about Councilman Miles Andre, I considered putting my fist through the canvas, but withdrew the impulse, thinking some art expert somewhere would lose a small piece of their soul if I did. Maybe I would, too. I put the painting aside, facing the wall.

Using the barbecue sauce squeeze bottle, and appreciating its rich, thick consistency, I wrote a six-foot-wide message on the wall opposite the elevator.


## I HAVE YOUR POLAROIDS


I STOOD BACK and studied my work. My elementary school teachers might not have approved of the medium, but they would have scored my penmanship well. A steady hand. Even block letters. Maybe I had talent after all.

I found a roll of paper towel in the kitchen and wiped down the bottle. Returning to the office with the security monitors, I tossed the open barbecue sauce bottle onto the plush white carpeting of a guest bedroom.

I settled into Councilman Andre's desk chair, a soft leather affair with electronic controls built into the arm. Mindful of leaving fingerprints and fearing I might be sitting in a massage chair, I avoided touching the controls. As it was, I worried that a wait of any duration might put me to asleep. The fatigue hanging on my eyelids felt like a crust.

I wondered if Andy had stayed with Lane. She could be assured Lane was in good hands with Rosemary II. My bet was that Andy would either go back to the squad room to monitor the planned drug raids or try to hook up with one of those raids. Even with Lane recovered, Pan D remained a target. I hoped for the former. I didn't like the idea of her suiting up and kicking in doors with trigger-happy sentries like AJ on the other side.

I rubbed my tired eyes. I had to blink several times to clear my vision. A blur on one of the screens snagged my attention.

Councilman Miles Andre stood smartly in the center of the elevator, riding up to his penthouse.

# 60

I hurried to the alcove.

*Fwooomp!*

I disappeared, pushed off the floor, and waited for him just below the high ceiling. I wanted to see his face when he stepped off the elevator.

His scent preceded him. The instant the doors parted he fixed his eyes on my message. A ripple of uncertainty distorted his handsome, groomed face. He stepped hesitantly off the elevator, eyes darting.

He turned. He shoved his right hand into the solid marble facing of the wall to the left of the elevator door. The illusion revealed itself as a hinged, hidden panel that swung inward. His hand disappeared to above the wrist. When he withdrew his hand, he held a gun. Another of those oversized, gaudy, nickel-plated semi-automatics.

Behind the big gun, he cautiously set off through the penthouse. I followed. It wasn't easy. The smooth ceiling lacked protruding light fixtures. The penthouse featured a sprinkler system, but there were no exposed pipes, and grabbing one of the little nozzles might have set it off. I used corners and room dividers to chart a course after him.

Andre did not speak as he searched his home for the intruder. He gathered in each room with his eyes, tracked the weapon across the dimensions of the room, then moved on. At the bedroom with the white carpeting, he saw the splatter of barbecue sauce and the discarded bottle. He froze and listened. He stood still for several minutes, breathing shallowly, turning his head to adjust the pickup capability of his ears. An ambusher might lack patience and make a mistake. He waited for such a mistake. I merely floated, watching.

When nothing but silence rewarded his patience, he moved on, slowly, methodically. He stopped several times to listen. Eventually, he arrived at the great room/kitchen combination where I had entered. There, he checked the sliding door to the balcony. When he opened the door, he found the broken latch. Behind the gun, he poked his head out, immediately checking upward, examining the squared edge of the roof above. Finding nothing out of place, he returned to the great room and closed the door behind him.

His search ended at the elevator alcove where it had begun. He read my message again. It had the effect I hoped for. He turned to the elevator wall and pressed the marble, replacing the gun and letting the panel snap back into place. Spinning on a heel, he marched purposefully through the great room I had entered from the balcony. I followed.

Andre moved into the kitchen space adjacent to the great room, a broad, open celebration of black speckled granite, silver fixtures, and expensive-looking appliances. He moved around a kitchen island large enough to park a car on, to the refrigerator built into the wall. He pulled the door open and stood examining the contents, cataloging the missing barbecue sauce, I presume. Maybe checking to see if the intruder had also disturbed his mushroom caps or herb mayonnaise. He closed the door.

Once again, he stood and remained silent for a long moment. Listening. At this height above the city, possibly thanks to the thick glass, the silence seemed to press on my ears. I found myself thinning my breath for fear he might hear the air moving in and out of my lungs.

When he moved, he did so abruptly. He stripped off his expensive-looking suit jacket, revealing a dense-thread white shirt over a fit torso and thick arms and shoulders. He tossed the jacket unceremoniously on the kitchen island and turned back to the refrigerator, to a smoked glass panel on the face of the left side door. LED numbers illuminated the panel showing a digital time display and digital temperature displays for the refrigerator and freezer compartments of the big unit. Glancing side to side, as if someone might be watching, he pressed his fingertips on the refrigerator control panel. I couldn't see what he pressed, or in what sequence. Only that his fingers touched the glass multiple times.

The entire wall, refrigerator, built-in freezer, a set of pantry cabinets, moved sideways. The motion carried no machine hum or gear grinding. Not even a distant hydraulic whisper. The wall simply moved sideways, with part of the pantry cabinet to the right disappearing into what I had taken for a large closet.

I pushed myself into a position to view the yawning space where the refrigerator had been. A room appeared, softly lit by recessed lighting. The room wasn't large. A person standing at the center of the space could reach out and touch all four sides lined with cabinets and shelves. Like the rest of the penthouse, however, it had a high ceiling, but not quite as high. I took that to mean it was reinforced above, below, and on all sides by steel or concrete. Because the entrance was an opening in a wall, not a door, the entrance ran all the way to the ceiling. I took advantage of the height and pushed myself in above Andre as he stepped in below me. He reached to one side and touched a simple red knob. The wall stopped moving.

Not a panic room. A vault. Neatly bound bricks of cash sat stacked on one set of shelves. I couldn't begin to guess the amount. Black velvet jewelry boxes occupied another. A set of drawers ran from waist height to the floor on the wall opposite the sliding opening. Above that hung weapons behind heavy glass with a lock at the center—half a dozen handguns of every possible size, including what I guessed was a fifty-caliber revolver. Above those hung semi-automatic rifles, the kind the news media mistakenly calls assault rifles. Mounted on one set of pins, he displayed a Thompson submachine gun, the ultimate gangster accessory. Mounded boxes of ammunition sat in tidy rows on a set of shelves. The ammunition easily totaled several thousand rounds. Another shelf held a row of cell phones with charging cables running through a hole to a hidden bank of chargers.

Framed photographs occupied one shelf. When I first glanced at them, I averted my eyes, expecting a display of his perversions. My eyes were too fast, however, and I registered that they were ordinary family photos. Andre with an attractive woman. The two of them with a child. Andre with a child. The child as a growing boy. I looked closer and saw that the child in every photo looked the same, a boy staring not at the camera, but at the space beyond the camera, with half-lidded eyes and no life in his expression. I recognized him and wondered if the Councilman knew his child had burned to death less than an hour ago.

Andre moved to the set of drawers. He pulled open the top drawer and removed a steel box which he took to a countertop next to the doorway. He flipped open a hinged lid.

The box contained Polaroid photos, scores of them, arranged in two neat rows.

He breathed deep relief and stroked his fingers over the deck of photos, then picked up the one closest to him.

Lane. Chained. Naked and clenching her arms around her knees.

Andre put the photo back and thumbed through a few more. Close-ups. I turned away. My attention fixed on the weapons hanging from pins on the back wall. The cabinet lock and glass looked impenetrable. I wanted to fill my hand with one of them. It would anchor me. The weight of it would take me to the floor. I would reappear, and the sound of the weapon being cocked would make him turn and see me. He would die never knowing how someone slipped into the room with him and pointed his own gun at him. He would die with one of his sick photos in his hand.

Unless he jangled a set of keys for me to steal or unlocked the cabinet himself, the weapons might as well have been on Mars.

Thumbing through the photos, Andre pulled a phone from his pocket and poked the face. He held it to his ear. It rang half a dozen times before he cut it off and stared at the face of the phone. He jabbed it again, held it to his ear, and got the same result. No answer.

Now he closed the lid on the box and gave his full attention to the phone. He called the same number again. Same result. This frustrated him. He tapped through several recent calls and touched another number. Someone answered. I heard the sound of a voice but not the words. Andre spoke angrily.

"Someone's been here."

He listened.

"Why? *Where are you?*"

He listened.

"With her?"

He listened.

"When?"

Andre glanced at his watch.

"Ten minutes. Fine."

He broke the connection.

Andre tidied the photos in the box and replaced the box in the drawer. He slipped out of the room, touching the red button on the wall panel as he went by. The opening began to close. He hurried out of my line of sight.

I gave a fraction of a second's consideration to trying to break into the gun cabinet. My mind blew through fast-forward frames of picking a gun off the wall, checking the magazine, and putting a bullet or ten into the walking disease that was Councilman Miles Andre. The wall opposite the gun cabinet moved inexorably, shrinking the opening to the kitchen. I gave up the idea for something better, if less satisfying.

Confirming that Andre had disappeared from my line of sight, I pushed off the ceiling. I maneuvered into the same position Andre had occupied a moment ago. His cloud of scent hung in the space.

*Really? Can you not smell yourself?*

I opened the drawer. I picked up the photo box. It didn't weigh much, but relative to me, it was more than enough to put my feet back on the floor.

The door had closed halfway. I had no time to conceal the box. I slid through the door sideways holding the box behind me. I hurried out of the room thinking that if Andre saw the box floating through his penthouse, everything would change. I scanned both directions. Andre was nowhere to be seen. I made a right turn, opposite the direction Andre had gone. My path took me out of the kitchen, into a broad room on the western side of the penthouse, where a wall of windows ironically offered the criminal owner of this penthouse a majestic view of the Milwaukee County Court House and jail complex.

A bar stood to one side. I stepped behind the bar and placed the box on a low shelf. With the box out of hand, I floated again. I pushed up to the ceiling. I worked my way counterclockwise around the penthouse circuit. At the open door to the master bedroom, I found the Councilman changing his clothes.

*Ten minutes.* Did that mean he planned to leave? Or was he expecting someone. Either way, my vague plan to murder the bastard now had a wrench in its gears. Andre had been disturbed by the message on his wall. He had called out for help. I assumed the unanswered call went to a melted phone in the pocket of Mauser's crisp corpse. His second call had to have been to another trusted underling.

Andre emerged from the master suite in a fresh set of casual clothing, looking like the poster child for country club membership. I wondered how he managed his crusader-for-the-poor image on the decaying streets of the district he served. The country club clothing did nothing to mask the tension in his face and the urgency of his movements. He hurried back to the kitchen and great room where he took up station, pacing. Twice he tried calls that didn't answer.

I found myself wishing Mauser would answer, so that Andre could hear him screaming from the depths of Hell. After the second call, he jammed his phone into the pocket of his creased slacks. At least he answered my question about whether he intended to stay or leave.

Someone was coming, someone he trusted. So much the better. It would reveal another cancer to be removed from the population. Even with Andre dead, the machinery of Pan D would need dismantling. The police would appreciate knowing the identity of those who served him.

Andre poured himself a drink in the kitchen, then returned to pacing.

The smooth great room ceiling offered nothing to grip. The adjacent kitchen area featured track light fixtures, vertical posts and hanging cabinets, all of which offered gripping points. I eased into position over the central island where a framework of elegant plumbing descended from the ceiling over a broad set of sinks. The position offered a view of the great room with easy access to the circuit going around the penthouse, and the vault if he opened it again.

I watched Andre pace.

A soft chime announced an arrival at the elevator in the alcove. Andre placed his drink on a coffee table and moved out of my sight to meet the visitor.

I heard his voice, his practiced warm greeting. Whoever came to Andre had his trust, which put them at war with me.

That's when I heard Andy's voice.

# 61

For a micro-fraction of a millisecond, electric shock hit me. My mind flashed on the idea that the person Andre trusted to walk into his luxury condo was my wife. The impossible notion hit like close lightning, the kind with no time gap between the flash and the thunder.

*It couldn't be.*

The notion passed in the time it took Andre to return to the great room below me. This he did carefully, walking backward, with his hands extended, looking down the barrel of my wife's service weapon, which she held in firing position with her finger on the trigger and the hammer pulled back. I knew the trigger pressure of that gun. It wasn't much.

New lightning thoughts flashed through my mind. Andy knew Andre's identity. Andy came to arrest him. Andy found something, solid as granite, telling her Andre was Pan D.

I realized I wouldn't be able to kill him. Andy would never allow it. I had been removed from the board. For the second time today, I was reduced to the role of spectator.

"Please, Detective Stewart, come in," Andre said casually.

Andy followed Andre into the room, moving the weapon as he moved, keeping her distance from him. He stood tall and fit. I suspected he could be dangerously quick. She took no chances. She let him have the center of the room while she worked sideways, putting a low leather sofa between them.

"I just came from the Pink House," she said. "You burned it. You're Pan D."

"You learned about the Pink House," he said with a hint of admiration. "That's remarkable, considering you only just arrived here today. You must be quite the investigator. I suppose that validates the idea of putting fresh eyes on a problem. Please, Detective, sit down. Tell me how you reached this conclusion."

"Not a chance," she said.

"Alright," he said pensively, "how about this? I'd like to confess everything to you." He gestured at the sofa. Andy made a face.

"Well then, if you won't sit, I will. Will you join us, Detective Martin?"

Martin entered the room from behind and below me, his own weapon drawn. From the elevator, he had circled around to clear the penthouse from the other direction. Good police tactics, I assumed. If I hadn't completely abandoned the idea of killing Andre with Andy here, I did now with Martin on hand. The two of them let the air out of my plans.

Andre picked up his cocktail and sipped.

I didn't like the way he studied Andy. I worried that any second now the person Andre had spoken to on the phone, the one he trusted after Mauser, could walk off the elevator and into the picture. If not for Martin's presence, I would have considered Andy in genuine jeopardy. The MPD couldn't be far behind, probably filling the lobby below at this moment. Andre's underling would likely make a pass on the building, see police cars and bolt.

Andre, the politician, ignored the fact that his world had collapsed around him. He sipped his cocktail and relaxed on an ugly, swept-back leather chair with one leg crossed over the other knee. His arrogant bravado annoyed me.

"Mr. Andre, you're under arrest for kidnapping, murder, arson and additional charges to be named," Andy said. She recited the rest of the Miranda warning and asked if Andre understood his rights. Her green eyes locked on him over the barrel of her weapon.

"Detective, I am better acquainted with my rights than most people. Moreover, I have a great deal of money and power, which gives me more rights than most people."

"Like the right to kidnap a twelve-year-old girl?"

"Ah, well, since you asked... May I guess your age? Twenty-six? Twenty-eight? You are unquestionably an attractive woman, and you may think you are well below your prime, but you are aging. You have produced eggs, I'm going to guess, for a decade and a half. Possibly longer. You look like the type that matured early. Do you have children? You don't, do you. The consummate and consumed professional police-woman. Each month you waste your opportunity. You literally flush it away. The child, Lane, when I met her, she had just ripened. I smelled it on her," he said.

I wanted to snap his neck.

"We men can do that, you know. It's not outrageous. For most of human history, scent guided a man to a woman ready for insemination. Civilization has imposed artificial restrictions, of course, but until quite recently, again viewing the grand span of time, a woman of twelve or fourteen offered the best opportunity to procreate. Healthy. Unused. The notions you have of pedophilia and rape are quaint affectations of our age. But it's self-destructive, really, as we have pushed women like you, a healthy specimen, into imposing artificial delays, into their thirties and forties. And at what cost? Autism? Birth defects? Risk? While excellent breeding stock is held out of reach by silly cultural notions. It's a shame."

Andy stared at him. She said nothing for a moment, then wrinkled her nose as if she'd encountered a foul odor. "Fuck you."

Andre laughed. "Oh, my God, I'm kidding, Detective!" He laughed and slapped a hand on his thigh. "I mean, the anthropology lends a certain verisimilitude to the argument, but even I understand the taboos of our culture. Seriously, Detective, I just like fucking little girls. Helpless little girls. It's fun. It's a rush. And a man in my position, well, I simply get to do it. One of those rights you mentioned."

"I think you should shut up," Andy said. "Martin, can you put some handcuffs on this—this shit."

"Yeah, I kinda forgot to grab mine. You got any?"

Andy glanced incredulously at Martin, who moved across the room to her side, his weapon pointed in the direction of Andre.

"Are you serious? This is your arrest. MPD's arrest. I don't have any handcuffs with me," she said.

Martin shrugged. "Somebody will have some. They'll be here soon."

"The part I like the most is the expectation, Detective," Andre continued. "The expectation that someone is supposed to protect them. Or save them. Daddy. Or Mommy. They cry out for them. They know this shouldn't be happening to them. There's a dawning, in their faces, when it becomes real that they are *owned* by me. You see hope extinguished. I like to try and time it so it happens right—"

"Shut up!"

"Oh, please, Detective. Andrea. You think I'm some sort of monster, but I gave every one of those young women meaning. I'm not some sick serial murderer. Those girls, I should say young women, went on to serve a valuable purpose in a vibrant service industry, satisfying the needs of many,

many men. Some of them still work right here, in the city. Some traveled to exotic foreign destinations. Did you know that in some cases, they were brought to me willingly, by their mothers? I had hoped Lane's mother would understand the opportunity availed to her little girl."

"Honest to God, I will shoot you where you sit," Andy said.

I wished she would.

"Or you could shoot me where I stand," Andre said, standing up. "I'd like another drink. Can I offer either of you something?"

"Do NOT move!" Andy said. She squared her shoulders, her knees slightly bent. She stood as tense as I've ever seen her.

"Where do you expect me to go?" Andre asked smoothly. "If I were foolish enough to pull a weapon out of the lettuce crisper your bullet would be through my brain and gone before I could bring it to bear."

Andre walked out of the great room space and into the kitchen where he drew another shot of amber liquor from one of half a dozen bottles standing at attention in a chrome rack.

"What does the training manual suggest for this? Do you shoot me for refreshing my drink? Do you both rush me? Throw me down and put a knee on my neck? Rod-ney-King! Rod-ney-King!" He turned, raised his glass, and laughed. "Or maybe I've lost all hope. Maybe I'm going for suicide by cop. I can't face what's coming to me. My political career! My reputation! I need you to end it all for me. What do you think?" He smiled.

Something about this felt wrong.

"I'd be careful, Andrea. How will it look? White cop kills Black civic leader? Riots in the streets! Millionaire athletes protesting the national anthem! So much to consider when you put weight on that trigger."

He wasn't far from me. I looked around the kitchen for a weapon. At the far end of the kitchen island, some sort of meat tenderizing hammer hung in a row with other serious-looking cooking tools. I pictured Andy and Martin seeing it float through the air on its own and killing their perp before their very eyes.

Andre stepped back into the great room.

"Jim, would you mind?"

*Jim?*

Martin, standing behind the sofa beside Andy, turned and raised his weapon to touch it to her temple. I nearly screamed.

"If he shoots you, he has to pay the cleaning bill. I'd rather you hand him your weapon, Detective," Andre said.

Andy's focus narrowed on the front and rear sights of her weapon. She thought about it. Andre stood, a dead man in her sights. Her finger had weight on the trigger. At this distance, she wouldn't miss. Andre saw the intensity in Andy's face, the rage in her eyes. He spoke up quickly.

"Jim, if she shoots me now, and she seems like the kind to make that sacrifice, I want you to find the mother and kill her, and then kill, once and for all, that husband of hers." Andre stared over the barrel of Andy's weapon, into her eyes, tense, working hard to fix a smug, cold smile on his face. "Kill him slowly."

*No no no no!* Andy started to fold. The rage in her eyes didn't fade, but the gun tipped up and she removed her finger from the trigger guard. Martin reached over and folded his hand over the barrel, taking it from her. He slid it into his belt.

"Can I take it, Jim, that she found her way here on her own? That whatever deductions she made that brought her here to me were shared only with you? Or will that fat ass Schultz and the whole FUCKING MPD COME THROUGH MY DOOR?"

Martin shook his head emphatically. "We're good. Nobody else knows we came here."

"Are you dead certain?" Andre asked, calm again, with emphasis on "dead."

"She told me on the way here—about you. She knows I really hate you around the office, so we're buds now. She's been all up in my shit all day. As soon as somebody tipped her to the Pink House she dove into it like a rookie. Too fucking much energy in this one. By the way, the Pink House is on fire."

"Yes."

"You might'a said something. Anyway, she came blasting out of there and told me she figured out you were Pan D and invited me along for the big bust. She's a good little police-girl, she didn't want to do anything without MPD blessing."

"Sit." Andre pointed at the sofa. Martin pushed Andy around the end of the leather sofa and made her sit.

I worked my way toward the meat hammer.

Andre sat in his ugly post-modern chair. He regarded Andy with curiosity.

"The Pink House," he said. "Who gave you that name?"

"Anonymous tip," Andy replied. "The Pink House. That's where you had your business partner murdered."

Andre smiled and nodded.

"He wasn't really a partner. More of an associate, a friend. I didn't gain anything by his death, I mean financially. That would have been a bit on the nose. I did, however, offer to help his estate sell that gaudy rubble heap of a house. The market has been soft. No viable offers forthcoming, so I've tried to make use of it when I can," Andre mused. "However, the savage way he was killed by evil gangbanger addicts—along with his poor wife and daughter— right there on Lake Drive, the very heart of white money. Oh, so tragic! So shocking! That! That paid dividends! I worked it for months. It landed me on the MPD task forces. I'm asking you again, who told you about the Pink House?"

"Really? You're going to sit here and do this villain schtick? I'm supposed to, what? Play for time? Tell you everything while I look for an out? Where do you get this stuff?"

Andre nodded. "It does seem a little theatrical, I will admit. But I'd like to go back to the deal you just made with this devil. The one where you handed over your weapon instead of using it on me, on the promise that Jim here would spare your friend and your husband. Here's the thing, Detective. I lost something precious today. Well, maybe not precious, but something I was *really looking forward to*, thanks to you. And while you're a little older than I would have liked, you're quite attractive. I think you're going to have to make it up to me."

"Delusional, too," Andy observed.

"Not so much. In fact, you're going to have to make it up to me and make sure I enjoy myself, or I will kill 'em all. Just, kill 'em all! So, that's what you're going to do, Andrea, with a smile on your face. You'll be dead when it's over. I don't think you'd believe me if I said otherwise. But it's the only bet you can make that I won't go after your friend and your hubby— which, honestly, is a lot of work, a lot of exposure. I'll let you buy their lives with your dignity, your humanity, and your womanhood. Oh! And your life. How's that?"

"Wow. That is the worst pickup line ever," Andy said.

I moved to the end of the kitchen island where the meat hammer hung. To pick it up, I put my feet on the island, otherwise I would have simply settled under the hammer's weight. I planted my feet and started to move it but froze when the motion caught Martin's eye. He now sat on the back of the sofa with his gun pointed at Andy on his left. His point of view carried past Andre on a direct line to me. He registered the movement and did a double-take.

*Dammit!*

"So, let's renew our agreement. And start with you telling me how you learned about the Pink House," Andre said, his voice growing colder.

Andy said nothing. I looked for a new option. A direct attack on Martin seemed the best idea.

"Well, no need to answer," Andre said. "Part of the fun will be getting you to say and do anything that comes to mind."

I worked my way into a new position above the island, then fixed a direct line for the space above Martin. He had one thigh on the back of the sofa. He sat sideways, resting his weapon in his leg, aiming it loosely at Andy. I saw Andy calculate the geometry of her position, Martin, and the gun. I hoped the math didn't work for her. I needed time.

"Your son is dead," Andy said as if reading my thoughts.

I pushed off. I crossed the great room space. As I passed where Andre sat, I glanced back at him to read his expression. He blinked. Andy struck a blow.

"Burned to death, this afternoon," she said. "Didn't Jimmy here tell you?"

Andre pivoted his frozen expression to Martin. "Detective?"

"I think the firefighters called him a 'Crispy Critter,'" Andy said. "What was it you called him? Mauser?"

Andre, still looking at Martin, asked again, "Detective?"

"She's full of shit," Martin said.

"Oh, you're going to lie to your boss now? He has you hanging out to dry here, exposing yourself, and you're going to lie to him? Do you have any idea who's next on the Too Inconvenient To Live List?" Andy turned back to Andre. "Mauser. He was your son, wasn't he?"

Andre said nothing.

"Yes. I found the Pink House. Obviously. I'm not lying, though. It was an anonymous tip. Somebody out there knows me and hates you." She wasn't lying about that either. "From that tip, I found the story about your 'friend,' and then the stories about you, moving up, moving in with the MPD. I got curious about you. I found out you have a son." Andy pushed harder. "The boy wasn't quite right. I saw his picture. I saw a lot of pictures today. Oh, they let me see their book on Pan D, and it had pictures, but not enough, and certainly none of you or your son. I think Detective Martin here kept it nicely cleansed. But you can't believe what you can find on the internet, and what we get now from Homeland. Detective Martin let me use his laptop. He was so busy he didn't see when I found the Pink House, and pictures of you grieving over your friend, then pictures of you making speeches, rallying the neighborhoods against guns, against drugs, against heroin, against pills, against prostitution. You were going around making speeches and in all those pictures and videos, you know what you didn't have with you? Your wife. Your son. Google says you have a wife and son, did you know that? Google has pictures. It seemed odd to me. Politicians love to trot out family. So, where were they? Well, as you well know, your boy was a guest of the state mental hospital, but they're a little vague on how he got released. I called. Somebody pulling strings, I imagine. And your wife? I have a feeling no one will ever find your wife, will they?"

Andre held a blank face.

"Your boy—talk about a purebred sociopath. The genuine article. Serial killer material. Perfect for the family business. Pan D and Son. You made good use of his—um, talents. He is—or was—quite the asset. His name was Alexander Andre when he was your boy. But I think Alexander Andre died a long time ago. He was Mauser when he worked for you. Undoubtedly some other alias by day. You ordered him to burn the Pink House, and Lane with it. Am I right? Don't answer that in front of Detective Martin. I'm not sure he signed on for burning a child alive. That's where we found your son. At the Pink House. His car. Him. Cooked. Your boy shouldn't have been playing with matches, Councilman Andre."

Martin's posture stiffened. He put the gun against the side of Andy's head and pushed.

I moved into position above Martin, but it was no good. If I dropped on him, she would die. He didn't even have to pull the trigger. A simple convulsion would do it.

I needed another way.

Andy continued. "Oh, don't blame Jimmy here for not giving you a heads-up. I didn't get a chance to tell him any of this. He had to *chase* me over to the Pink House. He handheld me all afternoon while I turned over rocks, but when I figured out the connection between you and—how did they put it in the newspaper article? 'A majestic pink stucco home in the Spanish tradition'—well, things sort of cascaded. Martin here, he was a little distracted by the raids he was setting up, and I assume by having to let you know which houses MPD had in their sights. You two probably had to work out which ones to leave on the vine, you know, so the MPD would feel they had scored a few points. I took off without sending Jimmy a memo, and he had to come chasing after me. And guess what—there was Lane!"

Andy looked at Andre pointedly. Andre blinked. She caught him unaware again. Good girl!

"Oh, you didn't know? Your princess is still alive."

I glanced at the elevator. Something about it, a thread, tugged at me.

"You know what? I think I'll pay the cleaning bill," Martin snarled at

Andy, shoving the barrel of his gun harder against her head. She leaned left, bracing herself against the pressure with her left hand on the sofa cushion.

My pulse thundered in my ears.

"Not here!" Andre barked at Martin. His polished demeanor rippled now with rage. He stood up. He looked at Andy with naked loathing.

It hit me. The thread tugging at me from the alcove.

*Keep talking, Andy!*

I pushed into the alcove, diving toward the elevators. Thanks to the geometry of an inner wall, Andre slipped out of my sight. I unfolded myself by the elevators. The hidden panel, the one with the gun—which one? I had nothing to prop myself against. If I tried to press into the panel, all I would do is push myself away. I had already begun to float. I thought about reappearing, but Martin might see me and react before I had time to find the gun. I couldn't start a gun fight with Andy directly in the line of fire. I'm not that good.

"Why, Councilman Andre, you do not seem pleased. I would have thought you'd be delighted to hear she's alive. At the very least, you'd want to be in on the photo op. Granted, it's Sunday, not the best news day. But you may want to rush over to the hospital for a picture with the girl. Or should I say, *another* picture with the girl?"

Middle panel. I was sure. I lowered my arm, put my palm against the top of the panel just below it, and curled my fingers against the hidden panel. I pushed the panel open far enough to gain a grip. I reached in and wrapped my right hand around the weapon.

"Funny what you find on the internet. Councilman Andre celebrating Arbor Day, planting trees in the park with all the neighborhood children. And there she was, bright and beautiful, and in awe of meeting someone so important. Twelve years old and full of trust. Standing beside you—you with that stupid shovel in your hand."

I pulled the big silver gun out. It gave me weight. I turned. Out of Andre's line of sight, but not Martin's. I aimed it at the back of Martin's head, about twenty-five feet away.

"You weren't leering at her in the photo, but you wanted to, didn't you?"

Martin's gun pressed into Andy's hair, forcing her head on an angle to the side. I wanted to fire, but what if he convulsed? What if his gun went off? What if I missed?

Andre turned his anger on Martin, "She's alive? When were you going to tell me she's alive?"

Andy interrupted. "Oh, I don't think he knew. I didn't know for certain myself until I found the girl. Jimmy ran into me as I was leaving, coming here. I guess he didn't see her, and I was so wrapped up in telling him I knew who you were—and trying to find you—I didn't have time to explain. I called your office. You make your staff pick up on Sundays? Somebody did, and they said you were probably at home. Here. Nice of them. You kept a straight face, Jimmy, I must admit, but it must have been a shock. His only move was to join up and come here with me. And he even volunteered to call Schultz and rally the troops. You did call, didn't you? On the way over here? I heard you talking to them. Schultz even called you back, just before we got here," Andy said, mocking Martin. "That was Schultz, wasn't it? That's who you said it was, *Detective*."

"You know, you are kind of a bitch," Martin said. He turned to Andre. "Miles, nobody knows. And if the girl is alive, she doesn't know anything."

"That's true, she doesn't," Andy said, leaning farther under the pressure of Martin's gun. "But you did leave a big fat clue and I'm not the only one who got it."

She wasn't.

I lowered the gun, curled myself into a cannonball, and stuffed the gun under my shirt, pressing hard. I felt a cool electric surge as *the other thing* wrapped around the weapon. I hoped it wouldn't be damaged—that it would still work. When I pulled the gun back out, it had lost its weight and vanished in my hand. I pushed off directly at Martin.

"What clue?" Andre demanded.

I floated to Martin and then stopped myself inches from his back by grabbing the sofa cushion. The leather dimpled. Andre's eyes darted to the moving upholstery, drawn by the motion. I let go. The upholstery relaxed. His eyes questioned but didn't linger. I pushed myself away from Martin, toward the wall behind him. Once there, I bounced back toward the sofa, stopping behind Andy's left shoulder.

"What CLUE?!" Andre demanded.

I laid the weapon on the sofa cushion next to Andy's left hand. I leaned in close. Her hair brushed my face.

"What fucking CLUE?!"

I whispered. "Dee, I love you. In two seconds—a gun by your left hand."

She stiffened at the sound of my voice. It played like a reaction to Andre's outburst. Her head pivoted, stealing a glance. Too soon. The weapon was still *gone*, wrapped in my hand. I leaned back.

I reached around her head and put my right hand under the grip on Martin's weapon.

*Please, God...*

I released the weapon in my left hand and felt cold electricity. It dropped out of the empty air onto the sofa cushion beside Andy's left hand. With my feet touching the carpet for leverage, I slapped my right hand upward.

Martin's gun fired.

Andy's head went down and for another micro-fraction of a millisecond my world came to an end. Then Andy's left hand swung around and up, and she smashed the flat side of the heavy silver semi-automatic weapon into Martin's face. I continued pushing with my right hand, closing a grip on his arm, angling his weapon higher. Andy pulled back and swung again, this time with the gun butt. It raked Martin's forehead, ripping the skin. I felt him take the jolt. With both hands now, I twisted the gun in his hand. It went off. Andy ducked. The slide burned and bit into my palm, and I nearly lost my grip. Martin tumbled backward and his hold on the weapon failed him. I yanked it free, but not before it went off a third time.

*Fwooomp!* Gravity gathered me. I wheeled and pulled Martin down behind the sofa. We both hit the carpeting. I had expected him to be unconscious, but he was far from it. He threw his hands up to his smashed face. Blood flooded through his fingers.

Martin howled like a child, "*Ooowww! Ahhhhhhh-owwww!*"

His face became a mask of red. Blood filled his eyes. Blind and confused, he kicked and flailed backward. I threw his gun over my shoulder away from him, then reached and pulled Andy's gun from his belt. He rolled away from me, howling.

Andre saw everything. His face froze in disbelief. I had appeared out of nowhere. Struggling to comprehend, his mouth hung open. From it, a deep moan grew into a howl, and from there, into a scream of rage. He threw aside his drink and lunged at Andy.

Twenty-one feet, they say. A gun is no sure defense against someone charging you inside of twenty-one feet. Andre stood less than ten feet from Andy. In two powerful strides, he reached her.

The big gun in her left hand barked once and the top of Andre's head exploded.

The rage in Andre's face winked out like a dying light. He tumbled onto the sofa. Andy rolled to the floor. His falling dead body caught her legs. His arms flopped at his side. She kicked and yanked herself free. In an instant, she rose to her feet, the big gun swinging between Andre, dead before her, and Martin, writhing on the carpet.

Andy's green eyes blazed. Her mouth drew sharp gasps of air with her lower lip extended just slightly. Her chest heaved. Allied with the rage, her hair shot down across one eye and flew like wild flags of war around her head.

I have never seen her so dark, so powerful.

She threw a wide-eyed glance at me as I skittered backward on the floor behind the sofa, away from Martin, who rolled back and forth, cursing, holding the flap of skin on his forehead and covering the smashed remnants of his nose with his hands.

Andy stared at me.

"Hi, honey," I said softly. I tried a smile, but it felt more like a grimace.

I didn't think it possible, but her green irises gained a light all their own and grow even wider when I spoke. She struggled to register that I was, in fact, *there*. The gun remained pointed at Andre, but I wouldn't have bet against her swinging it around on me.

She abruptly shook her head, the gesture of someone banishing a vision. I pulled myself to my feet, thinking if she got a better look at me, she might not shoot me. As soon as I reached a full upright posture, she bolted around the end of the sofa and threw her arms around me. I pulled her close, but just as suddenly, she pushed herself away and glared at me. I was uncomfortably aware of the monstrous gun she swung in her hand.

She pulled back her arm, balled a fist and punched me in the chest.

"Where in blazes have you been?!"

Then she hit me again. For emphasis.

# 62

"Look at you," Andy said, "you're not a complete moron. You had your handcuffs all along." She kneeled over Martin. The detective moaned on his belly. He bled liberally onto a very expensive-looking cream-colored Berber carpet. Andy clicked one ring closed on a wrist, threaded the cuffs through the steel frame of the sofa, then clicked the other. Even with his hands behind his back, he might be able to move the sofa, but he wouldn't get far. She did a thorough pat-down to check for a second weapon.

"Fug oooo!" Martin sputtered. "Ah kahn breed."

"Turn your head."

I held Andy's weapon and gathered up Martin's. She stood, reached out and took her own weapon back and handed me the shiny cannon she had used to take three inches off the top of Councilman Andre.

"Be careful with that thing. Both of them. Fingers away from the triggers, please." She gestured at the three bullet holes in the windows overlooking the balcony and glittering city beyond. Like they were my fault.

The complex woman that is my wife faced me, tense and professional. She nurtured a simmering anger. A moment after the dust settled, I went to Andre's limp body and swung a leg back to kick him with everything I had. Andy shrieked at me to stop. She scolded me. How was she supposed to explain a post-mortem injury like that? *Use your head, Will*! In that instant, I decided that if his remains found their way to a marked grave, I would visit once a year to piss on it.

I watched her closely. She had taken a life through violence, something she often told me she prayed would never happen in her career as a peace officer. I knew most of the other issues of the moment would pass, but she would carry this one with her, and she would try to carry it alone.

For the moment, however, the professional police officer took command and dealt with a crime scene and the knowledge that she, possibly more than Miles Andre or Detective Martin, would be the focal point of an intense inquiry into what, exactly, had happened here.

I wasn't helping matters.

"That's a long story and now's not the time," I said when she asked me how I managed to get behind Martin without Andre seeing me.

"I need to know everything, Will, everything," she said, letting the anger surface. As she said it, she fished her phone from her jacket pocket. "And quick. Because I need to get Chief Schultz up here, and—"

I put my hand on her hand before she could swipe the screen open. I looked at Martin, then gestured with my head toward the kitchen. Mildly exasperated, she followed me to the kitchen, and then with visible reluctance, she followed me around the first corner to the western room that overlooked the courthouse.

"Will, we don't have time for this! And I can't leave Martin alone out there!"

"We do. And you can. If he wants to try climbing down the side of the building, I'll throw the sofa over the balcony to give him a running start. Now sit down, here," I pulled a bar stool away from the bar. "You need a minute to—I don't know—to breathe. Martin's not going anywhere, and Andre certainly isn't."

She sat. Rigidly.

"I know," I said. "I know the shit is going to hit the fan and you're going to get swept up in it, fast. So, before that storm hits, give yourself a moment. Plus, there's something we need to do."

I went behind the bar and pulled two glasses off the shelf. I found an open bottle of something that looked expensive and poured two shots.

"I can't. The first thing they're going to do is test me. I can't."

She pushed her glass back at me. Knowing this wasn't the hill to die for, I raised my glass and clicked it against hers. "I love you more today than I did yesterday, Andrea Katherine Stewart."

The words melted her and irritated her equally.

I downed the shot. The liquor flowed smooth and warm. Being the first liquid I had consumed all day it radiated quickly to my extremities.

Andy fidgeted on the stool. She needed to be a cop right now. She needed to get back to the business of her profession. Despite her tension, she drew a long deep breath and took my hand.

"Thank you," she said, "for, um—you know—seriously, how did you do that? How did you get up here? And how did you find out about the Pink House? How did you figure out it was Andre?!"

"I knew it was Andre as soon as I found Lane because—"

"—of his COLOGNE!" We said it together.

"Oh, my God! Yes! I knew it as soon as I got near her!" Andy said, her face brightening for a moment. "But, wait wait wait! How did you—I mean, what did you—Jesus, Will!"

"Okay, you're not going to like this, but you really need to *not* know a few things right now."

"Will, I'm going to be the subject of an officer-involved shooting investigation. That means DOJ. On top of that, I'm out of jurisdiction. That means an inquiry that could put me in serious jeopardy. I have to know what you know!" The anger layer pushed to the surface again. "You've been running around all day, and I had no idea where you were or what you were doing, and you call me with that thing about the Pink House and then you end up— Oh, my God!" The emotional layer surfaced. "You saved Lane! She told me! How did you get her–? The fire! *You got Lane out of the fire!*" She put her hand to her mouth and again, her eyes went wet.

"Dee, slow down. Breathe. And listen."

She nodded. Took a deep breath.

"No matter what happens, ever, it's you and me. And I love you. But I'm about to piss you off because this moment isn't the time for me to explain— not any of it. I'll tell you everything, I swear to God! As soon as it's just you and me, just us—at home."

"Will, do you understand what is about to happen here? I'm going to be asked questions for which I don't have answers."

"But you do have answers. You got here on your own. Bringing me into it will create more questions than answers. Dee, trust me when I tell you that *what I have to tell you needs time* and right now, there's no time. You've got to call in the cavalry, and this place is going to be swarming with cops, and there's something that must be done. We've got to take care of this."

I reached under the bar and pulled up the box of Polaroids and opened it.

"Andre took pictures."

Andy gazed at the rows of photos. She shot a look at me as understanding dawned.

"Lane?"

I nodded. "I have to get rid of this shit before this place is full of cops.

He's got a whole vault you need to drill into. It's probably full of evidence. I grabbed these, thinking I might use them to prove it was him, but he took care of that. These must be destroyed."

"Will, you can't! That's evidence!"

"Evidence of what? That he kidnapped Lane? I think we know that. Evidence for his trial? Trial's over."

"But you—that's—"

"Dee, I will not have these pictures logged into some evidence locker so they can be digitized by some horny nerd who sneaks copies that wind up on some sick website. Not of Lane. Not of any of the children he—I won't let it happen."

"What if these aren't the only ones? Or he made copies? Or scanned them?"

I shrugged. "We gamble. My bet is that he had a reason for shooting Polaroids instead of using his phone or a digital camera."

The cop in her, running so deep, harboring such faith in justice and the system she served, grappled with process and procedure. The internal battle raged on her face.

"It's not just Lane," she argued. "There are others. These photos might answer questions. Offer closure."

"And will you be the officer that knocks on a door and holds up one of these and asks, 'Is this your daughter? Did you hand her over to Councilman Andre when she was twelve?'"

"Finding those he hurt might save them!"

"Then make it public, what he was doing. Put out a call. Let the ones who can face it come forward. Set up counseling. Advocate for his victims. But these—these will take them right back to the moment."

She opened her mouth to speak. The words didn't come.

I pressed my point. "He confessed. He imposed his own sentence when he gave you no choice. From this moment forward, the investigation should be about tearing apart the gang he created, the drugs, the distribution, and anything else he did. Not his sick—Christ! I don't want to give it words."

She reached for the box and pinched one of the photos from its row. I put my hand down on hers and pressed it back into place.

"Don't. You can't unsee it."

She looked at me. "Do you understand the position you're putting me in?"

"Dee, they will feel it. Every set of eyes that touches these, these kids will feel it. Somehow. Somebody has to protect them."

She held her ground for a moment, silent. When she let go, I feared what it cost us.

"Alright. Alright, go," she said tightly. "God, Will, I am trusting you on this."

"I know."

She closed the box. "Take them. But you can't just carry them out the front door. There are cameras. MPD will pull the building security footage as a matter of course. How do you plan to get out of here with them?"

I picked up her untouched shot and downed it.

"The same way I got in." I said. As her lips parted with the automatic question, I touched them. "Don't ask."

# 63

A ndy, channeling her anger at me, called MPD, declared an emergency, and told someone on the other end of the call to find Chief Don Schultz *now God dammit!* and that she would hold.

She made the call from the kitchen because Andre's blood and brain spatter, abundant in the great room, didn't quite reach the spotless granite and steel space. Before she called, I pointed out the location of the vault and the control panel on the high-tech refrigerator. Maybe MPD had a security system wizard who could break the code. Just before she touched her phone to call MPD, I took Andy's face in my hands and kissed her. She threw one hand up to the back of my head and kissed back, which told me we were good, even if she reserved the right to marinate anger over my refusal to explain myself.

"I'll be a while," she said, just a little testily.

"I'll be at the Hyatt, room 919, probably out cold."

While she made the call, I went back to the west room bar and wiped down the empty tumblers and the bottle I had touched. The police might not bother with a full forensic treatment of the penthouse, but a couple of freshly finished drinks invited questions.

From there I found a linen closet near the master bedroom. I stole a silk pillowcase and dumped the Polaroids into it. I tied it tightly shut and worked the sack up under my shirt, looping the slack end through my belt twice. I needed my hands free, but also needed to be sure I wouldn't spill the photo-horrors all over the street. I wiped down the empty metal box and left it under the bar.

Satisfied the package was secure, and looking like I had a new beer gut, I vanished.

I took the nearest exit to the balcony, out of sight of Andy, leaving through a sliding door in the west side room with the grand overlook of the courthouse. From there, in the cooling night air, I worked my way around the balcony, past where Andre lay with his brains spilling onto his expensive leather sofa and Martin lay with his face bleeding on the carpet. Andy kept watch on her crime scene from the kitchen, speaking urgently into her phone. She stood erect, radiating a powerful professional presence. Her badge hung from her belt and her weapon had been secured. She placed the silver hand cannon and Martin's service weapon on the kitchen island, minus magazines. Evidence neatly organized by Detective Stewart.

I paused long enough to whisper a prayer of thanks. If anything had happened to her…

The mind needs vaults. Thinking of the way Andre had threatened Andy, thinking of the gun pressed into her hair, thinking of what had been done to Lane and what lay in store for her, thinking of the photos I had seen—those thoughts and images belonged in a vault with the door welded shut. I vowed to build that vault, steel wall by steel wall, a little every day.

I chose not to go down the way I came, but instead used the balcony half wall to float myself to the east side of the building. Below, I spotted the side-walk where the dog-walkers had looked down their noses at me. I fixed a course to the fire hydrant beside the Crown Vic. I checked for trees, wires, streetlights. The course looked reasonably clear.

"This is just messed up," I muttered. Against ten thousand years of evolution and genetic coding, not to mention self-preservation and common sense, I grasped the balcony wall and hopped over into twenty stories of empty air. Calculating a trajectory, I pushed off.

The glide down was slow but exhilarating. Thanks to bad aim, I came down on the roof of the unmarked car with nothing to grasp. I ended up spreading myself out as my feet touched, coming to a full stop on my belly with my arms extended down the windshield and fingers gripping a wind-shield wiper blade.

I climbed behind the wheel, strapped in, found the keys under the seat, fired up the V8 and pulled what looked like a driverless car into traffic. I went several blocks before reappearing, just to see the look on the few faces that noticed.

The Hyatt stood only a few blocks away, but I headed north, back into

Pan D territory. For one thing, there are no gas stations in the center of the city. I cruised all the way to North Avenue before I found one. For a ridiculous sum of money, they sold me a plastic one-gallon gas can. I found it amusing that they also sold me a disposable plastic lighter without raising an eyebrow, even though I looked like I'd just come from a fire. Maybe I got a pass because of the obvious cop car sitting next to the pump where I filled the can with about seventy cents' worth of gas.

At first, deciding on a place to do the deed had me baffled. A park, perhaps? Some parks have public grilles and fire pits. But most parks are closed after dark. I didn't want to chance an encounter with a passing patrol car.

I sprouted a mildly brilliant idea.

The Polaroids burned in a pile of gasoline-soaked rags on broken pavement in an alley shielded on all sides by decaying garages and homes, in a decaying neighborhood, much like the one that Lane Franklin had grown in and laughed in and played in and had built a beautiful heart in. Perhaps it was the very same neighborhood. I really didn't know.

When all the photos had curled and melted and turned to ashes in that small pyre, I drove away with the silk pillowcase on the seat beside me.

# 64

I drove the stolen police car into the loading loop in front of the Hyatt. The uniformed bell captain recognized the car for what it was. He startled when I threw him the keys and said, "It's stolen. You might want to call the cops."

Fully visible, without crutches and surrendering my body to gravity, every move I made ignited pain. What I really wanted was for the bell captain to bring his luggage trolley over and offer me a ride to my room. When that didn't happen, I looked for a secluded spot to disappear just to get the weight off my body. I planned to skip the elevator and simply float up to the ninth floor. Twenty-four hours ago, the idea would have been exciting. Now, all enthusiasm for floating around in the Hyatt's atrium escaped me. I felt exhausted and I hurt everywhere.

My plan fell to pieces when Pidge hauled out the sliding doors to meet me. After one look, she wrapped her arm around my waist and hooked her shoulder under my armpit to help me walk.

"Jesus, Will! You look like wet steaming shit!"

"It's a fashion statement."

We limped awkwardly into the hotel.

"What are you doing here?"

"Earl told me to get over here and set everybody up with the company credit card. Can you believe it? The old bastard has an actual beating heart!"

"What do you mean, everybody?"

"Didn't you hear? They found Lane! She's okay!" Pidge slapped me on the chest. I winced. She paid no attention. "Fuck, yes! She and Rosemary II are over at Colombia St. Mary's getting her checked out, but the word is she's fine. I told Rosemary II there's a room here for them, but she wasn't sure if they would want to keep Lane overnight or not. Probably not. I had your room switched over to Earl's card, too. Have you seen the rooms? You gotta check out the fucking mini-bar!"

"You just get here?"

"Fuck, no. I've been here most of the afternoon after I brought Rosemary II back. She went with Andy to the cop shop. Earl said to make this our HQ until this shit gets figured out." I must have had the question on my face because she added, "Oh! Andy called. Told me you were coming. Told me to get some food in you and get you to bed, ASAP. I already called room service for you."

My wife. Not done with me yet.

"You smell like a fucking fire, man. What's that all about?"

I blew out a breath in a long sigh.

"What's in the bag?"

"Change of clothes," I lied, holding the re-purposed pillowcase at my side.

"I'll get you upstairs, but I'm not gonna tuck you in."

"I'd have nightmares. Just get me to the elevators. I'll take it from there."

"Good. 'Cuz I'm gonna hang here until I hear from Rosemary II. See if she's gonna come here or what. If not, I'm going to the bar across the street to find something long and hard and fu—"

"I don't need to know!"

Her cute pixie face beamed up at me.

# EPILOGUE

I t never gets old. Sitting on the farmhouse porch, watching the late afternoon sun ignite coronas of color in Andy's rich, dark hair. Staring at her when she's not looking at me.

She strolled across the lawn in animated conversation with Chief Don Schultz. She wore a new outfit and carried a sports bag she must have picked up after buying clothes and sundries for the four days she stayed in Milwaukee. She looked good as always, alluring, yet professional in a dark business-like skirt and white blouse. Her badge hung from her belt along with her service weapon. Her hair flowed freely down her shoulders, but she would have put it in her police bun or French braid for the meetings, interviews, and debriefings she attended over the last four days.

I struggled to stand on my replacement crutches and started toward the porch steps. I wanted to meet her on the lawn. I wanted to make the extra effort because I wasn't sure where I stood with her.

We never connected at the Hyatt. As I predicted, I was out cold when she finally arrived Sunday night. She let me sleep on Monday morning. She rose and slipped out before I pried my eyes open and took inventory of my damage. I found a note saying she had a meeting with Chiefs Schultz and Stiller at the ungodly hour of seven a.m. It was no small thing that she didn't wake me to demand the whole story. Again, I wondered what my secrecy had cost us.

Late Monday morning, I boarded the plane with Lane and Rosemary II. Pidge landed back in Essex just before noon. Rosemary II wanted her daughter as far from the city as possible, as fast as possible. Andy insisted I go with them. Lane and Rosemary II nearly tackled me in the lobby of the Hyatt and helped get me to the cab when they saw my pathetic movement without crutches. I avoided looking at Lane, who kept sending me wide-eyed knowing glances. Rosemary II wasn't much better, tearing up and taking my hand again and again. I squeezed into the co-pilot's seat for the ride home, just to get away from them.

Andy told me she would be endlessly tied up with police business. It went without saying that she thought it best that I avoid people asking questions. Not knowing what I hid from her didn't give her much choice. I could not decide if she protected me or protected herself. Either way, it cost her a small part of her professionalism, which made me feel worse.

Phone calls with Andy over the next four days were brief and carried a low-wattage undercurrent of tension. I didn't ask, and she didn't tell me about the investigation, except to say she'd kept me out of the official report, including massaging the story of Lane's escape from the fire, and dealing with my voice on the 9-1-1 call. She didn't say how or what was done about that. I'm guessing help came from the top.

It's not that we didn't talk. We talked daily. She mothered me about staying off my feet, resting, eating. She kept me up to date on Lane because she and Rosemary II talked several times daily. She ended each call with "I love you," which I fervently prayed remained true.

I noticed Andy started calling Lane's mother Rosemary II, honoring the woman who had, as much as anyone, saved a young girl and her single mom two summers ago.

I felt a little stab in the heart when Andy got out of Chief Schultz's car chatting energetically with him and she didn't throw me a wave hello. Maybe I was expecting punishment, and to be clear, I thoroughly deserved it. Maybe with Andy, I would always feel a little unworthy, a shade insecure and uncertain that she could feel about me the way I feel about her.

She melted my fears when she looked at me and smiled brightly with both her lips and her eyes. She dropped her sports bag to the grass. She hurried up the steps before I was able to maneuver down to her. Her eyes took me in. Her arms pulled me close, careful not to knock me off balance.

"Mmmmm," she hummed in my ear. Her embrace tightened. "Missed you."

"Missed you, too."

When we eased apart, I touched her hair. I studied her eyes. I found myself safe in those eyes, where I belong.

I wasn't off the hook, but at least I knew that the hook wasn't going to kill me.

"Thanks for bringing her home, Chief. Can I get you a cold beer?" I was not at all grateful that Chief Schultz had driven Andy back up to Essex. His driving terrified me. Earl offered to send a plane down to get her, but Andy told me the Chief insisted. I know she relished the time spent with a ranking officer, a fellow professional from a big city department. She probably talked his ears off, about the job, the tools of the trade, and the secret society that is law enforcement.

"I'll take one for the road," Schultz said.

*Great.*

"How are you feeling, Will?"

"Better. Sore. I was scheduled for physical therapy today, but I blew it off. I told them I had already done enough for this week."

Schultz paid me a knowing look. "That so?"

I looked at Andy. Andy looked at Schultz. Schultz looked at me, and then broke into a grin.

"Relax, Will," he said. "We have all the pieces in place that need to be in place. Even our pal The Ax is satisfied—although I think she has other reasons to feel happy with the way things turned out. Your wife helped us write a *really nice* report. That's what we aim for. *Really nice.*"

I felt relief. The last thing I wanted was to enter a discussion with the MPD about the fire at the Pink House, or bodies found in a cash house on the near north side. From the look on Schultz's face, he clearly knew or guessed more than had been neatly explained in his *really nice* report.

"I caught the news," I said. "Sounds like you're rolling up Pan D. Dumbest gang name ever, by the way. Latin Kings. Bloods. Inferno. I get that. Pan D?"

"Pandemic," Andy said. She nodded at me for emphasis. I liked that better than being punched. "It's all over Andre's videos and speeches. He talked about it all the time. Pandemic. The colossal ass was out whipping up the neighborhood to vote for him to lead a crusade against a pandemic he created and capitalized on. So, he used the name." Andy smiled like a girl wanting a pat on the head. I thought she might curtsey.

"Subliminal marketing," I said. "Or vertical marketing. Some sort of marketing. Chief, are you sure you can't stay for dinner? Seems a shame to drive all the way up here and then have to turn right around."

He shook his head at the offer. I was glad. "It was a good chance to wrap things up with your wife."

"Let me get you that *Coke*," Andy said, giving him a reproachful glance. She disappeared into the house.

"That's the trouble with cops. They won't let you drink and drive," Schultz said.

"You drive like a maniac, Chief," I said.

"I do," he agreed. "Beer calms me down. I'm a much better driver with a beer in my hand."

I think he meant it.

"Will, I offered your wife a job," he said quietly. "Just wanted you to know. She's good."

"The very best," I said. I didn't acknowledge that he currently had an opening for Detective. Martin would be a sore spot for MPD for a long time.

"She has a tendency to blow the living shit out of suspects, but I think we can work with her on that," Schultz said. An awkward silence settled between us. Andy reappeared and handed Schultz a cold can of Coke that rapidly coated itself with condensation in the summer humidity.

Schultz put out a hand and Andy shook it. "A pleasure, Detective."

"All mine, sir," she said.

When he was gone, I parked myself on the old lounge chair while Andy changed into denim short-shorts and an old Metallica t-shirt. She padded onto the porch in bare feet with two cold Coronas in hand. We were out of limes again. I might have used up our stock over the last few evenings, here on the porch.

She sat beside me and put a hand on my thigh.

"They let me work the case between interviews and debriefs," she said. "We think we found three more girls that Andre ... took. MPD has some good people working crimes against minors. They're reaching out to find more, to get them help. Chief Schultz is pushing hard on that."

She took a long pull from her Corona. I took it as her way of forgiving me for destroying the Polaroids.

"He told me. About the job. Well?"

"We'll talk about it," she replied. "But we have other things to talk about first."

"Yes, but before that I need to ask—are you okay? I mean, the shooting. Andre. How are you doing with it?" I hoped she didn't think I was trying to create a diversion. I genuinely wanted to know.

"It's ... um, hard to deal with."

"If I can—"

"No, Will. It's hard to deal with the fact that I honestly don't feel sorry. Or think of it as taking a life. Or any of what I have always been afraid I'd feel. It's hard to deal with the fact that I'm *glad I killed him*. I'm not supposed to feel that way. But everything he said—everything he did—plus ... I listened to the 9-1-1 tape." She shook her head, maybe trying not to hear it play again in her mind. "I heard what Lane said, to you—and I heard her crying for—you know. I honestly want to shoot the bastard again."

"Amen to that." We clicked our bottles and drank. "I wasn't sure you *would* shoot him. I gave you a gun and you turned around and used it as a club. I wanted you to shoot Martin, not beat him up."

"Well," she said, now the teacher, "you never trust a weapon you're not familiar with. I didn't know if it was loaded. I didn't know if there was one in the chamber. I didn't know if the safety was on, or if the gun was a piece of crap that would blow up in my hand. Better to club someone than to point a gun at them and have nothing happen."

"How did you know it would work with Andre?"

She shrugged. "I didn't. I wasn't really trying to shoot him. I had the thing in my left hand, and I was just trying to get away from him. I didn't know what else to do—I took a shot."

"Jesus Christ," I said. "One hell of a shot."

We clicked bottles again and drank.

I opened my mouth to speak but she put her finger to my lips, just as I had done to her Sunday night in Andre's penthouse.

"You'll get your turn and you better make it *God damned good*. But me first."

She lowered her eyes for a moment. Long lashes reached down for the light caramel color of her cheeks. When she looked up, I felt my breath go short as I always do when those green eyes fix on me.

"I know you," she said in that serene, melodic tone she uses to speak those words. "You know what that means to me. You know when I'm in something, I'm all in. But I want it both ways. For me. For us. For the important things. I mean, if you want your own checking account or you run out and buy a sports car without telling me, that's fine. But for the parts that connect us here," she touched her heart, "it has to be both ways."

I hitched a breath to say something. She waved me off.

"The police thing, that's my thing. And, okay, it bothered me a tiny little bit that you were running around doing *something* in Milwaukee, and that you wouldn't explain things to me—but I really do get that it was all about Lane—and Will, I am so proud and grateful that you were there for Lane, and there for me!"

*Here it comes*, I thought.

"But how could you pick that moment to not trust me?"

"Dee, you'll see—"

"Nuh-uh!" She waved her finger at me. She gathered herself again. "And it's not just that. I heard the 9-1-1 call … it, um …" her eyes welled up and her voice grew high and thin "… I heard it all, all of it and, um … okay, it's really hard to be mad at you—but *God dammit, Will!* Lane, she was trying to —um, she—wanted you to leave. And I know you had to do it, you had to stay and get her out, but—do you know what it would do to me if—?"

"Dee, I—" Finger to my lips. The anger layer rose.

"You call me out of the blue—you pull Lane out of the fire—you show up out of nowhere behind Martin—you tell me nothing! We are supposed to trust each other!" She punched my shoulder again, not as hard as she had at Andre's penthouse, but I began to worry it might become a habit. She blew out a cleansing breath and took a long pull from her beer.

"So," she commanded, "spill it, Pilot. Every bit of it!"

She nestled her bare leg against me. Her open expression made no pretense of expecting anything other than a damn good explanation. I really hated to say it, but…

"Um, not quite yet."

Her face clouded over. The anger flared. I grabbed her hands before she landed another punch. I nodded my head at the road beyond the lawn.

Lane Franklin pedaled her bicycle toward us in the late afternoon sunshine.

"I promised Lane I wouldn't tell you until she got here."

"Okay, you now have me completely confused."


LANE BIKED out from town after, she said, spending the entire day struggling to convince her mother she would be safe for a couple hours out of Rosemary II's sight. It had been a running battle. The last few days were crazy, Lane told us. It felt like her mother was afraid to let her go into another room by herself. I got that. The moment Lane pushed me to *Go!* and I didn't go— a bond had formed between us. It wasn't and never would be made of the same steel as a mother-daughter bond, but it was a bond, and it was ours. I understood Rosemary II's awareness of the terrifyingly fragile gift in such a bond. I felt it, too. I feared for this child, for her innocence. I knew that for the rest of our lives we would be linked, and I would have a hand in her path. Seeing her now, wearing clothes from The Goodwill Store and pedaling a fourth-hand bike bought from a rummage sale, I thought of the stolen silk pillowcase filled with rolls of cash sitting at the back of my upstairs closet. I counted more than sixty-three thousand dollars. It belonged to Lane. It was owed to her. Andy and I would work out a way to channel it into her life once I got up the courage to tell Andy about it. With it, I hoped, Lane would fly—literally or in any way she wished—and never look back on those hours in that room or feel that chain or any other chain.

Lane pedaled toward us in the summer sunshine, just a kid on a bike, not fourteen going on twenty-five, just fourteen. She had persuaded her mother to let her ride out to the farmhouse on her own to thank Andy again. In that regard, Lane bent her mother's trust with a partial lie. Because that's not why Lane had been so anxious to come for a visit and to come alone.

Lane hopped off her bike while it still rolled and took the porch steps in a single bound. She ran into Andy's arms. They hugged and held each other for a long moment, saying nothing. Then Lane threw a big hug around me and demanded, "Did you tell her?"

"Tell me what?" Andy wanted to know.

"Oh—my—God!" Lane exclaimed. Her smile lit up her face. Andy looked utterly bewildered.


I CHOSE the barn loft and led the three of us there on my crutches. I positioned Andy and Lane at the center, beside the worn ladder nailed to the vertical support beam. Wood smell and old hay scent added density to the hot, dry air. Dusty beams of sunlight streaming through the knotholes and cracked wood.

I turned to Andy.

"We've got a lot to talk about, and in a minute, you're going to see why. When I show you this—well, I think you'll understand that I couldn't just explain it to you while we waited for all the cops in the world to show up at Andre's place."

Lane bounced up and down beside Andy, grinning wildly. Andy looked at her as if the girl had gone mad.

"You know about this?"

Lane's head bobbed. Her eyes glittered. "Show her!"

I handed Lane my crutches and stepped directly in front of Andy. She looked at me with an expression that said if this went on much longer, the anger layer would rise to the top and stay there.

I reached for the ladder to fix a grip on one of the rungs.

"One question first. Were you serious?" I asked.

"About what?"

"I can get a sports car?"

I grabbed her hands before she could punch me again.

"Okay! Okay! Here goes. Whatever happens, don't freak out."

"Will, wha—?"

*Fwooomp!* I vanished before my wife's wide eyes. Her mouth dropped. Lane shrieked, clapped her hands, and began laughing.

Andy's hands shot out and hit me in the chest. She cried out. She groped up my chest to my neck, my face. She found and followed the shape of my head. Her wide eyes darted, searching empty air.

She stammered out sounds but couldn't connect them to make words.

*Fwooomp!* I reappeared. Andy jumped.

"Will!"

I took her shoulders in my hands, to steady her. I thought maybe she might faint. Or run.

"Show her the flying thing! Show her the flying thing!" Lane cried out, jumping up and down. "Oh—my—God! It's the most amazing thing ever!"

"Lane," I said, not taking my eyes from Andy's startled, uncomprehending expression. "Lane, could you give us a little while? Could you wait for us in the house? Get a Coke, and wait for us, okay?"

"Awww!"

"Please?"

"Can I have a turn?" The child whose childhood had nearly been stolen bounced up and down on the balls of her feet. Just a kid, wanting a turn on the ride.

"Yes, you can have a turn."

Lane skipped out the big barn door.

"Will, *what is this?*"

I shook my head.

"I don't know what it is," I said. "But I know how to use it. Come here. Put your arms around me."

She did. Andy looked up at me, trusting, fearful, expectant.

I pulled her close and said, "Hang on!"

*FWOOOMP!*

We flew.

DIVISIBLE MAN

Friday, June 2, 2017—Sunday, September 24, 2017

# ABOUT THE AUTHOR

Howard Seaborne is the author of the DIVISIBLE MAN™ series of novels as well as a collection of short stories featuring the same cast of characters. He began writing novels in spiral notebooks at age ten. He began flying airplanes at age sixteen. He is a former flight instructor and commercial charter pilot licensed in single- and multi-engine airplanes as well as helicopters. Today he flies a twin-engine Beechcraft Baron, a single-engine Beechcraft Bonanza, and a Rotorway A-600 Talon experimental helicopter he built from a kit in his garage. He lives with his wife and writes and flies during all four seasons in Wisconsin, never far from Essex County Airport.

Visit www.HowardSeaborne.com to join the Email List and get a FREE DOWNLOAD.

# PREVIEW

### DIVISIBLE MAN: THE SIXTH PAWN

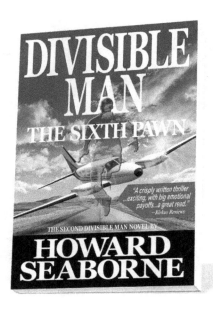

When the Essex County "Wedding of the Century" erupts in gunfire, Will and Andy Stewart confront a criminal element no one could have foreseen. Will tests the extraordinary after-effect of surviving a devastating airplane crash while Andy works a case obstructed by powerful people wielding the sinister influence of unlimited money in politics.

Available in print, digital and audio.

Learn more at **HowardSeaborne.com**

# DIVISIBLE MAN: THE SIXTH PAWN

## CHAPTER ONE

"I am so getting laid tonight." Pidge adjusted herself in the little black dress she had miraculously squeezed around her petite body. I doubted the structural integrity of the thing. Parts of her threatened to pop out. "Ten grooms-men, eight ushers. Fucking fish in a barrel."

"Half of them are married, Pidge," Andy warned.

"Good. Maybe they'll know what they're doing. I'm going to the bar!" She charged off toward one of eight bars on the perimeter of the wedding tent, a determined twenty-four-year-old blonde pixie in high heels.

"God help them, they don't stand a chance," I said. I looked at my wife. "What about me? Do I stand a chance?"

"Of what?" Andy fluttered her lashes at me. I made a show of examining her dress, a nearly-black, purple delight that shimmered on her curves and set off the warmth in her flowing auburn hair. Her structural integrity cried out for closer inspection.

"Of hooking up with a very hot woman tonight," I said.

"Depends." She moved closer and fidgeted with my tie. She pressed her hips against mine. "If I see one, I'll ask if she's interested."

"Oh, please, would you two get on with hating each other like a decent married couple!" Earl Jackson growled. He snagged a water glass from the round table beside us. The table seated eight. Folded place cards beside expensive-looking China displayed our names in gold script. A lavish centerpiece of sculpted white flowers dominated the table. "How long have you two been married, anyway? A week?"

Earl signs my paycheck as well as Pidge's. That and prize fighter stature topped with a permanent scowl makes him hard to ignore but I tried.

I put my hands on Andy's waist and pulled her tighter. "Has it been a week? Already?"

"Lipstick," she warned. I kissed her anyway. She kissed back. When she pulled away, she looked at Earl with green and gold-flecked eyes and said, "Three years, two months, and one day. But you're right. Hardly seems like a week." She smiled. Andy's smile and magazine model looks should carry a warning. More than a few men in the tent around us stole long glances at my wife.

"Get a room," Earl muttered. He twisted and tugged at his suit, which looked like it came off a rack in 1956. Andy threw him a loving look. A fissure appeared in his scowl. I feared if he smiled back his face might crack.

"I'm going to fix my lipstick." She gave me another sweet kiss. "Again."

"I'll stay here and count billionaires." I shamelessly watched her maneuver between the tables. Her combination of high heels, short dress, and inexplicable locomotion made me forget there were five hundred other people milling around under the gigantic tent.

Earl watched her, too. Earl Jackson loves my wife like a daughter, but also appreciates her architecture. When she slipped out of sight, he put one of his calloused claws on my shoulder. "You don't deserve her."

"Nobody does. I just try to keep up."

"So, whaddya figure? Half a million? Million?"

"What?"

He waved an arm in a semicircle. "All this. Senator Mealy-Mouth marrying off his little girl."

"I could not begin to guess. But I have to ask—how's he taking it that Sandy's marrying one of the governor's A-Team boys?"

"She would have been better off bringing home a crack addict!" Earl laughed. "Bob hates our pinhead governor. Speak of the devil."

Earl pointed at a cluster of guests. A short man held court at the center. His prominent bald spot reflected dots from the thousands of tiny white lights strung above our heads.

"If you want to count billionaires, go over by pinhead and swing a dead cat. There's half a dozen. Lester Brodling. Ira Waters. Bargo Litton, the energy guy. Couple of hedge fund guys. Fifty percent of the cash flowing into the Republican coffers in our happy 'swing state' is standing right over there eating bacon-wrapped water chestnuts."

"Your pal runs in quite the circle."

Earl snorted. "Bob? Bob may be a brainwashed elephant worshiper, but he doesn't give those kingmakers the time of day. In fact, he goes out of his way to be a pain in their collective asses. Oh, no. They're all here for the kid."

Earl might call State Senator Bob Stone names, but they had been friends since the first grade. Earl Jackson proclaims himself a life-long Democrat and keeps a framed picture of FDR on his office wall. Bob Stone waves the Republican banner, although in the last year Stone bucked his own party twice on high profile votes. Earl used it as merciless fodder for occasional Saturday morning breakfast debates with his friend at the Silver Spoon diner.

I didn't care one way or the other. Politics is the filler I mute on television while I'm waiting for the weather report. I had no stake in this extravagant wedding, either. I rode in as Andy's Plus One. She belonged to a book club with the bride, Sandra Stone, and the two had formed a friendship. I've met Sandy any number of times, but never the groom. Sandy teaches kindergarten at James Madison Elementary School in Essex. To hear Andy describe it, Sandy loves teaching as much as her adoring children love her.

Andy's invitation to the Essex County Wedding of the Century promised two free nights at the Cinnamon Hills Golf Resort, a lavish dinner, dancing, and other delights. I had no complaints. This was as close to a vacation as Andy and I expected to get for a while. We were broke.

In June, working as an air charter pilot for Earl Jackson, I crashed one of the company's Piper Navajo twin-engine airplanes. I have no memory of the event.

Three things emerged in the aftermath.

First, I became a minor celebrity. My fifteen minutes of fame came from the fact that I fell out of a disintegrating airplane at a hundred and forty miles per hour and dropped five hundred feet into a marsh. I wound up on soft earth, sitting in the pilot's seat with a broken pelvis.

Second, I spent a week in the hospital which ran up a huge bill. As a police officer, Andy enjoys health insurance through her employer, the City of Essex, but the major medical policy carries a five-thousand-dollar deductible, which wiped out our savings and put us on a payment plan. The broken pelvis still hurts, though they tell me it is healing nicely. I spent most of the last sixty days using crutches. I ditched the crutches a little over two weeks ago but don't have a lot of stamina for standing. Or sitting, for that matter. On the plus side, I can now tell when it's going to rain, and I don't have to drag myself out of bed and go running with my wife.

Third, I came away from the crash with something I can't explain. *The other thing.*

I vanish. When I vanish, I defy gravity and no longer obey the physical laws governing mass and inertia. *The other thing*, I am now convinced, accounts for me surviving the in-flight breakup of an airplane. Because nobody falls that far at that speed and lives.

As of the wedding weekend two months after the crash I still had no idea what it was or how it became a part of me. I do, however, know how to control it.

Only two other people know about *the other thing*. Lane Franklin, the fourteen-year-old daughter of Essex County Air Service's office manager, learned about *the other thing* when it saved us both from a burning building. The second person who knows about *the other thing* is Sergeant Andrea Katherine Taylor Stewart of the City of Essex Police Department—my wife Andy, or Dee as I sometimes call her. She learned of it after she killed the man who put Lane in the burning building in the first place.

Andy being Andy, she had questions.

The night I demonstrated *the other thing* to Andy she gasped at the impossibility of it. Not only because I vanished, but because I also took her in my arms and we both disappeared, then I showed her how gravity ceases to exist in the vanished state. We floated through angled sunbeams in the barn behind our rented farmhouse like a romantic pair of space station astronauts.

Afterward, we took up station on the farmhouse front porch and watched the setting summer sunshine kiss the corn tassels across the road.

"How do you know you'll come back? That you'll be visible again?" Andy demanded. "How do you know you won't get stuck that way?" Leave it to my wife to find The Worry. "Well? How do you know?"

"I don't," I said. "I just have faith that if I can turn it on in my head, I can turn it off."

"And you do that with the levers you described—the ones you imagine?"

"Yup. Push the levers up, disappear. Pull the levers back, reappear. It seems to, I don't know, *wrap* me up. You felt it, didn't you?"

"That cool sensation? Weird. Of course, what am I saying, this whole thing is weird...*Will, my God!* How is this possible?"

My wife, the cop, has a strong need to connect dots. I had a theory.

"I know you don't want to see Six Nine Tango." The wreckage of the airplane that had broken apart all around me at a hundred and forty miles per hour lay in a hangar at Essex County Airport. "But you heard Connie Walsh from the NTSB. She thinks I *hit something.* I think she's right. And I think whatever I hit—I think that's what did this to me. I think it saved me."

Andy's lower lip gained prominence, a sign of deep thought—or a signal to run for your life. I took it as the former.

I said, "You and I just floated around the barn like astronauts. I didn't want to scare you, so I kept us just above the floor. But I did some testing with this when you weren't here. I flew all over the barn, all the way up to the top, and then floated back down again. There's no way I survived that aircraft breakup and the fall—I don't care how soft the ground was—unless I *floated* down."

"The same way you got in and out of Andre's penthouse," Andy observed. She referred to the man who kidnapped Lane, the man she killed. She chased away the memory with a slug from her Corona.

"Yeah. Twenty stories up. Freaked me out."

"What did you hit?"

"Million-dollar question. Get out your science fiction catalog and pick a page. Wrinkle in time-space. Wormhole. Alien spaceship. Secret government test vehicle. Wizards flying through the RNAV 31 approach course on their brooms."

"This is insane," she said, not for the first time that evening.

We talked into the night. I flipped back and forth a few times, vanishing and reappearing, just to show her how easy it was. In retrospect, I think it scared her more than eased her mind.

Since that night, as summer slipped into fall, we talked about it often. We played with it a few more times, although Andy didn't like it when I took her along for the ride. Most of my practice sessions were conducted while she worked her patrol shift. She asked if I thought it might be radioactive and might give me cancer. She wondered if we should have a test done —at which point we both agreed we didn't want to share this with anyone. She didn't ask me to stop doing it, but I think she wanted to.

Lane often came to visit because the secret between us would have burst her open otherwise. When she visited, Andy and I took her to the barn and I let her throw her arms around me and we would vanish and fly between the rafters and beams with Andy smiling on the sidelines, tracking us by the sound of Lane giggling and laughing.

After one such session, Andy's posed another burning question.

"What are you going to do with this?"

I teased that I planned to go to Las Vegas to see how much cash I can carry out of a vault. She was not amused.

I wasn't *entirely* teasing.

During the episode that found me flying out of a burning building with Lane in my arms, I stole sixty-three thousand dollars in cash from a gang of drug dealers. I kept the money for Lane. Andy, heart and soul the professional police officer, frowned on my thievery once I summoned the courage to tell her. I reminded her the money came from the people who kidnapped and nearly killed Lane. They owed it to her. Call it reparations. Lane and her mother are not well off, so I convinced my wife we could slip the money into an education investment account for Lane, a little at a time.

Neither of us considered, even for a moment, using a dime of the money to deal with our health insurance deductible problem. I, on the other hand, wanted to go back to the hospital and have a heart-to-heart talk with a certain public relations executive who had hounded us during my stay, because of my celebrity survival status. One of the hospital's nursing assistants—later arrested for dealing drugs—swapped my pain killers with counterfeits. I figured a story like that might persuade the hospital to reduce the bill.

Andy would have none of it.

"The only reason we know any of that is because I was the investigating officer. I'm not about to use my badge to leverage freebies—not from anyone!" she declared.

*Well, when you put it that way.*

I could not answer her question. I had no idea what I planned to do with *the other thing.*

## CHAPTER 2

"Stewart!" I heard my name over the crowd noise and the string quartet playing in the wedding tent. Andy had not yet returned from the land of lipstick adjustment. A familiar face wove through the tables toward me.

"Jesus Christ," I said, "the people you meet when you haven't got a gun."

Dave Peterson, looking solid and tan in an expensive suit, took and shook my hand. He broadcast a smile from a wide, boyish face. An Essex County Air Service alum, Dave moved on two years ago, landing a corporate pilot job. Small air charter companies like Essex Air feed a steady stream of young pilots to the airlines and corporate flight departments. The latter had hired Dave. Before moving on to the big time, he and I did most of the flying for Earl.

"How are you, man? I heard about your fuckup!" He grinned.

"Yeah. I ruined my perfect record of one landing for every takeoff."

"Seriously, what happened?"

Most people don't ask me directly, but Dave and I flew a lot of trips and tipped a lot of after-hours beers together. Dave counted himself among the handful of people who attended the wedding when Andy and I married.

"I have no idea. Really. No clue. No memory of it."

"I heard in-flight breakup! And you wound up in a swamp? Is that really true?"

"Sitting in the pilot's seat."

"Wow. That's crazy!" He went on about it for a few minutes, interrogating me for details, for the status of the investigation, for a report on my injuries. I told him what I could, but often came back to the same blank spot in my memory. In the end, he looked at me with naked wonder. "I'm glad you're still vertical, man. Honestly."

"Not as glad as me."

He switched the conversation away from life and death—onto something genuinely serious. "I heard they pulled your ticket. What the hell for?"

"Mostly for the fun of it, I think. The NTSB people are great, but they're coming up with some blanks on this one. The FAA wants to fill in the blank with my name. And since I have this memory issue they're trying to pin 'Pilot Incapacitation' on me."

"Fuckers."

"It's not official. Temporary suspension, pending the NTSB report and review, and a medical eval. I already passed a new First-Class medical exam. The application is winding its way through Oklahoma City, I guess." I wished. Nobody had said word one to me about the progress of my application.

"Still working for Genghis Khan?"

"He hasn't fired me yet. I may be a penguin, but he's been trying to keep me busy. Wants to buy a King Air, so he has me doing a lot of legwork on that."

"A King Air! Finally!"

"What are you flying?" I jumped at a chance to change the subject.

"Falcon 20, but we just added a G-II. I'm scheduled for first officer school in December." Dave grinned.

"Gulfstream," I said, showing genuine appreciation. "The Rolls Royce of executive jets. Company must be doing all right."

"The company's opening up markets in South America, so we need longer legs. They told me to learn Spanish."

"I forgot ... what do they do?"

"Prisons. Private prisons. Huge and growing industry. We're one of the largest in the U.S. and they're tapping a big market in South America. Billion-dollar industry. People can't seem to keep out of jail. Here in the U.S. the state governments want to outsource."

I gestured at the tent above us. "What got you into this shindig?"

Dave pointed at a cluster of men in suits and women in elegant wedding wear. "That's the CEO, the guy with the perfect white hair. Pearce Parks. He's got the keys to the company jet. We fly him all over. He's pals with the groom, who pals with the governor, who's around here somewhere. We had his lordship on a flight out to California just last week, although I'm not supposed to mention that. We flew into Madison yesterday. Drove up here. They took pity on us throttle jockeys and let us tag along. I'm hoping to get in a round of golf in the morning. Say, how's Andy? Is she here?"

"She is. She went to fix her face."

"That girl's face needs no fixing. You're one lucky man. She still a cop?"

"Blue to the core."

"I believe that. And Pidge? Is she still terrorizing Earl?"

"Working on killing him. She pestered him to make her his Plus One. She's here."

"No shit!"

"She's looking to get laid, but don't get your hopes up. She's got a target lock on those guys in tuxedos."

"Ah, she brushed me off a couple years ago. I don't think she likes pilots." Dave took my hand again and shook it. "Listen man, it's great to see you. I gotta get back to the entourage, but let's grab a beer after dinner and catch up!"

Dave sauntered away, leaving me to think about the great division in my world—those who fly airplanes and those who don't. And how I was among the latter these days.

### CHAPTER 3

"I saw a guy with fucking makeup on," Pidge announced as she sat down and pulled her chair up to the round table. "A dude! And it was thick! What's that shit all about?"

"Where?" I asked.

She pointed at one of the bars on the tent perimeter. The guests stood three deep attempting to refuel before the big sit-down meal. I could not pick out a dude wearing makeup.

"It's a brave new world," Earl grumbled. He waved off the waiter who offered to pour dinner wine. Earl doesn't drink.

"Bald, Caucasian, medium build, wearing a brown suit?" Andy, seated beside me, asked Pidge.

"Yeah. Who wears a brown suit to a fucking wedding?" Pidge got her nickname—Pidgeon—as a teenaged student pilot. She talks dirty and she flies. She began flying at Essex County Air Services when she was sixteen and powered her way through her ratings and licenses. On the day she earned her commercial pilot's license she walked into Earl's office and told him to hire her because she was the best pilot he would ever have on the payroll. I think he would have flatly refused, if not for the fact that what she said was true.

"I think the makeup is covering up tattoos," Andy offered.

"All over his face? Who would fucking put tattoos all over their face?"

Andy turned her head and gazed at the bar. I assumed she searched for the man with the makeup, but the look on her face said she wasn't looking as much as pondering Pidge's question.

Andy the Cop, seeing things the way cops see them.

After a moment she turned back to me and seemed to let it go. I picked up the freshly poured dinner wine and raised the glass. She followed my move.

"To free vacations," I said.

"Free vacations." We touched glasses and sipped.

The string quartet broke into a classical version of "The Girl from Ipanema," a song that always reminds me of my wife, more so in the dress she now wore. Healing pelvis or not, I planned to dance tonight. And more. The *bossa nova* beat carried my thoughts to Andy, sitting so close beside me. She caught me looking at her as she flexed minutely to the music.

"Lipstick," she warned me, reading my mind. "And I'm not going to go fix it again."

She leaned over and whispered something in my ear as a consolation, something that made me wish the dinner and dancing portion of the evening lay behind us. She stroked my thigh as she sat back in her chair.

A moment later, the string quartet stopped, and the PA system began blasting a hip hop song I'd never heard by an artist I could not possibly identify. On a stage at the center of the tent, someone picked up a microphone and announced the imminent arrival of the bridal party.

## CHAPTER 4

"Andy!"

My wife pushed back her chair and rose to embrace the bride. Sandra

Stone, now Jameson, had been working her way around the room after her big entrance. A photographer trailing the bride quickly targeted the two. Behind him, an assistant with a note pad turned to a second assistant and said, "Who is that? I think that's somebody. Find out who that is."

"Oh, sweetie, you look absolutely stunning!" Andy gushed.

All brides look stunning, but Sandy Stone started from an advantage. Her light blonde hair had been spun up in a complex style accented with tiny blue flowers that caught and reflected the color of her eyes. She had sun in her skin, which set off a sweet crescent smile, framed in ruby red. I have a bias toward my wife, but seeing the two of them side by side, I had to admit that Sandy held her own. Together, they were show stopping, and the photographer snapped away, jumping from angle to angle.

"I cannot believe I made it this far," Sandy said. She flicked a bright smile at me. "Hi, Will! Your wife is gorgeous!"

"Said the beautiful bride," I smiled back at her. "All I can say, Sandy, is —holy crap!" I waved my arms. "Nice party."

She rolled her eyes. "Okay, so it's supposed to be the bride who goes berserk, right? What's the term for Groom-zilla? This is all Todd! He planned everything! I'm not even sure I picked the dress!" She laughed, an honest kindergarten teacher laugh.

"But it's beautiful. You deserve every bit of it," Andy said.

"I deserve to get out of these shoes," she said, making a face. She took Andy's hands. "I am *so* glad you came, both of you! Hi, Mr. Jackson! Don't you dare start a fight with my dad tonight!"

"Your dad and I never fight. I enlighten. He chooses not to be enlightened," Earl replied. "I promise we will behave in your honor."

Sandy leaned down and kissed Earl on his bald head. The blush that followed blended into his scowl and conjured a combination that camouflaged itself as rage. Pidge giggled.

Andy and the bride traded small talk before Sandy moved on to the next table.

"She wasn't kidding," Andy said, seating herself again beside me. "A couple weeks ago she told me she was *this close* to calling it off. It just kept getting bigger, and bigger. All Todd. Eighty percent of the guest list is Todd." Andy lowered her voice. "I was really afraid she would ask me to be in the wedding party."

"I could have helped you with that," I said. "Made you disappear."

## CHAPTER 5

"Seriously, what are you thinking of doing with it?" Andy asked one night, close to midnight, after her shift ended and we settled in on the sofa for a late snack. "*The other thing.* Assuming it stays. Assuming it belongs to you now."

"I think I did a pretty good job of busting up a drug gang," I said.

Andy frowned. When she learned of my role in rescuing Lane, while deeply grateful and a little impressed, a part of her was not happy.

"You're not trained for that," she said flatly.

"*No one* is trained for this."

"Suppose you did use it, undercover. Nothing you learn could be used to build a case for prosecution. You could not testify. It would be like planting a listening device without a court order. Not to mention you're going to want to keep it secret. Or else wind up in some government lab somewhere..." She trailed that last part off, like it had not occurred to her before.

"True, but information is information," I said quickly. "You work from anonymous sources all the time. Information doesn't have to be admissible to be effective—or preventative. I could work for the DEA. Get into cartel strongholds no one else can penetrate."

"God forbid! That's ridiculously dangerous!"

"Or be on call for the fire department if there's a high-rise fire. Just float people down to the street safely."

"This is not getting better."

"Infiltrate terrorist groups in the middle east? Dismantle rogue state nuclear programs?"

"I'm going to hit you. If you want to fight crime, how about white-collar crime? Sneak into board rooms when they meet to steal the pension plan. Catch the CEO plotting to violate SEC regulations or exposing himself to the office girls."

"Wouldn't work," I said. "It would be so boring I'd fall asleep and wouldn't be able to remember what they said. Let's revisit the Las Vegas idea. They wouldn't notice a few million missing from the counting room..."

"I would arrest you myself," she said. "Be serious, Pilot. This is a part of us now. So, I have a say."

"That's why we're having this conversation."

"Okay. Then, whatever you do with it, I need a couple promises from you." She squared herself up, facing me. "First off, no sneaking into the shower with me. I swear, I'll make you wear a bell."

"Damn. I hadn't thought of that..."

"And second," she grew serious, "I know you did some dangerous things to rescue Lane, but no more dangerous stuff. Deal?"

## CHAPTER 6

Gunfire ripped through the hubbub of dinner conversation. An automatic weapon. The rip-saw sound silenced the crowd.

"DOWN! EVERYBODY DOWN!"

A voice boomed, overly loud and distorted by the PA system that had been used for the wedding speeches and toasts. The command dominated the shocked silence suspended in the wake of the gunfire. Andy twisted, looking for the source. She reached for her handbag.

I followed Andy's searching eyes to the stage. Musical equipment and instruments stood at the ready, but the band had wandered off during the dinner hour. A man in a brown suit, his head covered with a black balaclava, held a microphone in one hand and a pistol in the other. Whoever had fired, it wasn't him.

"ON THE GROUND! COVER YOUR EYES! YOU LOOK, YOU DIE!"

The room rumbled as five hundred people squeezed out of folding chairs and found space on the ground.

Earl pulled out Pidge's chair and hustled her to the floor, then ducked down beside her. All around us heads disappeared below the table line.

Andy and I kneeled. She looked directly at me. I glanced down. She had extracted her Glock 17 handgun from her purse.

"You're outgunned! You can't!"

"I know. Too many people."

"I can." I held out my hand.

She knew what I meant. We had only seconds, time when the confusion would cover me. I reached for the pistol, but she jerked it away.

"Eyes only! Nothing else!" She gripped my arm. "Nothing else!"

I checked to be sure no one was watching. Everyone near us obediently pressed palms and fingers to their eyes. I glanced back at Andy and nodded. I made a motion as if to drop to the floor, then—

*Fwooomp!*

—I vanished.

# ALSO BY HOWARD SEABORNE

DIVISIBLE MAN

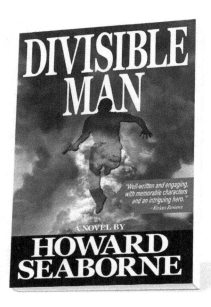

The media calls it a "miracle" when air charter pilot Will Stewart survives an aircraft in-flight breakup, but Will's miracle pales beside the stunning after-effect of the crash. Barely on his feet again, Will and his police sergeant wife Andy race to rescue an innocent child from a heinous abduction—*if Will's new ability doesn't kill him first.*

Available in print, digital and audio.

Learn more at **HowardSeaborne.com**

# ALSO BY HOWARD SEABORNE

DIVISIBLE MAN: THE SIXTH PAWN

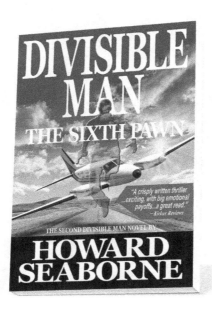

When the Essex County "Wedding of the Century" erupts in gunfire, Will and Andy Stewart confront a criminal element no one could have foreseen. Will tests the extraordinary after-effect of surviving a devastating airplane crash while Andy works a case obstructed by powerful people wielding the sinister influence of unlimited money in politics.

Available in print, digital and audio.

Learn more at **HowardSeaborne.com**

# ALSO BY HOWARD SEABORNE

DIVISIBLE MAN: THE SECOND GHOST

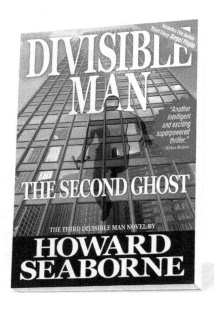

Tormented by a cyber stalker, Lane Franklin's best friend turns to suicide. Lane's frantic call to Will and Andy Stewart launches them on a desperate rescue. When it all goes bad, Will must adapt his extraordinary ability to survive the dangerous high steel and glass of Chicago as Andy and Pidge encounter the edge of disaster.
**Includes the short story, "Angel Flight," a bridge to the fourth DIVISIBLE MAN novel that follows.**

Available in print, digital and audio.

Learn more at **HowardSeaborne.com**

# ALSO BY HOWARD SEABORNE

DIVISIBLE MAN: THE SEVENTH STAR

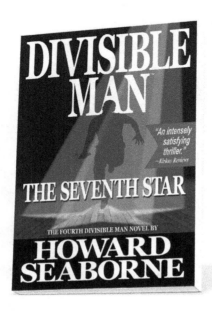

A horrifying message turns a holiday gathering tragic. An unsolved murder hangs a death threat over Detective Andy Stewart's head. And internet-fueled hatred targets Will and Andy's friend Lane. Will and Andy struggle to keep the ones they love safe, while hunting a dead murderer before he can kill again. As the tension tightens, Will confronts a troubling revelation about the extraordinary after-effect of his midair collision.

Available in print, digital and audio.

Learn more at **HowardSeaborne.com**

# ALSO BY HOWARD SEABORNE

DIVISIBLE MAN: TEN MAN CREW

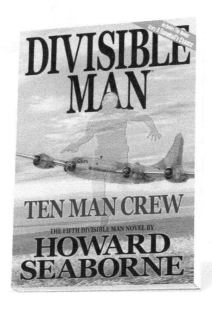

An unexpected visit from the FBI threatens Will Stewart's secret and sends Detective Andy Stewart on a collision course with her darkest impulses. A twisted road reveals how a long-buried Cold War secret has been weaponized. And Pidge shows a daring side of herself that could cost her dearly.

Available in print, digital and audio.

Learn more at **HowardSeaborne.com**

# ALSO BY HOWARD SEABORNE

DIVISIBLE MAN: THE THIRD LIE

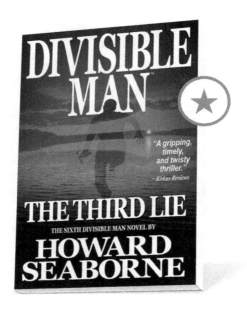

Caught up in a series of hideous crimes that generate national headlines, Will faces the critical question of whether to reveal himself or allow innocent lives to be lost. The stakes go higher than ever when Andy uncovers the real reason behind a celebrity athlete's assault on an underaged girl. And Will discovers that the limits of his ability can lead to disaster.

**A Kirkus Starred Review.**

A Kirkus Star is awarded to "books of exceptional merit."

Available in print, digital and audio.

Learn more at **HowardSeaborne.com**

# ALSO BY HOWARD SEABORNE

DIVISIBLE MAN: THREE NINES FINE

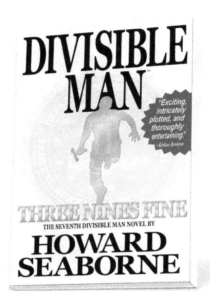

A mysterious mission request from Earl Jackson sends Will into the sphere of a troubled celebrity. A meeting with the Deputy Director of the FBI that goes terribly wrong. Will and Andy find themselves on the run from Federal authorities, infiltrating a notorious cartel, and racing to prevent what might prove to be the crime of the century.

Available in print, digital and audio.

Learn more at **HowardSeaborne.com**

# ALSO BY HOWARD SEABORNE

DIVISIBLE MAN: EIGHT BALL

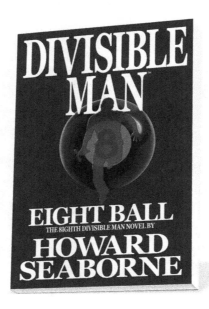

Will's encounter with a deadly sniper on a serial killing rampage sends him deeper into the FBI's hands with costly consequences for Andy. And when billionaire Spiro Lewko returns to the picture, Will and Andy's future takes a dark turn. The stakes could not be higher when the sniper's true target is revealed.

Available in print, digital and audio.

Learn more at **HowardSeaborne.com**

# ALSO BY HOWARD SEABORNE

DIVISIBLE MAN:

ENGINE OUT AND OTHER SHORT FLIGHTS

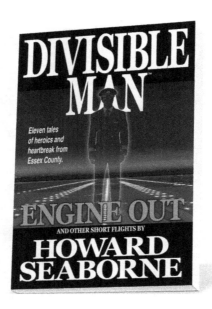

AVAILABLE: JUNE 2022

Things just have a way of happening around Will and Andy Stewart. In this collection of eleven tales from Essex County, boy meets girl, a mercy flight goes badly wrong, and Will crashes and burns when he tries dating again. Engines fail. Shots are fired. A rash of the unexpected breaks loose—from bank jobs to zombies.

Available in print, digital and audio.

Learn more at **HowardSeaborne.com**

# ALSO BY HOWARD SEABORNE

DIVISIBLE MAN: NINE LIVES LOST

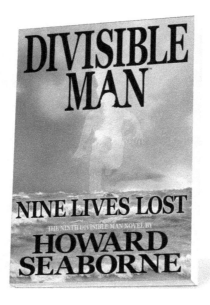

AVAILABLE: JUNE 2022

A simple request from Earl Jackson sends Will on a desperate cross-country chase ultimately looking for answers to a mystery that literally landed at Will and Andy's mailbox. At the same time, a threat to Andy's career takes a deadly turn. Before it all ends, Will confronts answers in a deep, dark place he never imagined.

Available in print, digital and audio.

Learn more at **HowardSeaborne.com**

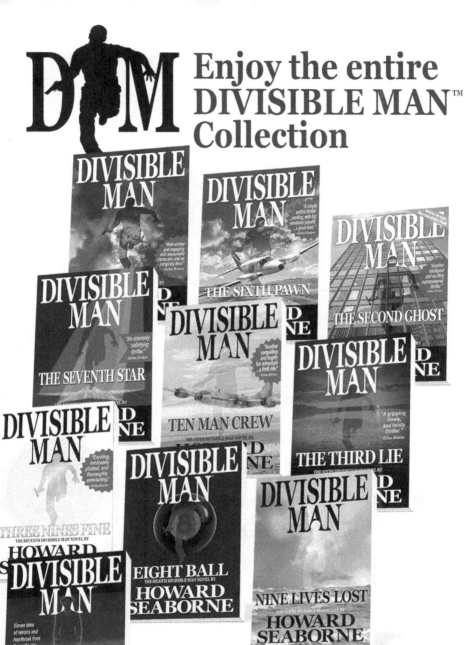

# Enjoy the entire DIVISIBLE MAN™ Collection

In Print, Digital and Audio

CPSIA information can be obtained
at www.ICGtesting.com
Printed in the USA
JSHW062059150922
30524JS00001B/2